CENTURY 21

By the Same Author

CENTURY 21

a novel by

Ewa Kuryluk

Dalkey Archive Press

Excerpts from this novel appeared in the *Gettsyburg Review, Formations, Storm,* and *Conjunctions,* to whose editors the author makes grateful acknowledgment.

Library of Congress Cataloging-in-Publication Data
Kuryluk, Ewa, 1946-
    Century 21 / Ewa Kuryluk.
    I. Title. II. Title: Century twenty-one.
PR9170.K83C46   1992
813—dc20   92-13244
ISBN 1-56478-012-0

First Edition, December 1992

Partially funded by grants from The National Endowment for the Arts and The Illinois Arts Council.

Dalkey Archive Press
Fairchild Hall/ISU
Normal, IL 61761

Printed on permanent/durable acid-free paper and bound in the United States of America.

CENTURY 21

SUNSET IN THE PERSIAN GULF. The red sea of my mind. Sailors sleep, their heads dropped between their fists. In empty coffee-houses marble-topped tables doze away. An oriental flower fades in a male hand. A small white dog licks Hostia's hands. Birds repose on a cherry branch. A veranda. A wooden bed. A woman pretends to resist her lover. A woman resents his measured caresses. Ideals of love, old-fashioned blossoms of sentiment. A collage of carnal decay. Prostitutes count their money and their years. Surprises await readers who reject surprises, pristine images, tints of many books, anthologies of fiction fused with poetry, shrines dedicated to Lowry and Conrad, and the name of Simone Weil knotted into Anna Karenina's black riband. In the Persian Gulf literature is born out of insufficiency and longing, writes Propertius, a notebook in his lap, his left hand resting on the windowsill in Hostia's room.

A burning fever eats me up. Wasps buzz in my lungs. A waterfall runs in my head. Sextus, says Hostia, why did you love me so little? Why did you see me only twice a month? Once I had clients every night, smiled with indifference and collected money. I banished them all because of you. The carnations you brought me are fading. I'm dying. Fever consumes me. But don't go away. Let us talk, until our voices turn to silvery bell tinkles. I want to tell you about my love for you. It's so repetitive, but you have to bear with me. Open the window, I'm short of air. Let birds fly in, so that my soul may join them. Dyspepsia tortures me again. Please pass me a glass of water. Forgive me for dropping it.

It all has happened so rapidly. Put away the flowers. Take my cold hands between yours. The same scene, it flashes in, again and again. Hallucinations of hearing. Delusions of smell. Black birds renounce massive harmonies. I implore you, Sextus, be tender with me. My hands tremble. Stay with me. The discourse of love is so boring. Remember Roland Barthes at a lonely table in the Café de Flore? You were moved by his account of Simone's and Anna's suicide, so you dedicated your verses to me and gave the collection my name. Why was the success of the invented *Hostia* followed by the downfall of the real one?

No, I don't expect relief, I expect death. The decline of my mind has begun. Memories jump. Thoughts are exaggerated by fears. Hours slip away. I'm dying, Sextus, bear with me. In my impotent anger I tell you again and again: bear with me. Bromide and potassium and Valium are of no use. But don't be alarmed. I promise to die by the end of this night. You are at the end of your patience? Ah, your presence will prompt my collapse.

My dreams are incoherent. I lose the notion of what I wish. But I love you, I cannot stop loving you, Sextus. Yesterday my urine was tested and they found blood. This is the chief reason for my collapse— loss of blood through the various openings of my body. The beginning of the end started with my miscarriage—and your absence. First I lost weight, then my mind. Don't get up, remain seated. I'll try to overcome my nausea and be kind to you. Sickness smells in the room. Please open the window.

IN URBINO, identifying with Simone Weil, whom she considers her alter ego, Anna Karenina writes: I feel a laceration that grows without surcease, both in my intellect and in the center of my heart. I am outside the truth, but I see Simone in New York. Since she doesn't want to be one of the privileged, she's depriving herself of food. In a state of growing melancholia, she eats less and less, because the children in France eat even less. There is no man in her life, and in her texts God alone is mentioned, and the hope of a bond between him and her. A mystic, Simone prepares to meet a self-chosen death. It's the end of February, and she's worn out and tense. She has been feeling exhausted for a long time. The continuous effort to gather her energy and direct it to what she has to do is killing her. She compares herself to a sterile stone and is looking for additional courage: to deprive her flesh of the last drop of water, to give herself away. She implores God to plunge her into slavery. She despises herself.

Every Sunday and often during the week Simone's steps lead her to Mass. She isn't baptized, but cannot control the intense desire to receive communion. Before entering the hospital she writes a theory of the Sacraments, in order to make them rocks of reality. When she reaches her limit of fatigue, God appears to her as an incarnated trinity. Absolute rest is ordered, but Simone is permitted to receive visitors. They promise not to tell her parents about her preparations for suicide. She gets thinner and thinner, speaks rapidly in a low voice, following the course of her thought, becomes interested in children, and disputes the dogma that unbaptized infants who die soon after birth cannot enter paradise but remain forever in limbo. Simone doesn't listen anymore, nor does she answer questions.

There is no man in her life, but priests visit her. She doesn't feel ready to enter the church but she hopes to join it in the moment of death. Surprisingly, she survives the winter and by the end of May goes back to her readings in Sanskrit. Ethereal and transparent, she looks cheerful—at last. She copies out a Persian poem: why, when I'm ill, does not one of you come to visit? Crueler for me than illness is your contempt. When she's finished with copying, she sees a bird flying in through the open window, its small breast covered with a strange design: a black-and-white pattern similar to the X rays showing the stationary condition of Simone's lungs.

The bird alights on the edge of a white breakfast plate, and picking up a few crumbs of bread, says: I won't bother you for long. But since you wanted me to come, I have come. The bird's eyes are golden, fire glitters in them. Now they converse, now they are silent. Why do you want to die? the bird asks.

I want to live, Simone replies, but eating disgusts me.

Do you remember Hostia, the bird inquires, the mistress of Propertius? Her lungs bore the same design as yours. She passed away in Rome, while he sat at the edge of her bed, a glass of water in his hand.

I despise women who die because of men. I wait for the hand of God to give me a glass of water, with a drop of blood in it. How can a woman commit suicide because of a man? I wait for the hand of God to open the window. And the window is opened. A black bird arrives in my attic and consumes crumbs of the bread I refused to eat.

My name is Simone, but I would like to be baptized and given the name Mary. Am I not Marie de France? Am I not the last saint in the secular provinces of the midtwentieth century? Do not mention Hostia to me. A courtesan who never worked in a factory, what did she know about life? Don't leave me alone, black bird. Stay with me. There is no man in my life, but a black bird has at last found my abode.

Simone lets the bird sit in her palm, and covers it with affectionate and bacilli-free kisses. The bird stays with her until Sunday, August 22. They suffer cardiac arrest, and looking perfectly peaceful, expire together at about 10:30 P.M. By that time Simone's brother is biking along the canal from the Institute for Advanced Study to Somerville, New Jersey.

E LEPHANT, PROFESSOR OF COMP LIT at Princeton University, sends Karenina a dissertation on Simone Weil. Please, writes Elephant, review it as quickly as possible. I'm afraid it's going to bore you to death. But since you need cash, do it, and I'll get you more stuff. Soon. I can tell you straight away what's wrong with the dissertation. Do you remember what Alfred Kazin said about Simone? A zealot with touches of genius. A feverish, inspired creature. A short life. But the dissertation is long, and evokes a revolutionary aunt, her hair oily, her spectacles too large. My Jewish princess wants to bring out the whole story. But what's the story, for God's sake? Simone's unbearable eagerness and her equally insupportable passion for geometry don't produce a story. Comment on the fact that she disregards the existence of Simone's unsympathetic brother and his daughter Sylvie, who's into French cuisine. In addition, Mlle la Ph.D. candidate ignores the existence of André's bike and fails to mention the path along the canal, autumnal trees reflecting their narcissistic beauty in the New Jersey water, and the appearance of the black bird. Instead, she dwells at length on the suicidal relationship of rational numbers.

When the Germans approach Paris, notes Karenina, Simone says to her parents: Germans are not savages. It will not be impossible to come to some understanding with them. I can't imagine, continues Karenina, what sort of understanding Weil has in mind. Instead I recall our last supper together. Simone sits to my left with her back to my new gas oven. Lowry opens a bottle. Conrad looks out of the window, and is drawn to barges floating down the Hudson River. We are all set, declares Simone. First, we will do away with Nietzsche's concept of Greek tragedy. Second, we will focus on the drama of Mr. Dow Jones. Third, we will interview Contras fighting Sandinistas. Fourth, we will establish a Nobel prize in philosophy.

Tonight Simone is into Sophocles and reads the Theban plays: where is the equal of love? In Antigone's darkening eyes. Where is her passionate haste? In the battle she cannot win. Where is Antigone? In a cave, walled up, without hope. Such is her story and the sleep that she will go to. No funeral hymn. No marriage music. No friend to weep at her departing.

Conrad follows the Hudson's flow. Lowry gulps down one vodka after another. Proust had an asthma attack and couldn't come, but he left a message on Simone's machine. A bloody bunch of immigrants, we are so sad tonight. Monstrosities burden us. By the gods of our fathers, what has happened to us? Time runs away. Manhattan doesn't stay with us. Guardian angels attack us on the subway. No ride is safe.

Our four topics remain untouched. Simone identifies with Antigone. We have only a little time to please the living, she says, but she means: who cares about the living? We are here to please God. There is no chorus, but two people quarrel next door—their voices rising and falling. Lowry plays with a plastic cup. Conrad folds a napkin into a sailing boat. André calls and insists somebody should give his sister a ride home. Buy me a Mercedes Benz and I'll ride her, shouts Malcolm, his voice violent with vodka. I'll get her a cab, Joseph pacifies the Princetonian. Don't waste your words on my scoundrel of a brother, Simone throws in. Let him sleep in a sacred sepulcher. This is the end of tears. No more lament.

Germans don't catch Simone, scribbles Karenina. She doesn't perish in Treblinka. She prefers to starve herself to death in an English hospital, sketching an essay on Anna Karenina.

THE SAME METAPHORS RECUR, writes Simone. Ships leave traces on the surface of the water. Airplanes trace the sky. Roads and railroad tracks meet and cross. Like all emigrants, I'm fascinated with places of transition, ports and airports, bus and train terminals. But terror arrives along with me at new destinations. Longing for context, I try to control panic and recall Nabokov's French governess at the little Siverski station, and Anna Karenina. One arrives in the Russian wilderness, the other escapes it. They don't meet, but for a split second, searching for adventure and independence, they face each other.

Anna arrives in Moscow, conquers Vronsky's heart, and a few days later returns to Saint Petersburg on the same train he is taking. In the middle of the night, agitated and sleepless, they walk out of the car at a provincial station. Anna wants to breathe air, Vronsky to buy seltzer water. Their coincidental meeting on the dimly lit platform is the first modern love scene in European literature. A pattern is set for eroticism, as we know it today: transient and casual. Locomotion causes motion. Motion stirs up emotion. Progressing machines speed up the progress of the self.

In love with Anna, Tolstoy contrasts her animated appearance with glimpses of domesticated females. Their names, pregnant with meaning, are foreign diminutives: Kitty, the pussycat. Dolly, the doll. Anna carries the name of her husband, but at least she has a serious first name. Who would dare to call her Annie or Annette?

Tolstoy makes Karenina break through social constraints, but he isn't interested in women's liberation. He is after the passion and agony of a soul drunk with autonomy. Freedom, a strong spirit, turns Anna into an alcoholic, makes her throw herself under a train. Imitating his heroine's daring, Leo escapes from wife and estate and dies in a railroad station. Life copies the artist's decisive text. Once in the open, no bird wants to return to the cage.

Compare Karenina, traveling by train, to Effi Briest, imprisoned in her garden's static nature. Rebelling against immobility, Effi swings into the sky, rides in the dunes with her lover, a suspect womanizer of Polish descent. But she doesn't succeed at breaking into the open, choosing her own death. Instead, she is trapped and punished. The fire of frustrated desire burns her out. Effi dies young, and her death arrests the author's heart. Not unlike Tolstoy, Fontane is in love with his heroine but doesn't slip into Effi's skin alone. Generous, he identifies with crushed femininity, accuses the iron male order of the Prussian state, and cries out for women's liberation. However, as a novel, *Anna*

Karenina is more to the point than *Effi Briest*. Fontane expresses compassion, Tolstoy passion and despair. But agony, more than any humanitarian concern, makes a text transcend its own time and space. Effi differs from Anna as much as an impressionist painting does from a black-and-white photo. The first belongs to the past, the second is our contemporary.

Lunch is brought in, but Simone refuses to touch it. She asks for a glass of water, empties half of it, and whispers to herself: remember Anna alighting at the railroad station, and her opposite, Madame Arnoux, in Flaubert's sentimental journey. Seated on the deck of a steamer, she embroiders something, surrounded by water, guarded by children and a husband. Cut out on the background of the luminous air and blue sky, she is an island and an icon, a painting by Berthe Morisot. Passivity personified, she makes men buzz around her like busy insects. She advances only when it's too late. Her hair is gray, and when she cuts a lock for her would-be lover, he is horrified. That much accomplished, Madame Arnoux returns to her invalid husband, and remains seated on a bench named after the man she never dared to love. Death tiptoes around her.

Simone raises the glass to her lips and tastes the liquid with the tip of her tongue. It tastes sweet, and she takes a few sips, but doesn't empty the glass. It's early afternoon but drizzle and low clouds turn it to dusk. Soon it will be over, but meanwhile you have to continue with the essay. Don't let suicide surprise you with an unfinished text. Write what you cannot say. Simone's hand refuses to hold the pen, but is forced to.

The story of a woman caught in total inertia, *Sentimental Education* doesn't progress into an erotic travelogue. The man sails around the woman like a ship around the earth. Suspended, love remains in limbo, it doesn't materialize. A novel about impossibility and impotence— Flaubert's prose mortifies my soul. I long to free myself, by whatever means, from the androgynous monster of a life that strangles Madame Arnoux—and me.

I cut some of my straight oily hair and put it in an envelope. But there is no one to whom I can entrust the treasure. Like too many female saints, I substitute virtue for love by abandoning my senses. I let go the trivia of common existence, refuse food, strive for utopia. I kill myself, in spite of my affection for my parents. A spoilt, selfish child, I have gone too far. Everything is out of control. If you let yourself go, you can't bring yourself back. I'm starving because it's the easiest way to die.

I never slept with a man. Why? I'm not that ugly. What prevented me from doing it with a male? The terror of being touched? The horror of being loved insufficiently? I, who am so passionate, why did I say no to sex?

It's World War II and millions are gone. But God has no pity on me. No bomb for Simone. No mine. I, the ideal sister Kolbe—the one who must step forward and offer her life to save *n'importe qui*—I have to die of my own mind. I'm a raindrop, why can't I join the rain? Does a crack in the windowpane separate me from the other drops? God, let me be drizzle. Let me fall to the ground. God, grant me what you grant others! I don't want to play the saint I am. Let me be Karenina and have a crush on Vronsky.

WHILE SIMONE STARVES, Anna is traveling through Spain, but she isn't in good spirits. The struggle to get up is harder every day, and as tension is added to hypersensibility, everything moves her to tears. Since last Saturday a Zurbarán painting has been on her mind. A picture about premonition, it shows Jesus with his mother. He is twelve years old and wears a blue outfit, plays with the crown of thorns and injures his finger. Mary sits with embroidery in her lap, her smooth peasant face marked with the fine traces of tears. The cloth she stitches is white, her dress is red. At her feet two white doves turn their heads to each other. A clouded sky is painted into the frame of a small window. Does the blue-grayish patch derive from the boy's garment? Is it the sky of early spring or late fall? A November day, heavy with rain, or a stormy April afternoon?

The middle of the painting is occupied by a wooden table. It has a drawer, and the drawer is open. Nothing is disclosed, but there is a hint of threat. Something is in store for mother and son, a pair accompanied by other couples: two pears, two doves. The red and the blue oppose and complement each other in the modest Spanish abode. The drawer protrudes from the belly of the table, the adolescent boy stays at his mother's side, while an abyss opens at his back. Envying their togetherness, father intervenes with violence. He loosens bricks, separates them from the mortar, squeezes a drop of blood from his son's finger. Wholeness is shattered, an ordinary day replaced with twilight. Firetongues taste the robustness of the roof.

Apocalypse, notes Anna, arises from our hearts' contradictions and nature's paradoxes. It's midday, but the house is lit. It's a cloudy morning, but the orgy of a sunset penetrates the room. It's nothing, Mother, I have just hurt my finger, don't weep. The two pears, don't they glow in the afternoon sun like two golden vessels? A drop of blood trickles from my finger. But a thimble protects the tip of your forefinger, Mother. Nothing will happen to you, don't be afraid of the needle.

Let crimson appear, prays Karenina, where the blue robe is creased. Where the red dress is folded, let black emerge. On the eve of passion and death, allow the mother to be with her son, the sister with her brother, the mistress with her lover. Oh, sacred time! Don't cut into the flesh of the profane. Don't replace the revolution of celestial spheres with corruption. Oh, God! Defend the definite from infinite vastness.

Reality is made, and in a split second, unmade, and in a split second, remade. But I'm so tired of the myth of the eternal return, of the *ad infinitum.* If time has a beginning, let time have an end. Oh, God! Spare me the sight of Vronsky entering the banality of a midlife crisis, a bridge from which you can see how parallels don't meet in heaven. Let me not witness Vronsky's age of panic, when forms dissolve, the annual rebirth of the cosmos is ignored, death is an indulgence. Oh, God! Since I have untaught myself how to hold to the world, let me not look into its face anymore. Instead, teach me to transform erotic relations into sacred conversations. Sacred to me alone.

Oh, God! Forbid me to talk to Vronsky. Teach me to talk to an anonymous young man, to be born on the moon a thousand years from now. It's for him that I'm writing this text. Oh, God! Preserve it, and have him, not Vronsky, homologate my words. My hands don't retain warmth. Oh, God! Supply me with hot water, let it run over them. I look for a place to settle in, but armies of suffering prevent me from finding asylum. Each night Proust is drained by asthma attacks. We don't visit each other anymore, but exchange correspondence. Marcel is aware of others growing old, but cannot understand his own aging. On the back of a postcard that shows a radiant young woman giving herself to a mediocre courtier, Proust scribbles, in his almost imperceptible handwriting: Vermeer must have been impotent, an invalid, or asthmatic. His painting transcends color, condenses light into longing. Only a cripple knows that blues originate in heaven, yellows in our brain.

Best friends go down the drain. But I, Anna Karenina, am still holding on to the world, even though I cannot hold it. Shielded by the curiosity of my mind, strengthened by the sharpness of my eyes, I structure my days as much as I can. But at night, when I wait for Vronsky, the primordial dragon of chaos tackles me with his tail. Then I fail to keep track of my irrationality and am swept away. My brain is inflamed, and to combat fever, I verbalize despair.

Does my ordeal produce worthless literature? Who am I to judge? On the whole, my genius is more versatile and assimilative than vigorously original. My writing is not without considerable imperfections, especially in the extremities and articulations. But, on the other hand, it's preeminently attractive with its sense of what is lively, intimate, and intense, and of what belongs together and what doesn't belong together but are fused in my text. My solitary mind unites the past and present into a pantheistic poem on the *Solidarität des Seins,* as Svevo puts it.

At this particular instant I'm on my way to San Gimignano, to a blind date with Benozzo Gozzoli. He read my piece on Simone and became interested in me as a woman. Now, I presume, he wants to impress me by showing me his house in Pisa and his tomb in the Campo Santo.

My studio, writes Benozzo to Anna, is located in the highest tower and thronged with birds and dogs. When you look down, you see more birds and dogs, and rejoice. Colors are vivacious and festive, herbs are aromatic, mercurial olive trees provide shade, and you may want to trace with your own fingers the face of a man who has been a distant but old admirer of yours, and to whom you may want to be connected by a brief affair either here or in the suburbs of Siena. There I have another atelier, paint angels, and have barely dressed peasant girls model for me. I cannot imagine a greater pleasure than portraying you amidst them, as a virgin or pietà—the *Santa Karenina di San Pietro Russo.*

Since Vronsky's image pursues me, the affair with Benozzo lasts only twenty-four hours. On Saturday morning I leave for Urbino to visit Raphael. He seems to be gay but he pays me compliments. As the polished white stones in Urbino's main street, where he lives, meet my feet, Sanzio tells me that I look as if I were eighteen. He has me paint on the balcony, and calls me Raphaella. Everything is still possible, says he, just try to avoid Vronsky, don't let him spoil your life. You're an attractive, ambitious woman. Be arrogant, don't admit him to your mind. Why don't you settle in Umbria, teach literature and art at our university, combine sculpture and painting into the next century's minimal art?

But I cannot settle anywhere. I am driven by an ontological thirst that manifests itself in different ways. One day I climb to the heart of the real, to the center of being, where I communicate with everybody at once and train for utopia. But the world doesn't appreciate my efforts and prepares for me the harshest punishment. Soon a dress, sewn from my nerves' endings, will shroud me, and people will have a good laugh seeing me turned inside out, the ontic substance staining the surface. I wonder: will Vronsky save me? How easy is going under? But meanwhile I'm still alive, and visit Campo Santo where, painted *al fresco*, angels flutter and frolic. I observe how people are rewarded for their religious nostalgia, while I'm dumped for my fervor. God prefers the moderate approach, I guess.

Nights are worse than days. I wait for Vronsky to come. Aren't these sentences suited to open every single chapter of every single book? Aren't they saturated with sex appeal? It's night, and I wait for the man to come to me. A million women wait for a million men to come. Some come, most don't. The night is quiet, or it is noisy. Trees throw shadows onto snow, or onto asphalt. Lights are reflected from snow, or from water. Come: Vronsky, Propertius, Jesus. Come now. Quickly. Let me not wait. Oh, come here now. I feel a panic that you might not come. Soon it will be morning. Another gray morning. Another day. I feel your skin on my face. I feel your hair in my mouth. Please come. Come quickly. Don't wait. Come! Now!

What are you doing? Where are you? I feel your head pushed hard against my breasts. I see you come barefoot, your white shirt open. I feel your feet. They're cold. But if you come, they will warm up. In no time. The adjective pursues the adverb, the adverb runs after the verb. Quick. Quickly. Come. Say that you love me. Now. Say it now.

I hear your heart beating. Why don't you come? I hear the elevator. Why don't you come? The blanket is soft and warm, but my hands are like ice. All by themselves they cannot warm up. Without you I cannot warm up.

I love you, my red rabbit. My posh pussycat. My coy kangaroo. I love you, my tiny tiger, my lonely lion, my honey Hemingway. I feel you against me, hard, solid, warm. You put your hand on my forehead. You drop your arm on my leg. Nothing else matters. Your shirt is open, and I kiss you. Where are you?

My hands are like ice, but I'm on fire. I'm an animal. I become one with you. I give you my heart. Can you hear it pulsate in your palm? We could become one, why don't you come? My mini-mouse. My frothy frog. My rubber robin. We are an animal, with four feet, and two heads. We are Siamese twins. I press my lips against your shoulder. I press my lips against your belly. We are different, but really we are the same. And if you ever change, I'll be glad to change as well. Into a corny crocodile. Into a green gazelle. We will never be separate again. I love you so much, I cannot speak. The night is so cold. But we are so close. So warm. Why don't you come?

My hand touches your cheek. Come. I'm so glad. I'm so happy. Come. I want to die. Now. Before I lose you. Before it's all over. No, you don't have to say it. I know what you mean. I love you. I love your name. The line of your neck. Let us sleep. But without you, I can't sleep. And even with you, I can't sleep. I wake and hold you tight, as though you were all of life that is to be taken from me. I hold you feeling that it is all of life, but that I can only hold to you, I can't hold you. You sleep soundly, and I kiss you. You don't wake up. Then I roll away onto my side, pull the blanket over my head, and try to sleep. But I cannot sleep. I kiss you on your neck, and lie in the night thinking.

I lie beside Vronsky, who's sleeping. He's turned away from me and I feel his body against my back. I watch him sleeping and watch time passing. His head is under my chin. I hold my arms around him. I put my lips behind his ear. I run my tongue along his neck. I turn myself toward him and he, sleeping, holds me to him. And now, stretched out on a sheet, I see the earth. Ships leave traces on it. Birds ascend from it. Butterflies fly up. And I'm dissolved in a single longing—to hold him tight. To hold Hemingway chasing his rabbit through Spain. To hold Propertius weeping at the bedside of his dying mistress. To hold back Dow Jones from falling and rising. To hold the universe in all its clarity. The Florence of the Medici. The moon. Therefore: come now. Please come. If you don't come, a locomotive will run me down. If you don't come, Simone is going to starve.

So little is required. So much is required. Coincidence of feeling. Coincidence of language. They coincide in literature, they coincide in dream. They coincide so rarely in life. Now! Touch me now. Don't rush away. Sleep with me in the morning. So little is requested. Too much is requested. Coincidence of chemistry. Coincidence of mechanics. What makes it so difficult to achieve coincidence? I cannot comprehend. I'm going out of my mind.

Now. Please now. Not tomorrow. Not in a week. Not in a month. Now. Everything else means pain. Everything else means torture. If it doesn't coincide, we shouldn't try. If it doesn't coincide, we have to give up.

Sex is a deadly poison, scribbles Simone. The risk of love is really too high. But what's the alternative? If you're afraid to eat bread, you must die.

BUT NOT EVERYBODY AGONIZES and dies for eros, writes Karenina. The world is populated with jovial gentlemen and robust females consuming sex like crabmeat or caviar. Last Sunday I met Goethe, a middle-aged German genius. He cruises through vaginal waters with his anima at ease, his face sunny as Lake Leman on an August afternoon. His penis is lazy, but watches out for adventures, his animate fingertips sift through the soft silk of imaginary skirts. Although Elephant's academic friends maintain that from the day of his entrance to Rome Goethe was given to the experience of rebirth, this, as Simone's brother pointed out to me, is just another piece of Princetonian sleaze. The answer is not rebirth but birth.

Upon his entrance in Rome Goethe enters Roma, an obese former girlfriend of Fellini's, squeezes deeply between her fat thighs and, experiencing a moderate thrill, inseminates her. An overweight imbecile, Roma gives birth to a mongoloid. But this bad news never reaches the poet's ears. His son is adopted by Roma's new lover, a superintendent, and dies at five. The day he is buried, Goethe describes his Roman mood, swinging between elation and depression, in a letter to Charlotte.

I have become more introvert than ever, Goethe informs her. Even women, with the exception of you, do not interest me anymore. Preparing for a subterranean journey, I get increasingly secretive and am about to fall in love with archeology. My bed stands next to a colossal cast of the head of Juno, a mysterious mask of a woman. I wish we were looking at it together. At last my lips are unsealed, and I can communicate with you in the right mood.

The lie, remarks Karenina, flows from Goethe's pen but not without a certain unease, since he would prefer not to communicate with Charlotte at all. But guilt, an emotion often stronger than love, moves his hand. Charlotte has turned forty-four. At thirty-seven, Goethe feels like her grandson. He wonders if Lotte has stopped menstruating but refrains from inquiring. However, the interest he takes in her flow inspires his studies in alchemy. He inscribes a leather-bound notebook with *Panta rei,* and begins to note his dreams about shipwreck in the Red Sea, sanguine sailors saving him from drowning, and his escape on board a steamer from the barren Charlottenland to the Virgin Islands. Examining the cause of his moodiness, Goethe confesses: I want to hold to my anima, but I cannot hold her. She flows out of me, a leaky vessel, and yet this gives me more pleasure than worry. It would help me so much to hear a friendly word from a female at this strange period of my life. Shall I invite Lotte here? No, at present I have to bear it all alone. Let me follow my heart and finish my course in silence.

Lotte keeps writing, and Goethe answers her letters, humidified with tears, with entries in *Panta rei:* Lotte's letters give me both joy and pain. All I can say is this: I have but one life, and I have risked all of it on this throw of the dice. If I come out of this alive and sane, if my mind, my constitution, and my good luck get the better of this crisis, I will be able to make everything up to her a thousandfold. If I perish, I perish.

If I come out of this alive and sane, my dear, writes Karenina to Vronsky, I may be able to finish my text on Goethe whose midlife crisis begins to ebb in Naples. Your love accompanies me. Wherever I am, I feel my need of you.

I am in a mood of great doubt, Goethe remarks, but I will let things resolve themselves, as they have so well done recently. Moreover, I have made the acquaintance of happy people, who are so because they are whole. The humblest human being, if he be whole, can be happy and attain perfection in his own way. That is what I will and must strive after. And I can do it, for at least I know wherein it consists and how it works. I have come to know myself better than I can well say. Karenina's hands tremble, and she spills her cold, sugarless coffee.

Goethe sketches *Faust,* unsuccessfully. But that particular evening he begins to write at 8:00 P.M. and spends the entire night at the desk. When he falls into bed at 6:00 A.M., the "Witch's Kitchen" is finished. But on the morrow depression returns and remains with him for five months. Stoned with anxiety, Goethe suffers the most severe writer's block of his life. But he continues to write letters and journals, the best of the best he is to produce.

My strange and undisciplined nature, which has made me suffer so much even in complete freedom and in the full enjoyment of every desire, will make it necessary for me to find my way back gradually even to you, even into the domain of your affairs. In these months of solitariness I have found my true self again, and that self is the self of an artist. Goethe considers this an important letter and waits for Charlotte's confirmation. He expects her to write: yes, that's what you are, an artist. But she doesn't answer and a long silence follows. Meanwhile

Goethe's relationship with a younger woman becomes known, his son is born, and a tone of resentment begins to mark his correspondence with Charlotte.

I must tell you that I cannot endure your recent treatment of me. When I am talkative, you close your lips. When I am eager, you accuse me of indifference. You criticize my every expression, every gesture. How are confidence and sincerity to flourish between us, when you have made up your mind to repel me by your mood? Goethe moves to a new paragraph and adds: I do not wholly abandon the hope that some-day you will see me again as I am.

I see you in the arms of a younger woman, writes Charlotte in her journal. How can I see how you are? You are opaque, I don't see through you. What do I mean to you? You sleep with so many women, and I'm about to lose my period. How can I not repel you? Since I love you, what else can I do? You hurt my pride. You humiliate me constantly, with your expressions and gestures. You don't tell me the truth, open your heart to me. How can I judge you properly? But I do not wholly abandon the hope that one day you will return to me.

A man—a woman. Two species with different speeds whose al-chemies fail to coincide, Karenina types. In agony, a woman asks a man to open his heart. He does, and emptiness is disclosed. In despair, a man begs a woman to open her heart. She does, and indifference is uncovered. But, on the other hand, emancipated women love and go mad, modern men go down the drain. But they don't wholly abandon the hope that someday they will see each other as they are.

H ow are they? asks Anna in a letter to Ann Kar. And Ann replies: As of here and now, none is whole, everybody's in pieces, suffering from neurosis, afraid of AIDS. In Manhattan there is an urge to get love under control. This makes eros sick, deaf-mute, and blind. When it's strived for, coincidence doesn't occur at all. Too much trying deregulates the mind. In Manhattan love grows into a destructive migratory locust. I wish I were with you in Urbino, could assist you in this period of stress. Forget about Vronsky, he isn't worth your agony. Sleep with other men, but don't get pregnant, you cannot afford a child. Use what I'm using. Ann ends her letter to Karenina and encloses a brochure on diaphragms:

Some couples want to separate the insertion of the diaphragm from their sexual activities. Others want to make the insertion part of their sex play, with the male helping. The diaphragm makes it easy for both types of insertion, since it can be put in any time before intercourse. But sexual excitement changes the anatomy of the vagina: the vagina expands and the cervix is pulled back and up. If you insert the diaphragm at this stage, the vaginal landmarks may feel a little different than usual, so be sure the diaphragm is positioned over the cervix. If your partner is not supportive of your use of a diaphragm, discuss the subject with him. You may find that a change in the jelly or the time of the intercourse may be the answer. If your partner understands your vaginal anatomy and the mechanics of insertion, the use of a diaphragm becomes a shared responsibility. You should never share needles with your partner! But share with him the secrets of the diaphragm.

Ann inserts the letter and the brochure into a large manila envelope, and returns to her essay on Picasso.

In Paris, Picasso's best friend shoots himself in a coffeehouse. In front of a woman who doesn't return his love, and three men who share her. Transforming himself into a corpse by means of a single boom, the man hopes to render the present four guilty for the rest of their lives. We don't know if he succeeds, but the boom does something to Picasso. The painter isn't present at the marble-topped table. But in the past he participated in the erotic division of the charming Germaine. After the suicide he paints her as his friend's anima, a ghost escaping from his dead body.

A dark-haired professor from Barnard claims that this picture expresses the artist's mourning for the only human being the piggish Picasso ever cared for. Listening to her argument, Ann thinks about death cementing what life cannot bind, the hardness of the neon light, the seminar members' faces resembling bad Xerox copies, and the beginning of her life in New York—in a new setup and tongue.

How many years have passed since? Five? No, six. Leaning back in a Proustian mood, Ann reflects on the half-lesbian, half-gay semi-utopia of eros, the way sex is sliced into the sandwiches of academic subjects, and how out of old taboos' dissection, new taboos are born. Her musing is interrupted by a flippant request addressed to the seminar members by a gay squirrel from the *Village Voice:* If you masturbate in front of mirrors, or while reading porno magazines, please raise your hand. While all hands go up, Ann ponders on the omnipotence of the party line. As in her homeland's Central Committee, nobody dissents, including Ann Kar, and the seminar's maternal chief leads her sheep safely into the eternal Roma of sex. They enter through the Porta del Popolo and head for the *nox ambrosiana* of a leftist bordello—to deconstruct male dreams and indulge in a female reverie of erotic liberation, lunar and down to earth.

In Barcelona, the Barnard professor explains, Picasso and consorts engage in sex in front of each other, sharing the same women. A couple of pillows are slipped under a prostitute's head, while another prostitute submits her cunt to be licked by male tongues. At once, they dart to their delight within the vulva, while Picasso rests his chin just above the prostitute's clitoris, and calls her to come on. From this position he can see what is going on. He is equipped with neither sketchbook nor brush, but his penis is hard as a pencil. Although he is less excited than his colleagues, his eyes are lit with curiosity. He watches the movement of soft red lips, and his friend's successful attempt to enter first one woman, then the other. He observes the powerful thrusts of female bottoms, the prick penetrating the cunt. Picasso's eager eyes take it all in and, at last, he springs up from his position and, profiting from the prostitute's outward motion, bends down between her and the man, and pushes the point of his tongue under her clitoris.

The documentation of Picasso's Saturday orgies isn't exhibited by Barcelona's cultural institutions. The young artist stores his drawings in the drawers of his mother's bedroom. A hundred years later the Barnard scholar digs them out, and presents them in a New York sex seminar. A thousand years from now, thinks Ann, my stepsister's moon scholar will masturbate in front of a drawing where Picasso's prick is one-third of the distance from his chin to his navel. To his left a prostitute studies the article's impressive size, another measures it, and two of his friends, watching the proceedings with an air of amusement, shout out: Take it between your breasts! You'll see a difference then. The prick is introduced into the cleft of a woman's bosom and, in rapture at the touch of soft flesh on either side, assumes even more satisfactory proportions. But he isn't up to his full height yet, she exclaims. Come and help me! Stand behind Pablo and frig him, while I work on him in front. That's the way to get him up to concert pitch. When I feel him long and stiff enough in my mouth, I'll get up and take his measure. The success of this plan is immediate, and when the measurements are taken, the proportions are found to be exactly twenty-one and seven inches respectively, while in the drawing they are three inches to one inch.

THE BARNARD PROFESSOR interprets Picasso's eminent erection as a representation of Pan and points out that panic seems to bend his neck, in accordance with the politics of the anarchists who caused panic in Barcelona. Listening to the Spanish specialist's strained staccato, Ann Kar recalls Count Panin, and his statuette of Pan. Subsequently her mind wanders away and encounters Moses Maimonides on a cubist beach in Spain. Strolling along the sea, they engage in a discussion of all the names of God occurring in the Scriptures.

I maintain, says Maimonides, that names are derived from actions. But there is one distinct and exclusive designation of the divine which does not descend from activity, namely the tetragrammaton, consisting of the letters *yod, hè, vau,* and *hè*.

It's a mild autumnal day, and Maimonides praises the excellent visibility. Perfectly smooth, the sea reflects two clouds. In his last letter from Denmark, says Moses, Hamlet compares one cloud to Elephant, our mutual friend from Princeton, the other to El Weasel, whom I don't know, and likens his father-in-law to a double-folded curtain.

Ann walks at Moses' side, keeping a certain distance between him and herself. She assumes that he's scared of women in the state of uncleanliness, in which she happens to find herself. Visibility is excellent, and the imprints of their shoes can be seen all the way back. Maimonides communicates the meaning of the tetragrammaton with increasing intensity. Every intelligent person knows, says he, that a word of forty-two letters is impossible.

However, Wittgenstein defines words with forty-two letters as particularly suitable for philosophical disputes.

For God's sake, Ann, don't bring in that assimilated Austrian Jew! Let him hibernate at Trinity. I dislike weak-minded men, but too-bright fellows bore me as well. And Ludwig in particular gets on my nerves. If he could, he would simply wipe out my tetragrammaton. *Schluss! Aus!* Then he would undertake the *Anschluss* of my thoughts, while sitting around and drinking tea with Russell.

As the day progresses, and the sea transmutes from silver to gold, Moses' excitement grows, and his voice rises: Today a heavy rain of gold coins falls between Danae's thighs. But you and I, we must oppose cheap glitter with true illumination. Look how the impressions of our shoes unite into a path, a thread of golden light—not metal, Ann— running through Spain's sand. Easy answers, so attractive at first sight, have to be reexamined, sudden emotions must be mistrusted.

Like falling in love at first sight?

Eros, Ann, presents us with eternal dilemmas. Don't you think it's just a vapor exuded by the brain? A *danse macabre* of intoxicated selves unable to discriminate between inside and out? In respect to love I happen to agree with Wittgenstein, it's something we should be silent about. To fall in love at first sight is as embarrassing as to boast about one's brain tumors or a cancer of the liver. You, such an intelligent woman, how can you even mention love at first sight! Your words make nonbeing triumph over existence, the indeterminate preside over determination, the impossible annihilate the possible. Oh, don't torture me with what is philosophically impermissible and, in addition, privately problematic. You say love at first sight, but mean a particular man you are involved with, an almost illiterate type who, at best, before going to bed reads a paragraph from a second-rate novel. Believe me, Ann, he'll never touch the texts you write, and should you ever try to read them to him aloud, which I hope you'll never do, he'll fall into deep snoring.

Dusk encircles them, and Maimonides' arguments flicker in the air like fireflies. Now they rest on his irritation, now they are propelled by his affection for Ann, a woman in love with another man, but who shares with Moses what her lover refuses to share with her—the salty air of a short sea vacation.

There is something to what you say, Moses, he doesn't give much of a damn about me. Last summer, night after night, I dreamt about going with him to the sea. I even bought a black bikini, but he didn't take the hint.

Let's not talk about him, Ann. Will you have dinner with me? I know a place close to the beach where they have first-class lobster. It's called Sarcástica Seductora, and the shellfish there is as fresh as in Boston and as tender as on Block Island. If you want an appetizer, they have exquisite oysters, and a good local wine, the Mocero. But now do me a favor: sit down and contemplate the setting sun, the best spectacle life can offer us.

It can't be better than Brook's *Mahabarata* at the Majestic.

I have nothing against Peter, I like his heavenly blue eyes, and when he has a hunch, he can direct the devil. But I still prefer the sun. Every time I watch it set, I feel as if I were confronting ideals, abstract beings which are neither bodies nor forces dwelling in bodies. Sterile commerce endangers the ideal, Ann, but we shall defend texts that don't sell, pictures nobody buys, inconvenient theories—the hardly perceptible charm of the sublime. You and I, we must preserve the sun's after-image under our lids!

The owner offers Moses and Ann a table in the corner, and as they sit down, Maimonides inquires about the Museum of Extinct Race— planned for Eastern Europe—Ann has mentioned to him in a letter from New York. What's the race?

Jews.

Jews? repeats Moses, and a shadow of perplexity covers his face. I thought this part of the world got rid of them. Who wants to bring them back?

Absence creates presence. In the minds of people who have never seen a Jew, they're already back. Schoolchildren draw Jews, the males in green, with red hair and flaming beards, reminiscent of Tasmanians, the females as turquoise-colored Salomes stripping their veils. Gentile priests and theology students are very much into Semites. And some survivors are into them too. A Holocaust vogue of scholarship and business is about to take off—and a Study Shalom Center to open on the shore of Lake Genesareth. You may be asked to contribute, Professor Maimonides. Why not prove that not only Jesus but virtually every Jew can walk on water?

The arrival of oysters interrupts the chat. Their fishy, bloodless flesh scintillates, and Ann observes with admiration how Moses digs in, consumes a dozen in no time, and wipes his lips with a paper napkin.

Recently I have been rereading Aristotle, Ann. There is no evidence of a theory of the eternity of the universe, neither in his writings, nor in the general consensus of the ancient people. Lobster arrives and is strategically positioned in the middle of the table. Moses takes a leg and sucks it out: wonderful, perfectly soft, Ann. He washes it down with a sip of Mocero, and points out to his companion the graceful silhouette of a waiter. She calls the boy, orders an espresso, notices his beautiful hands, and says: he must be an actor. That evening only two more couples are dining in the restaurant, and both are twice as old as Ann and Moses.

Will you meet me here two years from today, Ann?

In two years? What's the occasion, Moses?

I'll be twenty-five, a quarter of a century old. We will order oysters with Mocero, and you'll tell me more about the Jewish venture. What are they going to display in the extinction museum? The famous head of the herring Bruno Schulz's dad traded for the soleless shoe of my mom? Anyhow, if you have a say in this, make them choose the right spot. The top three on my list are Brody, Drohobycz, and Frydek Místek, to appease the Jewish Czechs discriminated against by the Galicians.

Can I walk you home? On the promenade along the shore, close to the harbor? asks Maimonides, taking Ann's arm. It's longer, but I'm sure you'll enjoy the moon set against the maze of masts and ropes, and the canvas blowing out in the breeze. Have you ever met this writer of Polish descent, what's his name?

Conrad?

Yes. Whenever I smell the sea, the symbolism of his ships pops up in my mind. Lonely pyramids and aquatic insects, they meander through sunlit mists and escape with ineffectual effort into the gloom of the ever more distant self, searching for a place to rest. The Nigger of a self encounters the Narcissus of a self, and together they head for the sea. A slight haze blurs the horizon, water sparkles like a carpet of pearls, the short black tug gives pluck to windward, paddlewheels turn fast. Reading Conrad is as good as reading Aristotle, a sea of ancient metaphors unites the two. The sky and the earth, normally unfaithful to each other, in his novels they sleep in a tight embrace as the tides carry them to the end of the world. There is no better refuge than the sea, no better grave. It leaves no room for doubt, and one desires to be a mouse in the food-closet of the *Narcissus,* to live there as long as the ship sails, and to be buried in its wreck when it sinks.

We have to part now, my dear. Many thanks for the dinner. The lobster was excellent, and so were the oysters. No, don't accompany me to the airport. See you in two years, Moses, at the Sarcástica Seductora.

BACK IN NEW YORK, Ann inspects the deteriorating seascape on her bedroom's ceiling, smells coffee, listens to the sound of a flute, thinks of Picasso as Pan, and remembers Pound in China, climbing up a steep mountain path and talking about a white pelican under an hibiscus tree. Relax, she admonishes herself, lower your expectations, don't mistake your man's mishmash for the mind of a Maimonides.

It's morning and Ann should get up. But she dozes and dreams of white silk curtains painted with white leaves. White elms on a slope. White chestnut brush in a valley. White stone elephants in the suburbs of Nanking. Victims of the Cultural Revolution—pairs in a park seated on newspapers, the safe distance of a page between their bodies. Bike rides with Karl along dusty roads. Their journey to China and their lack of intimacy—caused by too much closeness.

Opening her eyes, Ann recalls a middle-aged couple in profile, the man's tiny nose touching the woman's soft mouth, his hand unbuttoning the top of her silk blouse. A daring piece of clothing, it's embroidered with two dragons, each of them placed over a breast. Catching a phoenix, they signal the advent of a post-revolutionary period, when flirts begin to replace the study of the red scriptures. Ann closes her eyes and the spring in Nanking begins to unfold. In May Mao's portrait, a cup of tea in his yellow hand, comes down from the main wall of the central railroad station. *The Devil Incarnate* with the smashing Gérard Philipe is playing at the cinema The East Is Red, and a long line forms outside.

My God, which way will it go? a university bureaucrat whispers into Ann's ear the day a pupil of Matisse returns from the rice fields and is reinstated as the dean of the art school.

My God, which way will it go? the pupil of Matisse whispers into Ann's ear. *Plus ça change, plus c'est la même chose.*

Everyone in the university learns English. Mao's portrait, a cup of tea in his hand, disappears from the main wall of the university library. In the middle of the campus wild doves build a nest in the old mulberry tree.

Do you know about the campaign against doves? the pupil of Matisse whispers into Ann's ear. Mao accused them of consuming too much grain and ordered constant noise to keep them in the air. They couldn't come to rest and dropped dead from the sky. It went on for months, the campaign against doves. And here they are back with us. Survivors of a holocaust, they build their nest in the middle of the campus. What do you think? Is this reinstatement of mine just a trick? Do they want to test me in order to get me? I'm seventy-six. How much more can I take? The room they gave me is the size of a closet, I can't paint in it. I don't have a table. I have only a bed. Is it genuine? They really want me back? At the beginning I thought you were part of their game. That they brought you here to test me. But it's all right now. I trust you. I enjoy your company.

Tell me, how's Paris? How's Montmartre? No, I didn't live there. I dreamt about having a studio at Montmartre, but I couldn't afford it. I stayed in a small sublet around the corner from the Gare Saint Lazare. A very noisy place, with little light. Downstairs was an Italian restaurant, and the owner let me have the room for free in exchange for all kinds of jobs I did for him. Cleaning. Washing up. It left me hardly any time to paint.

Oh yes. In those days there was great interest in Chinese art. But nobody gave a damn about a young painter from Nanking. It was so hard, I began to despair. Then, suddenly, I had such incredibly good luck. A waiter cut his finger and I had to replace him. That evening I served a well-known art critic. He was gay and took an interest in me. No, I wasn't gay. I didn't even understand what it was all about. He was very gentle. He didn't force me into anything. He kind of accepted me as a friend. No, not as a friend. Rather as a protégé. He started to invite me to his studio in the Quartier Latin. Once, when I visited him on a Sunday afternoon and was about to take the first sip of tea, the bell rang and a short man entered the room. Matisse—Mr. Chou from Nanking.

Yes. It was meant to be a surprise. This was my twenty-first birthday. You see, goodness exists. I'll never forget it. I had a portfolio of my work with me. Small things. Pencil drawings of dry leaves. Of roofs. Of the dirty dishes in my restaurant. *Mais c'est charmant,* said Matisse. Can you imagine? He said my work was charming, lovely. Of course, said he, you must study. You're an artist. You may become a great painter. Why don't you come to my studio? Tomorrow night. There'll be a model and you can draw. He was so simple. So modest. I'll never forget the way he behaved. Never.

No. I can't show you anything. All of my work has been dispersed. It has disappeared from museums, and private collections no longer exist. My old studio? The house has been razed to the ground. I don't know what happened to my work. I don't know. Maybe something has been preserved in Shanghai. And there is this old friend of mine in Peking. A lady. Very old and sick. She has been spared. She hasn't been thrown out of her apartment. Yes. That's a good idea. I should give you her address. Perhaps you can find her when you go there. She was such a cultivated woman. A poet and a beauty. But I haven't seen her for twenty years. However, the other day somebody mentioned her to me. It's a miracle she's still alive. It's a miracle I'm still alive. In fact, I'm only half alive. A painter who has lost all of his work is as good as dead.

Oh, no. I don't want to complain. I was in Paris. I met Matisse. I became a pupil of Matisse. I painted many good pictures. I was counted among the best painters in this country. But, on the other hand, life has been hard on me. My work has vanished from the surface of the earth. That's what I mean when I call myself half dead. I'm alive as a man. Dead as an artist.

Oh I believe you're right. Some things may surface again. They might have been preserved. Somewhere. Miraculously. No, I don't exclude it.

It's possible and I'm grateful you want to look around. To search for them. But we have only one life, and I'm seventy-six. My heart is bad. Asthma plagues my lungs. After four years in the rice fields my hands can hardly hold a brush. You saw my room—like a closet. And you know how slowly our bureaucrats proceed. It will take them years to provide me with a proper studio, if they ever do it. My life is over. But I'm so glad we've met. Now tell me, how's Paris? Is Sacre-Coeur still so white? Its domes, like white eggs, remind me of the doves in the mulberry tree. It's so sad. Two of their eggs fell from the nest. What bad luck. First holocaust and now a new misfortune.

It's like the Jews in Poland? What do you mean? You must forgive me, I know so little about European history. I left Paris in '31 and haven't been back since. So you had a holocaust as well? Oh, how sad! Millions were exterminated? Like here? Like here. Yes, who knows how many millions. This country is so overpopulated. Life is so cheap. If I could give you an estimate? How many millions? I have no idea. Some say two. Others say ten. But many who were meant to perish, survived. I returned. Others return from the rice fields as well. And from the camps. Doves exist still.

You know, I believed wild doves were extinct. But I was wrong. Here they are. Life continues. We've met. Tell me, is Matisse finally appreciated as he should be? For many years he was in the shadow of Picasso. And Braque. But really, he's so much better than the two of them. He's at ease with himself. He's at ease with color. Don't you think he's the greatest colorist of this century? A truly painterly painter, not just a devourer of everything, like Picasso? Of course, Picasso is great. A genius. But he's possessed with malice. No, no. I don't imply that an artist should be decent. Artists are swine, you know that as well as I do. But there is more to Matisse than just decency. He's at ease with art. He doesn't force it. He's gentle. Generous. Intense. But not too intense. *Nonchalant,* as they say in French. Picasso's always so hectic. Matisse's always so calm. Of course I idealize him. After all, I was his pupil. He took an interest in me. The only French painter to take interest in a Chinese art student from Nanking.

THE DEAN OF THE ART SCHOOL in Nanking is dead, Ann Kar writes to Karenina. A million people are dead in Afghanistan. An extinct nation joins another extinct nation, an extinct species shares its fate with another extinct species. An ever-greater army of black derelicts begs at Manhattan subway stations, ghettos are depopulated by AIDS. But people mind their own business, expect the world to be saved by politicians or human rights advocates. When we were young, Anna, we believed in a solidarity of common sense. But where are we today?

Two weeks later an answer from Anna reaches Kar: The question you ask, Ann, is purely rhetorical. Personally, I'm at the end. You and I, we're just two hysterical females, making noise like bugs in the grass, cooking a sentimental bubbling soup in an old caldron. Our love for humanity resembles our affection for the Vronskys. Neither mankind nor men want us to agonize for them, they want us to accommodate them—to stop complaining about the broken seals and the smashed bones, about virtue rushed into destruction and the honored sin. Read Trakl, Ann dear, read Kafka. Accept the futility we're part of, the meaninglessness of the little good we discover within ourselves. It won't save anything. Look around, Ann. Corpses rot away. Arrogance sprouts by the roadside. Crimes are called errors. Errors are excused. Facts are forgotten. Illusions are treasured. Truth is mistreated. And we keep making useless noise, as if we were Saint-Simons. But our words, sweetheart, are mere words, we're old enough to know better.

Let us come to our senses, Ann, and stop telling stories that embarrass people. Drop China, Afghanistan—and our men, good for nothing. Let's turn silent, strive for oblivion, present good deeds as charity or sheer madness. We're adult females—let's go for adolescent pleasures. Let's track in Nepal, exercise, diet, practice safe, part-time sex, paint our lips, make up our brains, henna our gray hair. Well-groomed and fit, our selves will learn how to put up with the world's approaching collapse. Let's grow up and accept the wisdom that a superintendent whispers affectionately into his spouse's ear: life is about solitude. Life is about egoism.

Anna, dearest, answers Kar, don't lose your spirits. In Riverside Park leaves fall, lovers outline themselves. Before going to sleep, I read Confucian odes and dream of hibiscus under my black Chinese comforter. Dust accumulates in our eyes, Anna, but don't despair. In this zoo of a life we have more freedom than most animals. October expires and geese fly south, resting on their way at the shore of the Raritan canal, or at the banks of Carnegie Lake. Seasons change. Performing in pantomime, trees dress and undress. As dew turns to frost, pears burn in the branches of pear trees. A small white dog barks at the geese, and cheap metaphors swirl in my ears. Each year the fall feels more like a cardiac arrest prompting a flood of penultimate recollections. Matisse's pupil is dead, and so is Mandelshtam, I guess. Why do I want to write a requiem for them? Why do I insist on composing epitaphs for the best minds of every generation?

Why? replies Karenina a month later. Because there is nothing more beautiful than to recover the memory of people whose integrity is stronger than fear, who can live through horror without giving themselves away. There is nothing more exhilarating than speaking with the dead whose words we know by heart, whose texts we admire. It's like going to a sanitorium where nothing is demanded of us but to regain health. It's like going to the south with old friends and paying homage to the perfect proportions of Agrigento's Greek temples. It's like receiving a certificate of the absolute at the entrance to the shadow cave, or a Siberian camp.

By the way, Mandelshtam has a problem. He lost his right glove on his way from chopping wood, and his hand is turning blue. This new disaster proves how utterly helpless Osip is in the face of the life the common nobodies have assigned to him. The cold damages his hand and for a week he cannot hold a pencil. When his fingers are revived, the pencil cannot be found. Ten days pass until a few friendly prisoners begin to whisper into each other's ears that Mandelshtam needs a pencil. A guard is bribed, and in the wake of Osip's birthday a pencil arrives together with a piece of paper in which the officers' uniforms were originally packed. The paper is brown but of good quality, and its smooth surface with a few darker dots appeals to Mandelshtam. But the too-hard graphite produces a very light gray. There is little contrast, and Mandelshtam cannot read what he writes. Nevertheless, he scribbles away, likening his lost glove to his fate. He sees himself lost in the snow, paper is covered with his footsteps, nobody is interested in his verses, but a kind guy bribes a guard in order to smuggle them out. But does the guard forward the stuff? Or does he take money, cigarettes or bread, and throw the papers away?

Writing is a compulsion. Although unable to decipher his poems, Osip keeps covering the brown paper with imperceptible script. He compares snow to a shroud that will envelop him, crows to messengers from heaven, upright pines to females, fallen trees to corpses. He perceives air as a kiss of death. Ice-cold, it kills you when you breathe. But the air resembles Nadia's hands as well. It touches you, and you feel alive. At night, Osip keeps turning from one side to another. An avalanche of images keeps him from a sound rest. Sleepless or half asleep, he sails to Byzantium, crosses black and red seas, admires chestnut-colored women on the terrace of a beach café. Aphrodite meets him, her mouth opens in a smile, her right hand balances a fan, her left hand carries a rose.

Heavy with lice, blankets contribute to Mandelshtam's fever. He scratches himself, hurts his skin. The phone rings in his Moscow apartment, but he cannot reach the receiver. The Underwood is typing and he wonders: who's using it at midnight? He listens to men snore and around four o'clock in the morning, just before falling asleep, becomes aware of Olga's head against his chin, and thinks: I'm still alive. They haven't finished me off.

Yesterday, writes Karenina, I received two sheets of brown paper I cannot decipher and a letter from Nadia. She writes her memoirs, in order not to abandon hope and to recall what Mandelshtam told her about literature. It's a keyboard of references, he said, a keyboard of cross-references, and we're a bunch of borrowers. Poets steal from each other *wie die Raben,* and so do painters. I chat with Dante, you gossip with Laura. Multicolored birds, we hum to each other. Grasshoppers, we inspect the same grass blades, smell the same metaflowers. Word is culture. Culture is image. Milton recites Ovid, and when he stops, I continue. A glove retrieved from Siberian snows, our text never stops. Banned from the earth, it continues on the moon.

Mandelshtam's wife warms water and pours it over her cold hands, again and again. The faintest noise of Leningrad makes her tremble. She can hear grass growing in the streets, a virgin forest whisper. Eating bread with homemade black currant jam, Nadia licks the spoon and is comforted by its roundness, drinks strong Russian tea and is consoled by its bitterness. So little is needed to survive—a cup of tea, a piece of bread. So much is needed to continue—good health, good luck, the skin of an elephant. But what's the sense of it all? I live to write, but am not a writer, just Mandelshtam's wife reminding herself: it's the last glass of jam, leave some for tomorrow, the last cigarette, smoke half of it, save the other half. Give the crumbs to sparrows, they expect affection as well. Don't indulge in weakness, mourn friends who were killed, who killed themselves. Why can't the righthand glove be worn over the left hand? Why are you punishing us so much, God? Why have you chosen me to endure, me of all people?

I reread suicide notes from too many friends, see too many people whose legs are as thin as matchsticks. They can barely walk, even with a stick, and I watch them fall down in the corridors and streets, and being dragged away. I count death warrants. But why I? People die of disease, are arrested and rearrested, curse fate, pass away. I curse fate too, but I stay, visualize the stage, see actors failing in one drama after another, and think: it pays to play the public. Shakespeare may be our contemporary, but that which is acted here is superior to Shakespeare.

A man who argued in favor of a decree disappears. A man who argued against it disappears. Men who didn't argue at all disappear just the same. The game is called secret disappearance and half a century from now will be imitated in Argentina. A children's game, here it's played by adults with confused minds, palms stained with blood. They consider their failures a success, their successes a failure, camouflage themselves as much as they can, bury each other in silence, silence themselves to death. Their faces make me shiver. But isn't my vulnerability an idyll of the past?

DEAR ANN, WRITES KARENINA, my imminent suicide is an idyll of the future past. Against the gold mines of Siberia, the mine of my mind is a laughable affair, but it will bring me down. I am a sucker for erotic continuity, and now I have become hooked on Vronsky's blue eyes, so young and full of expectation when he wakes up in the morning. His gaze belies his age—he'll be fifty next December—and reminds me of our first spring together, of bluebells sprouting from the ground. His look warms my heart, but, alas, his words freeze it. Yesterday, coming out of the bathroom, he confessed: when you rang yesterday, I was talking to somebody else. I put you on hold, and by the time I was finished, I had forgotten about you. Did you realize it?

I did. In the last two weeks I have been considering calling you no more, and seeing what happens. Will you call by yourself, or use the opportunity to get out of my life? But I decided that life is too short for experiment, that I'm too old to be a guinea pig. What shall I do, Ann? I try not to complain about the little he consents to share with me, but I live on the brink of despair. Why does love render me so frail? A Russian Lady Chatterley, I eye the cosmos from a noble angle, but give myself away—oblivious of my position and pride. I, the modern Karenina, long to suck my keeper's prick, to soften and open up. All desire and fire, I turn my back on Vronsky—and leap over to him. I fall at his knees, hold his hands, bend forward—blindly, trembling, and hold him as if he were the atoms of my life.

My dearest, Ann answers, a similar misfortune has befallen me as well. Where are the good old days of masturbation in front of a dim mirror? Of games without any royal claim? What was dormant is awake again. What seemed quiescent shoots anew through my body. Mute and forlorn, the middle-aged hen has her bowels inflamed, her beak averted. Cackling in anguish: my heart is broken, she cares for nothing other than his hand to smooth her skin in a slow journey, starting at the neck and descending all the way to the toenails. Then up and down again. Up and down again. She closes her eyes, stuffs her brain with unspeakable rubbish or switches it off, loses weight, and submits herself to a cock who craves another chicken. Shut the door, she begs, lie down in the dark, grope me, soothe me, reassure me, cloud my mind, clip my wings, pet me to death. Has biology caught up with me finally? Am I to return to the prehistory of our sex?

Yes, dearest Anna, I too want his body on top of mine—and not once in a while but every night. I too want him to abandon the world for me the very moment he prepares to conquer it. I, an ex-erotic friend of Djuna Barnes, scream for bluebells which refuse to blossom in our midnightwood. Still, I waste my time looking for them with infinite patience or, worse, I invite D. H. Lawrence for five o'clock, and ask him, the stiff-upper-lip Brit: Will my agony be good for something? No doubt, he answers, putting on his heaviest Oxbridge accent. There is no better lens for the study of suffering than our own sick stomachs. Vulnerability illuminates. The strongest light is provided by the fire burning within. Good luck numbs, misfortune makes us discover a lost glove and a frozen hand. The blinding white of a Siberian day, Plato or Kant.

Dear Ann, Karenina answers on a postcard of Red Square. I'm not a great fan of Lawrence, but he may be right. Recently the heat and hot water were shut off in Moscow. Instantly I found the right words to deal with Mandelshtam's right hand and the hot water Nadia was pouring over her own hands, her fingertips returning from blue to pink.

Your last letter, Anna, Kar replies, was truly a consolation. You mentioned Mandelshtam, and opened my eyes to Manhattan: brain bits splashing onto asphalt, bad teeth, scraps of skin at the foot of a skyscraper. I saw with fresh eyes a legless black man, his breast tatooed with AIDS, at a cash-machine center, and I overheard with fresh ears a well-dressed man's reply to his *spare a quarter, sir*. Stuffing banknotes into his pocket, he said: I have to take care of myself. But on the subway I saw a black girl forcing her mom to part with a dollar. You helped me, Anna, to take my gaze off myself, face what's worst and what's best, detect this city's readiness to explode—on the Lower East Side, the Upper West Side, and everywhere else. The horrors and delights newspaper headlines announce here daily require the pen of a Suetonius. While delicacies dissolve on the tongues of financial crocodiles, a pizza crust is fished out of the garbage, devoured by a hungry wolf. The more money is spent on top, the less money goes to the bottom. You can skate in the SoHo lofts, or share your hole with roaches. Junk is sold as art, life is disposed of like junk. Do slavery and the laissez-faire of freedom meet at a subtle junction?

HOSTIA IS DEAD and Propertius, trying to forget her, studies Egypt at his patron's library. He reads about Erasistratus who, discarding the prejudices to which he was born, begins dissecting the human body in the schools of Alexandria, where the mixing together of Greek and Egyptian corpses has weakened those religious feelings of respect for the dead that make anatomy shocking. So here this art flourishes because of the low moral tone rather than from a search for knowledge. Currently Erasistratus of Cos is occupied with curing Antiochus, the grandson of Aristotle. Antiochus has fallen deeply in love with his young stepmother, and is pining away in silence and despair. Used to cutting flesh, in no time Erasistratus takes apart the young man's mind, diagnoses the illness and, in accordance with the principles of removal and transplantation, finds a cure. The father is to give up his wife to his own son. Within hours, Antiochus's health is restored. Within days, the name of his father is on everybody's lips. A famous general who once conquered his enemies, Seleucus is now praised for conquering himself.

It's a good example of how anatomy can influence and improve morality. Freud should have dismembered the body instead of the mind. Neurophysiology, not psychoanalysis, is the answer. You dissect cells, and the soul reveals itself. But to study the psyche with a knife, one has to be bold enough to face the mob's outcry, says Erasistratus to his friend Philadelphus, a learned pharaoh who, however, does not achieve much as a scholar since he succumbs to laziness and love of pleasure.

It's Saturday night, writes Propertius, and I imagine Erasistratus and Philadelphus sitting together and sipping wine. Gout plagues me lately, complains Philadelphus, I'm tired of luxury and wouldn't mind changing places with a beggar. My concubines bore me increasingly, the Egyptian as well as the Greek ones. I feel best when I'm completely immobilized, like now, and have my favorite slave read me Aristotle. Then I'm at ease with myself. I'm tired of ruling this country and all the annexed territories of Arabia, Lydia, Phoenicia, Coele-Syria, Ethiopia, Pamphylia, Cilicia, Caria, Cyprus, and the Cyclades, our most recent gain. Wars bore me. I would like the cities of Greece to be bound to me by ties of friendship, not by conquest. You think it's possible? To cultivate the art of peace instead of plunging people into the miseries of war?

It's not impossible. But to pursue peace with the military budget skyrocketing and the army having too much to say isn't easy either.

That's the problem. Our forces are too enormous. Two hundred thousand foot soldiers, twenty thousand horses, two thousand chariots, four hundred Ethiopian elephants, fifteen hundred warships. But in spite of it, Egypt will fall, like all other empires. No matter what they do. No matter how hard they try. They may fall apart because they fight, or because they relax. But for my part I would rather sit back, see you more often, drink wine, discuss philosophy, get acquainted with anatomy. I admire your mastery of dissection, the way you cured young Antiochus, so quickly, so elegantly. Were there more men like you, the world would take a turn for the better. By the way, are you interested in any of my concubines? I could easily spare some. Gout makes me woo muses, not women.

It's no good passing on to a friend females who love you. They are human too, although we're always forgetting it.

You're right. If I had more energy, I would set up a school for girls at my harem, like the one we have for boys. I would like my daughters to be as educated as my sons. It's a long time since you told me about the significance of women's education as the only way to bring them closer to men, to close the gap between the sexes. The idea appeals to me, and I'm the right man in the right place to take the first step. But gout deprives me of all energy. I don't supervise anything properly anymore, not even the finances.

How are they?

This year our income has tripled and amounts now to fourteen thousand talents, a million and a half artabas, five million bushels. To this you have to add gold, silver, precious stones and other valuable assets in the treasury. Trade down the Nile has increased, and we develop the new coasting trade on the Mediterranean. People get richer and richer, and inflation is down. Presently this is the most powerful country in the world. But it will go down the drain, although not during our lifetime. When exactly will it fall? I can't prophecize. But what has risen must corrupt. It's a simple deduction but, naturally, the limited brains of my generals cannot grasp it. They believe soon the entire earth will be ours, the whole disk will be called Egypt. How childish of them! Of our recent glory only some stones in the desert will remain, a few frescoes and texts. The memory of how you cured the young Antiochus by means of his dad's generosity.

Look at the swift cangias rushing down the river. I love the Nile, Philadelphus, with all its lotus flowers and hippopotamuses.

Panta rei. Everything is in flux. Tomorrow nothing will pass what is today. In a split second, present becomes past. Birth and death embrace.

While a crocodile devours a pig, another pig is born.

Divine wisdom! So I avoid splendor raised on the ruins of somebody else's home and want to permit the Greek settlers to form their own free state in the Nile delta. I would like to be remembered not as a military despot, but as a philosopher and poet who, a thousand years from now, could still be counted among the minor Pleiades of Alexandria. May posterity judge me from the epitaphs I had rhymed for my beloved wives. May I be praised as a good pupil of yours—and the first instructor of girls.

A WEEK LATER, continues Propertius, Philadelphus dies in the thirty-eighth year of his reign, in the presence of Erasistratus of Cos, his best friend. The eminent pharaoh leaves Egypt wealthier and more powerful than when it came to him from his father, and is succeeded by his eldest son, Ptolemy. He assumes the name Euergetes, marries Berenice, the lovely child of a princess, and starts his rule with the Assyrian war. Aware of her husband's deadly struggle, Berenice sacrifices a bull to the gods and vows that if her husband survives, she will cut off her beautiful blonde tresses and hang them up in the temple—a token of her gratitude. Euergetes conquers Syria and returns home safe, and the queen's locks are yielded up to the knife, while Conon, the imperial astronomer, is grouping fixed stars into constellations. Since one of the many clusters discovered by him is as yet unnamed, he marks it out on his celestial globe and calls it the Hair of Berenice. Subsequently the queen's tresses become the subject of a poem by Callimachus. Catullus translated it into Latin and read it to me last week. One of its metaphors, notes Propertius at the edge of his manuscript, struck me as particularly shocking. Callimachus makes Berenice's locks swear by the head from which they were cut that they had rebelled against leaving the queen and being raised to the stars. But, alas, the hair couldn't prevent the cruel separation, and this provoked de Sade's famous saying: Long before the divine Marquis, sadism was practiced in Egypt.

In addition to the constellation, a city is named after Berenice. To commemorate the queen's golden tresses war prisoners, criminals, slaves, and dissidents dig gold from the mines of Berenice, three miles outside the town's main gate. Men and women alike crawl with lamps on their foreheads searching for gold veins, tunneling the quartz by hand. The hewn stone is dragged out by children, and old men break it with small hammers. Younger girls wash the fragments and grind them to dust in spar mills. They are turned not by oxen but by older girls and women, three to a spar and naked. Armed Nubians guard, fetter, and flog them. All work without rest, and welcome death like a mistress.

Poor Berenice, whispers Propertius, she's appalled by her husband's misdeeds but still in love with him. Touching her absentmindedly, Euergetes keeps thinking of ways to lower production costs. Obviously, the pool of labor has to be enlarged, while food supplies are cut. One must introduce a new tax—whoever cannot pay it will be sent to the mines, his family included—and a language decree. Come here, my cutie, I'll confiscate the property of non-native speakers, and ban them to Berenice. This will provoke uprisings, and put more slaves into my hands. Pressing Berenice's tits, the pharaoh hisses into her ear: you're dying to be fucked, but I prefer my mines to your cunt. Their ceilings glitter with gold, your hair turns gray. The older you get, the more you thirst for my prick, but I'm about to stop entering that foul mine of yours! I need fresh blood—blonde, young. Seven-year-old kids are on my mind, all golden locks and pink, peachy skin.

Stop it, gray pig! Don't touch my prick or I'll kick you. Tomorrow is a hard day. I'm inspecting the gold mines, the pride of Egypt, the glory of the civilized world. No, you aren't coming with me. You bitch in heat, you stay in your pig bed. Stop pestering me, or you'll regret it.

You stink, you disgust me. It's the last time I consent to receive you. From now on I'll ride baby calves, not a putrid cow. Kids, that's what I need, tight green nuts, firm rosebuds. I'll crack them apart, crush their petals. Blood will splash out of their cunts, they'll cry. But I'll pacify them with sweets, and go inside once more, scratch their alabaster skin, bruise it all over with my nails, suck their unformed breasts, bite through their nipples.

I'll have them, my pig queen, brought to me in pairs, dressed in white, like little girls. I'll bolt the door and throw them upon the lounge, or throw myself upon the lounge, and let them explore the bedroom. Soft like mice, they'll tiptoe around their daddy cat. Aroused by their puppy smell, I'll lift them, light as a feather, first one, then the other, play with their ankles, knees, glue my lips to their mouths, invade them with my tongue, feel them about under their clothes, slip my hands between their thighs, find their slits, their tiny cozy holes, start opening them up.

By then my prick will be fully erect—a steel soldier ready for the battle. I'll direct their precious little hands to him, loosen my robe, let it fall from my shoulder, teach them how to pet him, promise them cookies if they do it right, undress them, one by one, and inspect their slits with every single finger. Oh, how warm and soft they feel! No hair obstructs the entrance! Nothing obscures the view. I drive into them like into a gold mine, pulsating amidst the belly of a desert, draw apart the pink lips, divide each pear into two halves, split the babies with my pistol, force them to their knees, make them kiss the weapon, push into the mouth of one pussy, make the other lick my balls, spread them out on the sofa, eat them out biting through juicy membranes, place their slits on my mouth, drink them out. One by one, their legs apart, their small feet around my neck. I deflower them by hand, one by one, squeezing them out with my forefinger, cleaning them out with my tongue, feeding on their tasty blood, the sour-sweet cherry marmalade. Watch out, Berenice. See how I do them in? One with the right, the other with the left forefinger. They squeal, but I shut them up with a sodomite cocktail, position them on top of cushions, one next to the other, and get ready for the final destruction. Oh, how tight, how incredibly tight the baby harlots are! You princely swine, you were never that hard! Your softness appalled me the very first night. But they are coconuts, rendering my prick a hammer. It's too big to fit into them, and they groan and weep for their lives, and excite me even more. My screwdriver continues the attack and, getting sleepy from the alcohol, they bear the end. A few more strokes, and my prick disappears wholly in one slit, one climax is reached. Instantly, I transfer my sword to the other little beast, reach out even deeper, divide her as well, and consume another feast. But I don't stop at this. I go on, repeat myself, don't rest until the last drop of my milk fills the baby bottles.

By that time they are blown apart, without consciousness, half dead. I have them removed, take a nap, and at night recommence with another chicken pair. I finish off four kids a day, and this rejuvenates me, infuses new purpose into my life, makes me exploit new gold mines, expand Egypt to the stars.

Excited by his vision, Euergetes throws himself onto Berenice. Excited by his vision, Propertius interrupts, and finds himself aroused. The rapture is followed by dinner and a drink at his patron's house. By eleven o'clock Sextus is back at his Underwood, and resumes typing. But he is tired from Euergetes' pornography and remembers two Jewish slaves in Alexandria speaking about Josephus, the son of Matthias, who works for the emperor:

He's the worst traitor the world has ever seen. Ninety-seven thousand Jews were made slaves when Jerusalem fell. Ninety-seven thousand, and he grows fat eating from the Roman hand. My entire family perished in the gold mines of Berenice, and he calls himself Josephus Flavius and stuffs himself as if he were a pagan pet. You know how he survived? By trampling into the ground forty Jewish leaders. He persuaded our best boys that they should rather die than surrender to the Romans. His voice is as seductive as a nightingale's, and so he sang to them: God would never forgive us a suicide, we must not kill ourselves. Let's ask fate to determine who should die first, and by whose hand. Brothers, he chanted, let's cast lots on the understanding that we will kill each other, the second the first, and so forth.

The fox, he drew the last lot, but that's not the end of the tale. Roman soldiers brought him to Vespasian. Yes, the one who ordered the slaughter of all Jewish men, the commander in chief. But Josephus invented another trick. Counting on the general's superstitious nature, he fell to his knees and cried out: Soon you'll wear a crown. Two years later Vespasian became emperor, and his patron. Skunks have such good luck!

It's because destiny has been replaced by Fortuna, a Roman harlot, who likes Jews best à la steak tartare. Now we have them both in Alexandria, the fox of a scribe and the donkey of an emperor. My kid was tortured to death because he refused to acknowledge Vespasian as our king and god. At thirteen he had more courage than this son of a bitch. This, phooey, Josephus, who licks the hangman's asshole clean.

Shit is sweet. Just wait and see. He'll be rewarded with Roman citizenship and a solid pension. Once the mines of Berenice are a mass grave, he'll settle in a nice estate at Gethsemane and write our history—from the Roman point of view—looking out the window at the ruins of Jerusalem. I have survived the death of my son, wife, two small daughters, grandparents, uncles, aunts, cousins—first, second and third. I have witnessed their end, and remained whole. But when I recall Josephus at Vespasian's court, I want to die.

So do I. The smell of his ink poisons the air. Because of this scribe we won't be able to bear it.

Willy-nilly I have crossed the line from the private to the public, notes Propertius. I set out for Egypt to find consolation in the exotic, and forget Hostia. Now I find myself tête-à-tête with Josephus, a man involved in politics, something I hate. I can draw the outlines of a woman's mouth but the headlines of history escape my notice. My pen conveys the ephemeral and erotic, but refuses to track the decisive and brutal. Since Hostia is no more, I should find myself another mistress, make her inspire new sonnets. Josephus disgusts me, but I understand him all too well. He doesn't give a damn about anybody else's skin. He prefers his script, drying on a papyrus leaf, to the salvation of his people. Still, morality isn't my cup of tea. Who am I to judge him?

I N NEW YORK, losing hope of having her love returned, Ann Kar lets her mind travel, highlight distant tragedies, project onto the walls of her studio the muddy streets of Peshawar, which lies within a horseshoe ring of hills at the edge of the mountains separating India from Afghanistan. It's autumn and povindahs, the traveling merchants, bring their caravans from Kabul, Bukhara, Samarkand, and unload goods in the markets: sheepskin, wool, silks, dyes, gold thread, carpets and precious stones, dried fruit, glass pearls, knives and small arms, brightly colored scarves called lungis, wax cloth and embroideries. Peshawar is packed with people. The shallow river hardly moves. In the middle of the market tea with milk is boiled in a huge caldron. A nest of wasps, the crowd buzzes and glitters.

British have to get out of here, a beautiful young merchant says to another male beauty, his slender hands playing with an exquisitely ornamented silver knife. They have been here too long.

How long, exactly?

Over half a century. They took the whole of the Punjab in 1848.

How do you know?

My father told me. The British have to go. But when they go, he says, there'll be new bloodshed. Ours is a place at the crossroads. It has changed hands in the past, it's going to change hands in the future. Alexander came here. Other empires will set their greedy eyes on us as well.

But that's the past, Ann reminds herself: 1900. That's not the Peshawar I visited on my way to China. No caravans reached the city anymore. The border to Afghanistan was closed, and disquieting news was arriving from the other side.

It's late October, and Peshawar is filled with Afghan refugees and weapons. At the outskirts of the city camps rise and expand. Tents are put up—blankets supported by poles. Drained by the heat and a throat infection, I interview an old man. His clothes are dirty, he leans his back against the trunk of a dead tree. I could be his daughter, I think, smile at him, and ask: How old are you? Where are you from?

I'm seventy-three. A painter from Kabul. I studied there at the Industrial High School in the time of King Shali Khan's rule. One day the king came to visit the school. He was about to leave for Europe, and seemed tense and tired. He sat down in the studio and watched us working. Quickly, I painted him, and he was so pleased! He gave a hundred golden coins to his son, and his son gave the coins to me.

His son was with him?

Oh, no! It was a big ceremony. The best pupils from all over Kabul were invited to our school and Faiz, the Minister of Culture, presented me with the coins in the presence of Shali's son. I graduated from the school with honors.

Were your parents artists too?

My father, the director of the Kabul museum, was a miniaturist, and my mother dabbled in painting as well. But then a woman was not taken seriously, although she was an excellent artist, particularly gifted in painting flowers and birds. Often my father made a pencil outline of a landscape or garden and my mother executed it. She had an incredible sense of color and detail. Peacocks' tails—no one painted them better. After graduation I was first employed as a teacher in my own school.

But then my father became sick and I was hired as my father's deputy at the museum. But the work didn't appeal to me. Administrating doesn't suit my temperament. At that time theater interested me, and I started an experimental group.

In Kabul?

Yes, in Kabul. But then the school hired me again and I began teaching theater also, and popularized theatrical ideas, not entirely without success. The Ministry of Culture gave me a grant to develop what I called educational theater. Oh, how busy I was in those days! A *Hans Dampf in allen Gassen,* as a German friend of mine used to say. I had hardly any time to pursue my career as a painter. I also traveled a good deal.

Ours is such a beautiful country. Wild. Untamed. Theatrical. The drama of nature is performed day and night. Every sunrise is a gala spectacle, every sunset a tragedy. When the red ball vanishes behind the mountain peaks and blue darkness seeps down, the heart leaps up and seems to stop.

The government sent me to Kandahar to paint historical pictures of Afghanistan. To document the past. Where are my paintings—the ones of Kandahar? First they were at the home of the king. Then the authorities moved them to the National Gallery where two entire rooms were filled with them. But who knows what has happened to them since I left Kabul, whether they have been preserved or broken.

After my return from Kandahar I was assigned a peculiar job. For three years I designed postage stamps. Oh, I enjoyed the work, but it was bad for my eyes. So I quit and became the teacher of King Shali's family. I gave art lessons to his children and also painted them. Squirrels with black, velvety eyes, how lovely they were. Finally, thirty-six years after my own graduation, I was appointed the principal of my own old school. But it happened too late. My health bothered me constantly and after I had a heart attack the government retired me. I expected the end but recovered, opening my own private art school, and also taught in the Fine Arts Department of Kabul University.

When the Soviets invaded us, nothing much changed, at least not at the beginning. For another two years I continued with my classes and felt relatively safe. Then, unexpectedly, a Russian artist arrived at my place. He was the vice-chairman of the Soviet Artists' Union, with a name something like Voronskoy. He stepped out of a black car, accompanied by six armed guards. A pretty theatrical sight! The guards encircled the house and he bumped into me. A huge blond block, twice my size, his blue-eyed gaze slightly out of focus, this Soviet colleague simply pushed me aside and began examining whatever there was on the walls. Silent as a fish, he looked twice at everything and left without a word.

Two weeks later I was summoned by the Party's Central Committee. Artists from all over Afghanistan were gathered there, and since I knew most of them I had a strange sense of dejà vu. I remembered how boys from all over Kabul were gathered at our school, how I was given the golden coins. And I thought: they're going to present me with something. So it was. I was offered the chairman post of a new fine arts association that was to be established, with sections for music, theater, cinema, architecture, and painting. I stood there and saw myself reflected in the eyes of friends and students, their pupils widened with anxiety. With the exception of a few mediocre actors and an architect, no one was eager to join the association. But nobody had the guts to admit it. Not a hero either, I mumbled: I'm an old man with a very bad heart. A new job would kill me. When I said it, I saw in the corner the Voronskoy jerk and realized he was the one who selected me for this Soviet smoke screen of an art union.

Walking out of the Central Committee I exchanged a few words with a friend of mine. That's it, I concluded, and he agreed: yes, we have to leave. The sooner the better. A few days later he disappeared, and I haven't heard from him since. Like myself, he was an old man, but braver, and his health was better than mine. He did what I wasn't ready to do, not yet, and must have died on his way to Pakistan.

I, instead, applied for permission to go to India, under the pretext of seeking medical treatment. But I was refused the passport and told: If you want to go abroad, you can go to East Germany or Czechoslovakia.

Could you go to Poland?

No. But since my wife was sick as well, we began thinking about going to Prague. As a young girl my wife was acquainted with a Czech architect who told her about Prague. What a lovely city it was. So we were preparing to go there, but delayed our departure, and meanwhile things were getting out of hand. One evening I had dinner at a friend's house and wanted to go to the bazaar to buy medicine. But as I wasn't feeling well, my friend asked his nephew to fetch it for me. The boy went and never returned. Military police arrested him on his way and he was forced into military service. My friend, who inquired about him, also disappeared.

The number of funerals increased in those days, and while attending them I dropped a word here and there. Soon I was summoned to the head of the Khad, our secret police, whom I have known forever. He wrote his dissertation on Descartes and once taught Basic Marxism in our art department. When I entered his office, he greeted me with: You act against us.

I'm too old to act, I replied, but I don't like how you treat people, my friend's nephew, for instance. He went to get drugs for me and hasn't returned since. I wonder why? He didn't answer but gave me a long look, and groaned: Ostad, here's my advice. Keep out of it.

I returned home and found my wife crying. She isn't a hysteric. Far from it. But she hadn't expected me to come back. When I saw her in tears, something cracked in me as well. Suddenly I had a vision of bombed-out villages, bombed-out towns, bombed-out mountains, and a dear friend, a former reporter, shouting: Hiroshima is being born at the foot of the Himalayas.

The hallucination passed, and I sat down next to my wife and began to weep. An old man, I behaved like a child, scared to death by what I had been ignoring all that time: nails torn out, skewers pushed through private parts, electrical shocks, people buried alive.

Then my wife wiped the tears from her face, and whispered: Ahmad was here and told me about his son. His feet were tied together. Closely. A stick was hammered between them. They brought him home yesterday, crippled for life. He's only eighteen, and such a bright, handsome boy. But Ahmad praises God that he has him back. So many never return. They are blindfolded and dropped in the fields. Tractors bury them like living seed. So Ahmad rejoices, but feels condemned at the same time. He can't abandon his only kid, leave without him for Pakistan.

She paused, and then resumed her talk: After Ahmad had left, a registered letter was delivered to me. They want me to join the Party. We have to get out of here, forget about Prague.

It's strange you received the letter and not I.

Oh, you'll get one as well, she answered, and was right. Two days later a soldier came with a green envelope, and said: Open it. Inside was an application for Party membership, and he uttered a command: Sign it.

Young man, I answered, I'm an old man who can't sign anything. He looked at me, hesitant, and said: Here, write that you can't sign it. This I wrote and he asked me for one of my pictures. I gave him a sketch, and he went away. It was two o'clock in the afternoon. I put the application on the dining table, and we left. I, my wife and our two children, with just a few belongings, and some of my drawings. We headed for Kot-e-Sangi, in the suburbs of Kabul, where we stayed overnight with my wife's family. Then we proceeded to Logar. Ten days later we arrived in Peshawar.

When exactly?

In the first days of October.

How did you come here?

We walked. All the way down. And what we saw on our way affected me more than anything else I had seen in my life. Once we slept in the ruin of a house, with nothing in it but a vase with dried flowers, a little barley, clothes smeared with blood, and a page of the Koran that some-one had used as toilet paper. I sat down and stared at the scrap of the Holy Scripture, I don't know for how long. After a while I heard a noise and a young man entered the room. I remained seated and he stopped in front of me, silent. We stayed like that for a minute or two, then he asked: Where are you from?

From Kabul.

Heading for Pakistan?

Yes.

What's your job?

I'm a painter.

What do you paint?

I used to paint historical sites and shrines. But that, I guess, I won't do anymore.

Yes, everything is ending. I'm from Kabul myself. They forced me into the army. I deserted. Now I'm on the run, trying to make it to Peshawar.

We can go together.

No, it's too risky. If they catch me, they'll kill you as well. I must do it on my own. But, if you don't mind, I would like to talk to you. I haven't spoken to anybody from Kabul for a long time. How's the city now? I studied philosophy but to earn some extra money I worked as a night guard at the National Gallery.

Then you must know my paintings.

Your paintings? But of course! That's why you looked so familiar. There was a photo of you in the catalogue. Oh, I have always wanted to meet you. What good luck! Something good comes out of this war after all. People move around and become acquainted with each other. I'm an old admirer of your art, and of your wife's work. Once she taught an evening class and I wanted to attend it. But I'm not talented, so I felt too shy to enroll.

Sit down, I said. You must be tired.

Thank you, but I would rather stand where I am. I have to tell you about something I saw yesterday. Near Musavi a Soviet convoy stopped a bus to search the passengers. There was a young couple among them. You could see they were recently married. The young man was literally beaming with pride as he helped his wife down the steps. The moment she alighted, a soldier uncovered her face. She was not older than fourteen and had a childlike face. The soldier pushed her husband aside and took her away, laughing at her, as she was trying to cover her face, her cheeks turning red, tears appearing in her eyes. The man tried everything to get her back, but they all laughed at him: Tomorrow morning, come here at eight, and you'll get your wife back.

The man was from the local village where I hid for a few days. He went home, told his parents what happened. Next morning he arrived at the bus stop with a big knife, and waited for the Soviets. They brought his wife seated in front of a tank. Her face was uncovered and bruised all over. Her clothes were torn. When she caught sight of her husband, she cried out to him: They took everything from me. Kill me.

The man began killing his wife with the knife he prepared for the Soviets. They fired at him with their Kalashnikovs. To revenge the son, his father came running from the village with an ax in his hand. So the soldiers fired at him as well. All three perished. The girl. The young man. The old man.

Promise me that if you get to Pakistan you'll tell the story to others, exactly as I told it to you, with all the details. Do you know Ammilah? He taught part-time in our department. Greek philosophy. Of course they removed him. He was jailed for five months and when he returned from prison he was a different man. But before his arrest, he was for us a kind of Socrates, repeating one thing: To be a decent man you have to complement philosophy with compassion. While philosophy strives for synthesis, insight into life's meaning is gained through analysis, through focusing on particularities. Not unlike the Truth with a capital *T*, generalities don't break our hearts. But in order to be good for something, we have to have our hearts broken. History is a series of holocausts, and in their essence they resemble each other. Therefore, when we consider just the essence, we aren't moved. Our consciousness hibernates. To feel the victims' pain, we have to recall their faces and fates, slip into their skins. Philosophy can make us comprehend why we should act. But, ultimately, only a sense of identity propels us into action. Therefore we must remember the details. Clothes covered with blood. Dead flowers. The page from the Koran, its letters effaced by excrement.

I'll never forget the expression on that girl's uncovered face. She had the eyes of a baby rabbit facing the knife. All women look alike when you hurt them. But until the end of the world no one will bear her features. If I were an artist, I would paint her face. Perhaps you can paint it one day.

Carol Kar puts aside Ann's Afghan interview, wipes her eyes, and sighs: My sister makes me cry. I, a bit of white shit prone to overreaction, I live through her words and the ordeals of others from which I have excluded myself. Yet I long to belong and she provides me—with what? Tears of terrestrial togetherness, I guess. Salty water, you're my last tie to this world! Carol has been born with an allergy to life. But Ann carries on, brings death to my bed, hammers out my headache.

I'LL BE GOING NOW, THE YOUNG MAN SAID. But before I leave, let me try to decipher the page of Koran. He picked up the dirty sheet of paper, and I saw his lips moving. The first paragraph is illegible, but then it reads: In the name of God, the Compassionate Compassioner, the Sovereign of the Day of Judgment. Thee do we worship and of Thee do we beg assistance. Direct us in the right way. In the way of those to whom Thou hast been gracious. On whom there is no wrath. Who go not astray.

He paused, and I said: It's my favorite sura. The thoughts are so simple. No explanation is needed. You know, once I considered myself a modern man. Before the Soviets came, before the slaughter began. Then I called myself an agnostic and read the Koran from the point of view of an artist. I enjoyed its poetry, praised the subtlety of its metaphors. But now, as we walk from Kabul to Pakistan, I behave like the strictest believer. My feet are bleeding. My wife has lost her toenails. Now I say my sura regularly, and repeat twenty times a day: Compassionate Compassioner, direct us in the right way.

The same has happened to me. At high school I considered myself a Marxist, and communism attracted me so much. But now I wonder: Is it worth anything at all? But maybe we're wrong to turn to God, like children afraid of darkness. I thought of myself as a modern man. Now

I pray all the time. But since I don't know the prayers by heart, I beg: God, forgive me my ignorance. I haven't read the scriptures, and so I address you in my own way. Be compassionate, God, listen to my unschooled words. Direct me! Pity me. Help me. *Rahman. Rahman. Rahman.* I repeat it all the time, and now I realize that I have been praying in words so similar to the sura. Can you believe it? I must have been guided. God must have been with me all those days. Oh, how happy I am that I found this page! Now I have the proper words in my hands. The sacred words. You don't mind my taking this page? To me it's a miracle. Now I'm certain we're going to make it to Pakistan. You and I. Your wife and kids.

Did he make it?

No, he didn't. Next afternoon we found his corpse by the roadside. They shot him from a helicopter. Right in the head. They just about blew it away. But the rest of the body remained intact, and his fist was clutching the page of the Koran. The sun was setting, and we stood there as if fixed to the ground. The entire sky resembled a battlefield, and I heard my wife whisper: Blood, blood, blood. Let us say the sura, I said, and we prayed aloud: Compassionate Compassioner, Sovereign of the world, direct us in the right way. In the way of those to whom Thou hast been gracious. On whom there is no wrath. And who go not astray. *Rahman. Rahman. Rahman.* We walked all night and in the morning, without realizing it, we found ourselves in Pakistan.

The encounter with the young man has marked me. His words are imprinted in my mind. The face of that newly married girl, it haunts me, and I sketch it every day. I'm an old man, but perhaps I can still be good for something. I'll paint the ruin of that room, the flowers, the half-effaced page of the Koran, the emaciated figure of the philosophy student, his lids heavy, his lips trembling.

In Afghanistan there are no photographers. No cameramen. Hardly anything is recorded. But I'll paint it with the tip of my old brush. My mother metamorphosed peacocks' tails into rainbows. I'll paint pain. Disgust. Disaster. The end of our world. I'll keep it alive. May God give me strength, good health. I don't doubt His existence anymore. I believe He'll assist me so that I can document it all: Girls without fingers, boys without feet.

No, I don't hate the Soviets. I'm too old for that. But the young ones dream about revenge. But even I, whenever I wake up in the middle of the night, I am in rage. On fire. Then I pray: God, have compassion. Preserve me from going insane. Let me paint.

LET US NOT LOOK BACK. Let us start from scratch, was the motto of the first moon president. That's why Earth history has been obliterated to such an extent. That's why so few relics have survived to our day, an older colleague says to the young moon scholar curating Paths of Prehistory, a new exhibit of Earth art, which includes two recent arrivals: an extremely well-preserved picture dug out at the foot of the Himalayas, and a silk scroll from the territory defined as China.

SCIENCE FICTION IS CAROL'S FAVORITE GAME. It complements her attempt to escape from the Himalaya of suffering, from her planet of pain. Out of neurocells, which keep splitting, her twin, a young moon scholar, is born a thousand years from now—to probe not the exile she's best at, but a return to Earth. Meanwhile, he needs a place to live. So Carol has an architect, whom she deeply mistrusts, don a dome on the moon's head. The asylum for lunatics will be round and white, she announces. Fighting anguish with mortal disgust, Ann's sister jumps around, and cries: Hurry, hurry! It must be finished before dead seals begin to surface from the plutonium sea. Before Berenice is poisoned in her pyramid. Oh *terre du mal*, I, Charlemagne the Last, I shall save some of your dust in my fallout shelter.

Carol doesn't go out anymore. She drives in the spaceship of her bedroom—its ceiling crumbling, its windows overlooking Hispanic slums—to the *luna libidinosa* of delight. At night, cosmic rays transport her to the top of the Lunar Love, the highest summit of her satellite. Time is white, mosquitoes bite. Carol quotes Lorine N, and scribbles to Ann: I've spent my life on nothing, but mankind won't fail to imitate me. A certified schizophrenic, I'm a medium of the future. Shortly after my own escape, ten survivors of the collective suicidal act will flee to Luna, Terra's outer womb.

IN THE DARKROOM the two moon scholars analyze the laser prints of the Himalaya picture. It's a still life, the younger man says to the older one, but an unusual one. It encodes a portrait, hides a face. Let me show you how it works. First you see only a vase, with a few dried flowers. I found their name in the *Atlas of Earth Flora*. They are called lion-hearts, and lions are listed in the *Atlas of Earth Fauna.*

How did they look?

I assume lions were small and fragile, and thus prompted a botanical analogy. Either insects feeding on these mountain flowers, or tiny birds, or fish living in wild torrents, their shape or color reminiscent of lions' hearts.

The vase of flowers is depicted against a misty background. Neither walls nor a floor or ceiling can be detected. But the space opens up at the top into a sort of sky, at the bottom into an abyss. When I examined this still life for the first time, I asked myself: What does it signify? Soon it captured my imagination. I had the picture cleaned by our best art-historical team and began to study its fragments by enlarging them. Gradually new impressions were added to my original perception. Here, for instance, do you see this piece of paper, covered with half-effaced script? It's Arabic, a major Earth language. In our Earth Library we possess books written in it, among them four copies of the Koran. But only one of them is complete. Two are partly burnt, the third—radioactive—has to be kept in a safe.

It must have been an important work.

As important as the Bible of which we have five copies, all slightly damaged.

Was the Koran considered a sacred scripture as well?

Absolutely. The dirty piece of paper is, in fact, a page from the Koran corresponding to page 44 of our edition. So far I have been able to decipher two words: Compassionate Compassioner.

What does it mean?

Our Arabists tell me that it's a name, one of many, given to the god of the Koran. In original it reads *Rahman.*

Still, I don't see the portrait you're hinting at.

You have to focus on the two dark dots, to the left and right of the flower.

Eyes?

Exactly. Dark, wide open. Do you see the rest? The stalk of the central lion-heart delineates the nose. Petals outline eyebrows, and where you expect the mouth, clouds seem to part. The light patch is shaped into a neck. The arm reaches down. The hand picks up the page from the Koran. Our specialists suggest that it's the portrait of Rahman, the holy script in his hand. But to me, it doesn't make sense. The features are so delicate, childlike. It could be the artist's son or daughter, but why the face is so sad I don't know. The eyes are blank with horror, as if they couldn't endure what they beheld. The lips seem to tremble. But I may be just projecting my reverie onto this enigma of an image. I am trained as a scholar but, unfortunately, I'm too much of a dreamer. I should have been born on Earth, a poet or stand-up comedian. Do you want me to screen the other picture as well, the one from China?

Next time. I must run now. My lecture starts in a minute.

What do you teach these days?

Oh, I read with my students boring Earth texts, classify and date them. Today we're going to analyze our ancestors' view of the moon. If you have nothing better to do, join us.

What you see in front of you is the enlargement of a semi-scientific paper or review article. The top is erased, the text begins at line sixteen, in the middle of a sentence. I suggest we read it first and then attempt the textual analysis. But keep in mind that our ancestors' perception of the moon was different from the way the Earth appears to us. An unknown celestial body, the moon was for them about the future, while the Earth is for us about the past. So let's begin:

. . . the existence of dark and bright regions, irregular in form, on its surface. The other is the complete illumination of the lunar disk when seen as a crescent, a faint light revealing the dark hemisphere. This is due to the light falling from the sun on the earth and being reflected back to the moon.

To an observer on the moon our earth would present a surface more than ten times as large as the moon presents to us. Consequently this earth-light is more than ten times brighter than our moonlight, thus enabling the lunar surface to be seen by us.

The surface of the moon has been a subject of careful telescopic study from the time of Galileo. The early observers seem to have been under the impression that the dark regions might be oceans. But this impression must have been corrected as soon as the telescope began to be improved, when the whole visible surface was found to be rough and mountainous. The work of drawing up a detailed description of the lunar surface, and laying its features down on maps, has from time to time occupied telescopic observers. The earliest work of this kind, and one of the most elaborate, is the *Selenographia* of Hevelius, a magnificent folio volume. It contains the first complete map of the moon. Names borrowed from geography and classical mythology are assigned to the regions and features. A system was introduced by Riccioli in his *Almagestum novum* of designating the more conspicuous smaller features by the names of eminent astronomers and philosophers, while the great dark regions were designated as oceans, with quite fanciful names: *Mare imbrium, Oceanus procellarum,* etc.

More than a century elapsed from the time of Hevelius and Riccioli, when J. H. Schröter of Lilienthal produced another profusely illustrated description of lunar topography. The standard work on this subject during the 19th century was the well-executed description and map of W. Beer and J. H. Mädler, published in 1836. It was the result of several years' careful study and micrometric measurement of the features shown by the moon. The text gives descriptive details and measurements of the spots and heights of the mountains.

Here the text is damaged by a large hole, and we have to move to the third line from the bottom: ". . . irregular character of the surface is most evident near the boundary between the dark and illuminated portions, about the time of the first quarter." A few sentences are effaced here and we have to go down even further: ". . . most frequently exhibited changes in appearance are near the center of the visible disk, marked on Beer and Mädler's map as Linne. This has been found to present an aspect quite different from that depicted on the map, and one which varies with time. But the question still remains open whether these variations may not be due wholly to the different phases of illumination by the sunlight as it later strikes the region from various directions."

What boredom, the young moon scholar whispers to himself. What unspeakable sterility. Since only a few texts from Earth have been preserved, each is treated as if it were a treasure. Who cares how some backward Earth scientists interpreted the moon, the place of our exile, with whose monotony we're confronted every day? I'm not interested in the intensity of moonlight as it was measured by G. P. Bond of Harvard and F. Zöllner of Leipzig, the result being 1:570,000. What fascinates me is the intensity of sunlight on earth, and the way its burning power inspired the Chinese and Greeks. It's enough to know that the intensity of sunlight is somewhat more than half a million times that of the full moon. Darkness rules here, and obscurantism is our daily lot. This sad fact of our lunar life isn't relieved by the knowledge that the proportion of light reflected by a region on the moon is much greater when the light falls perpendicularly, which is the case near the time of a full moon, and rapidly declines as the light is more oblique. Here we simply need more light. Why don't I try to join an Earth exploration team, instead of dreaming of terrestrial existence?

IN ORDER TO SAVE HERSELF for a little longer, Carol Kar assists her lunar twin, meanders with him in the same blue-and-red labyrinth she's lost in. Once it was a drawing, now it's a drawriting she projects onto the white seascape of her room. The paint crumbles and no man wants to cross her ocean. No one, with the exception of the moon-man. Only he isn't scared by her growing fondness of the cotton curtains opposite her, the young *los Americanos del Sur* playing in the yard, the rats. Confused and caged, Ann's sister identifies her lunar twin with the Underwood, a noble dinosaur, dedicates to him each black sign, and touching his keys with her sweaty fingertips coos: Woody, Woody, Wood. You alone aren't appalled by my oily skin, swollen eyelids, smelly cunt. A perfect Under-Companion, you return my love and never boomerang your Caroline.

THE STRONGEST IMPULSE TO WRITING is provided by anger and love, writes Ann to Carol. But even better is the combination of being in love and growing old. As the eyesight fails, the past is paraphrased into the present. I'm in Trieste. It's All Souls', and I encounter an aging writer by the name of Italo Svevo. In love with a young girl who doesn't give a damn about him, he walks around the dull city on the brink of bursting into tears. His constant expectation follows the luminous shape of his young mistress, but the pathos of growing old disgusts her, and she refuses to share it. She's a superficial girl, with sparkles in her eyes, but Svevo dies to transport her to the top of a glacier, to guard her in an Alpine hut. He dreams of the total you-and-me in a mutual space. But the frivolous Angiolina won't go there. Poor and pretty, she wants to consume oysters and champagne, dance, flirt, have sex with sexy guys.

Like the architect who abandoned first me and then you for the swirl of accidental skirts, she has the same appetite for life. But you, I, and Italo are ascetics to whom bons vivants can never adjust. Thus we must break up the real pairs into imaginary couples, force our ex-man to hook up with Svevo's mistress, catch Italo for ourselves, engage him in endless conversations, quote, prove the point, compare him to William Burroughs, compile with him a report on aging, and transcribe the scribbles of the three of us into a hermaphrodite of a text—with two heads, four hands, and two Jewish brains. As a first step towards an affair with Svevo we must arrange a blind date that would acquaint our lost lover with Angiolina. Then we have to get for ourselves an academic appointment at Trieste. There, strolling through the chestnut woods and passing a shrine of the Virgin, her scroll inscribed with *senza la mamma la vita non ha scopo,* you-and-I will become Italo's middle-aged brides.

Indeed, Carol replies, your solution solves everything. In no time things coincide. I'm no longer a fortyish girl given to silent despair, nor is Svevo an impotent fiftyish man. Together we strive for the Faustian monologues buried in Helen's glove, transmute to clouds, support granite. You-and-I, we discover the sublime in our common heartbeat, as we rest our heads on Svevo's shoulders, while he rests his head in our hands. Ours is a supreme incest, with more distress than sex. A union of destruction and death in Detroit—and everywhere else.

Dearest Carol, Ann cables from Trieste. What happiness! I and Italo, we transgress the smooth ice surface, discourse without thinking, think without conversing. Our senses, attuned to each other, ascend to symphonies, roll in remarkable reveries. Finally we are free from plight, desolation, menial jobs, money worries, and transform our Alpine hut—somewhat suggestive of Heidegger's Schwarzwald cabin—into the sixth station of the cross where, as you know, Christ met Veronica. From now on we will carry her cloth beyond the limits of defeat and desperation to the top of the world where at dawn the stock market is discussed and at night the short-term CD of amor.

Don't you think, Ann, Italo asks, that it would be safer to climb up all the way to the Khyber Pass rather than rest here?

Oh, how foolish you are, dear. On top even a needle is spotted in no time, the imprints of your shoe soles are identified as made *in Italia.*

What about Tibet?

Where Soviet satellites take pictures of every hair on your head? Red guards track you down, a Dalai Lama's spy dropped from the sky? Believe me, Italo, the higher you go, the more likely you are to be gunned down. Mont Blanc is safer than the Himalayas.

You're right, *carissima.* So shall we just dream of being snowed in, or surviving the last nuclear winter west of Schwanensee? Shall we remain in Trieste or move to Manhattan? Since we can't escape to the moon, we might as well land at the Kennedy Airport, settle on the Upper West Side, ski in Riverside Park. The Big Apple noise may jam the helicopters you hear since your last visit to Peshawar.

Every night they hide in my earmuffs, like the sound of the sea when you travel by ship.

I realize this, *amore,* but it's bad for sex. Afghanistan turns me off. It's either erection or helicopters.

It's nine o'clock in the morning. A squadron of gunship helicopters comes into view above the village of Wonkhi, sixty miles southwest of Kabul. They fly high over the village, and its inhabitants, experts in guessing the intention of aircraft from their height, are confident that they will be spared. The copters pass very fast. It's a reassuring sight, and people start on their daily routine. But soon they return at a low height. The villagers assume they are going to Kabul, since they usually keep at that height on their journeys back. However MIGs, which precede the copters, begin shooting missiles, and when the planes get out of the picture, helicopters replace them. Their task differs from that of the MIGs, which destroyed houses, shops, and the mosque where most of the villagers hid. By now they are all dead, but in the fields there are still people, children, mules, donkeys, dogs, and chickens—to be gunned down now.

Try to sleep, Ann, put your head on my breast, press your belly against mine.

Ann falls asleep, and finds herself in the iron grip of a dream—a Himalayan valley. Sumptuous foliage overgrows a brook, stillness and solitude rule. Suddenly a scythe strikes the bottom of her ear, and a buzz is released. To escape from it, Ann begins to run. But the sound comes from within. The faster she runs, the louder it is. A cloudless sky reflects itself in a lake, and she feels lighter and lighter. From an adult she turns into a two-year-old in a blue nylon dress from a U.S. parcel, her very best. Don't get it dirty, Mom shouts across the valley, just as the sound hits her elbow. Too late. Can blood be washed out with cold water? It hits again. The buttocks are ripped off. The belly is perforated. Raw flesh is bad for you. A third hit, and Ann cries out: Italo.

A bad dream? Copters again? Wake up, Ann, I'll warm you a little milk.

I 'VE COME TO SEE THE CHINESE PICTURE, the older colleague says to the young moon scholar.

I'm so glad you remembered it. It's painted on a silk scroll with a very fine brush. According to the *Atlas of Earth Fauna,* the bird alighting at the edge of the nest is a wild dove. The plant resembles a mulberry tree. Seven young doves open their beaks, impatient to devour the gray-green insect, possibly a grasshopper their mother caught for them. The foliage is rendered beautifully. The leaves—are they veined with gold?—remind me of a little piece of Chinese embroidery exhibited in the Earth Museum. The China experts assume it comes from a silk sash or cap. The young doves look so fluffy and gay. At first glance it's a simple watercolor. But the more I scrutinize it, the more I'm intrigued. For instance here, at the bottom of the tree, I have discovered the faint outlines of an old man, with a lean face and long white beard, leaning against the trunk.

He holds something in his outstretched palm. What can it be? Flower petals? Pieces of silk? Tiny insects? Pebbles? Grains?

No, the shells of two broken eggs.

The eggs in which the doves were hatched? But why are there only two of them? Aren't seven small doves sitting in the nest? Besides, the young ones seem to be some weeks old, so the shells should be no more.

Exactly. But look what I have found here:

> Dove in the mulberry tree
> I mourn the children you have lost:
> A daughter and a son.
>
> But soon young wings
> Will flap over the plum tree.
> Silk sash and silk-spot cap
> Still in the old precinct of mulberries.
>
> Down from the spring
> the knife-sharp water run
> Flooding the wolf-grass.
> By night I wake and sigh
> For Chou's lost life.
>
> Chou's down.

A beautiful poem, did it inspire the painting, or was the painting inspired by it?

We'll never know. But my intuition tells me that the two are related to each other. When we read the verses, we understand the picture. It shows an old man mourning the death of two young doves, a brother and a sister. Their death reminds him of his own ruined life. The scroll is signed. I deciphered the artist's name.

Is it Chou?

Yes.

How extraordinary! And who's the poet?

It's Es-ra Pon-du, the author of *Confucian Cantos,* a rather distinguished author. In our *Earth Literature Encyclopedia* his entry consists of a whole paragraph, describes him as the greatest poet of the Mao dynasty, and mentions Chou. An excellent painter, he was Pon-du's best friend. However, during a period referred to as Red Culture Revolutionary Era, he fell into disfavor and was sentenced to five years *hard labor.* No, no idea what he was forced to do, but his health was destroyed. Still, after his return from banishment, Chou experienced an outburst of creative energy, rendered his mistreatment in allegorical pictures, and inspired Pon-du's poems.

AGAINST THE BACKGROUND OF HER HUSBAND'S MONSTROSITIES, Berenice's eyes behold landscapes of desolation: hills consisting of rubbish from excavations, blocks in the middle of nowhere, conflagrations, crumbs of stone. Slopes are X-rayed and etched with the deadly heat of black suns. Mounts, humped and deformed, are stained with the greenish excrement of decaying clay and bloodred ruddle. Steep skeletons of pink-colored granite and bone white tufa open black mouths with elephantine teeth.

A wholly unrelieved aridity, the queen whispers to herself. No foliage, no oasis. In a desert of rock, blades of gold are excavated in the gold mines of Berenice. How could I be so foolish? I should have offered my hair to the gods for the privilege of having Euergetes slain. I should have prayed for his death, saved Egypt from his sword. Instead, I saved him for myself. So now don't complain, just contemplate his crimes. Today he rushes slaves to the desert to erect gigantic propylaea. Tomorrow the project is abandoned, water and food cut off, thousands are wasted, and a debauch of stone is left to mark the disaster. After tomorrow, slaves are transported to the banks of the Nile to build a bridge in the marsh. He wishes it to stand on sphinxes, sculpted in black basalt veined with white. A whole mountain is moved to the river, an army of artisans assembled to carve the colossi. In a couple of months most of them find their way into a mass grave and the project is killed. But before the unfinished beasts sink into the ground, the pharaoh has himself photographed in front of them in the disguise of a sphinx. He wears a helmet with lappets, his paws are crossed, his huge breasts project sharply, his eagle's pinions are extended, his artificial eyes, inlays of alabaster, protrude, and he crouches, ready to attack.

The Nile is my only consolation. I rejoice hearing at intervals the hippopotamuses wallowing by the banks, the sound of ibises whipping the air with their wings. They abandon their hunting positions in the swamp and fly off to perch and dry their feathers on the balustrade of my balcony. But at noon, when the sun reaches its zenith and the raw glaring whiteness pours down on me, I rage with the gods, doubt their existence. Obsessed with steel, I see it everywhere. The whole world changes into a single steel fist, stretching out from the smoked sea shores to the clear-cut edge of the sky.

Reading *Anna Karenina* in the original, I was struck by a name: *Stalin*—a man made of steel. That's how my husband should be called. A Stalin of the Nile, he personifies the evils of solar energy. Caught in his fist, Egypt cannot breathe, the river comes to a halt. A sheet of molten tin, water refuses to wrinkle. Lotus flowers freeze into obscene cups, imitating the vegetal vaginas Euergetes likes to cast in cement. Life copies the cruelty of his politics and art. The heat of his neurocells exfoliates the country. How can a son be so different from his father?

I fell in love with Euergetes, seeing in him the mirror image of the gracious Philadelphus. A poet and womanizer, how human he was! A man who felt compassion for the humblest creature on earth, how could he engender a dragon? How could the gods play such a dirty trick on him and me?

I'm so agitated. Scenes change constantly in front of my eyes. Now I see ocher-hued riverbanks unrolling themselves rapidly like a serpentine scroll. Now I watch myself as a child, swinging in a hammock and waving a large fan of snow white ibis feathers at Euergetes, crawling in the grass. Now I spy on myself at twelve, a month after my first period, two months after my wedding, arranging a bouquet of lotus blossoms in a bloodred vase. Now I escape from the palace in a solitary cangia, flee from my husband into the depth of the Nile, the coolness of the moon.

Oh moon, the last goddess I'm still attached to! Your hand touches my temple, and the fever goes away. Waning and growing, a maiden and a pregnant wife, you stroll in the night sky, your face delicate and pale. More feminine than earthly females, protect me, a scarab, locked in dust and dirt, play with my locks. My hemicycle of hope, let me fall asleep on the lounge of underwood and night. Romans call you Luna. Do you prefer to be addressed by that name? I hear you murmur yes. Oh, Luna! Change me into a cangia gliding on the Nile to the gates of another empire, free me from Euergetes, and from being queen of Egypt.

Looking out the window, I envy beggars and prostitutes who sell their bodies at the port, their bellies bruised by brutal sailors, their skin coarse, their bowels plagued by parasites. They are further away from badness than I am, outside the wicked walls of his fortress, where lions imitate the shapes of birds, papyrus petals dwarf the pyramids, crabs copulate with frogs, double-tailed crocodiles feed on fat gazelles—their mugs modeled after the oldest whores. In a few years all symmetry has been lost. Egyptian art—a microcephalic stillborn.

S HOULDN'T YOU LEAVE FOR EGYPT, ITALO? Assist not me but Berenice? Afghanistan recedes. For an entire week I haven't dreamt of copters. But she's in the desert. Hippopotamuses barricade her bed. She needs a decent man to reassure her now, or else her face will be disfigured by despair. Embark for Alexandria as soon as you can. Go, comfort her. No, not by boat, it takes too long. Consult the list of charter flights in the *Corriere*.

M Y QUEEN, THE YOUNG GREEK SLAVE SAYS entering Berenice's boudoir, a man wishes to see you. A foreigner.
Young?
No, he's growing old, has skin like ebony, and light gray eyes. Not very tall. Quite short, but kind. A little sad. He resembles someone, oh yes, the Jewish slave who escaped from the mines, was caught in front of our gate, and executed the next day. You want to change before I ask him in? Paint your lips, powder your temples, pomade the blue network of veins, put pearls into your curls, wax into wrinkles? Fine, my queen. But, in your place, I would limit the effort. This stranger isn't elegant. His smile is soft, and he's aging. Finding out that your legendary hair has turned to gray, he may feel more relaxed, closer to you. His own hair is *grau meliert,* as in the book by Schnitzler we're reading. Therefore, if I were you, my queen, I wouldn't dress in the silver silk skirt. It may intimidate the foreigner. Why don't you wear the linen tunic with the cape? It drapes you well, makes you a marble Aphrodite—and me a homesick Greek.

There are so many unbearable things here: the heat, the horrors of your husband's politics. But it's your art that really drives me crazy! The way talented sculptors unteach themselves how to carve a wrist or the eyelid of a girl. The way painters unlearn how to paint a petal, the neck of a gazelle, the feathers of an ibis, the ebbing of the Nile. Once so exquisite, today Egyptian art is an abortion. An eyeless statue blinding us in Gaza. Where rotten contours please only a sadist, nature begins to imitate your art. So beauty withers, ugliness mushrooms. Fine hands are rare, slim figures are no more. Egyptian males are mammoths, if not whales, females are chunks of chopped mutton or pork. But you, my queen, you can't be blamed for that. So let me not complain, but help you with the dress. The stranger shouldn't wait too long for your attention. I praise the gods for having sent him here. His presence may prevent your summer melancholia, when sunrays shoot us in the boiling sand. I sympathize with your bad luck, queen Berenice. But, on the other hand, I ask myself: How could she sacrifice the best of her to save a criminal?

R AISING HIS EYES TO POPOCATEPETL, looming above them, Lowry remarks to Ernestine: Isn't our volcano a Moby Dick? It has the air of beckoning us on, as it twitches from one side of the horizon to the other. Does it signal disaster?

The disaster is already at our side. It has just arrived from Acapulco, concentrates on you, Ernestine, and carries a Polish-English name: Korzeniowski—Conrad Joseph. We, the Lowrys plus disaster, sit on the terrace of a café, across from a drunken *pelado*, a serene little thief. I find myself in the right alcoholic equilibrium, oscillating between a state of subconsciousness and a state of surconsciousness. Hardly aware of what's going on, I, nevertheless, control events, although so far there are no events. I declare this country a land of nonevents, and watch Conrad pouring coffee into your cup, Ernestine, bending over you more than he should. This is a place of disastrous nonevents, of unsuccessful politicians and penniless writers. I wonder, Korzeniowski, what's the purpose of your coming here?

A crowded bus arrives from around the corner and an accident occurs. A peon is gravely injured. When his sombrero is lifted, a bloody mess appears where his face had been. Conrad jumps up and wants to offer first aid. Lowry stops him, saying: It's against the local law to touch the victim. It's a country of death and he's meant to die. The *policia de seguridad* will be here in no time. If you help him, they'll arrest you, something I would welcome. Therefore I just want to warn you. It's better to jump into the Popocatepetl than to be thrown into a Mexican jail, black as the lava of legendary nonevents. So I suggest you keep drinking and blinking at our best friend, the white killer whale. Instead of playing the samaritan, just tell me: what's the purpose of your dandy visit, Korzeniowski? I hope it's not us, since we're about to go go go. Tomorrow we head for Vancouver, that Salome of a city where my sweetie is supposed to dance the symphony of the seven veils—composed by Hugo Hitler, with a libretto by Musa Lini—and earn us a fortune. My plump pudding, she'll buy me that villa of an island entitled l'Isola d'Archangel Gabriel. Don't interrupt me, dolly, or otherwise I'll forget the sonnet I composed for our *sehr verehrter Herr Doktor* Korzeniowski, my old pussy dog or, if you prefer, *polski pies.* Where was I? Oh, yes, that prepaid and premailed paradise over-shadowed by the pinions of my vulnerable wife Angelica d'Angèle we desire to acquire. That piece of poetry and fiction and belles lettres and essay in one. *N'est pas, mon ange? Mój aniel.*

No, *mon cher collègue,* I'm not *alcoolique.* Molly Moll, ignore what K says, and shut up yourself. I like you best silent as a carp *à la polonaise,* and that's what our distinguished guest fancies as well. Isn't that so, *mon auteur polo-anglais?*

Don't cry, cookie, don't mourn the bad bad bobby-boy of your husband, unless you want to perform the role I adore: Lady Xantippe in *The Dead Drunkard of Novogorod,* or is it *Malcolmovitch, the Vampire of Dnepropavlovsk?* No, that's not what you want? You wish to complain about the brute Lowrowski, spending his dolly's dollars on boozy booze, to Jossif Jossifovitch Konradowskij? Do tell him the truth! Penniless, broke, bathing in booze, I do spend your bucks on cheap whores and don't even enjoy it, while you howl at home. Go ahead, K, exude pure gold. She'll collect it between her thighs. Danae sweetheart, catch all our dear C ejaculates in Mexico. He, after all, is neither broke nor a Brutus. To the contrary, ours is the pleasure to sit at the table with the very best-selling *Pan Cogito Koryto.* Your anthem, *vive l'Angleterre! Ecrire c'est mourir un peu pour mon pays polonais,* extracts a Yangtze out of my bladder.

I beg your pardon, sir. Your name isn't *Korytowski?* No roots in *koryto,* the till you have your snout in? No? You swear to God? Why, then, does your pen drip with porcine ink? Oh, come on! Admit that you're a hero. Haven't you fought your way to the feeding trough? Don't go away, cookie! No, I don't insult our Anglo-Pole, I'm absolutely unaware of harming him. I just want to know: how do you make it? That way, sweetie, we can try to barge in as well, instead of waltzing through the night with *Jean Bautista decolté.*

You want to go? But where to, dearest Ernestine? To Cyprus, Cythera? Maybe you want to join us, Joe? I, my delicious wife, and you, Konrad Patriote, we would make a superb triangle—drunk, romantic, and satanically angelic. Shall we embark for Madagascar, the New Palestine? Take a scooter to Panama? The Transsiberian to Vancouver? A yellow submarine to Zakopane?

No? You don't want to come? Damn it, Conrad, nothing works out. You're right, sweetie, all coincidence is fucked up. Look at her, Joseph, a pretty one, she has come here because of me, a *cochon de mal* she loves so much. Why can't she stop fondling my ass? Why do I have to abuse her all the time? I'm not even intoxicated with her charm, as are you, Korzeniowski, the *prince charmant* whose peripathetic eyes peregrinate between my wife's front door and her rear one.

Tomorrow, first thing in the morning, I want to read you, Prof. Cock, a novella I'm expanding into a novel-in-progress. Since I have enrolled in your writing workshop, it progresses so well that I should be able to finish it after my death, perhaps while traveling first class by the October ferry to Gabriola, the isle of the dead world literature. My stuff is awfully good, almost as good as Pearl Buck's, whose crap my bingo spouse takes in and excretes *en passant.* Oh, don't cry, Ernestine. I'm a drunk old fart, envious, without talent, neither a Conrad nor a Melville, although I too love the sea, especially the mystic waves of Bloody Mary and gin. I too would like to be rewarded with a Nobel's dynamite, enjoy publicity and big bucks, play the noblesse oblige of a well-to-do guy, day and night pay compliments to my sweetheart. Unfortunately, noble committees don't go for drunks.

When I hurt you, Ernestine, it's like cutting into my own flesh. You saw the blood under the sombrero? You saw the police mugs? It's all such a *Scheisshaus,* and I'm a big *Scheisser* whom God presented with the gift to narrate a disaster. An alcoholic who bullies his angel of a spouse, I'm nevertheless capable of spelling shit out. Screwing it in and out, I release the real thing, the odor we shall smell on the day of our last judgment.

Isn't she a Fra Angelica, Conrad? The way she bears with me. Convince Ernestine that she's an angel, Joseph, tell her that in my name.

She needs to be reassured, or else she'll go down the drain, like myself. Bend over her, Conrad. Pee coffee into her teacup. Be kind to this sweet-sour puppy of mine. Let her share with you the *sauerkraut* of her life with me, the unsuccessful scum. I too scuba dived in the sea, but compared to your nautical sensibility mine is a big minus. No Copernicus, no King Sobieski behind me. Besides, I'm as fluent in English as you are in Polish—a plain disadvantage. But how did you dare to run away from your mom's po-la-ca right into the Anglo-ass of my legal spouse?

No, dolly, I don't insult our guest. I just spill out some questions and, exceptionally, reasonable ones. Why did you sack, my lad, your parents' rural pol-pot for the sake of the urban Mr. Shake and Mrs. Spare? Believe me, Jan Kott was mistaken, they aren't our contemporaries. Come on, Korytowski, confess: What made you desert *maman?*

MY QUEEN, PLEASE LET ME INTRODUCE MYSELF. My name is Propertius. Propertius Sextus. I'm a Roman poet traveling through North Africa on assignment. My patron wants me to compile an encyclopedia of African culture, with emphasis on Egypt. Obviously he has heard about the colossal development of recent years, about the hectic architectural activity of your husband. During my journey on the Nile I passed a lot of the building sites, some of which, if I'm correct, have been abandoned.

Did I like what I saw? It's a delicate question, it needs a diplomatic answer. But I'm not a diplomat. I'm a poet, and I trust you: no, I don't like what I saw. I'm not drawn to the gigantic. I'm into neither monumental architecture nor big sculpture. I love painting, the sort of painting that flourishes in Rome. Swift, casual, impressionistic. Pictures that show a room like yours. The silhouette of a charming woman, like you. A flower vase. An open window. A bird flying in. Things that are light and gay. But really, my queen, the more you look at them, the better you see that they aren't gay. The swift strokes of the brush catch time that is running away from us. They pinpoint the eluding present, the beauty of a mistress we have lost—before we have learned how to treasure her.

Oh, don't accuse me of melancholy, my queen. In my essence, I'm not a melancholic. But I have been through a lot. Through what? It's not easy to explain, since I don't know if you are familiar with our history. A history of wars, not unlike your own. Of course the entire world remembers the Assyrian war and how you sacrificed your hair in order to save your husband. You regret it? Well, let us not dwell on the past. When we're young we commit many mistakes. We trust instead of mistrusting, fall into traps we set for ourselves. You trusted your husband. I trusted our emperor Octavian. I thought him a decent man. But after the battle of Philippi I realized that I was wrong. To provide his veterans with land he confiscated my estate as well as other poets' property—that of Virgil and Horace, you might have heard their names. But while they had support at court, I had only myself. Within days I was reduced from relative opulence to sheer poverty. Did nobody protest the confiscation? Oh, there were protests. Octavian's injustice provoked an insurrection, with its center in Perugia. One of my uncles was involved in it. He was killed by brigands while escaping Octavian's lines. But I don't want to bore you with the story of my misfortunes. You have your own troubles, I'm sure.

Do you read Latin? You do! Your erudition equals your beauty. In this case let me present you with a book of my verse. *Cynthia.* Yes, it's a name, a woman's name. Someone I loved. No, not her real name. She was called Hostia. A woman of many accomplishments, and a poet in her own right. Yes, she meant a lot to me. She encouraged me. She gave me deep intellectual sympathy and genuine affection, without any jealousy. However, I didn't return her feelings, as I should have. I regret it still. Yes, she's dead. She died young. In despair. It was my fault. I left her for another woman. I was so immature, unable to grasp the real nature of her feelings. But I did keep loving her. Each of my poems is a product of this love. Each line, each word is dedicated to Hostia. When I wrote *a rose,* I saw her face before me. When I wrote *a face,* I saw her eyes fixed on mine. When I wrote *eyes,* I saw myself reflected in Hostia's translucent gaze. Oh how we err when we're young.

You're right: *errare humanum est.* We never stop doing wrong. Never. Now, for instance, I shouldn't be listing your monuments. I hate totalitarian architecture. I hate it when sculpture is used to glorify politics. I'm the wrong man in the wrong place. But maybe, my queen, I really took this job in order to get acquainted with you. It didn't occur to me before, but I see it now. The moment I entered your room I knew we were going to be friends. After all, this journey is an escape as well. From Rome. From Hostia's grave. Yes, I have come to the Egyptian wilderness to forget. But I cannot forget.

It's so terribly hot here. How can you bear this climate? My brain is boiling. At night I am feverish and find myself in a hallucinatory flux.

Don't you all hallucinate here? Don't you all go mad? Oh, my queen. This country disgusts me, but your person fascinates me. Or does your bad luck draw me to you? I know what's going on here. I'm aware of your husband's cruelty. But despotism isn't limited to Egypt, my queen. Don't idealize the Romans. They suffer from monomania as well. The big little caesars, they too are infected with the bacillus of the colossal. Yes, I agree with you. In this dreadful heat, in the middle of a desert, everything is aggravated. Contours are incised with a sharper knife. But basically, my queen, it's the same everywhere. Rulers conquer and exterminate. Men torture women. Even I, a rather civilized guy, even I made my mistress grieve.

Oh, how sorry I am today. She was so tender. So bright. Easygoing and cheerful. Oh, how I long to undo what I did to her! But in this world nothing can be undone. I deserted Hostia for a stupid, worthless female. Why? She was younger, sexier. You know how we are: younger women, faster horses, more money. For a while Hostia put up with my lack of tenderness. She shouldn't have been so tolerant—that was her mistake. Oh, how I long to undo the pain I inflicted on her. I try to do that in each poem. But papyrus remains papyrus, and Hostia remains dead, worms consuming her body. Where is her tomb? She's buried in Urbino, a small town in Umbria, where we spent our first summer together. Our best time together.

H OW LONG IS IT ALREADY SINCE YOUR ARRIVAL IN EGYPT, Sextus? Two years! How time flies when you're with me. It seems as if you came only yesterday. It seems as if I have known you for-ever. How is your compilation going? Is my monster of a husband not in your way? Is he helpful? That's good. Out of an inferiority complex he has developed enormous respect for the Romans. He sees himself immortalized by your study. And I am so happy to have you here. Let me confess something. It's childish, but I have to tell you: before I fall asleep and after I wake up, I thank the gods, your Roman divinities and my Egyptian idols, for intervening on my behalf. Why? I'm convinced that they made Hostia die young to make space for another woman. That way Berenice could join the orbit of your life. You don't realize what you mean to me, Sextus. You don't know the creature I was before we met. Humiliated by my husband, I wasn't a queen but an outcast, doubting the existence of gods.

It's strange the way we average humans are. When terror governs, we pray to gods, like children afraid of the dark. But we believe in gods only up to a point. There is a limit, a line we can't cross. On the other side, despair erupts, black lava poisons us, and we can pray no more. Then we begin to doubt the existence of gods. Don't we invent them when we're faced with misfortune, and hold to them when bad luck comes and goes? But when it stays too long and hardens into facts—facts that imprison us in subterranean mines, facts that make us bury too many people we loved, facts that force us to walk by new extermination sites, facts that relate us to a despot's misdeeds—then the gods begin to slip. Our better selves slip out of our skins and we abandon humanity. Then distortions stop bothering us, and we stop comparing the deformed with the harmonious, the depraved with the perfect. Correct me if I'm wrong. But after all I have gone through I tend to believe that people of integrity and courage can do without gods.

The question is if anybody is that strong.

Such moral giants don't exist?

They may, and some of them are, perhaps, our gods: people we divinize because of their goodness—or wickedness. Don't you call Euergetes a steel dragon, and mean: he isn't part of our human lot? Indeed, one day his name may signify the devil, while yours may stand for the immortal, faithful spouse. Finding the Hair of Berenice in the sky, people will be reminded only of your love, regard you as a young goddess of marriage: Saint Berenice who sacrificed the most outstanding section of herself to save Egypt's chief exterminator.

Oh Sextus! Stop! You make me cry. I was so young then. I was only twelve.

You know how much I honor you, my dear. Of course, you were only a child, overflowing with feeling. It's not your fault that you were given to a demon at that tender age. You shaved your locks for him, and showed them to the world. When we're in love, we all want to do that. But fate tricked you. Out of devotion crime was born. Still, Euergetes is not worth your tears. Come here, my dear, let's observe from the window the game your husband has devised for us. Really, his taste is the worst this earth has ever seen. Here's a Kleenex, dry your eyes, and tell me: what is he celebrating on this Saturday? Why can't it be the annunciation of his death! Aha, it's his ascension to the throne. Give me your hand, we shall ascend to the top floor, inspect the troops, and amuse ourselves.

Oh, that's unbelievable! Really, Berenice, we may be underestimating him. What a performance! No, it's not just kitsch. It's the kitsch of brave new worlds to rise—a thousand years from now. Look, Berenice. Look and count. One. Two. Three. Four. Thirty-two. Sixty-seven. Eighty-eight. And more. A hundred of his portraits afloat on the Nile, each of them fêting one of your husband's aspects. Here he's Osiris. To the left he subdues Assyria. To the right he consumes virgins. *Et voilà.* A patron of the arts, he distributes pencils and papyrus. Architect-General, he carries pyramids in his palms, while cannons perched on his shoulders proclaim him Military Head of Earth. Well, I must say, Berenice, he goes too far, ignores that Rome has dispatched fifty spies to gather news of his extravaganzas. Really, you should advise him to restrain himself. Otherwise, we may want to clip his elephants' trunks, sell him into slavery. I say, I say, what an outrageous joke. A million soldiers, each of them a lotus in his mouth, setting a million false icons afloat.

They aren't soldiers? They are slaves? Jewish boys dressed in military outfits? All camouflage? At midnight they'll be executed, all of them? Forgive me, Berenice. That's why you didn't want to join me at the window. No, it wouldn't have crossed my mind. But that's the problem. He belongs to a different species, I can't read his brain. And when I try, I feel as if I were deciphering an alligator's alphabet. No? You're right: no beast can aspire to his cruelty. Yet the power of Euergetes is derived from beastliness. *Cultus animalis*—there's no better word to render his rule. Perhaps I should ask Octavian to include my bon mot in the New Roman Dictionary Virgil is working on. In Rome we suffer from the *cultus personae,* here you're closer to the ape. But I ask myself: is our emperor more advanced than Euergetes? Besides, the cult of some duck or mouse may still await us. You're unwell? A glass of water? Aspirin? Lean against me, dear. You need fresh air. Shall we go for a walk? Later, when it's over?

Hold me, Sextus. See the green snouts? How they surface? To be fattened up with human flesh. Bones are washed clean, fall to the Nile's bottom, while its waves regain their usual shade.

Yes, life continues, although you consider ending yours. I know, you cannot bear it anymore. But you must, dearest. You must report to me what he tells you, what you learn from your servants. There is no other way to trace the present. No, not for ourselves. For posterity. It sounds pathetic? Yes, perhaps. Your ibis pet scratches your leg with its long beak. Listen to me, my dearest, dearest queen: you are the message, I am the medium.

Is that why I'm still in Egypt? Yes and no. Please, Berenice, don't twist my words. You are the best friend I have in the world. And I pursue both you—and my profession. I'm a poet with the soul of a reporter, a hunter of rare rhymes and curiosities. Under your husband, Egypt has become peculiar, a sinister spectacle of our age. So I'm here—using your eyes, ears, tongue, brains—to hear it clearly, describe faithfully. The two of us, we have a larger scope. Fondness is good, but it's not enough. My mindless talk makes you turn pale. You would prefer me to love you just for the sake of you, not for the sake of something else? But I do love you, Berenice, in my own way.

No, my interest isn't erotic. I admire you but avoid sleeping with you. No, not because you're too old. Sex is a mystery. When I recall some of the women I've had a crush on! Believe me, I despise myself. Some were stupid and vulgar, others without affection, drawn to me because of my position or money. What attracted me to them? The thrill of flesh. But you aren't a young girl, Berenice. You have your own experience. Didn't you agonize for your husband's caress? The mere touch of his fingertips? Oh, don't weep, Berenice. No man is worth your tears. No, I'm almost certain it's not your age. That's not the reason I didn't fall in love with you, I swear.

Do I find you pretty? Oh, I find you gracious. Exquisite. No, you're not too thin, your breasts aren't too small. Don't be ridiculous, Berenice. Hostia, she was as slight as you are, and no better endowed. No, I don't know why we haven't become lovers. No, I wasn't afraid of the risk. In sex, risk adds thrill. Your hair? I love women turning gray. Anyway, in my own way, I love you, Berenice, and would like to stay with you forever. Why we haven't become really intimate? It's rather strange, but that's how it is. We can't change it. Or can we? You believe it's possible, you hope that I can fall in love with you? Still? Well, the idea appeals to me, but how shall we accomplish it? What do you want me to do?

Leave me, Sextus. Return to Rome. Remember me there.

You want to turn me on by your absence? You want passion to be born, like a phoenix, out of Egyptian sand? The concept isn't bad, but life may be too short for that sort of experiment. Many things may happen on my way back. Pirates may capture me. I may contract an illness. You're right, I may meet another woman, fall for a teenager. You really want me, you really want us to engage in such craziness? Your plan may not work out and, forgive me, dear—it's a very female strategy. For some reason women tend to think that what cannot be achieved in reality will be fulfilled in dreams. But there's no guarantee.

No, I don't discard dreams. After I left Hostia, I dreamt about her every night and in the morning translated my reveries into rhymes. But in the afternoon I edited my verses, eliminating, replacing, adding new details. What did I do exactly? Well, it would be fair to say that I removed some of the dream events in order to make room for what occurred when, dreaming about her, I slept with someone else, colder and more casual than my mistress. Hostia would virtually melt in my arms. Caressing her, I was constantly afraid that she might lose consciousness. The more she burnt, the colder I felt. Too high-pitched, she rendered me almost frigid. The truth is, I prefer the type of sex we find in streetwalkers who just open up and provide us with professional pleasure. They don't tremble, don't whisper diminutives into my ear. They earn their income and help men to get on with sex, a sweat-sour business.

Am I too sincere with you? Making you sad? Well, you wanted me to open my heart to you, Berenice. Infatuation doesn't equal affection, dear. Certainly, I wouldn't mind falling in love with you. But I can't promise it, I can only try. Hostia is dead, and you aren't unlike her. You could be a Hostia resurrected. You don't like that. Oh, I'm sorry. No, it's not because of her that I adore you. I love you for yourself. No, I don't want to leave Egypt. But if you insist, I'll obey.

Oh, Berenice! Don't torture me. I'll go where you want me to go. To Moscow. To London. Yes, Rome is OK with me. I agree to be a guinea pig in this experiment of yours. In this sex trial. All right. I'll leave next Saturday with Aristotle's nephew who's heading back as well. You would prefer me to travel by myself? Oh, don't be such an incorrigible romantic. You know the social animal I am—I can't do without company. But since we are about to part, keep your promise. Let us finally go for that little expedition along the Nile, in a simple cangia. Only the two of us.

F ROM THE DECK OF THE CANGIA they enjoy the glory of an Egyptian sunset. A band of violet, tinted with rusty spots, occupies the lower portion of the sky and meets above zones of azure and shades of blue into which a clear lilac is infused. Tints of pearl and gray mottle through it, and where the red ball casts its reflection, the darker colors give way to pale yellow hues and sparkles of turquoise. Under the beam of light, water ripples obliquely, and shines with the dullness of an old quicksilvered mirror or a new razor blade. Against the lemon-colored glow, the sinuosities of the bank and all objects along the shore are brought out in black relief. In the crepuscular light, eyes are misled and perceive things where there is nothing. You take a little brown speck trembling in the net of luminous waves for a tortoise lazily drifting with the current, or for a crocodile raising the tip of his scaly snout above the water to breathe the cooler air of the evening, or for the belly of a hippopotamus gleaming in midstream. Or you mistake a rock, left bare by the falling of the river, for the ancient Opi-mou, father of the waters, who sadly needs to replenish his dry urn. But it is none of these. By the atoms of Osiris so deftly resewn together! It's a man who skates on the surface of the Nile.

Isn't Gautier a wonderful writer, Propertius remarks, interrupting his reading, raising his eyes, and focusing on Berenice. Isn't his text the exact image of what we see around us? Or, more exactly, what you see, while I keep following his words. As he says it, it occurs to him: I try my best to amuse the queen, but I don't succeed. It's our last trip together, and she has sunk into the solitude that from now on will be her daily bread. She presses my hand lightly to acknowledge that she appreciates what I'm doing. But her gloom isn't diffused. The sun is half sunk below the horizon. In two or three minutes it will disappear for good. Everything comes to an end, I hear her whispering, but she doesn't whisper to me anymore. She talks to herself. But let me not be easily discouraged, Propertius admonishes himself. Berenice, who, do you think, is the man skating on the Nile?

I couldn't care less, she wants to reply, but checks herself: I'm sorry, Sextus, I don't know. But I'm interested in what you're reading. I'm paying attention. Who's the man?

It's Cleopatra's lover. In a nutshell of a boat he sails to the queen desiring an adventure. He is a handsome youth of twenty, his hair so black that it seems blue, his body so blond and so perfectly proportioned that it might be mistaken for a bronze statue of Lysippus. Although he has been rowing for a very long time, his slender figure betrays no sign of fatigue. Not a single drop of sweat bedews his forehead.

As Propertius continues reading, Berenice becomes caught in the French reverie of Egypt. She sees Sextus returning—his face pale, his expression exhausted by her absence. She dreams of him on the deck of a ship. Emaciated. Looking younger. Desiring her. He's sailing back—on fire, in love with her. And she dreams of herself at twelve, her hair golden as on the day she met Euergetes. Her cheeks have regained their peachy texture. Her teeth are all in place, glittering like pearls. Today she's going to be wed to Propertius, Propertius Sextus, a promising Roman poet whose first book of idylls has just been published under the title *Berenice*.

T HE SUBLITERARY SENSATIONS OF GROWING OLD! How shall I translate them into texts? Svevo asks Propertius.

Oh, Italo! How can I take you seriously? Compared with me, you're a young man. You still engage in affairs with women. But look at me! Since my return from Egypt, I simply vegetate. Oh, Berenice! She was unsatisfied with my moderate affection. She wanted sex—at our age!—and got rid of me, in order to turn me on. Women are such dreamers! They don't grasp life's transient ways. A few days of roses and wine one has to drink at once. Nothing lasts. Hold to the sparrow in your palm, don't long for the hummingbirds of El Dorado.

Women have a better memory than we do, Sextus. Arteriosclerosis affects them less, and so they rely more on their recollections.

True, Italo. My memory is like Emmentaler, full of holes. I recall what happened half a century ago, I forget what I wanted to utter this instant. My souvenirs of Egypt are a bleached sheet, my childhood—a fine etching. I can distinguish every single pebble in the garden of my parents' villa in Perugia. It's my fifth birthday, and the evergreen pine trees stand out against the late November sky. Or I'm two and watch from the veranda the first snow of my life fall in infinite silence. Snow-flakes, each of them a heavenly star, melt on the dark blue bag I'm packed in. I see this in all clarity, while after six months Berenice's features fade away. She has deeply touched my soul, yet my retina hasn't retained a distinct image of the queen. Or is it my brain that can't hold her? Tomorrow she'll be a shadow. An *animula vagula blandula, pallidula rigida nudula*. A stain on my skin.

Why don't you return to Egypt?

To Berenice? Never. I couldn't face her again. Framed by her bed-room window, set against the Nile's changing tones, she appeared so fresh. But from the distance she is what she is: a menopausal female on the verge of suicide. A battered wife. A desolate queen of the desert. She should imitate Cleopatra, ask for a viper, and end her visit on earth. You disagree, Italo? You're against suicide? But isn't the best of our literary tradition based on our taking our lives? Remember Menippus? Or the elegant exit of Petronius Arbiter? His wrists were slashed but his fingertips still fondled his lover, the tiny Greek boy—his blond locks beautified for the occasion with poppies. Isn't that how we all desire to die? Only most of us cannot afford it. For my part, I'm afraid of slipping out of the role, committing a minor mistake, surviving as a plant. Suicide requires skill, style, and a grain of cynicism. Petronius wasn't bad at that. But what compelled him to go for the final experiment?

It might have been his last contribution to the policy of enlightenment which Petronius had pursued all his life. He was the right type to witness the gradual extinction of the physical, the penultimate flickering of the mistress anima.

Suicide as a scholarly study?

Yes, his last literary essay on the irregular verb *mourir*. A contribution to the grammar and syntax of dying. A footnote to the *entreprise mélodramatique* of opening one's veins. In fact, Petronius's boy was there from the beginning to the end, a pencil and block in his hands. So we have everything on paper. Alas, the stuff is so boring. Booze and drugs, drugs and booze.

To die by one's own hand is one thing, to produce literature another. A *dea ex machina* is needed to make the two coincide. What were his last words?

Sich im Denken orientieren.

Goethe? Schopenhauer?

No, Nietzsche.

Oh, the old snob of a *Satyricon!* Not even *mehr Licht!* That's not sufficiently sophisticated for him, an Arbiter. *Sich im Denken orientieren.* After a life of sodomy at Nero's side! If that's what his suicide amounts to, then indeed suicide isn't an answer. But what's the answer? I'm so tired, Italo. But in Rome, so far away from Berenice, I can't fall asleep. I'm in panic. She's persecuting me.

She? Who?

Signora Panica, a mix of Sylvia Plath and a queen worried about menopause. A relative of Panin.

Count Panin?

The very same. Nikita Ivanovitch, who placed Stanislaus II on the throne so that Poland might be drawn wholly within the Russian orbit. He was irresistibly attracted to women and his Moscow cook was the best. In the last quarter of the eighteenth century all Russian diplomacy was intimately associated with Panin's name.

Wasn't he born in Danzig?

Yes. But let me look up in the *Britannica* when he died. Here it is. March 31, like my uncle. In Italy. He met there with Karenina, and shortly afterwards experienced panic for the first time. It happened in Rome, the capital of panic, according to Pnin. In a *pensione* near the Colosseum Panin dreamt about himself as a boy, creeping under the skirt of Catherine the Great and finding in its depth a Polish king. Scared to death, the count mentioned the dream in a letter to the empress, and passed away the following night.

Am I going deaf, Sextus, or have the birds in your cherry orchard stopped chirping? Has water stopped streaming from the penis of your marble Pan? What's this sudden silence?

Don't panic, Italo. Birds go to sleep at dusk. Slaves turn off the fountain. It's evening, my dear. We have been talking and talking and talking, and the day has gone by. Do you want me to continue, or shall we have dinner?

All right then. I'll finish the story of Panin. Shortly before his death, he became interested in Greek art and bought at an auction a small statue of Pan, not dissimilar to mine. His Roman mistress wrote to Anna Casimirovna K, an ex-friend of Panin, that the count had spent too much money on Pan. She herself liked the body of the goaty god. He reminded her of the first boyfriend, a Sicilian.

Anna K was of Polish descent, and Panin addressed her as *Pani*. She, in turn, called him *mon ami russe*. Their romance remained an interlude, since their contrasting temperaments could not agree with each other. But in his latter days Panin recalled *Pani* frequently, and had a miniature of her face painted on the ebony cover of his watch. I presume he bought Pan because his name reminded him of *Pani*. His love for her was the only affair he kept secret all his life. Anna was married to an Austrian baron who, well established at Schönbrunn, spun intrigues against Panin.

On March 31, at midday, Panin's last mistress found the count in his bed. He failed to come to the breakfast they used to take in her small silk-lined boudoir. He seemed asleep, and his right hand rested on *Hymn to Pan*, a Russian version illustrated with engravings by the artist who painted Anna's portrait. Pan was depicted with horns, a goat's beard, and tickling with his hairy tail a naked nymph. She fled his embrace and was transformed into a reed. From it the shepherd's pipe was produced, the musical instrument Pan supposedly invented. Both the pipe and the reed could be perceived between Panin's dead fingers.

But as his mistress panicked at that moment, this escaped her attention.

On my way back from Egypt, when we were passing the island of Paxi, our pilot Thamus heard a mighty voice proclaim *Pan is dead.* Nobody could identify the voice and during the rest of the journey we kept discussing the meaning of this miracle with Aristotle's nephew. According to him, the strange message might have announced either the birth or the crucifixion of Jesus, or the end of the ancient world and the beginning of modernity. However, the majority of Romans traveling with us maintained that the name they heard was not *Pan* but *Tammuz,* and several women went so far as to lament the death of Adonis, their darling. Our sailing near the island of Paxi was also shown in the book that supported Panin's dead hand. The artist juxtaposed Jesus and Pan. After Panin's funeral, his mistress spent a sleepless night looking at the engravings of Pan. At dawn she discovered Anna's picture in her ex-lover's watch and was moved to tears. She decided to visit her Viennese friend and present her with the miniature. But upon her arrival in the Austrian capital she learned that *Pani* had died as well—on the morning of Panin's death.

Svevo has gone home and Propertius finds himself in the night's deep throat. I can't sleep, he repeats, can't read, can't write. I doze away, waiting for the night to end. And it ends. Bathed in the honey-colored light of the late September, Sextus wakes up as a sunny morning arrives at the porch. His eyes take in the light and his poetical nature begins to warm up. He associates the flaming red beech in front of his window with the Russian tail of Yesenin's fox and catches a glimpse of Rilke, disappearing at the end of a chestnut alley or in a manor house whose color—*Marientheresiengelb*—Sextus prefers to all other colors. Smiling to himself, he reaches for a pencil and composes a poem, born out of too much worrying, to his Berenice.

My dearest queen! I have lost interest in life and wander around wondering: why here? Where shall I go next? Sextus pauses, then adds further questions. Am I really Propertius? Or is this Thomas Wolfe in the village of Mornaye? He shares my sentiments but sets them to prose. Or am I Trakl who, indeed, is into verse?

And how he can write! Propertius whispers to himself. Trakl doesn't suffer from Rilke's cultivated *Prager Deutsch,* or from the empty rhetorics of too many question marks. He never asks: why here? why now? He doesn't dedicate a poem to a queen, fall in and out of darkness. He resides in it permanently. *Nimm dir ein Beispiel.* Observe how he holds to the flaming beech leaf, as if it were his sister's heart. In Salzburg, Trakl looks neither for a place to live, nor for a place to rhyme. He looks for a place to die, and his resolution is mirrored in his lines. World War I has as yet to break out, but he epitomizes it already. A poet of few words, he is faithful to the same adjectives, nouns, and verbs: black, blue, purple. Shadow, dusk, night. To sink, fall, perish. September's last glitter. A stony brook. A red leaf. Rats. Earth. Tree. November destruction. A 2705-days-long night shoots through his head. Brain splashes out. The poem hugs the page.

In Salzburg Trakl doesn't accompany the countess on her visit to the marquise. The chateau is a ruin, rose petals reside on the ground. He doesn't desire to settle in a quiet place. Incest is his crime. The name of his sister is Margaret, Sextus reminds himself. Treblinka is born out of her broken eye. Women stand naked in line, menstruate, throw up. Read Trakl and remember: the wolf is out everywhere, undoing humanity the moment you choose not to care. Holocausts come and go. Berenice's tresses are golden, and so is her constellation. But her roommate's extermination is hatched in the Egyptian mine of a heart.

June too soon. July gone by. August you must. September remember. October all over. The letter to Berenice is typed, but Sextus continues to abuse his Underwood, and starts a new one: My dearest queen. We wish the little universe of our lives pleasantly compact. But life is a meat grinder making us into pulp. Back in Europe, I watch another Euergetes preparing to set the world on fire. He's a petty bourgeois from Linz, but his neurocells give me creeps. He talks bombs, gas ovens, dear. His name, you better memorize it, is Hit. A *Nichtl* who in his heart's abyss is a builder.

Oh, architects are so dangerous! Think of Speer, such a cultured *Herr*. We read his memoirs together, remember? But he's an architect, and now he can't resist Hit's reverie of I-and-You, the two of us. We'll raze the world to the ground—re-erect it from the ground. From the suburbs of Salamanca to the salt lakes of Kazakhstan. From San Francisco to Shanghai. Hit-and-I, the associates of all times! Hit barks, kicks Speer, and erupts: ha-ha-ha-ha. History requires, Albert, that I disguise myself as Adolf the Great: author, linguist, politician, super-duper, *alles sehr schön*. But you know who I am: architect, buddy, architect. Take a glance at our gray, rainy Berlin. A shabby shtick. *Eine komplette Null.* But I-and-You, we'll ouch the *Schweinehund*. Here the Goethe, there the Schiller, in the middle Adolf Hit. First year: German Acropolis in Minsk. Second Year: Germanhattan in Madrid. Third year: Gerld World Center in Hitler, Missouri. Twenty miles high. *Architektur macht frei.* Once we're done with the bugs—Semites, Stalingrad—we'll pound out of the ground a great new planet, as *teutsch* as on the first day of creation. I-and-You, the divine Aryan-Adam-dvoika, we'll munch Eve's cunt, spit out her blood.

Without you, Berenice, I suffer from nightmares. Pricks turn pistols, split the earth. When it's over, women appear: you with your locks, Veronica with his photo, Magdalen with her pyx. The male instant of crucifixion is followed by millennia of lamentation. But the salty excretion of our better selves doesn't save the world. Because of my weak constitution and innate horror of hitting back, I feel like a fe-male, and willingly join the ranks of mourners. As a result, women mistake me for a womanizer, men for a feminist, while you, sweetest, you simply dismiss me.

Not to endanger you, my queen, I report on Egypt under various pseudonyms. But my words lack the necessary strength hatred alone hacks out of language. It's hard to admit, but some thoroughly evil men may be great writers. Oh, Berenice! I'm utterly confused by your absence, hallucinate more than I ever did in the desert. Is Hit really a major threat? Why do I see myself entering Rodin's studio in Paris and meeting Rilke whom, by the way, I consider an extremely overrated poet?

ITALO, WHISPERS PROPERTIUS, I'm being alienated from myself. I frequent unfamiliar places and feel a foreigner where I am. Tonight I dreamt about a September afternoon at Riverside Park. Seated on a bench, I contemplated the Hudson River, an unbroken road of golden light.

Sextus, I have to tell you something. Angiolina is back in Trieste, and has a new gadget. Now she can be phoned by several people at once. When I called her today, she talked to somebody else.

So you spoke with her?

Just for a sec: Thanks for calling. I'll call you later. OK?

Did she call?

I don't know. I preferred not to wait. Her joviality drains me of the last drop of cheerfulness.

It fits my theory, Italo. The jovial is the enemy of the good. It pretends to be nice but is incapable of true kindness. A jovial character stores the taste of sauternes and oysters, obliterates other people's pain.

As long as you provide Angiolina with pleasure, she tolerates you. The moment you let her glimpse your agony, you're out—a mad dog, free to roam the streets. But can I continue with my Manhattan dream?

I remained seated on the bench and saw Jason traveling down the Hudson, while Faust and Helen played basketball. Two classmates, tall and black, they were drawn to each other without realizing it, and infused into their game the solemn joy we possess only when we're very young. They exposed their youth against the autumn's sorrow, and I had to compare their shiny strong bodies with my own decrepit flesh, a papyrus palimpsest with layers of texts, one more impenetrable than the other. Yet I didn't pity myself. I felt sorry for them, imagined them scarred and hardened, separated, discriminated against. But I enjoyed watching their game—untouched by my own weariness.

You must have read too much Wolfe, Sextus. Behind the murmur of your words I hear the soundtrack of his rivers and times, and the hysterical fits of his American anima, a provincial soul in pursuit of a capitalized Truth. Instead of hanging around Riverside Park and complaining, you should take a few manly steps: talk to Horace about reissuing *Cynthia,* start to write *Berenice,* the book you're pregnant with, book a trip to Egypt.

IN STRASBOURG GOETHE ENJOYS THE ATMOSPHERE of medieval Christianity, for he's staying in the neighborhood of the cathedral. The old fox is in top form. His tail, bushy and glowing, is saluting every woman in the street, and there's nothing that doesn't interest him. If he could, Wolfgang would reform the Venetian sewage system, improve the efficiency of female genitals, change the course of history, restructure Original Sin. But in Strasbourg he lives not only in proximity to the sacred, but close to a cemetery as well, and remarks to himself: better a view of a graveyard than a view from it.

American academics claim that in Strasbourg Goethe doesn't part company with art and science, Karenina mumbles, but I have posted my own private eyes all over the city and gathered different information. Mostly he consumes food and femininity, and tries to conceal his appetite behind mystical speculations he stuffs into his letters. Here's a typical example, an undated postcard to Lotte: Dearest! Womanhood is our eternal goal, even though a man may be seduced by a fair Ecclesia today and tomorrow fall for a charming Synagogue. He should alternate between both and arrive at the microcosm of the pleasurably divine by adding a reasonable number of dishes to a good quantity of wine. Where was I? Oh, yes. Your love accompanies me everywhere.

My research reveals the card's date. It's written before Goethe goes out with the innkeeper's daughter he met the previous day at the cathedral entrance. After spending an enjoyable night with the restaurateur's only child, he cables to Lotte: For wherever I am, I feel my need of you. More in a letter. He fails to compose one, but a card is mailed: *Gnädige!* Last night I dreamt of the old familiar faces. It seems as if I could not unload my boat of pheasants' feathers anywhere but among you. May it be well loaded.

It's well loaded, Karenina notes. Wolf consumes a rich dish of tender pheasant legs cooked in Alsatian wine and unloads himself, gracefully and without too much ado, between his young concubine's thighs, smooth, hard, and sufficiently spread out.

On the morrow, right after breakfast, Wolf sketches two copulating goats, and scribbles: The soul is endowed with an upward tending nature, but it likes to sink. After lunch he sets out for Rome and in the last days of September arrives in Lausanne. From the terrace of his new companion's villa, situated on the shore of Lake Leman, Goethe contemplates the Devil's Peak, Mont Blanc, and lemon trees which, mistaking the autumn's exceptional mildness for spring, blossom in the garden. In the Swiss woman's oily skin a Hebrew past is hidden. A widow in her early forties, she is a skillful watercolorist and instructs him in the art of aquarelle.

Karenina contemplates two unfinished paintings of lemon blossoms presented to her by Vronsky, and writes: I assume that the one to my left, a rigorous and pedantic rendition of the flower's anatomy, comes from Goethe's brush. The watercolor to my right amounts to a pale patch of pink seated on a gray line. A Chinese-looking composition, it's almost imperceptible by now. Vronsky acquired the pictures from a schoolteacher in Weimar who, mistrusting Marxism, wouldn't entrust this most valuable item in his art collection to the local *Goethehaus*. Why? Because of its director, an exceptional ass, famous for his attempt to bury two East Germans—our Wolf and the author of *Das Kapital*— next to the Lenin mausoleum in Moscow. Anyhow, my ex-lover hid the sketches at the bottom of his suitcase. While it was being searched at the border, he addressed the guards as comrades, acted like an apparatchik—he may well be—and smuggled out the artworks.

Goethe's affair with the Swiss woman, Anna continues, doesn't last.

On the wings of the freezing north wind, Charlotte arrives in Lausanne. Disguised as the poet's muse, she puts the watercolorist on the defensive. The widow realizes that Goethe could use a few more painting lessons, but doesn't insist. An amateur, she's intimidated by Lotte's professional handling of the affair. Soon Goethe departs for Rome, alone. Back in Weimar, his official mistress blots out the Lausanne episode. Thus the two sketches I own are the only proof that the watercolorist's modest path crossed the road of the monumental *Mann*. What a pity her picture isn't signed! One more woman artist who tries to obliterate herself.

D EAR ITALO, WRITES ANN KAR. Yesterday I returned to Manhattan from a provincial university where *La senilità* provokes the provost to narrate the story of his Sicilian great-aunt's stroke. What a relief to be back! The plane flew along Broadway, from south to north, passing the brownstone of a man with whom I have a part-time affair, and my own building. I must arrange for you to come here. This city releases cascades of feeling even in senile farts. All steel and glass, Manhattan hits hard. This island of a town has appropriated even me, an eternal exile, woven my life's many threads into a fabric, reconciled the red with the blue. For a while. But now everything seems to fall apart again.

Oh my dear specialist in aging, tell me: how shall I control myself, come to terms with menopause? An emancipated woman, I'm becoming obsessed with menstruation. Does it happen to all females at a certain age? Why do I want to have sex during my period? Can the longing for the ultimate intimacy of blood exchanged against sperm be explained by my Jewish descent? My need to tackle a taboo? My atheist upbringing? In my younger years I never let a man enter me while I bled. Now I'm a bitch in heat, and my pride alone prevents me from begging for love. I lose weight, want to be licked clean. He? He postpones every date, withdraws his hand from mine, sleeps with me three times a month.

Oh, Italo! This late love of mine is a cup of sugarless chamomile, getting cold in my hand. My confidence is undermined, puerile nightmares permeate my solitary nights: a medallion with my dad's portrait is hanging from my neck. I unfasten the chain, throw his picture away, and encounter his headless body. It's stained with fresh blood and resembles a sanitary napkin. While I try to pick it up, an ambulance arrives and two men carry it away on a stretcher. I hear the siren and see myself returning home. At the doorstep my brother awaits me, a healthy, handsome boy. We embrace, he evaporates, I wake up. My feet are cold, my lips are sealed, my tongue is salty and stiff. Oh what a burden aging is! Sunlight solidifies into a bloody hematite—etched by memory. So I recall the morning we went by *vaporetto* to Torcello. You glanced at Venice's hazy silhouette and pressed my hand: *come è bella.* Then life was still a vessel filled with mercury. You bought me a lemon-colored blouse near the Ponte di Accademia. Karl waited for me in the open window of a small hotel on Campo Santo Stefano. Carol painted on the balcony in Urbino. On the boat you told me that the best fiction is produced by us, the middle-aged ones, out of flesh going bad and bold. Damned souls, caught between hysteria and sclerosis, you explained, excrete eminent texts. I disagreed, and a few days later we returned to our topic in the Trinity School swimming pool where we used to meet on Mondays at eight, remember? But that night the lifeguard's absence prevented us from jumping into the water and your mood turned philosophical. Anguish dictates the best lines, you said, taking off your bathing cap. Fear exiles us from the blah-blah-blah of verbal commerce.

My notes on our dear band of aging dinosaurs, sacked by sex, are meant for you, Svevo. By the way, Berenice is very sick. Breast cancer. Transmit this to Sextus. He shouldn't delay his journey back. She refuses to yield to the knife, but nothing else can save her. Once Propertius is with her, she'll agree to the surgery. Poor queen, in her despair she has taken to writing. I enclose a copy of what I received from her yesterday. Give it to Sextus, it may prompt him to act. Since Berenice is about to die, you shouldn't wait. By the way, the queen told me Sextus was at the verge of converting to Isis, the moon goddess she trusts more than the rest of the Egyptian heaven. May she preserve you in good health.

S EXTUS, ANN SENT ME A TEXT BY BERENICE I would like to submit to Virgil's new magazine.

Pro Arte? It hasn't really taken off.

It will, Mezoros is promising to finance it. I would like you to read her text and, if you find it suitable, recommend her to the board. Since it's partly a travelogue, it would fit into the fall issue and complement

Broch's inner journey to Brindisi, a metaperegrination across the androgynous land of the self which Virgil wants to publish in September.

Propertius's hands tremble. He takes Berenice's papyrus scroll but doesn't dare to unroll it. He stares into the dusk, switches on the radio, and rejoices. Like a sequence of raindrops running over a windowpane, Schönberg's twelve-tone tune accompanies an ode to Laura, and reminds him of a trip to Calabria, together with Petrarch, with whom he quarreled about what really cements love: *amore? more? ore? re? iunguntur amititiae.* Remembering the old argument, Sextus listens to his old friend's words set to music:

My inner eye that now feasts upon her only, and turns its back on all that is not hers. I sought a valley, ringed around with mountains, in which my weary sighs might find some solace. And slowly, musing on my love, I reached it. No ladies did I see, but rocks and fountains and that day's image, which my constant spirit holds up to me wherever I may look.

Miraculously direct, the voice echoes in Sextus. The walls dissolve, all knowledge is dispensed with. The little *Lied* envelops him in silence. When we're injured, only the ardor of a childlike song comforts us, a rondo for the glass harmonica, an adagio for flute, oboe, and viola. Let me retire to my Berenice's writing, no longer fear the impact of her words, unroll the scroll. The sight of his beloved's handwriting gives him shivers, and he begins to read aloud:

Alas, a single happiness remains for me, my dear. When you were close at hand, I dreamt you away. But once we are apart, we really are together, and our life is an eternal pact. Do realize it, my dear Roman: no woman loves you more! Meanwhile, I do as you told me. I keep my eyes open and must report: under the disguise of *glasnost,* the KGB is sending spies to Egypt. But is it good or bad for Euergetes? His health, I'm afraid, is best.

The prerequisite of happiness is too little. Too little money, a too small apartment. Too little work, it makes people converse. These words, I guess, define a queen, who in too-much can never find her rest. Looking out of my bedroom window, I see you in Rome. Lemon trees blossom and you dine with Wolf, Lotte, and Kowalski right at the corner of the Via dei Polacchi. This spring, I hear, Goethe pursues biology, and Sartre with de Beauvoir have joined you for a while. I recently saw their photo in the *Cairo Times.* Jean-Paul, a wreck, takes a sip of beer, she reads to him from *Le Brigate Rosse.* Something trickles out of his nose, and I ask myself: what will become of his philosophy? Not much, my queen, Propertius whispers. The radio sings from *Boy's Magic Horn* and he can hear how Mahler, haunted and depressed, probes exile and escape, and heads for heaven. There I'll dance with Berenice, jump, hop, have John slaughter the lamb, drink wine, have angels bake us bread and flesh. Do I really want to read her text? I must, I guess.

Last evening the imperial architect acquainted me with plans ordered by Euergetes. He wants a crystal cube to house his tomb—a sort of a cubist ice palace. An English gentleman, the builder isn't without irony and has the nose of Ben Nicholson. Talking to him, I pondered your description of the old painter, a tiny man in a thick blue sweater. Didn't he share a wife with a Cambridge professor? Dance with her last tangoes at Highgate? Meanwhile his children from various marriages broke in and stole his work, correct? I wonder: what happened to Carol Kar's portrait of me in Ben's collection? She painted me elongated and absent, dressed in blue silk, against the blue of the Nile.

Following Berenice's lines, Propertius steps into a London critic's house, spacious and dark and filled with tons of art. There he met Ben, a million years ago, had health biscuits with jam, and was attacked by a Burmese cat. What was the address? Oh, yes. From Belsize Gardens he returns to the queen's boudoir. They sit together on a cotton couch and a Greek slave takes a picture of them. Both wear black kimonos and resemble a couple. Sextus's right hand rests on Berenice's shoulder, the queen's right hand is hidden under his left arm.

A FOREIGN CORRESPONDENT FOR U.S. JOURNALS, Karenina travels around the world, meets men, separates from them, and still waits for Vronsky to write her a word. It's mid-October, and she finds herself in Buenos Aires, sightseeing, visiting the pastel-colored Bocca, a cemetery of ocean liners and artists. Anna touches the elephantine skin of bottle-shaped baobabs, the trees of local drunkards, and dines in the Esmeralda Verde where for a dollar one can eat as much as one can. On a Sunday morning Karenina takes a tourist boat to the sleepy country of Uruguay, rents a bike, and rides along paths, winding and pink like the necks of flamingos.

In the Museum of Postmodern Art, black as a Nigger, soulless as a Narcissus, Carol Kar, her friend's stepsister, exhibits veils and shrouds. The museum is owned by a Jewish merchant from Kiev. He has the art dust of all continents shipped, unloaded, and stored in a sort of submarine, an electronically supervised gallery with a mysterious and unholy spell. A nymph, slender and insecure, answers red and black telephones, pasting together contradictory messages. In front of her desk a crowd of artists competes for the golden rain of fame.

The boat is maintained by an underpaid Indian mate. All day he polishes steel bridges and ladders, cleans the perforated plastic floors, switches the video monitors on and off. He took to me and I took to him, Carol tells Anna. He, the Nigger sailing on his hands and knees through the sea of art, and I, the Narcissus of an artist. My Spanish isn't good, his English doesn't exist, but we reach out to each other. His face, still and sunken, reminds me of a mask. A shadow inhabits his eye, and he holds on to a small canvas bag, bleached and dirty. An unbuttoned striped cotton shirt discloses the boy's rachitic breast. He's under-nourished, has oily hair, drops of sweat cover his forehead, shadows outline his hollow eyes. Soon we'll part, Carol whispers, but now we would like to go ashore together, desert the ship, forget about the fixed arrangements of our separate lives. This instant isn't about sympathy or sexual attraction. It's a rare moment of solidarity in a divided world. In a split second, Anna, we will be outmaneuvered. Reality will cut through our togetherness, common sense will lead us apart. But for the time being I partake of the boy's nature, mournful and silently accusing. He stands in the open doorway, his arms crossed, his nails dirty, and he surrenders to weariness. Motionless, blank, he accuses his alter ego— the civilized world. You are a journalist, Anna, why don't you respond to his accusation, repeat my silent words?

What do you want to say, Carol?

I, a suicidal New York neurotic, want to address him in a way so pathetic and tasteless that only a Karenina could bear it. I want to say: I see the slender hair holding a sword suspended over your head, my boy. But a day will come, although it may arrive after your death, when your hands will grasp the sword. I wouldn't mind preventing this, but I know that it cannot be prevented. All humiliation ends in fight. During summer vacation, I saw Polish solidarity rise. It rolled like an avalanche, you'll roll like an avalanche. Therefore grant me permission to include you in a sheet I draw and fold for posterity. A shroud, where people meet and part like solitary ships, it will outline what is obscured today. The high cannot ascend, but the low can rise. It sounds like religious rubbish, but you shouldn't laugh at my words. I'm mad, but wise as well. Your steamer goes down the river, dredging with the anchor down. My boat sails swiftly, ignoring pilots, beacons, buoys. You discharge cargo,

I glide on the surface. But we're both sailors.

You must forgive me for speaking in metaphors, Anna. But they create the intimacy we both thirst for. In this whale's stomach of a world, we could have a drink together or a smoke. Instead we opt for images rushing us around. You and I, we're an opium den where Chinese sailors chitchat and play cards. Billiard balls click and loud smacking noises come from men's fat lips as their tongues embrace liquor glasses and lick ice cubes. Suddenly, a windowpane breaks, splinters cover our table, and the sound of riot and devastation encircles us.

DEAD DRUNK, HIS TEETH CHATTERING, Malcolm Lowry meets a sober Conrad dressed in a fancy flannel suit. Dr. Conrad, I presume, says Malcolm, and has a big sip of gin. Are you in business? Joseph inquires. Certainly, replies Lowry. I had a novel rejected by fifty-five publishers, lost my only disk with another one. To fulfill my felicity, a donkey from *New American Lit* accused me of plagiarizing the Nigger of your Narcissus. I wait for my wife, the apple of your eye. She's due in a minute and I hope to be able to stand up and kiss her on the right spot, though I doubt I can find it. It's tough to have a wife.

It's tough not having one.

Is that so? What's up?

Shanghai.

The only place they have decent bars and girls, let me tell you before she arrives. The woman who isn't really my wife, but to whom I consider proposing tonight. Not a good idea? You're probably right. But here she comes. A beauty? Yes, she looks fine. Maybe slightly too fine, and too difficult.

And, indeed, she comes in, Conrad notes in the evening, beaming with ostentatious charm. A stout piece of a woman, ready to plough the literary Lowry marsh, a suggestive, rustic, and homely nature. I immediately identify her as a vessel for male longings, a bosomy boat with glazed cabins and windows protected by tiny white curtains. A robust round arm. A watering pot. Bowing her sleek head of a maiden, she pronounces her name with pride: Ernestine, making clear that with her fair skin, hair, eyes, and little knobby nose, she knows nothing of the wicked sea and the corrupt world. Pretty, touching, vulnerable, thoroughly feminine, she walks into the bar and all men's eyes focus on her. She addresses Lowry as sweetheart. She calls me a dear friend.

Her teeth are white and smooth. Her tongue—an advertisement of perfect pink. She wears a blue dress with white polka dots, and white high-heeled shoes. In her large and comely face lips are outlined with crimson lipstick. She has a good complexion and the paleness of her skin reminds me of the white, empty candor of a statue. The simplicity of her apparel, the opulence of her form, her imposing stature, and the extraordinary sense of vigorous life that seems to emanate from her like perfume exhaled by a flower, makes her beautiful with a beauty of a rustic and Olympic order. I imagine her reaching up to clotheslines with both arms raised high above her head. And this causes me to fall to musing in a strain of pagan piety.

While Conrad continues writing, Lowry fails in one attempt after another to lay his future wife. No way. He fancies a bottle, not a female.

Projecting the image of the future Mrs. Lowry onto the formidable Mrs. Hermann of his Nigger and Narcissus, Conrad masturbates that night and wakes up to a creative morning. When Malcolm wakes up, he finds at his side a creature dissolved in misery. She wept all night and is asleep now, her red and swollen face buried between the pillows.

Ernestine is earth, young and fresh, as on the first day of creation, writes Joseph. Meanwhile Malcolm contemplates his bride with fear, gets up, and proceeds to the kitchen to fix himself a drink.

A virginal planet, Conrad mimics himself, undisturbed by a vision of a future teeming with monstrous forms of life, clamorous with the cruel battles of hunger and thought. Ernestine—a modest, silent presence.

I draw no great comfort from her company, Lowry remarks to himself. Just the opposite: I draw comfort from her absence. Having established this, he returns to the bedroom, absentmindedly fondles Ernestine's big tits, and when she opens her eyes, proposes to her. She accepts and goes to the kitchen to prepare breakfast.

I wouldn't mind embarking with Ernestine on a long sea passage, muses Joseph in the evening. To Uruguay, for instance. We would arrive there in early October, when lemon trees blossom and give off heavenly smells. We could walk hand in hand along the shore, rent bikes, and ride on the pink roads, lie in the warm red sand, make love in a cheap hotel in Montevideo, and eat enormous, inexpensive steaks in Carmelos. I would spray seed into her sad tropics and play my favorite game, the *post-coitum-animal-triste*. But do I really want to sleep with this girl for the rest of my life? To produce offspring? Take care of some drug addict of a son? In the long run I couldn't draw comfort from

Ernestine's company, Conrad scribbles on the edge of a newspaper. Then he takes out his stationery and composes a letter to Lowry:

Dear Friend: I encourage you with all my heart to marry Ernestine, a wonderful piece of femininity, to be treasured and guarded. My departure for Shanghai is imminent, and so I take farewell of both of you. Sincerely, J C

That night Malcolm succeeds in getting an erection. Once. His effort at ejaculation remains, however, only an effort. But he's pleased with himself, less drunk than usual, and writes:

Mom, kiss me good night, says Aeneas to Venus before the decisive battle. Next day corpses litter streets, his saffron dress edged with acanthus is torn, and Peter Brook's *Mahabarata,* performed at the BAM, makes the point that in the age of relativity time is a snowball, a hot-air balloon, a harbor where sails are pulled down, a missile inspected on site.

We head toward the land and the land dissolves. Like the curve of a bow the port disappears in the waves. Cliffs of the east meet the waters of the west. Manhattan's towers bow to Moscow's golden onions. Good omens abound, as do bad ones. Both hemispheres forget the Afghan holocaust and admire two horses grazing in a meadow. One is tattooed between his ears with a red star, the other wears starry stockings and striped shoes. Oh, what a wonderful view! Recently they got hemorrhoids from drinking blood. Recently they fed on grass. God bless them, the harmless creatures! Earth and oceans, support them! Winds and storms, help them forget that Troy was razed to the ground. The Trojan horse is such a dandy animal, its belly filled with the promise of peace.

But why is Aeneas's fleet holding a sure course over the sea, cutting through the waters that darken under the wind? Why is Venus driven by worry, pouring out complaints? Not satisfied with bones and ashes, Miss Universe requests a flood to sweep Troy away. Gods grant her request. Once the apocalypse is over, funeral games are organized for Anchises, Venus's dead lover.

But who cares anyhow? The world is a cage of wonders. Cancer genes yield practical applications. Oncogenes are believed to trigger cancers through different mechanisms, and clever strategies show promise against common colds. Everything happens at once. Reactors are built in space. Schoolchildren from Mississippi meet their schoolmates from Vitebsk to organize a Chagall show in Pennsylvania.

Useful medical applications begin to emerge. Cancer is the answer to the question of metaphor, and so is AIDS. Tunnels can shelter us from nuclear waste. Tunneling efforts are scheduled to begin December 24, and giant tunneling machines are being specially designed to fit the geology of our planet. Nearly two zillion zillions will be required to tunnel us under. But tunneling represents the priority of our age, and the Grump Transtunnel Corporation is expected to do a good job. It will take them thirty-three years to complete the project. In the process eighty-eight zillion cubic meters of soil, enough to rebuild three hundred great pyramids of Egypt, will be hauled to the surface. The project is headed by the distinguished terra-engineer Faustophilos, and the consortium plans a crucial twenty-zillion stock offering in November.

It's September, and Underwood, my roommate, revels at my side. An alcoholic, he creeps slowly through the enchanted nightwood of the mutual text that writes down the two of us. Psyche and Techne embrace, as things wander in and out of our twin machine-minds.

In Milan short skirts inspire inventive spring openings. It's a wonderfully brave world: spring occurs in October, the fall fashion shows are fixed for February. When the earth is frozen, print dresses with shirred bodices and the over-the-knee stockings and soft silk blouses with tapered trousers gathered at the waist appear in collections that could have been put together by committees on cultural thought. An important innovation is shorts, which are skintight in stretch fabrics and paired with a low-neck camisole and a long jacket, or tailored and cuffed in linen or leather. Oh what a dazzling universe of wild colors and offbeat shapes, which take the rich by storm. Clothes are fitted so snugly, no bulge goes undefined. Short tight tops bare a sliver of flesh at the midriff. The newest creations fall from small natural shoulders and billow out around the hips, the shape reminding men of an upside-down flower. The sexy models on painterly ciba-chrome prints have blurred faces, their hair slicked back into knots and anchored by many silver-colored headbands, combs, and barrettes, all worn at the same time. But the thighs are naked and invite my gaze and tail. Finally Ernestine is asleep and I can be by myself. Gin keeps me company and I savor the press-speak, which acquaints me with the world. *La Prensa* reopens in Nicaragua. A celebrated Chinese painter, who has immigrated to the United States, can't sell his work. He has enrolled in a multidisciplinary mental health program serving the homeless in Manhattan, and hopes for the best. I'm in love with Ernestine but neglect her. I don't want to hurt her but all the time I do.

THE MID-OCTOBER EGYPTIAN LIGHT FILTERS THROUGH the colored windowpanes and, lovesick as well as increasingly ill with progressing cancer, I, Berenice, stare at the ceiling, oblivious to the world. The ceiling reminds me of polar plains and glacial seas, of Greek peninsulas and islands in the Antarctic, ice caves, ice stalagmites, frozen streams and fountains. Soon I'll depart for the winter islands, go to sleep in an igloo situated at the seaward end of the glen of the Mylopotamus, and named Santa Sophia. Is Propertius waiting for me in that hole of holy wisdom? On a small platform covered with snow pebbles? It's a windy spot and he's afraid to leave the tent. He presses it to the ground with the weight of his body. Oh how light you are, Sextus, a snowflake melting in my hot palm. It's dissolved, but a mark remains—a stigma of your presence. It's beyond words what I owe you. Beyond sex. Beyond the solid state. Our fluid affair solidifies in a split second into a bit of amber in which two insects are trapped. A thousand years from now the relic will be exhibited in the Luna Museum of Terrestrial Pain, together with a piece of cotton glued into a shell—my portrait by Ann's stepsister.

THE YOUNG MOON SCHOLAR'S EYES are fixed on the screen, where a three-dimensional Earth map, illustrating the political geography of—presumably—the early twenty-first century, flashes on and off. Was Manhattan then the capital of the United Earth States? Was banking the main resource of the UES? How did it all end? What's the significance of Dowjones? A central concept, omnipresent in the sources, how is it connected to the final collapse? To a salty pebble? To a transparent goldstone? To a likeness in a shell?

The moon scholar wears a purple sweater and his profile is cut against the luminous screen in all its youthful clarity.

IT'S A PITY, WHISPERS BERENICE, I can't explain it to you. Time, my young moon-man, is a mouse. It consumes all. When Michelangelo sculpted me and Sextus as night and day in the Medici chapel, he intended to place a marble mouse on top of the sarcophagus. But I asked him not to, and he consented. Later he mailed me the model of the tiny beast with a nice note: *To Regina Nox—from a modest maestro.*

But where was I? Oh, yes, on the moon, at the moon scholar's side, in front of the Earth globe. Your eyes move around it, gliding over Cyprus and Cythera, which both claim that Aphrodite was born there. Then you become fascinated with Cyprinodont, a little nest in Egypt, named after a fish. Once a close ally of the pike, cyprinodont was the favorite fish of our time. It was characterized by a flat head with projectile mouth beset with cardiform, villiform, or compressed, bi- or tricuspid teeth, large scales, and the absence of a well-developed lateral line. Inhabitant of the fresh and brackish waters of Egypt, cyprinodonts, cooked or grilled, provided the main course of many suppers I had with Propertius—Propertius Sextus, a great Roman poet, whose name, I presume, is known on the moon.

To get away from cancer and depression, I am studying the Egyptian fauna, the innumerable species, which are threatened by my husband's rule. Steel mills pour poison into the Nile. Fish die. Hippopotamuses go blind. Crocodiles alone survive and flourish. Scavengers and executors, they fill their bellies with the flesh of crippled creatures, condemned humans. Cyprinodonts are just about extinct—the last couple lives in my aquarium. They are a loving pair but too old to mate, and so all I can do is to record that in cyprinodonts the sexes are dissimilar, the female being larger and brilliantly colored, with smaller fins. The anal fin of the male can be modified, it's a queer detail, into an intermittent organ by means of which internal fertilization once took place, the ova developing in a sort of uterus. When Propertius first arrived in Egypt the Nile was still populated with the *genus analebs* cyprinodonts, in which the strongly projecting eyes were divided by a horizontal band of the conjunctiva into an upper part, adapted for vision in the air, and a lower for vision in the water. The pupil was separated into two parts by a constriction.

Many years ago an American zoologist, Professor Claudino Schwarz from the Manhattan Animal College, provided me, upon my request, with his paper on Egyptian cyprinodonts, published in *Me. Mus. Comp. Zool.* XXI (2001). A correspondence developed, and I learned that he and his wife Amelia, a professor of neurology, were not only distinguished scientists but also art collectors. Among other things, they possessed several shell-portraits by Carol Kar. They were the first in Manhattan to recognize her talent, and introduced her work to me. After Carol's suicide they commissioned a Greek stele. It represents Pan mourning the nymph he killed, and marks Carol's grave in Tribeca Cemetery, on Manhattan's southern end.

WHY AM I SO OBSESSED with this guy Conrad? Malcolm asks the four walls of his room. What is it about him that makes me mad? Why do I oscillate between classifying him as a fake, and giving him the credit of being a genius? Why do I put together the facts of his life, and then disperse them?

At Constantinople, where Conrad has gone with the intention of joining the Russians against the Turks, he joins the French merchant navy. That's how it starts, and continues: he keeps running away from noble obligations into the arms of commerce. In Lowestoft, Suffolk, he gets hold of his mate's certificate, sails for the East in an English ship, describes this voyage and the rest of his travels, and achieves success, despite his all-too-vigorous style. In pursuit of his alter ego, the *anima polacca,* he explores the tropics and participates in exotic adventures. Afraid of women, he reserves for them his brain. A Pole, he insists on penetrating into the heart of darkness. But unlike most of his countrymen, good at going under, he's spared—shielded from malaria and stopped from hitting the bottle by a curious charm: the English language, a foreign bride, bought at a slave market in Malay. With her at his side, he can bear the sight of his mirror image in the golden sea at sunset, as he heads for Shanghai, crosses the bloodred Panama Canal.

Do I resemble him? I don't. But we have mutual interests. Our eyes rest, again and again, on people marked by the desolation of time. Turning our eyes around the world, we catch glimpses of ourselves— familiar strangers, faded and grim, with a mingled expression of fatigue and eagerness. But it's not the fatigue, Joseph, it's the eagerness that's killing me. I'm forty-one, and starved for the love I neglected in the past. It's the appetite of a man approaching menopause, and it's the fall: the autumnal light Bruno Schulz speaks of, the fox of Yesenin, the *animula* jumping out of my skin. The bloodred leaf that holds to the branch but is blown to the ground. The lemon tree, mistaking mid-October for March. It's the widow in Lausanne who hopes to attract Goethe's attention by means of aquarelle. It's the eagerness that's killing me. That's making me write.

EAGERNESS IS DESTINY, Carol Kar scribbles. Sixty-eight is a memorable year and the number of a two-story wooden house in the suburbs of Vienna. I approach the house, and my nervousness increases. To soothe it, I buy cherries coated in chocolate. The wooden fence around the house is held together with rusty wire, dwarfish cherry trees move their branches in the November wind. I pass through the half-open gate, climb three wooden steps leading to the porch, and ring the bell. A middle-aged woman opens the door and hearing my request, shouts Herr Géza in the direction of the staircase. Silence follows, and she shouts again. Then, turning to me, says: He isn't home.

How can he not be at home? I'm eager to lose my virginity, and that's why I'm here, a fourteen-year-old, to visit you, a Hungarian refugee, more than twice my age. How can you be not at home? Refusing to believe in your absence, I walk back slowly. Soon I'm reassured, and stopped by your voice. In a white unbuttoned shirt, without an overcoat, the middle-aged man is running after me. He runs against the wind, but when he reaches me, his hands aren't cold. Why has he changed his mind? I wonder. Thirty years old, lonely, good-looking but not talented, he's after me, the Lolita who hasn't read Nabokov, and perhaps because of that, has no desire for sex. But in order to comply with life's course as it's rendered in books, she considers it her duty to be deflowered. A devourer of fiction, she knows that lovers who don't sleep together aren't real—and it's the reality, not the man, she's after.

As they meet, she hands him the chocolate box, wrapped in pink paper. He tucks it under his left arm, puts his right arm around her, and they rush to his upstairs sublet, unheated and dirty. Brushing aside rubbish, Géza deposits the gift on the table, declares that cherries in liquor are his favorite sweet, brags a little about photos he took at the Academy. While his low-contrast pictures glide through her fingers, he steps behind the girl, lifts her green woolen skirt, undresses her, lowers her into his bed, positions himself on top of her, and whispers: The bed stands above their kitchen table. Let's do it quietly.

Is it the first time?

She doesn't reply.

Don't be afraid. It won't hurt. I won't make you pregnant.

His Hungarian accent comforts her but it does hurt. In. Out. His penis isn't smeared with blood and—half relieved, half disappointed— he murmurs: I see. You have done it before. Want a cherry?

He doesn't accompany her home, and she returns alone—the adult female she plays. When the tram comes to a sudden halt, she feels something drip out of her. It's blood. It's over.

WHAT'S OVER? this Carol hides from her friend Elephant. It's Sunday morning, and they bike along the Delaware & Raritan canal through the forty-first fall of their lives. Elephant gossips about academic intrigues, deadlines, tenure. Seasons change, positions are cemented, or undermined. Junior profs try to outfox each other, the senior faculty wives are into alc and loud talk. On Saturdays spouses visit their respective shrinks, because of sleep or sex disorders. A successful treatment restores hibernation and monogamy. Salaries rise, houses are bought and sold for a quarter million. Scholars invest in the stock market. Babies are born with life insurance. Why then does the quiet absence of joy obstruct the rhythm of hearts? Why are Psyche's wings turning gray when she overflies Carnegie Lake? Why isn't Amor with us?

Academic wives, says Elephant, pry into the nature of their unhappiness, and bring suffering upon themselves. Oblivious of life's proportions, they fall into insanity. But, indeed, here in the paradise of the learned and wealthy, it's hard to not lose perspective, to not go somnambulist. Too comfortable, the soul is converted into a captive, and doesn't know it's caged.

Light passes through the negative of the self, and the film is hardened. But I can't bear the developing process anymore. The dark room. The smell of ink. The bath of cold water. The dusting of the lines with asphalt, Carol wants to confide in Elephant, but bites her tongue: I can't frighten her with the imperceptible etching away of my own substance. So she says: Wandering around, the mind encounters no borderlines. How can feelings, expanding and reaching out into the void, be described? Why did the great poet Propertius fall for Hostia, a courtesan of Tibur? Left her, came back, deserted her again, to and fro, between ardor and disgust? Did they ever reconcile? Or is it all a myth, prompted by the well-preserved mosaic of Hostia's eyes in his villa? Perugia is in one pupil, Persia in the other. Propertius stands at the window, a lotus in his hand, a small white dog at his feet, a bird on his shoulder. Vapor escapes from his mouth and forms into two commands: Lick her hands, fly.

Did you know, Carol, Elephant asks, that Marie de France saw the mosaic when it was first excavated, and was inspired by it?

Yes, she composed her famous lays about a wife locked up by her jealous old husband in a high tower. Young and flirtatious, she dreams about a secret lover. He flies in, disguised as a bird, and once inside, turns into a radiant youth. They screw each other secretly every night, but their love doesn't last. The husband discovers the nightingale, lines the entrance with glass splinters. The bird flies in, has his wings wounded, bleeds to death. Deeply moved by the mosaic, Marie mixed some of its elements with Propertian verses into an elegy of unsafe sex—enslaved, injured, extinguished by the evil eye. Like Sextus, she was attracted by excessive vagueness and immoderate indulgence in allusions and phantoms. Egotism and vanity sparkle in her poems. Words are electrically charged. My stepsister and I read her poems and cry.

E ACH NIGHT, with exhilaration and frustration, I read Berenice's incoherent text. Clearly, it's written by an amateur. A woman who's out of breath. It's night, the moon shines very bright, and the voice of a nightingale can be heard from the garden. Has the bird freaked out? Or does the world come to an end? A nightingale in mid-November sounds like a Neronian joke. But as I look around, nothing is as it should be. Lemon trees blossom in the fall. Beech leaves turn red in May. Desperate females dabble in literature. True poets shut up. The market plunges in a tumultuous wave of selling. Fall coincides with depression, as frenzied trading on the stock exchanges lifts volume to unheard-of levels. The earth is exhausted. A desert. And even the moon appears deformed, elliptical and shady. Oh how I long to get out of this. Tell me, Italo, why do all late civilizations resemble each other? Replay the same records? Produce cotton sculpture? Compile Assyria, Babylonia, and Egypt onto a single compact disk? Lack in intimacy? Abound in impotence? Let entire continents go broke? But coming back to Berenice: her writing is unprofessional, but good. *Pro Arte* should publish her in installments. We need to listen to women's voices. Let Berenice replace Propertius and join literary Rome.

It's too late.

Too late? What do you mean by that, Italo? Is she sick? Breast cancer? Radiation? Chemotherapy? Why didn't you tell me at once? How can you make me read her text, and not tell me she's about to die!

She needs surgery.

And? She refuses to submit to the knife? Can you blame her! But if that's the only way to save her life, she has to be cut. Of course I'll go to Egypt. Take the next available flight. Maybe it isn't too late. Something can still be done. Oh, how could I ever leave her alone? Be so weak, moody, unreliable? How could I desert the only creature I care about? Mother died when I was three. When I was thirty-eight, Hostia passed away. And now Berenice! How can I survive the women I love? Berenice, she is so selfless. She suffers, and I read her text, instead of holding her in my arms.

Unless you accompany me to the airport, Italo, we may not see each other before my departure. So let's say farewell now. And greet the rest of Italy for me. What my intentions are? I don't know. If I can come here with Berenice, I'll return. Otherwise, I'll stay with her. And if she dies, there's no life for me either.

Forgive me, Italo. I'm a hysteric, I always talk about suicide. But believe me, the big talkers never kill themselves. I give you my word, I'll be back. Soon. After all, am I not number three of our local Olympus, obliged to make public appearances and mix with the plebes?

P ROPERTIUS DEPARTS, writes Ann Kar, and on the same day I arrive from New York on the strength of a grant I have been awarded to study Saint Veronica. Tonight I and Italo head together for a Japanese movie in the Metro Theater, right off the Via Appia. *The Muddy River* captures the awkward gestures of a ten-year-old. It's 1956 but the boy isn't aware of the Polish Spring, unfolding in October, of Khrushchev alighting at the Okęcie Airport to reinstate Gomułka, and of Gomułka appointing my father his minister of culture. Ten years old, I'm in Warsaw, unaware of the Japanese boy. But after all those years we finally meet in Rome. Two war kids, morons with adult faces and nightmares, we're rachitic and neurotic, succumb to rheumatic fever, develop myocarditis.

Ann talks too much, thinks Italo, interrupts me all the time. But I enjoy her animated art of associating and turning everything upside down. I like her black-and-white outfits, the way she outlines her lips with crimson pencil. It's December. Mornings are gray, days lack brilliance. I listen to Ann as to my own body's soundtrack, and feel as if I were in the cargo of a boat, crossing black seas, and white seas, and yellow seas, and the ultimate red sea. Her presence reshapes reminiscences, collects them like a lens, and makes me remember Lowry and our journey on board the *Ultramarine,* the old Greek steamer reposing on the bottom of the Panama Canal. When she's with me, I find it easier to grow old. She shelters me with her metaphors, some superb, some so-so. In her company I'm warm.

What you expect never happens, babbles Ann. It's the unexpected that makes you go on. Two years ago, after I had reconciled myself to masturbation and the insignificant quickies in town, I met a man at a party. He invited me for dinner, served pasta with sauce Alfredo, inspected the slight territory of my body. That evening I was menstruating and when he touched me, I said: I should be going. He accompanied me to the subway, put his arm around me, kissed my hair, and said: Let me guess what kind of shampoo you use.

His guess was right?

Yes. Two weeks later I invited him to dinner. When he finished eating, he asked me to sit on his lap. We may as well go to bed, I replied. He laughed, brushed his teeth, entered me, fell off, was asleep. Strangely moved, I listened all night to his snoring, my hand on his neck.

What kind of a man?

Ordinary. Decent. Nothing to write home about, and midway between paradise and hell.

Paradise and hell?

Come on! Don't you remember your own joke, Italo? In paradise bankers are Swiss, lovers French. In hell—the other way around. My catch was from *Suisse Romane*—and on the soft side. But I shouldn't be too hard on him. A hard prick isn't all there is.

Indeed, dearest Ann. Want a real boom? Do it yourself with a kitchen spoon. And that's the *individuum* whose offspring you miscarried? I say, I say. Well, the moon reflects herself in the black mirror of the Tiber, and Rome's arrogant beauty strikes me as out of proportion.

A good line, Italo. I'm ashamed to admit that the guy is the chief reason for my being around. I had to escape from his brownstone. But you should visit Manhattan, see the skyline unfold as the bus drives from Port Authority to New Jersey, hear the asthmatic city breathe heavily, note the feet of a black wrapped in paper—against the blurb of late capitalism, all smooth and steel. See, he devours a pizza crust he has fished out of garbage, guards the door to Chembank, scratches himself, grimaces, shouts. He cries, his eyes turned inwards. He suffers from skin disease. His forehead is slashed. He's lame. Insane. A bum. He's about to freeze to death. He's dying from thirst. He's approaching the abyss. He's there. The Jewish slaves who perished in the mines of Berenice are easier to account for than this black. I have written about China, Afghanistan. But a more experienced pen is needed to describe the waste of Manhattan—and its *danse macabre* of success. The sacred cows sipping seltzer at Castelli's.

Mailer's good at that.

A hell of a writer. Remember his American dream? A diaphragm a guy takes out of a girlfriend. But too much skill kills. What hits doesn't expose.

Expose what, Ann?

Conversations you overhear: Today I shook hands with Rauschenberg and Lichtenstein.

And with Warhol?

Don't you know he's dead? He wished to become a ring, and I tell you: I saw him glitter on Liz Taylor's forefinger when I shook her hand as well. May the sweet sweat of fame sleep with my skin tonight!

And who are you?

I'm nobody, but this is So and so. Yes, he's ancient, but he still paints, writes, dances, screws around. And the other guy?

Alzheimer? Oh, I see. And to his left: is it Ginzberg? Dead, doesn't he look dead? But his sweater is by Dior, his pants by Crazy Horse.

Were you Frankenthaler, you could come with me naked. But since you're a nobody, you either put on some decent crap or stay home. I don't give a damn about the reason you wear black pants. Your beautiful soul is shit to me. Damn it, I'm not going to be embarrassed by you at a black-tie dinner party. I want a woman that looks like a whore. Pantyhose, high heels, and so on. Were you Rauschenberg, your slacks would be smashing.

A pity Proust is dead.

Broust who? Oh, I get it. The French asshole. He's great. Mustard with your Virginia ham? No? Do I remember what? The parable of the mustard seed? The Bible? You wrote the Bible? You're writing it now? How fascinating! I can't wait to read it. Who's your publisher?

Lichtenstein?

No, I'm not Lichtenstein. Over there, with the red tie, talking to the guy in the silver skirt. No, that's not the composer. The one who did *The Beach?* His name is Einstein. And didn't Glass dance in it? Or was it Reich? Oh, I see, they're both here. Glass in his fabulous black velvet suit, Reich in his gorgeous tweed jacket.

Who's the man with the withered hand? Picasso's grandcousin? That's why he looks so familiar. The same nose, sick. See his pants? Empty. Laser surgery? Looks good to me. I see, and that's his spouse? What's her name? Herodias? Could you spell it for me? Reminds me of my girlfriend in Sweden. Henriette.

Often, upon returning from a SoHo opening, my sister opened the

Bible, to read about the mustard seed. How it grows and puts out branches. How birds rest in their shade, fly off into the world, and proclaim: The smallest has become the biggest—our new tree of life.

That's how an unsuccessful Jewish Polish Communist artist turns into a Bible scholar.

Sure. Or looks for consolation in the heartbreakingly obscure biographies of Van Gogh or Vermeer.

For PEN members it's Joyce—and the chicken stew he couldn't afford.

Or, closer to home, Svevo. To recall how genius fails in this world does help, dear Italo.

But it corrupts as well, dear Ann. Famous or not, as long as we're alive we can't sort it out. Hoping to contribute to algebra, Piero della Francesca abandoned his art. Instead of providing us with a few more pictures, Leonardo tried to fly. Nobodies, on the other hand, suspect that they are nothing—and therefore seek the company of giants. Or their recommendation, as in the story of the Viennese art student who begged a critic to visit him in his studio. Was it Gombrich?

Of course. And the student was Géza. A refugee from Budapest, extremely handsome. Carol knew him rather well. He dabbled in everything—from film to relief.

That's him. But do you recall Ernst's point?

I recall nothing at all.

So don't interrupt me anymore. One Sunday afternoon Gombrich climbed to the top of a suburban villa. Géza opened the door, led him into an untidy attic with a little something in the middle, wrapped in a rag, and removed the cloth. A lump of clay emerged. Gombrich walked twice around Géza's would-be oeuvre, plotting an inconspicuous escape. Noticing his embarrassment, the artist handed an envelope to the young critic: It's for you, read it. Gombrich obeyed. The letter praised the Hungarian sculptor's abstract work, and was signed Michelangelo.

Gombrich was so gossipy! Carol must have heard the story from him. That's why she entitled her Big Curtain *Michelangelo,* and dedicated it to *Herr Géza.*

There are so many ways to be in touch with fame.

Think of libraries, Italo, where you swim in an ocean of famous published words. This reminds me of my days in the Public Library at 42nd, swarming with exiles and self-appointed scholars, the heads of asses next to the elbows of geniuses, lips moving with solemnity, eyes raised to the half-effaced fresco on the brown ceiling. Striving for sacred knowledge, bag ladies write in mirror script, survivors study the Gnostics. Light radiates from the pages of the Nag Hammadi Library in English, as fame is retrieved through texts, and addressed:

Do not be arrogant to me when I'm cast out upon the earth, up on the dunghill. Find me before the kingdoms, open their gates for me, make ladders appear, help me climb them. Reward me for digesting unwritten documents, stored only in the software of our guardian angels, as a short man from Kielce calls the computers. Oh God, be my twin! Assist me in getting my text typeset in Siamese.

I feel shameless and ashamed at once, the shorty from Kielce whispers into my ear, when my bag is inspected at every door. Did I escape from the Warsaw ghetto to teach at the Y? I, the greatest living authority on Julian of Norwich? His lips tremble, mystical blood drips from his fingertips. Can medieval essence justify my vegetation? Unpaid bills, returned manuscripts? Can my fourth-rate existence be replaced by the first-class text I intend to create, and now sketch in contours and convolutions? I'm here from Friday afternoon to Sunday night. All the time. I hide on top of the wooden gallery, where Migne is pickled in dust. A Mauss, I acquaint myself with the meandering of Saint Dionysius, fondle a privately printed translation of Plotinus, where love and soul, angels and spheres are capitalized, and eye an older individual, who is also leafing through Migne. He responds by making a strange noise at the end of the table, and rushes to excuse himself. Waiting in expectation, I wave my hand with a never-mind gesture. But he minds, and I'm dismissed. He descends to the ground floor. But no, he hasn't given me up entirely. I feel his gaze glued to me but don't return it, keeping my own eyes fixed on the page where Plotinus is accused by Porphyry of sucking his maid's breasts at the age of eight, washing only once a month, and declining to have his bust sculpted. In Kielce. . . .

Ann, you really go from *Hundertstem ins Tausendste.* But I'm glad to learn that neo-Platonism is linked to lack of hygiene. It makes sense. If you dwell in the house of the ideal, you don't spend money on soap. If you're all soul, you don't mind the stench. By the way, I just received a letter from Malcolm announcing his arrival in Rome.

SAILING TO EGYPT ON BOARD THE SUPERSONIC MARZ68, whose ideal comfort makes him refer to the plane as Plato, Propertius enjoys the sound of the spheres and recalls Mary Magdalen, whom angels fed music through her ears, keeping her alive for thirty years. His return to Africa reminds him of the last journey with Hostia. Following an invitation of the Chinese PEN, the European delegation flew to Nanking and went by boat to Wuhan to attend the first international congress to be held after the book burnings of the Cultural Revolution.

I went with Hostia, but I never slept with her, not once. Excited, Sextus feels like urinating. But *occupato* flashes at him in big red letters. He waits for his turn, chatting with a black stewardess, and finds blood in his urine but isn't alarmed. Back in his seat he closes his eyes, and Yangtze appears under his left lid, Nanking under his right.

The sun sets, junks float by. Playing with paper sails, the wind produces an odd noise. The *Mao Tse-tung* passes under the enormous Nanking bridge, erected in pink sandstone by the Soviets, and embellished with colossal statues of workers, male and female, schematic and stern, each of them ten times the size of the average Chinese house. Arranged in couples, they represent various divisions of the proletariat, display muscles, hold hammers, hacks, and barrows, and guard the river from the crawling class enemy, their faces washed blank by utopia, their gaze fixed on the *futurum exactum* of a dawning age.

Drawing Hostia to his side, Propertius tries to face the doctrine that bore the red giants, but he's disturbed by the babbling of his colleagues. I'm smashed and overjoyed, he overhears Simone de Beauvoir exclaim, leaning on Sartre. Here *les chemins de la liberté* are cut into granite, comments Aragon, his eyes feeding on the statues. Elsewhere the sun may set, but here it keeps rising, Elsa Triolet remarks to Sartre's wife, pointing with her manicured hand to a female proletarian holding an ax, and adding: Doesn't she remind you of the Nike of Samothrace?

Yesterday I shook hands with Mao. I haven't washed them since. I wish his salt could penetrate through my pores, fuse with my blood.

That's what I feel, replies de Beauvoir. I hung on a red string the wishbone of the duck Mao shared with me in Shanghai, and I've been wearing it around my neck ever since.

Isn't this a honeymoon! Haven't we been wed to the Revolution!

Remember Ulan Bator at dusk? The powerful profile of the First Secretary? The smell of Mongolia?

The entire east is red. The forces of history dwell in us.

Humanity's avant-garde, we step onto the red bridge, participate in the long march.

Our generation's best minds are baptized in blood. We empty the cup of victory. We're betrothed to the sun.

Aren't you embarrassed, Sextus?

No, Hostia. I'm amazed. Our fellow travelers are drunk.

With power. Peripheral at home, here they sit in the imperial lap, and play with the globe, mistaking it for the earth.

Hostia's hands are cold and Sextus warms them in his own. They exchange views on Shanghai where at the promenade, running along the shore, couples, tucked into each other, behave with greater freedom than anywhere else. It's late afternoon and Hostia feels worn out and sweaty. She washes her face in a little fountain and returns to Propertius, who waits for her on a green wooden bench. As she joins him, he closes his eyes and says: Embrace me. She puts her left arm around him, unbuttons the top of his shirt with her right hand, caresses his neck, but doesn't have the guts to kiss his ear—since she perceives a policeman blowing a whistle. This is the pinnacle of their China journey, and they both realize it. To please his mistress, Propertius begins to improvise:

Oh, Hostia, my paper moon, my silk kimono, my rice screen. Don't you sense that I'm all ink, ready to impregnate you with my calligraphy, to taste your granadilla, the oblong fruit of the passionflower, a tropical dessert. Its flesh is lavish and sumptuous, lofty and sublime.

Sextus feels Hostia melting at his side and is relieved: it's good we sit on a public bench in Red China, and I can mislead her. In theory I wouldn't mind having sex with her. In practice, I couldn't. My limbs are tired, my senses don't desire the grain buried under her tongue, and my cock is so soft that if we were in bed I would have to invent a headache to get away with it. Instead of giving her pleasure, I would again get on her nerves. Here at least I can soothe her with my words.

Chinese fishermen unload blackfish and killer whales. Children surround Propertius and Hostia, showing each other the strange white couple on the green bench. Don't be afraid of kitsch, Sextus murmurs to himself, continue:

Hog suckers grow in your garden, Hostia. Ho hum. Oh, how high and hard is the roof of your mouth. How green, a meadow of a thousand flowers, how puffy is the pouch into which the ball is to be played. Do you want me to drive it in? The hard, hard ball? Is that what you want me to do? To hole up. Ho hum. To place it in, as if in a refuge? But is it really a good hiding place? Can you guarantee that the ball won't be stolen?

Hostia laughs. She does it so rarely these days. She laughs, presses Sextus's shoulder, makes him smile.

How is it? Sextus teases her. Hollow and open and deep in a body of water? And will you offer cooperation as well, form a supporting team? Faceup, and exposing every inch of the matter? Hold out for a prolonged period of time? Can you hold me? Hold out?

And what if I can't? whispers Hostia into Sextus's ear, while he listens to a hobo singing in the streets.

WITH SUPERSONIC SPEED Propertius's body is carried to Egypt, but his mind—an independent yellow river—empties itself into the estuary of the Yangtze, overflies Shanghai, its wall pierced by seven gates, and explains to Hostia that the rich alluvial plain stretching from the city's western suburbs all the way to Suchow is a garden of Eden famous for its exquisite teas and silks. There the PEN delegation visits a silk factory. In the silent incubators eggs are hatched by artificial heat. In the rearing house, a well-lighted and well-ventilated home, the larvae, crammed into a million paper apartments, munch mulberry leaves. In the extermination quarters the silkworms are hardened by steeping in strong acetic acid, have their glands separated from their bodies, and their viscous fluid drawn out. A death factory, Hostia whispers to Sextus at the exit.

It worries Propertius to observe how his mistress compares everything to the human condition. But don't succumb to futile sorrow, Sextus admonishes himself. Behaving as casual as possible, he leads Hostia gently to the bus and draws her attention to the forthcoming trip to Hangchow and the excellent weather forecast.

Wasn't it magnificent! Aren't you impressed! Aragon's bearish voice hits Sextus's back. Don't you feel like falling on your knees and chanting: the progress made by socialist China is out of this world! I have always thought of life as the vulgar, which is fed to the poor, and the sublime— devoured by the rich. But here everybody's existence achieves a monumental scale. Gorky alone knew how to put it: Mankind! Your name sounds proud.

Damn it! No day without this bastard perverting the French *esprit!* As anger attacks his brain, Propertius notices Hostia's sudden paleness, and murmurs: I have always assumed that vulgarization and sublimation are not states of the human condition but figures of speech. There's no subject we couldn't either sanctify or debase. The victor's glory is the victim's end. Losers, even if we aren't introduced to them, perish here as elsewhere.

You speak like a petit bourgeois, Sextus, and that's what you are: a villa in Rome, a dacha in Perugia, women, good food, erotic elegies, compassion with silkworms. And you, Mademoiselle Hostia, you pity them too? Aren't they pretty, the cream-colored larvae? Haven't they produced this *vraiment joli* scarf tied around your neck? It's made of what they have eaten with healthy appetites, and you must admit that unlike beggars in Calcutta, silkworms don't starve here. Oh, Madame! On the little couch of your heart the silk moth yawns, has a good time, is taken care of, and resembles your *petite charmante existence. Monsieur Properce,* why don't you feed your *chérie* with *fruit de* mulberry?

Since we consider ourselves your class enemy, we love to be insulted, Hostia answers, and Sextus's spirits rise: doesn't she have class! Besides, his mistress continues, you misquoted Gorky who wrote: Oh God! How proud *Man* sounds. So long, Mr. Aragon.

This intermezzo improves their mood. Stepping into the bus, Hostia whispers: Let's sit in front, enjoy the view, ignore our comrades, and talk seriously about the vulgar and the sublime. When Aragon mentioned it, your predecessor came to my mind. A man I expelled from it a long time ago because of his vulgarity. It surfaced whenever I was in a perfectly sublime mood. As I expected him to whisper: Honey, I treasure you, he was certain to say: Last night I had a drink with Bombatius, and asked him: Who's your squeeze these days? Popetta, Bombatius replied, and in turn inquired: And you, old fart, whom do you brush nowadays?

Each time he managed to hurt me so hard that I almost fainted, but I hid my pain. The more vulgar a man, the less a woman can play the weak female. Thus I used to counter my lover with some sort of brave question like: So what did you reply to Bombatius? hoping he'd either stop or try to repair the damage. But he never took the hint, and went on hitting me: Oh, dear, I screw Aldona and Fiffi, or: There's no shortage in part-time whores in our old Rome.

There's something to it.

Of course. But when it comes from your lover's lips, then it kills you. Do you remember Hofmannsthal's poem on episodes and agonies? We all know what amounts to just an episode for you may be an agony for me. Vulgarity can assume a deadly touch, as does the sublime when it's applied to the wrong person. I left the man after he described his crush on somebody else in sublime terms. The combination of his vulgarity—vis-à-vis me—and his sublimity in respect to another female tipped the balance. Oh, I'll never forget that mid-January morning! He told me the story of his great love at the breakfast table—after a night he refused to make love to me. Ready to break out in tears, I got my heart broken right there.

Hostia, darling, don't excite yourself. Couldn't we change the subject?

No, Sextus. I must tell you. After I had left his house, I suffered a minor heart attack. Had I not encountered you a month later, I would have surely died. But at least I learned from this—his episode and my agony—what power the words of those whom we love have over us. The picture of that last morning with him—it still floats in and out of my mind. We sit at the table, drink coffee, nibble at fruit. Suddenly he asks: Did I ever tell you about that girl from Folignano I fancied? No, I reply, alarmed.

Don't dwell on this, Hostia.

I'll make it short, Sextus. Ours was a strange relationship. In two years we strolled only twice along the Tiber. We never went together to the sea, walked together through the snow. All we did was to meet once a week, have a pizza in a trattoria or at home, drink a bottle of Beaujolais, chat, have sex. You know what a cheap date I am. The most I ever dared to ask of him was to spend an entire Saturday with me—a favor I obtained on the strength of a recent miscarriage, followed by pneumonia. A little guilty, he wanted to compensate me with a small gift. It was mid-May. We met in the morning and he said: You're so beautiful tonight.

A Freudian mistake.

And the best compliment he ever paid me.

The weather was crisp and sunny, and we walked for hours in Parco Centrale, embraced many times. He kissed my hands, even squeezed my small breasts. And when we sat on a bench near the Lago Minore, he whispered into my ear—the only whisper I ever heard from him—It's like a midsummer daydream. On that Saturday we did so many things together! We visited the Museo delle Terme, had strawberries with liquor on the revolving terrace of the Café delle Muse.

An imitation of the dining room in Nero's Domus Aurea, a new amusement then. Didn't the Muses close down last year? The man must have been a great love of your life, Hostia. A small remark by that imbecile Aragon, and he was resurrected. But how's the January morning related to the May day?

In January he narrated his first visit to Folignano. How he and his mistress went north, to the misty Lago Maggiore, strolled along the shore, made love in a hut. Like in a Petrarch sonnet, said the man I considered completely apoetical, and smiled. His smile moved me. I got up, kissed him, and tried to erase the effect of his words. But the scene at the foggy lake, which he had described with so much ardor, stood between us like a sheet of glass. Looking into it I realized that his tale was the mirror image of what I had secretly wished for myself. Then the glass broke, cutting right through me.

But you survived, my dear. We're sightseeing in China, Sextus says, remembering Goethe's words: Great passions are illnesses without hope of recovery. What might heal them, does in fact make them worse.

Hostia's hands tremble. Taking them into his hands, Propertius says: Calm down, darling, it's all over. But he knows it's a lie. The disease has rendered his mistress's mind a silkworm. Spinning and spinning, it eats itself away. She's so tense, so terribly sensitive. She's losing weight. How long will she last? Reminding himself that there are many false alarms in life, Propertius tries to silence his panic. But it speeds up his pulse.

They're heading home, and he stares into a starry night in the Persian Gulf—tight as an envelope—and asks for the hundredth time: Are you all right, sweetheart?

I'm fine, she replies, but the end is at hand. Day and night touch each other. Open the window, Sextus.

He does. When he returns to her couch, Hostia is a corpse.

In ten minutes we'll land at the Euergetes Airport in Cairo, a female voice announces, and Propertius, struggling with his belt, gathers his thoughts, scattered in all directions. Pound paces in Torcello. The sumptuously blonde Mary Magdalen visits the obscene emperor Constantine in order to hear his opinion on her empty purse. Is it really as worthless as the Holy Virgin *post partum?* How can that which was pregnant with meaning yesterday be empty tomorrow? How can sense be extinguished in a split second? Where am I? With Aragon in Shanghai? With Ezra in Rome? Why does one poet speak on the Fascist radio, the other adore Mao? Why do my colleagues make such fools of themselves? I buried Hostia in the Persian Gulf, now I'll bury Berenice in the sands of the Sahara. Is that what fate has in store for me? Must each of my lines be born out of love missed and misused? Must ink drip to the ground?

I F I MUST TAKE MY SHIP DOWN myself it's my duty to procure some knowledge. But that's not easy. That's as difficult as the English language when you begin to dabble in it and don't see yet what a devil of a current it is. No end of shoal places, too many awkward turns between the tongue and the mind. But no matter what, English is so much better than Polish. A compact piece of canvas, strong and subtle, it carries a detailed map of the world but fits into my pocket. A language to the point. But what's the point, Conrad? Why do you want to carve for yourself a niche in somebody else's home?

An adolescent, I try to puncture time, create a small spot in it, and fill it with my essence, so that the point of my humble existence isn't missed. Not missed in its physical condition and not missed as a project, the Heideggerian *Lebensplan* no one can accomplish.

At school I delighted in geometry as much as Simone Weil. No navigation without geometry. An empty page and the surface of the sea resemble each other. Pens and ships draw lines, their traces cross and meet. Sailing and writing are the work of the eye and mind, extended in time. My point is the geometric element of which it is postulated that at least two exist, and that two suffice to determine a line. A loner and dreamer, I pursue the other point, the point beyond the horizon. I, *Punctus,* I'm after *Puncta* whom I hope to join at the point of death, merge with her at the point of eternity, become a dot in the needlepoint of her texture, the embroidery of her landscape.

I wish to furnish my life with a point: to scratch out the mortar from the joints of the old Polish brick wall, fill in new material. That's why I have placed myself at the point of a ship, sailing close to the wind and training for the contest of life. But, simultaneously, I consider pointblank refusal, I play with the idea of abandoning all *points d'appui.* However, suffering from an inferiority complex and hurt ambition, I want to be pointed, and a real pointer, drawing people's attention to what interests me. A draftsman but not a pointillist.

A stranger, I study dictionaries, where *point* is followed by *poise* and *poison.* Poisoned with the worst premonitions of failure, I enrich my vocabulary. The English section of my brain, never at rest, strives for the poise of a native speaker. I sip tea, cultivate stiff upper lip, fight Slavic sentiments, and fear that in spite of my efforts, English, an oversized glove, won't fit over my right hand. I dream of losing my glove and hand in Siberian nightwoods, where my British passport either isn't recognized or becomes a source of trouble. Waiting for my stepparents to intervene in my internal exile, I explain to the least brutal Russian guard that English is an excellent language. Precise as a polecat preying on chickens, it effaces the Polish effects, a diffuse aristocratic mode of talking too much, saying too little, an unfortunate tradition that makes me miss the point.

Impersonal as an autobiography seminar, English makes me adjust my features to the narratives of a culture I only half comprehend. It's like an affair of a Pole with a Czech, when *laska* means love in one language, stick in the other. A Polish acrobat, I balance the pole on top of my nose, and hope for a reward. And I'm rewarded, but with a carrot only, and not with the *pomme de paradis* we Poles long for.

In my motherland life deteriorates as pollution, mismanagement, inflation increase each day. But I'm on my way to America where Chinese peasants are brought to work in American fields. I see them, seated on a Sunday afternoon in front of their houses, sad but satisfied with their achievements, reminiscing, holding on to their photo albums, like my Chinese mistress in London. Each time I visited her, she was dying to show me her pictures and explain them in identical words: Here, you see, that's my first husband. He doesn't look at me but I look at him. Here, that's him again, with my uncle, and mother and the dog, in the village where we used to go for summer vacation. And yes, that's me. And here—can you find me?

At the center of an exiled identity resides the photo album. Yes, that's mother, and that's me in the garden of roses, my Chinese mistress whispers, her face a mirror image of the communion with the past she experiences. Shadows solidify to bodies, enigmas regain substance, and the bleached wallpaper in her house of time is refreshed. She goes on, and I pause, watch her passage between *puncta* and *punctus,* desire to touch her hand with my fingertips. But I don't dare to disturb her trip to the sacrosanct commonplaces of her former existence. Perhaps, after the album is closed, we'll be able to converse? Perhaps there will be a moment of confidence?

No, I hope in vain. Already, the streak of a shadow disturbs her face. A faint signal she tries to suppress, but I perceive it, and know: she doesn't return my love and wishes to be left alone. She's ready to share, but to a point only. She desires to keep to herself what animates her at that instant. Don't be scared, my dear, I want to tell her. Don't fear my insistence. I'm at once too proud and too modest to claim you for myself. Where others insist, I withdraw. Right now I'm ready to dissolve in the air. To disappear for good, leaving you to yourself. But I reconsider. Not so young anymore, I'm afraid of letting you go, an unwilling sparrow scratching nervously at my palm. So I pretend to have the skin of a hippopotamus, remain silent, listen to police car sirens. Oh, don't remove your hand from mine. Don't turn me into a pariah: a Polish writer blind to the fact that he has no chance. Your Chinese fingers tremble, and I see through you: a stranger, you're sad as well. Disoriented, you doubt my affection because you don't trust yourself. How can I convince you? Our mutual silence stimulates the uncontrollable. This moment of love missed has its piquancy.

As the text proceeds, my English improves. It gets *flott,* as Goethe would say, makes the most of the little that there is: dim daydreams, the claustrophobia of chemistry. Without expanding, the text becomes refined, although no ways from means to ends are revealed. Visiting Psyche, Eros moves in circles and hides from her his essence. But little by little, she succeeds in stealing upon his heart, his middle-aged heart clogged with cholesterol, and upsetting her own heart as well. Perceiving the cardiac turbulence as the last ebbing of her fortune, Psyche begins to learn the truth of a late love: it's all about growing old, forging phantoms, fabricating lies, reheating the soufflé you can't redo. An adventure in neurophysiology rather than eroticism, it reflects how lack of energy leads to overproduction of meaning. Lowry is right: a late affair is a night-study of my favorite verbs: to fall, sink, die. An experiment in reduction and loss. As usual, Psyche has the courage to admit what Eros prefers to ignore.

It's Psyche who makes me list female ships that, at one point or another, I'm convinced, would carry me to heaven. She points out cracks on the ceiling of my bedroom, and shouts: Soon, in the full morning light, you'll see what you escape from: the ruins of Warsaw.

While Eros busies himself with business as usual, Psyche takes time, prepares to depart, links the beloved figures of the past to abstractions and colors: red to blue, blue to red, red to blood. She perseveres and transcribes what is happening, before the heart bursts. She arrests the moment, stretches seconds, fetches warm wax, presses her fingertips in it. One day she's agitated, another day she's calm. She may go as far as dusting her bookshelves, as if she had changed her mind. But she's ready to depart, and dreams of dust.

Psyche isn't subject to regret. Shrouded in sentimental moods, clothed in emulation, she enjoys the sleepless succession of images, larger contexts, fresher scenes, performances in future fame and money. As nights turn whiter and whiter, her appetite for self-destruction grows and grows.

Late love probes annihilation, flirts with nothingness, embraces death. It waltzes on blue waves to *les isles macabres des polonais.*

It's the hysteric and ecstatic in my character that make me go English, head for the sea. Conrad-Korzeniowski, a bilingual schizophrenic, I'm a Nigger and a Narcissus—fond of blackness.

Eros is absent, but Sex visits Psyche, and she knows the difference his touch makes to her breasts. Yes, she can still part her legs at a 45° angle, imagine a prick as long as the distance from her chin to her navel, experience electric effects at the edge of her clitoris, raptures of flesh, shivers of delight. Indeed, all this can be accomplished without Eros, as violet eyes of desire flush, nipples swell.

While Eros absents himself, Psyche visits brothels, throws away her civilized shell. She doesn't fear disease, and has her better self raped. She asks Sex to enter her—not to sleep at her side, snoring and wearing Eros's pajamas. Freed from excessive sublimation of youth, Psyche longs at last for a knife to cut her apart.

Yes, my dear Sex, Psyche says. It's you and me. Only the two of us. My breasts are underdeveloped, but they catch light from the shaded lamp. Please Sex, put your arm behind my head, turn your arm around my thigh. Look and remember. Nudity is speechless, and so is delight. Chestnut-colored hair, before it turns gray, will be in your mouth. My bedroom has an old mirror. It reflects Eden—the pink between my parted legs.

Alone at sea, I watch out for Psyche. Oh, how gifted she is! Endowed with a sense of the ridiculous and serious. I watch her naked in the bathroom. White foam of her salty smile seduces me, and I forget the ocean.

Believe me, dear Sex, Psyche cries, you're robust and jovial. But really, oh great love of my life, it's all very fragile. You make a mistake and lose everything. But don't you want to keep Psyche forever? If yes, go ahead, Sex. Drop your pragmatic interests. Psyche and Sex are here to screw up their lives—cheap, but thorough and tough.

Come. Come. Come. Push. Push. Push. Faster. Your tongue in my mouth. Drive, my red automobile, all the way in, long and hard. Fear nothing. Night draws a silver coverlet over us. Ambrosia falls from the sky. Faster. I want to drown in the red sea of your heart.

Whom do you squeeze full-time? Eros asks Sex. Whom do you squeeze part-time? Psyche, you know, is growing old. She isn't eighteen, next spring she'll be forty-four, and I don't really go for her anymore.

Making money these days, Sex? Yes, but not enough. That's what I really need: more money, younger women, faster cars. Psyche is younger than I, but not young. And your Animula, Cupid? Sweet, but difficult.

Dear Psyche, says Sex, stop typing. Forget about the new strategies of prose. Don't consult English dictionaries and, in particular, don't wait for my call. I won't phone anymore. Dial my answering machine. The honey of my business voice will drip into your ear. It's not ideal but better than silence. This Psyche knows and calls Sex twice.

Eros interrupts Psyche's typing. He calls from Venice, and she rejoices at the tone of his voice. Like a Chinese comforter, Eros keeps Psyche warm. Without Eros, Psyche would be as unhappy as Persephone.

The extent of Eros's affection for Psyche cannot be described. He lives in her mind. To Eros Psyche dedicates the air between words, the white between letters. Her memorial to Eros is made of silence and trust. Eros is Psyche's Siamese brother, but she can't live without Sex—who doesn't give a damn.

Eros-Narcissus, Nigger-Sex, and Psyche, the twins' mistress, we are the trinity of endless sleepless nights. Trotting around the globe, we cannot come to terms with one another, nor can we part. We undo and harm each other—it's a pretty ghastly sight. But the voyage is ours. Ours is the night. Conrad bites his pencil, doodles, scribbles, tears page after page, and around 3:00 A.M. groans: God! Punish me for plagiarizing Malcolm, make me write on my own.

O N NOVEMBER 4TH, Professor Bel Bonafiducci, Department of Psychology, Princeton University, receives a registered parcel. He isn't surprised. Two weeks ago the Science Section of the Manhattan Echo published his *Amor & Suicide in Literature & Art: An Academic Analysis of the Devil Incarnate of Eros,* an examination of mental states, leading from love to self-destruction, which ends with an appeal to support his research by supplying him with unpublished texts by unknown writers and artists who either committed suicide or played with the idea of killing themselves. Since then Bonafiducci's correspondence has tripled. More than pleased with his text, Bel cannot restrain himself from rereading his conclusion:

Not unlike every human being, an author or artist erects in front of him or herself a persona, a mask which absorbs or hides the critical states of mind he or she succumbs to. Distinguished creation results from deep psychological crisis or *furor divinus* (*Phaedrus*, 5.7.b), and is not unfrequently prompted by an author's or artist's involvement with the representative of the same or the other gender. *Furor* may lead to great achievement as well as suicide, and this can be studied best in texts by unknown authors and artists, beginners or amateurs, who cannot smooth out successfully or digest feelings aroused in them by the drama of gender.

Eros and *Thanatos*, in English love and death, are the twin brothers responsible for artistic or literary creation. But true insight into the agonies of human nature, excited by the erotic *furor*, is best gained when we consider the unpublished, unexhibited, and generally unknown but, nevertheless, available creative products which record, like a seismograph, the way the mind suffers and creates. Unlike a professional, an amateur does not control his or her brain but simply registers impulses, without ever comprehending their meaning. Such a brain, comparable to an extravirginal forest, yields higher scientific returns than the camouflaged minds of well-known authors or artists.

An Amateurish Suicidal Brain, or ASB, isn't aware of borderlines. It acknowledges neither past nor present, oscillates between the prehistory of submerged continents and the distant future on new planets. The ASB floats freely in space, unhindered by gravity and pragmatism, and represents a simultaneous entity that encompasses the entire universe and encodes humanity as a whole. There is nothing an ASB cannot relate to, since its structure is totally interconnected and, in this capacity, resembles the inter-phased quality of the postmodern age, and the avant-garde literature or art in particular. Today still an exception and pathology, the ASB reveals patterns which will rule the brains of future humans, and is thus of enormous scientific interest to us.

From the experiments conducted at the SLab, Princeton University, it can be deduced that the ASB is determined by extreme neurophysiological stress. What causes it? The new triadic syndrome of the modern age: erudition, freedom, and solitude, or EFS, which envelops the brain in the fantasy of the everywhere and nowhere. As long as this condition of the educated, emanci-pated, and solitary self remains latent, it amounts to a malaise. However, in certain acutely sensitive individuals the malaise develops into an illness which, after its main symptom, *omni*present *det*achment, has been termed OPDT.

As of now, OPDT seems to affect only ASBs. But I expect it to spread with the speed of AIDS and become a major epidemic in the mid-twenty-first century. For this reason OPDT has to be studied without delay. Creative products of ASBs have to be analyzed and evaluated to prevent disaster. Let me end my article with an urgent appeal. Anyone possessing a literary or artistic creation by an ASB is kindly requested to contact Bel Bonafiducci, Ph.D. Princeton University.

Rereading his text, a brief summary of his third book to be published next month by South North Carolina University Press, Bel discovers formulations which strike him as particularly felicitous. For instance eros and thanatos in italics prove that he's at ease with antiquity, and add to his scientific quality the charm of a humanist. Happy with himself, Bel murmurs: This should get me tenure, turns his attention to the shabby manila envelope addressed in red, pulls out a pale printout, and begins to read:

It's October 15, and ninety-two-year-old Martha Graham is carried onstage by her dancers, their bodies perspiring. Persephone presents her belly against a blue silk background. Judith kills Holofernes with a wooden sword designed by Noguchi. Tons of thrill swirl in the forest of long legs and necks. But, at the end, a simple pas de deux makes me submit to fate. When the ballet is over, I hurry uptown on Broadway. The city is noisy. Near Lincoln Center I slow down, listen to a street cellist playing Minute Valse, catch a glimpse of Combat in the window of LOVE DRUGS, recall our last supper together—and the cockroach you crushed flat above your dining table. Combat, a chain of elegant black motels—you check in but don't check out—is a capital investment. No cock to creep into your bed, no roach to rub your back for the rest of your day. Reduced to $2.99, Combat is on sale, and that's why I can't resist buying it for you, my dear. The last economy of my life, it highlights my style. Too poor to throw away a cent, I'm rich enough to throw away myself.

My black backpack is packed and tied to my chest with red rope. My text, wrapped in cotton and plastic, sits in the main bag. Left and right two bricks keep an eye on every letter. From where I live the Hudson can be reached in five minutes. I see them—whom exactly?—fish out my corpse, untie the backpack. Now a man's unknown face emerges from somewhere. He unwraps my paper and begins to turn the pages.

Strong stuff, Bel murmurs to himself, and what I need. He takes an Earl Grey tin from the top shelf of the kitchen cupboard, opens it, smells the tea. It storms, and large hailstones mixed with snow hit the pretty box he built last week for his new air conditioner. Just on time, and against her advice. His Roman wife, she expected winter to be late this year, and wouldn't even consider looking at the black squirrels, their tails so bushy since September. Of course, it's early. Every beast knew it, with the exception of Silvana, God help her. Bel cuts a thin slice of health bread, tasteless but the only brand with no saturated fats, according to her wisdom, spreads a soupspoonful of honey—*strengstens verboten*—over it, and licks his fingers. Luckily, Silvana doesn't discover his crime, and he can sail away on the supreme tide of sweetness to Italy where Goethe greets him with the words: *You're a Winnie the Pooh, Bel.*

Yes, I'm a Trinity type of bear, not too bright but very English, Bel admits. Alas, this truth has to be concealed from my wife: for her I'm into suicide, a Princeton prof, up for tenure. Have providence guide me, Goethe, against her deadly current. A potential ASB, Silvana has OPDT, and may infect me. Perhaps I'm sick already, even though nothing is stranger to me than suicide. The rubbish I have to study drives me nuts. Who's Martha Graham? What has ballet to do with cockroach traps? Who would ever conceive of a more ludicrous death? A backpack. Two bricks. A river. What dreadful taste. But, on the other hand, my dear wife could come up with something like that. First buy Combat for me, then kill herself.

Be cautious, Bel Bonafiducci admonishes himself. It's more than suspect, a trick Silvana plays on you. Doesn't she run around with a backpack, like a bloody sophomore? Isn't her birthday on October 4? Isn't Combat a clear hint? Isn't she setting a trap for me? Didn't Pooh and Piglet prepare one for Heffalump, and fall into it themselves? What-shall-I-do-about-you-know-what? Bel panics. But he is calmed by the growing whiteness of the garden. It snows, and he muses about what Pooh likes doing best in the world: a walk with Piglet. A little something with Lotte in Sextus's cherry orchard. A hummy sort of day outside, and birds singing.

Oh goodness me! How can a friendly animal specialize in suicide? How can a Pooh be married to an ASB? If I don't get tenure, she'll commit suicide, or murder me, or do both. It's not the text that is a trap. I have been trapped already, and robbed—of our au pair. So sweet. Blonde and pink, a true Piglet. When I told her that she reminded me of that old roommate of mine, she laughed, and said: *Monsieur, collez-moi Piglette.*

Oh Piglet! You were so gay, and such a smart Small. My only consolation in this net of invisible intrigues. We biked together along the canal, and twice I invited you to the Pancake House off Nassau for Pineapple Jumbo with a double portion of maple syrup.

Carissimo! Are you working on the text you received today? Silvana's superloud voice interrupts Bel's reverie. I do! I do! He shouts back, and rushing out of the kitchen returns to his desk. Damn it! No honey. No peace. Study suicide and shut up. The slimness of the printout encourages him to take it up again. He skips a few pages, and begins to read at the bottom of 15:

Who's the suicidal author? A female. How old? In her early forties. Alone? Semi-alone. Into sex? She masturbates. Her life? A cozy cocoon of broken glass. Her temperament? That of a punk silkworm, or a female Petrarch. Her mind? Focused on art which brings her neither success nor money, and on an impotent man who doesn't care for her. Her origins? Obscured by the part of the world she has exiled herself from: *Osteuropa*, a backwater that cannot be bettered, an outpost prone to the unbearable banality of the bad-or-bad. Gas ovens-or-potato shortage. Pole-or-Jew. Leave it-or-die for it.

Si, Bel murmurs to himself. Haven't I become a Pooh because of how cold and miserable it would be being lost all life in the Pole-or-Jew sort of thing?

Thin, blue-eyed, bursting with nervous energy, she likes men more than is good for her. Their slightest interest inflames her imagination, carrying her straight into the arms of eros-thanatos.

Bel sighs, and skips a page:

An artist-author, I have confined myself to the maze garden of the English-American language hoping that the vastness of my experience will render insignificant my vocabulary's limitations. May the tolerance of a multilingual empire be extended to me. My name starts with a C, but I am no Conrad. He was shipwrecked in the Shak Sea at nineteen. I was shipped to the West Side at thirty-six. A middle-aged Mistress Anima, confused in the morning, lucid after five o'clock, I entertain my guests with slide shows on China or Afghanistan, the gold mines of Berenice or the bridges of Prague. Proust, Propertius, and Karenina go in and out of my door, even though I am a Freudian joke and a compulsive liar. Alive with anecdotes, I talk like an Australian parrot, hop like a kangaroo, quote Plato in Hebrew and Czech, and attract weasels and elephants who take my fakes for fairy tales. A sex maniac, I choose the most unsuitable objects of desire: photographers without talent or money, revisionists converting from socialism to science fiction, decorators of mosques and synagogues who waltz, professors of metaphysics who are ladies' men. A stand-up comedian, I am all soul—and a pain in the ass.

Tutto al posto? Silvana's voice echoes through the house. OK, OK, I'm working, Bel shouts back.

So much for my psyche. Now bear with me, the suicidal blind amor. I'm four, watch my brother arrive and occupy my room, retire to the kitchen, squat under the table. Born with a deformed head, and allergic to animal protein, he cries day and night, and I'm mortified with melancholia. A dense chain of shapeless instants, my childhood passes slowly as a life sentence. A toddler has no business, no friends call on her, nothing illuminates the void.

My only joy is the Sundays I spend with Dad, a silent listener whom I nickname Ear. We stroll through the zoo or botanical garden, hand in hand, and savor the sight of the nonhuman world.

At five, I discover sex. It's summertime, and in a small resort a band of kids runs around, and giggles: a Negro, hee-hee-hee, scratches his ass, hee-hee-hee, a bimbo, hee-hee-hee, licks off his nails the sweet chocolate. We're looking for turkey eggs, want to come? Intrigued, I follow them into the brush. They take off their panties, and so do I. It feels fine, and soon I figure out more ways to pleasure. It's hot, and I'm still a babe. So I sit cross-legged in front of men—with no panties.

My infancy lacks entirely innocence and beauty. But from bad it goes to worse. The kindergarten slavery is replaced by the drill of a Stalinist school. At seven sudden seizures of sadness solidify into a depression. Tired of life, I wish to lie down, and be left alone. One morning, while I play piano, a strong pain attacks my left breast and throws me to the floor. When consciousness and speech are regained, I ask: Can I stay in bed? Yes. I thank God. In one instant atheism is swept away by faith.

Yes, Bel whispers, I also prayed, my prick in my fist, when I couldn't sleep because of my back. The bundle, thrown out of the train, had a little injury, but kept it to himself. Yes, there's something to suicide. The film is replayed, and finally we face the past without terror. The storm has stopped and large snowflakes fall solemnly. But within Bel a tension begins to rise. His heart goes bing-bang, bang-bung. Tea comes to his mind, but he dreads an encounter with Silvana. Changing to the couch, he skips the rest of her childhood, and starts reading on page 39:

Tea is a good drink. It wakes up ghosts, elucidates memories, makes me peregrinate across this opaque continent women label Man. Is it a homogenous land? My own experience excludes that. The males I had share little in common. Invited together, would they be able to converse? I wouldn't mind assembling them at a party in paradise where caviar, cognac, and cigars would loosen their tongues. Fluttering around as an angelic butterfly, I would over-hear their comments on my body and soul. I suppose Europeans would spare me less than Americans, and all would gossip about my too soft thighs, minute breasts. Even in heaven we like best to discuss the deficiencies of others, the splendors of ourselves. Life isn't about paying compliments to those who aren't present. And after life? It's about the same.

Bel smiles. He has become reconciled to the suicidal author, and wouldn't mind resurrecting her. I must find out the exact story of this text, he murmurs. Maybe it's just fiction. She never jumped into the Hudson. It would be nice to meet her in New York. Have supper with her. We are from the same part of the world, and could be friends. There may be a sympathetically porcine edge to her. The end may be a happy one yet. Bel gets up, the last page in his hand, and leaning against the window frame reads the end:

I'm still alive but Tempus runs out of my blue house of time. But without you, dear, I can't survive. I beg you, wait. Don't desert me yet. Look at all the drawings in red I did for you. Oh darling, stop running out. Don't shout *Tempus fugit.* Great love of my life, how can you desert me? Are you not ashamed of yourself? I'm not that old. I'm still attractive. Why are you so feverish? Why do you burn day and night? Come here, sit down. Let's talk. Let's go to Hawaii. Oh, Tempus! If you only knew how I love each atom of your *Sein.* I outline the imprints of your feet with my fingertips, the contour of your ear with the tip of my tongue. I trace the impression of your lips on crumbling walls, on my heart's membrane. I'm like Peter—when an unknown man passes him, he asks *Quo vadis?* But the moment the question is out, he sees how the man's soles imprint themselves on stone, and knows: master has appeared to teach me about memory. No faith without remembrance. When you forget, you betray.

But, my ex-erotic friend, Tempus exclaims, the contrary is true as well. You have to forget! Men are right to obliterate what women retain. Too many tokens in the mine of your mind are in your way. *Tempus fugit!* Throw away old memories, run. Or I'll overtake you on the *via crucis,* kiss you good-bye. Eros and evil in one, I'm all life. A Judas, I move, I touch. Don't accompany me to Golgotha, Veronica. Don't electrocute your brain. Suicide isn't a final solution, it's a blind date.

Wait! If you stray, Saturn, I'll go down the drain.

IT'S MID-NOVEMBER, and the smell of decaying leaves permeates the air. Berenice's breasts have been removed, Propertius is with her. He has left his Roman villa to Italo who shares it now with Ann Kar, Goethe, and Charlotte. A social cat, Goethe has designated Tuesday as the *jour fixe.* Between 8:30 P.M. and midnight Sextus's studio serves as the salon de Madame Verdurin, with Wolfgang playing her.

What's on the agenda *ce soir?* asks Svevo.

You, my *senilus,* have you forgotten? Goethe replies. You on Petrarch. It's ages since you promised our ladies to scrutinize the genius of Madonna Laura.

How unfortunate, I'm completely unprepared.

So you'll improvise.

Are many people coming?

Lowry may drop in, if he isn't too drunk, and I expected Conrad to be back from Stromboli. But he cabled that bad weather prevented him from boarding *Aeolo*. The island has no natural harbor. It's so stupid to visit it at that time of the year. I presume that's why Ernestine pretended to be sick.

Sure. Otherwise Malcolm would have joined Joseph, and either slipped into the volcano or drowned near Strombolicchio, the rock of drunkards, where Ulysses wined with sirens.

Does Mandelshtam plan to make an appearance?

You never know with him. When I phoned him ten minutes ago, he said: Let's leave it open. *Tout le monde* is talking about his imminent elopement with Olga.

Osia is begging everybody not to tell Nadia about the poems he's dedicating to his new girlfriend.

But, *vorsichtshalber,* he's writing verse to Nadia as well.

Let's not stand judgment over poor Osia. Duplicity is the nature of such affairs. Who can deal with them decently? But I'm certain he'll come back to Nadia.

No doubt. Olga isn't his type. *La salsiccia non è per il signor gatto, la morta-della non è per il signor uccello. E la nostra carina Olga non è per il signor Mandello.*

Did you invite Kowalski?

Of course. He has been offered an assistant professorship at Princeton and is about to desert us.

Tenure track?

Apparently. But meanwhile he's a *Jammerkater*. For two hours he meowed about passports, visas, work permits, and all the rest. How capitalism suffers from a lack of identity, communism from a lack of identity cards. Bored to death, I was close to pooh-poohing him a bit. But he's too *lieb*. So I advised him to marry a reliable Roman girl. This would entitle him to a proper document, since what he has is not a *Pass* but a Polish swindle. It expires, I quote him, the very minute a Hebrew crosses the border of his official non-fatherland. But, among us, Italo, there's a woman who could solve his problem.

Silvana Bonafiducci?

I agree, she's a hysteric. But, on the other hand, he's such a Winnie the Pooh, so they may match. She'll replace the urban *Mutti* who flung the baby out of the train and into the charming birch forest near Treblinka, and the childless peasant *Mama* whose mushroom-hunting resulted in finding a fair infant.

Is that the story?

Se non è vero, è ben trovato, but I believe it. Henryk acquainted me with some of his *Rassegenossen* who as kids missed our good German gas oven by an inch. All of them struck me as somewhat strange. One resembled Piglet, another Tigger, and a woman physicist with a tot introduced herself as Mother Kanga with Baby Roo. Perplexed, I mentioned them to Moses, but he kept his lips sealed, as he so often does, and upset me even more. On my way back from his shack I strolled on the beach and, lost in thought, stepped on a crab. Hearing its shell crack I shuddered, and it dawned on me: were you in their skin, wouldn't you want to slip out of it? Abandon mankind, head for the animal paradise at the river Cam, grow fur and feathers, go for animal talk, have five-o'clock cream tea with Eeeyore?

Translate *Winnie the Pooh* into Polish? Of course. And do you know, Wolf? The bear has a place named after him in the middle of Warsaw— and Henryk a photo at that street's corner. He wears a sailor suit, holds a hula hoop, and poses under a sandstone plaque with Pooh and Piglet— in relief.

But coming back to Henryk and the little Bonafiducci. She's rich, and her dad's connections are worth more than money can buy.

Isn't she too cold for him?

She'll cheer up. During the honeymoon he'll force-feed her with his sweetness, pretend to be a bear with very little brain who has to be managed, and melt the ice. Weak women love to protect strong men.

A manic-depressive, isn't she treated with lithium? Didn't she try to commit suicide last December?

Are you certain, Italo? Well, in that case, I won't encourage the marriage. Henryk's such a dear, who wants to ruin his life! But tonight we must bear with Silvana. It's too late to disinvite her.

MY DEAREST PUSSYCATS, Goethe says. Welcome to the humble abode of a major Roman poet who for the duration of his visit to Egypt has kindly permitted us to use his place for small public gatherings. How is Berenice? I hear her breasts have been removed. She feels better, although radiation and chemotherapy undermine her immunity. Her hair is falling out. No. No, she hasn't lost all her locks, but there are problems. With skin and nails as well. And teeth, I guess.

I see a few old friends arrive. They don't need an introduction. And some precious guests are with us tonight. Henryk dear, don't hide in the corner! Stand up. The handsome young man is Dr. Kowalski, or shall I say Professor K., a brilliant Polish scientist on his way to Princeton, where he has been offered a chair. I beg your pardon, Henryk, in what? Psychology. Well, my dear, may I ask you to refrain from reading my brain? And, perhaps, from tracing the difficulties senility causes me in switching from the left to the right hemisphere. To my right I have the pleasure of seeing Signorina Bonafiducci, a doctoral candidate at the University of Rome. What department are you in, Silvana? You're a neurophysiologist. Congratulations. And what's the subject of your dissertation? Chemical changes in suicidal brains. That's fascinating, my dear girl. But you shouldn't get too much absorbed with death. After all, it's life we're into. Or not? And who's coming here! Nadia, darling! How wonderful you could make it this time.

Our topic tonight is a ladies' man—Petrarch. And Svevo, our senile Renaissance genius who, as usual, forgot about his assignment, will improvise on the subject. Come out, Italo, you're going to overcome your adolescent shyness and sit in front, and not in the last row where nobody can see you. Don't argue with me, Italo, you're not great enough to be so modest.

Ladies and gentlemen. As most of you recall, the most famous event of Petrarch's life happened on April 6, 1327. That day he saw Laura for the first time in the church of Santa Clara at Avignon. Who Laura is remains uncertain still. Our sweet de Sade claims that she is the daughter of Audibert de Noves, and the wife of Hugh de Sade. However, this claim rests on obscure tradition, on documents which the most unreliable Marquis professes to have copied from originals no one has ever seen. There are very good reasons for suspecting that he fabricated a romance flattering to his own person, or was duped by some previous imposter. Nothing is now extant to prove that if this lady really existed, she was the Laura of the *Canzoniere*. Skeptics, including my friend Henryk, seated in the darkest corner of this room, treat Laura as a mere figment of Petrarch's flowery fantasy. If we join you, Henio, we're done with her. However, my intuition tells me that it would be wrong to subscribe to Dr. Kowalski's pessimistic theory. As a poet of a rather conservative Italo-Swabian breed, I'm inclined to believe in Laura's reality and picture her as a married woman with whom Petrarch enjoyed a respectful relationship.

What do you mean by respectful? asks Charlotte. There was nothing between them? They just talked, as we do here all the time?

I assume that's all it amounted to.

Strange.

It's not strange, *liebe Lotte,* Goethe intervenes. *So ist das Leben.* Let Italo continue.

After April 6 Petrarch's inner life is given over to his passion for Laura. Historians of literature maintain that this infatuation must be seen as the chief cause of Petrarch's solitary life. I don't share this opinion but the fact remains that in 1337 he established himself at this godforsaken hole Vaucluse.

I wouldn't call it a hole, Goethe explodes. It's an extraordinarily beautiful spot which Charlotte and I visited last week. I could settle there immediately, and live finally in communion with nature in her loneliest and wildest moods, if only Lotte would agree to that. Oh, I know, my child, you never will. But still, it's the choice of Vaucluse that distinguishes Petrarch in so remarkable a degree from the common herd of medieval scholars. That's all I wanted to add, Italo.

In Vaucluse Petrarch spends his time mostly among books, meditating on Roman history, and preparing himself for the Latin epic *Africa,* which isn't my cup of tea. In his hours of recreation he climbs the hills or traces the Sorgues from its fountain under the limestone cliffs. He never leaves home without a pencil, so at least the legend goes, and most of his odes and sonnets to Madonna Laura are committed to paper during his excursions.

May I ask you a question?

Go ahead, Charlotte.

Is Petrarch all by himself? No woman in his life?

It's a very good question, Charlotte, although nobody wants to tackle it. But the fact is that in 1337, at the pinnacle of his passion for Laura, Petrarch becomes the father of a son.

Giovanni?

You're right, Wolfgang.

Five years later a daughter is born, probably by the same woman. Francesca?

Yes, that's her name. Petrarch uses his connections to the Holy See and has both children legitimized by papal bulls.

I saw the bulls at the Marciana, Goethe exclaims. But the name of the mother isn't mentioned in them.

It's not mentioned anywhere, Wolfgang. A case of perfect obliteration. Children in, mother out.

Had this been the age of photography, Petrarch would have doctored all photos as well.

I imagine so, Henryk. The woman was no Trotsky but you can't find her name anywhere.

Not even in letters? Diaries? Scribbles at notebooks' edges?

No, Charlotte, I'm sorry to disappoint you. Nothing has been preserved. Inner censorship works miracles, and you must take into account the fame and power of this man. A declared genius, he could promote you to the top of Olympus, or crush you like a worm. The whole of Europe was excited about his love for Laura. You had to be a hero to come up with another woman's name.

And so she remained nameless? All the way through history?

It's unfortunate, Charlotte, but that's what happened.

But he had two children with her, I don't comprehend.

But that's how men are, Lotte. Career first, children second, wives and mistresses last. Laura was the moving spirit of the poet's worldly success, the mother of his children a stone around his neck. If there is any deep passion in this pig of a man, it's the desire for laurels, not Laura. Brainless critics compare Petrarch to Propertius. But the two have nothing in common. An opportunist, Petrarch has built his career on Platonic adoration. Only his reverie was allowed to flow onto paper. The women he impregnated had to remain a blank. It's a mistake to call him an erotic poet. His verses have no sex appeal. To get the thrill, regret, and sorrow real love inflicts on us, we have to read our Sextus-Sexus.

Bravo, Svevo. Bravo!

Don't get so emotional, Lotte. So *gefühlsbetont.* I strongly disagree with what you say, Svevo.

You do, Wolf?

I do, my young old man. Petrarch suppressed the existence of women in order not to contradict the image the world had of him. But his poems do have an erotic quality. Naturally, they reflect every single affair he had. Every single embrace. What difference does it make if we know his women's names or not? They have been all subsumed under a single metaphor: Laura.

For me, Goethe, this single metaphor is *poeta laureatus.* One who cares only about fame. Accordingly, fortune prefers Petrarch to others. When the first drafts of *Africa,* that tasteless *Schinken,* began to circulate in 1339, it became manifest that no one had a better chance to obtain the laurel crown than Petrarch. But let's quarrel later.

In Petrarch's life two threads intertwine. The surface is embroidered with the finest sacred *amor,* the gossip of all courts and brothels of Europe. But underneath a spider web of intrigues spreads out. At the age when others go through a midlife crisis, Petrarch begins to exert his influence in several quarters to obtain the honors of a public coronation. He succeeds in his machinations and on a single day, September 1, 1340, receives two invitations, one from the University in Paris, the other from the king of Naples.

I presume he chooses the king?

Petrarch's psyche isn't alien to you, Wolfgang. Yes, that's what he does. He departs for Naples, is entertained by the king as if he were the emperor of China, and sent with magnificent credentials to Rome. There he receives the poet's crown upon the Capitol from the hand of a Roman senator amid the plaudits of the people and the patricians. I'm certain Wolf remembers the oration Petrarch delivered on this occasion. No, you don't?

But I do, throws in Virgil, It's composed upon these words of mine: *Sed me Parnassi deserta per ardua dulcis, raptat amor.*

The old hypocrite! Lotte erupts. No oration without *amor.* Amor— Laura. Laura—Amor, that's the trick he plays, and the whole world falls on its knees. *Raptat amor.* Really, he has no shame.

Petrarch is great! Goethe's bass resounds in the room. This day on the Capitol the ancient era meets modern times. His coronation initiates a new stadium for the spirit. From that point on the Renaissance is in, the Middle Ages are out.

I appreciate your enthusiasm, Wolf, but to this I want to add that the coronation opens a fresh chapter in Petrarch's biography as well. Henceforth he is ranked as an international celebrity, the guest of princes, the ambassador to royal courts.

Oh, I adore the poet-ambassadors. In Poland we had a couple of them, Przyboś, Miłosz, Kowalski whispers to Lotte. Catching the names, Goethe mumbles to himself: Miłosz was only a cultural attaché.

As Petrarch's fame grows, so does his vanity. In addition to his house in Vaucluse he acquires a pallazino in Parma. So now he has two headquarters and refers to them, with his usual modesty, as my Transalpine and Cisalpine Parnassus.

Isn't that the period he gets involved in politics?

Yes, Henryk, now I enter your territory. The wedding of *homo poeticus* to *homo politicus.* It's a pity Mandelshtam isn't with us tonight. Anyhow, when Cola di Rienzi's revolution breaks out, Petrarch behaves like a Mayakovsky. He rushes to Rome, hails the leader, and throws himself into the dream of reviving the republic, without considering the absurdity of it all. He calls the medieval mob *populus romanus,* and sacrifices his old friends of the Colonna family to what he judges a patriotic duty.

Faithfulness has never been Petrarch's strong suit, Lotte sighs.

You're really too hard on him, Italo, Goethe erupts. You run down an enthusiast, a born visionary.

All right, Wolf. I'm coming to the end. In the autumn of 1347, around mid-November, Petrarch begins to build a new house in Parma. There he hopes to pursue the avocations of a poet honored by men of the world and by the men of letters. However, this agreeable prospect is over-clouded by a series of calamities. On April 6, 1348, at the twenty-first anniversary of their first meeting, Laura dies of the plague and Petrarch ponders a plan of quitting the world and establishing a kind of humanist convent, where he could spend his last years in the company of kindred spirits. Nothing comes of this scheme. But his writings change percep-tibly. There is a certain gravity in the poems Petrarch writes in *In Morte di Madonna Laura* and I must admit—reading the late verse, I'm ready to forgive him all the minor and major sins. Unfortunately, his arrogance doesn't decrease and he begins to behave like a real bastard. At the occa-sion of Charles IV's passage through Mantua, he offends everybody at court, declares Charles unfit for any enterprise, and declines attending him on the trip to Rome. When Charles returns to Germany, after assuming the crowns in Rome and Milan, Petrarch addresses a letter of vehement invective and reproach to the emperor. But by that time his fame is such that this doesn't prevent the Visconti from sending him on a mission to Charles. In 1356 he finds himself in Prague, is charmed by the city and dispatched with honor and the diploma of Count Palatine.

As the years elapse, Petrarch turns increasingly restless. He moves about all the time. He abandons Parma and settles in Padua. Troubled by thoughts about immortality, he makes a donation of his enormous library to the republic of St. Mark.

Why does he give his books to Venice?

In that Boccaccio plays a role. They are quite close for a while. Petrarch wants to learn Greek and Boccaccio introduces him to a Greek teacher.

For God's sake, Greek at that age?

He is like you, Wolf. Eager to acquire new knowledge. Either how to paint watercolors, or how to read Plato.

By the way, Italo. Didn't Petrarch possess some remarkable manuscripts of Homer?

Correct. But his Greek was too basic to understand them. So he used to complain: Homer is dumb to me, I'm deaf to Homer. Before his death, Petrarch sees his daughter Francesca happily married.

Does her mother attend the wedding?

What mother, Lotte? Oh, the anonymous female by whom he had her. No, of course not. She does not exist for the public eye.

Oh, Lotte. *Kapier's endlich!* When we say Petrarca, it echoes Laura.

H OW LONG IS SEXTUS GOING TO BE AWAY?

Why do you ask, Wolfi?

I wouldn't mind turning our volatile literary sessions into something more permanent.

An institution?

Why not, Italo? Don't we have enough first-class names to come up with impressive stationery? Svevo, Mandelshtam, Virgil, Lowry, Conrad, Goethe. Since it's Sextus's house, we could add Propertius to our list.

What about women?

Karenina phoned me from Urbino. She isn't my glass of *Sekt.* No discipline, lack of form. A typically female writer. Don't protest, Svevo. *De gustibus non disputandum.* You hate Petrarch, I'm allergic to Anna. But that's not the point. Her texts make sense. There is even something to the nonsense she writes about me and Lotte, though I pray to God to direct her to a less delicate topic. Maybe when we elect her a member of our Institute, she'll finally leave the two of us in peace.

Our institute?

Yes. Why don't we call it the Institute for International Vanity?

Von mir aus. But back to women. In the age of affirmative action one isn't enough, and I happen to like the co-ed aura. Don't you?

I could do without it. But who wants to be called names? *Male chauvinist pig. Sexist. Macho.* Lately—under the pretext of enriching my vocabulary, would you believe it?—Lotte presented me with a feminist dictionary. What a pest! So who else? Weil?

Simone's so difficult!

She doesn't have to be with us all the time. And this *ami* of hers, Proust, isn't he from Paris too?

Yes, but he isn't a woman.

Oh, you're really giving me a hard time, Italo. Well, there is this girlfriend of yours from New York. What's her name?

Ann Kar. But you have stubbornly refused to recommend her to Virgil.

I'm so busy. But if she's OK, she can be a member. I rely on your taste. And Berenice? I hear she has taken to literature as well, or rather, to a flow of free associations. But that's secondary. She's a queen and an immortal, and we'll make Sextus happy. It's a pity Hostia is dead. She would make a good Vanity Fellow. But we have Nadia, she is such a dear. It may cement their marriage, when she joins us together with Osia.

And what about Charlotte?

She isn't an author.

But the whole world knows her letters to you, and they aren't bad. Anyhow, you can't exclude her, Wolfi. If you do, she'll eat herself to death. Why not make her the secretary?

This may offend her. She may insist on being just an ordinary member.

Leave it to me. It's still the best solution.

Make her an éminence grise?

She'll be in charge of us as long as she's alive, and I expect her to be around for quite a while.

Well, shouldn't we then have Junior Fellows? To be dismissed the moment they get on our nerves?

It's called rotation, Wolfi. There has to be a selection process, a committee. One must review submitted applications, and so on.

Oh the bureaucracy! No, Italo, it will spoil the good time we're supposed to have, and our health which crumbles already.

So why go public? Why not keep everything the way it is?

No, the Institute is here. Next year we'll start with proper procedures. For now I'll just propose Kowalski and the Silvana girl to be our Junior Fellows. And to bring guests, young, bright. They may delay our going under in a sea of senility.

WHILE GOETHE AND SVEVO PROCEED with the foundation of the Institute, Osip, Nadia, and Olga eat dinner in a small *pizzicheria* at the corner of the Via dei Polacchi. They empty their second bottle of vodka and approach the dessert, a homemade pumpkin paste served *à la Cracovia,* with whipped cream and *Blood of Christ,* a drop of beetroot brandy. They gossip, discuss the Polish pope, and try to ignore the rising temperature of their triangular setting. While Nadia and Olga electrify each other in turns, Osip is stuck in the middle of a magnetic field whose tendency is determined, perhaps, by his mistress's spotless skin.

Lately, muses Osip, I have been able to inspect some of Ola's lovely complexion. But the examination isn't completed. Will it ever be? Charming she is, but her hands look only half human. On the other hand, Nadia's front is an ironing board. I enjoy Ola's pneumatic feel— she does have a lot of sex appeal—but can't bring myself to forget about her paws. Could they be repaired by cosmetic surgery? She also is so unpredictable, opaque. Not easy to manipulate. Not likely to listen to my poems with Nadia's intense glow. Does each love have a beginning and an end? Shall I leave my dedicated wife for this mischievous girl? I have always imagined my passion for Nadia wouldn't last. But is it really so? Ours has been such a precarious marriage. She has taken my eccentricities with remarkable patience. Has life really forked down like summer lightning? Am I obliged to move out of our comfortable flat to Olga's suburban attic? Have I not written to Nadia: Gentle hands of Europa, hold me forever?

Is Osia going to leave me or stay? Nadia reflects fixing her eyes on Ola's fingers. Short and deformed by arthritis, they are extended by artificial nails—in blue and red. Why has this girl to be so extravagant? To attract men? Obviously, Osia is taken with her. Who would blame him? She's young, has a splendid figure. Why did he choose me in the first place? My only trumps are my hands. Shall I stand in his way or pack my suitcase? What glues me to Mandelshtam, anyway? It may be destiny rather than affection. If he's in love with her, I should let him go. But why did he write in his last poem: Life has forked down like summer lightning, and an eyelash fell into a teacup? Clearly, love is the lightning, Ola the cup, he the eyelash. So they must have slept with each other. Now he's rhyming for her, while we exchange vacant glances. Love is a play of blind chance. We have been together for seven years. Now we're about to part. Had I a revolver, would I put a bullet through my head? No, neither would Osia. But Ola, with her paws and peacock nails? An actress, turning her inside out all the time—she might. What does it mean: an eyelash foul to the root? Is he not being sincere? Just flirting with Ola?

WOLFGANG ASKED ME to offer you a membership at our place. Will you accept? Svevo asks Ann Kar.

The International Vanity fair? Sure. Where's the woman who would say no to Goethe & Co.—a male Olympus and Parnassus in one? Sure, I feel flattered to death. But let's talk about something else. A photo I want to show to you, Italo, of two men and a seven-year-old girl. They were shot in front of the Warsaw Palace of Culture, a Soviet-style monster, on a sunny but crisp spring morning.

A strange picture, Ann. The hair of all three of them flies in the same direction, creating an art-nouveau wave.

An excellent photographer took it on the first Sunday in May, during a book fair organized on the large square around the palace.

A personal gift of Stalin, if I remember well.

Yes. While it rose amidst the ruins, the capital joked about his largesse: when your best friend presents your spouse with a rose bouquet you appreciate his attention. But when he arrives with a diamond ring—God help me. Yes, the man to the left is my dad. I could have gone with him to the book fair, but I preferred not to. At nineteen, I enacted Bartleby. So I remained at home—a book in my lap. But I was too tense to read. Instead, I produced rabbit shadows on the soft pink curtain, shrunk and bleached by then but still my favorite object in the entire flat. We moved into it in '47, when heaps of bricks and carbonized trees surrounded the building. But soon grass and wild chamomile began to overgrow the mess, and I developed a passion for excavation. I amassed a big collection of bits and pieces—porcelain and glass, door handles, spoons, and a silver knife, just one. Are there more spoons than knives in the world? Yes, perhaps. They can more easily slip away. Soon I turned from an archeologist into a thief, and my skills were applied to my parents' pockets, bags, and drawers. A natural transition, don't you think, Italo? I stored the banknotes and coins in the corner of my room, behind a white pre-war cupboard. Then the currency was changed—and my fortune gone. No, I was never caught. My parents were too busy. Dad was rebuilding the outer world, Mom was setting herself on fire. So I grew into a scavenger. Yes, I stopped stealing, but ever since I have been into garbage—and finding things. In Manhattan I furnished my flat with junk. In Central Park watches and gold chains, lost in the grass, caught my eye. I pick up every cent. Why? I'm too afraid to pass it up, to forget who I am.

That's how you write too, Ann. You appropriate other authors' texts, recover characters from the bric-a-brac of literature. Your mind is a regular archeological site.

Don't forget, I was born right after the flood. At the epicenter of an earthquake. Inspecting the torn Japanese rice-paper shades in my bedroom, a lover asked me once: Where do they come from? From the street, I replied, and he laughed: You have surrounded yourself with found objects. Am I one of them? No, I replied. You have been with me from the beginning of time. I just unearthed you.

Yes, you find, save, assimilate. Mix Afghanistan with Egypt, Poland with Japan. Antiquity—with the future on foreign planets. It's exhausting, Ann, I must say.

Literature can't be the story of that weightless, short-lived particle, the I. No, not anymore. Now it's the past-present as it unfolds in our heads—a *Sprachfest* of survivors. The world is broken, and so am I, but I keep talking with immortals. They are the ones who write my texts, adding fragments to fragments. My reality is all fiction. A *Luftmensch*, I'm ready to dissolve in air.

Aren't you contented, Ann? Attached to nothing, you flutter around, a cheerful butterfly.

No, a moth—who still has some possessions. But you should meet my stepsister, Carol, from my mom's first marriage to a Jewish bank clerk. She owns nothing but her life—a life sentence.

Where's she?

In New York. An artist, she produces almost imperceptible drawings on unbleached cotton, with rusty felt pens and white acrylic paint, turns out scholarly books on esoteric subjects. The shroud of Turin. Paper theater. The kiss of Judas. Quite a character, she's always dressed in black and white, has a pageboy haircut, and looks like a boy. No, she isn't completely unsuccessful with men. But it would be better if she kept out of their way. Someone flirts with her and, hopla, she's burning. Am I close to her? Yes and no. She's shrouded in secrecy, and such a rare bird. Right now she's agonizing over somebody who may be her final catcher. What do I mean? His skin is ten times as thick as hers. How she survives? A few cognoscenti buy her work, she publishes here and there, gets a grant. A shadowy kind of life. No, I can't figure it out, but asking people, even one's own sister, about their bank accounts is even more difficult than inquiring about love. Luckily, Carol's so minimal. No radio, no tape recorder, no TV. She doesn't read the papers, has only a slight idea of what's going on in the world. Alas, the past never leaves her. She's four years younger than I—and still in Treblinka, if you know what I mean. A sort of Simone, but gentler and not so bright, Carol identifies only with losers. Afghans stepping on mines, black bag ladies in Riverside Park. You must meet her, Italo. Before it's too late.

Too late?

She's an endangered species, and she'll never ask for help.

Calm down, Ann. Let's go back to the photo. Who's the younger man?

One of my dad's authors. A Marxist philosopher.

He looks fragile.

Yes, but he'll persevere, while Dad has only one more year to go.

Some twenty years between the two of them?

Yes, two generations—of belief and repression. Dad obliterated the Moscow trials of the thirties, his author the chilliness of the Moscow Party School in '52. But that May they both began to examine the causes of their respective amnesias. For Dad the exam turned out deadly. But the younger man built his new career on it. He became a revisionist.

Didn't I see his face in the *Corriere?* Is he a member of the papal commission on the Holy Spirit? Yes, he's brilliant, but something is missing. A personal touch, I guess. He decided to dissent at a conveniently late moment, didn't he?

Don't blame him, Italo. A career revisionist cannot dissect himself all the way to the bone. Then no one would buy his version of history. But is he that different from you and me? Had we the nerve to keep our texts in a drawer until our respective deaths—our insides could be made transparent. But since ambition prompts us to publish our confessions, a lot is censored and stored away. But aren't you hungry, Svevo?

I wouldn't mind a little something.

Semolina with shredded apples, cinnamon and sugar? Or coffee with Argentine biscuits? Or both?

Sounds wonderful. But I can't take my eyes off the photo. Your father and the philosopher remind me of two spies in a Le Carré novel, with the girl—is she the Marxist's daughter?—serving as decoy. Really, Ann. You should tear it in two, keep the half with your father for yourself, send the philosopher the other half, and remake the episode into a thriller—without a single digression. You write every day, don't you?

No, I don't, my friend. No *Chartreuse de Parme* per month. But it's only because I mistype every second word. Still, Mr. Underwood 700 I found on Broadway and 116th is a genius. At night he corrects my spelling.

Djuna Barnes told me exactly the same. No *Nightwood* without my Underwood. Mandelshtam types on one as well. Is it an epidemic?

Yes, and there's another one. We all visit a sick grandmother and fail to return because the little Redhood we meet on our way leads us to Wolf's Winter Sanatorium. Didn't Mandelshtam tell you?

He did, Woof, woof, how are you today, Osip Emilevich? Very well, Dr. Stalin, thank you for caring in advance.

Wouldn't you like to try our world famous ice bath? It will do you plenty of good. Oh, thank you! I'd love to be made into a *gelato*.

Italo laughs, while Ann fills his mug with coffee, adds a splash of milk, and shakes her curls. The setting sun shines through the branches, a sparrow chirrups, spreading its tail, a rook caws, the wind rustles among the cherry leaves. Aren't we a handsome couple, Italo thinks, feeling a pang of sadness. Their eyes meet and she hurriedly gets up, squeezes his hand, fetches a bowl of sugar. No, nothing will come of it. Already her lips part, and she asks: Do you know, my dear, who invented the ice palace? Annoyed, he just stares at her. But there's deep sorrow in her undertone and he regrets being obstinate, even for a moment, and answers: Russian boys, I bet.

No, a girl, Ann exclaims, and sits down. You missed the first prize, Comrade Svevo, but you won the second: a frozen banana split, awaiting you in my freezer. Like most good things on earth, the ice palace was invented by the *imperial mistress of fur-clad Russ, thy most magnificent and mighty freak, the wonder of the North, who made thy marble of the glassy wave. Ice upon ice, thy well-adjusted parts were soon conjoined, nor other cement asked than water interfused to make them one.* By Anna, your favorite eccentric, at whose accession the Dolgoruki family was exiled to Siberia. Do you remember? In September 1739 the empress recalled Prince Sergei Dolgoruki under the pretext of charging him with a special mission. In high spirits he returned to St. Petersburg to learn that he and his family would go on trial.

Ann, my Scheherazade. . . .

Silence, Italo. In no time Sergei was found guilty of concocted charges of treason and beheaded. Prince Vasili was broken on the wheel and Prince Ivan quartered. But in November poor Anna was faced with another trouble. A Ukrainian peasant proclaimed himself the tsarevich Alexis. Three soldiers believed him, and a priest held a mass for him. Blank with rage, Anna had the imposter impaled alive. The village was razed to the ground, the peasants were resettled, and the coldest winter in history arrived. The Seine was transformed into solid ice. In Versailles champagne bottles burst. In Lübeck a seven-foot-long ice lion was fed with frozen lamb. In Moscow doves fell dead from the sky. And Anna was inspired with the idea of an ice palace. So she ordered the architect Eropkin. . . .

Ann, is there any more coffee? No, but you can boil more water. Oh, God, she's angry with me. So what! How long can I play a column of salt? Italo sighs, excuses himself, disappears in the bathroom, lights himself a cigarette, relaxes. Soon the sound of her musical kettle and the smell of fresh coffee reach him. Finished? Can I come in? Ann scratches at the door. Back in the kitchen, he sees a banana split on the table, and whispers to himself: Dig in, let her talk.

Can I go on, dear? Eropkin created a midwinter night's dream—a Palladian ice villa with frozen fireplaces guarded by naked caryatids, beds with ice-hard mattresses, night tables with caviar and strawberries in their natural tints, and a grotesque garden with a fountain, a life-size seal surrounded by nymphs. All this for a wedding of Prince Mikhail Golitsyn, an out-of-favor courtier, to an imperial dwarf, a Kalmuck woman nicknamed by Anna *Buzhenina*—roast pork in onion sauce. The couple was married in Saint Mary's and stuffed into a cage. An elephant carried it at the head of a procession and was followed by Lapps in sledges, drawn by wolves and pigs, Khirgiz cripples on Bernardine dogs, and Siamese twins on ponies and ostriches. The bridal pair was bedded on an ice sheet and soldiers were posted to make sure they didn't escape.

They froze to death?

Oh, come on, Italo. Russ are tough. That night Golitsyn impregnated Buzhenina, and she bore him two sons.

Dwarfs?

No. Normal size. On the day of their birth the architect was executed for high treason. But for a month he enjoyed incredible fame. His villa on the Neva was the talk of the town. Crowds assembled to admire the ice mansion and its garden, with palm trees and parrots—tiny talking robots. The walls were left transparent, only doors and window frames simulated green marble. The façade was embellished with six niches containing obscene ice statues of Pan and the satyrs. At night candlelit lanterns rotated in invisible hands and amused the populace. On February 1st the ice palace was attacked and defended for a week. Trapped in an alcove, five officers had their extremities frozen off. When the villa fell, the news hit the world press and a new entertainment was established in the west: the storming of the Winter Palace, a sham battle.

You know what comes to my mind, Ann? Euergetes. The extremes of climate seem to inflame men's brains. The Siberian snows and the sands of the Sahara breed similar excess.

It's a smart thought, Italo. But aren't humans capable of anything at any time? Now let me cook more semolina, it will calm us down.

When you spoke of the exotic ice birds, Ann, I had a vision of the *Tiergarten* in Berlin. Mother took me there on a Saturday afternoon and the zoo infected me with a sad reverie. Sorry for the captured animals, I began to dream about myself as a cub separated from his family during the hunt. Shortly afterwards I read Hugo's *Miserables* and was moved to tears by Gavroche, the homeless orphan who was killed on the barricades, remember? The belly of a bronze elephant was his hideout. To save the boy, one night I metamorphosed into a living elephant. While he was sound asleep inside of me, I marched out of Paris.

We share our loves, Italo. At eight a heart disease kept me in bed for a year and every night I dreamt of visiting Gavroche in the elephant— sleeping at his side, protecting him from a bullet. But in the morning I used to reread the description of his killing—to convince myself that nights count less than days.

But they don't, Ann. We're the captives of the night—and of our animal selves.

Perhaps, but kids more than adults. That's why the zoo affects them so deeply. Dad and I, we visited the wild beasts on many Sundays, while Mom cooked chicken for lunch. The zoo—spread out on the east bank of the Vistula we had to cross by tram—was directed by Dr. Frogman, Dad's old pal. Baby tigers slept on his couch, and snakes, their lazy bodies wound around the pipes, shed their skins in his bathroom. Caressing a boa's head, Frogman once said to Dad: Look, my beauty menstruates, and shook with laughter. *Menstruates*—the foreign-sounding word stayed with me, and so did his sudden outburst of hilarity. My curiosity was aroused. Soon I linked it to blood in the lavatory. But whose—Dad's or Mom's?

When I saw my mother's menstrual blood for the first time, I was stiff with terror. I thought she suffered from a fatal disease, and was going to die. At night, each time she went to the bathroom, I woke up, seeing blood flowing out and leaving her an empty sack. Once I ran out of bed and waited for her in front of the toilet. She stepped on me, and cried out: What's the matter, Italo, can't you sleep? Mama, I whispered, tell me the truth. What truth, dearest? Are you very sick? I'm not sick at all. Tell me the truth, I repeated. At last she understood what I meant, and mumbled: Come, lie down in my bed. Such was the climax of my childhood—and its end. Next morning I felt like an adult man.

What happened?

She took my hand and placed it first on her breast, then on her belly. Women are different from men, Italo. They bear children. Before you were born, I carried you here for nine months, feeding you with my own blood. When you came out of me, I had milk in my breasts and you drank it. Women's bodies are filled with extra fluid and when they have babies, it's used for their nourishment. But they can't be having them all the time, so each month some blood is released. It hurts a little, but it's natural.

This illness, will it ever stop, Mama?

When I'm old, it will. But meanwhile, don't worry, dearest. Go to your bed and dream of the *Tiergarten* we're going to visit next Saturday.

How serene. And perhaps a key to why you're so good to women, Italo. But, on the other hand, you cannot bear the sight of blood. Why?

Because of a summer day that linked blood and death. I wasn't yet four, and walked with Mama in the forest. Suddenly a rabbit hopped across our way, touching my legs. Its fur electrified my skin. Elated, I kept talking about the animal for hours. In the afternoon I had a nap and dreamt of it. We picnicked on the beach and at dusk began to return on the same path. Mama carried me for a while, but when we came near the spot of our morning encounter, I demanded to be set free, and asked: Is the rabbit still here? It may be, watch out, she replied. But first a butterfly, later a large brown bird diverted my attention, and only her ah! ah! brought me down to earth. Letting my hand go, she put her hand in front of my eyes. Her fingers trembled and between them I saw the rabbit. His fur was crumpled and empty, his blood was feeding flies. *Aus,* I heard Mama whisper. *Aus, so rasch.*

Beasts and blood. The bathroom and the kitchen. That's how death introduces itself to kids. Every Christmas a rabbit, sent from the countryside by my grandpa, was skinned by Mom. While the hide dried on the balcony, carp were hit with a hammer on their heads, and cut. Their slices jumped in the frying pan, their blood turned brown. For me even suicide is a kitchen business. When I was four, the husband of a neighboring vacationer killed himself in Warsaw, and everyone talked about *the gas oven.* It made sense. The rabbit pâté was baked in it. But how could an adult fit into one?

Who was he?

The author of a Holocaust classic and the father of a baby I saw once or twice. A handsome, witty guy, so I heard, in his early thirties. He and his wife were Auschwitz survivors.

He felt too guilty to stay alive?

Please, no stereotypes, Italo. He cheated on his wife, and worked for the Polish branch of the KGB. That's why, perhaps. Anyway, they enlisted him right after the liberation, in Berlin, where the couple had trotted along with the Red Army. How? Why? Oh, the famous banality of evil, I guess. They must have tempted him with cash, two valid passports, a flat in an ex-Gestapo residence in the center of Warsaw. He was seduced, but not for good.

No Josephus, but a Jew, I presume.

No, Italo, a proper Pole. But his boss, the renowned Moskvitch, was a rabbi's son who had changed his name from Mäusling. His deputy, on the other hand, was the feebleminded Ninel—from Lenin, reversed—a Catholic ex-priest.

What a collection! No wonder he wanted to get out of it.

No wonder, Italo. But enough of that. Last night I reread your *Senilità,* the passage where Angiolina rises to the level of your feelings for her. She doesn't strike false notes, doesn't even once tell you that she loves you. It's superb.

Is it where I hold her closer and closer to myself with my left arm?

Yes. You have your head in her lap and you're overwhelmed with a feeling of deepest compassion for her. That's what I felt whenever I met with my last lover. But why do we pity people who hurt us? Whose victims we are? It's idiotic. We take their hands, put them against our foreheads, and in that attitude of adoration tell them that we would give them up altogether rather than that any harm should happen to them through us. We tell them what we want them to think, but what they don't think and will never say. We lose so many words for nothing. When you have Angiolina utter with a smile: We seem to make a fine couple, my heart almost stopped. Once, on a chilly Manhattan evening, we passed a beggar and, as always, my sweetheart refused to give him change. I have to support myself, he shouted. More gracious than my boyfriend, the bum paid us a compliment: What a pretty couple you make! Pleased, my egoist laughed: Repeat it, man, and I may consider sparing a quarter. Of course, I was immediately flooded with hope: he may be generous, after all.

Is he the one whose child you miscarried? You were half dead, Ann, when I visited you in the hospital. And you chatted like a madwoman. To stop you from asking, again and again: What do you think, Italo, will he take off a whole Saturday to reward me for what I have been through? Will he, once I'm out of here?—I force-fed you a pudding, and kept repeating: I'll kill the bastard if he doesn't.

And so he did. I bought myself a new pair of pants and woke up every five minutes—that Friday night. Rushing to his place on Saturday morning, I was almost hit by a car.

Poor darling!

No, Italo, this one time he didn't disappoint me. He must have noticed the glow of my skin, the fire in my eyes. It was midday, but he took me in his arms, and said: Tonight, you're extraordinarily beautiful, realized his error, laughed. I'd brought fresh strawberries, and we ate them. He lifted me up, put me on his knees, fondled my breasts. The beginning of the end. Before, I only had a crush on him. That Saturday I fell in love. We walked through Central Park, watched people dancing, playing ball. We sat on a bench, and again he kissed me, and whispered: It's like in a French movie. Yes, I chanted, *Last Year in Marienbad* with a Polo-Czech cast.

D EAR FRIENDS, GOETHE SAYS. I have the privilege to introduce to you Simone Weil, who has just returned from Madrid, our most precious co-Fellow, distinguished philosopher, and a woman, no, rather a person of the world. Woman still doesn't sound proud enough. Yes, Lotte, you desire to contribute to the semantics of femininity? Simone, would you mind letting my spouse speak before you begin?

Forgive me for forcing myself to the foreground, Dr. Weil. But I would like to clarify what you mean when you say *woman,* Wolf. Do you imply *das Übliche?* That female thinkers are saturated with emotions? That they mirror themselves in male intellects? Neglect politics and economics? Lack design and construction? Fuse, instead of differentiating? Use metaphors, not abstractions? Have weak brains? Are bad in geometry? Don't engage in combat? Try to please? And that, by contradicting women's weak strategies, Mademoiselle Weil places herself outside of us?

Ms. Goethe, may I answer instead of your husband? I believe my reply will be more to the point, since I have chosen to be a male French intellectual with a classical background—and to starve to death the Jewish woman I was born. Life isn't about what we are, I believe, it's about what we want to be. A moth could live the life of a beaver, if she desired it with all her heart. I, Weil, I wish to be neither a woman nor a female eunuch—worshiping a Sartre. I want to be a follower of Socrates, a Christian martyr, a medieval monk, a Byron ready to die for the freedom of some irrelevant Greeks. According to all past and present definitions, I'm not a woman. I allow myself, if at all, to be female only in dreams. For the duration of a sleepless night I may be Karenina stepping out of the train and meeting Vronsky on a platform. But my life is that of a man.

When a war breaks out, I go to war—refusing to wait at home. Striving for an anti-female utopia, I would rather kill myself than resign. Mine is a performance in autonomy women are either forced to deny, or prefer to deny—it's safer. But I, Ms. Goethe, I have left the herd for the cold. That's why your husband dislikes and honors me. I get on his nerves, but he recognizes that, not unlike himself, I'm myself to the point of destruction. I accommodate no man. I don't peek in a beloved pair of pants, and sigh: Shall I be with male A or male B? For me the dilemma is: To be or not to be? I'm interested in geometry, divinity, and communism. Women's issues? I plan to confront them on my deathbed. Therefore I have decided to acquaint you not with my own views on this topic but with the opinions of a colleague of mine from the Ecole Normale, Dr. Saint-Simon.

Presently Saint-Simon is trying to formulate a paradigm of how nobility, loyalty, purity, and happiness can be restored to the relationship between the two sexes. I won't hide from you that my sex life equals zero and that in respect to my own ambition love and marriage possess less substance than the concepts of heaven and hell. But that's not Saint-Simon's position. He believes that the first step towards a general betterment has to be the modification of the marriage laws—established by Christ and his successors—in order to eliminate whatever is contrary to human nature. My main problem with his approach is that I don't know what human nature is. Personally, I neither resemble most humans nor would like to resemble them. But my colleague seems to know what he's talking about. He postulates that the old laws be replaced by a new law based on the social equality of men and women, and by the rehabilitation of the needs and pleasures of the flesh. As for equality, I'm all for it, even though, in the short run, it will change nothing. As for the needs and pleasures of the flesh, I consider them a secret territory nobody understands. The more the world talks sex, the more impotence I suspect. Recognizing needs and pleasures is one thing, satisfying them another. It's good to abolish taboos, but when they are gone we may have more problems than before. One can turn eros into a sip of Pepsi—only to discover the taste of brandy.

Like most reformists, Saint-Simon deals not with the future but with the past. He disputes the fundamental principle of Christian morality—exclusive love, followed by the indissoluble and eternal union of the espoused. But who believes in that anyhow? The idea that a male virgin will make a female virgin happy for the remainder of their lives has always been just a fantasy. Saint-Simon thus proclaims the need for generosity and tolerance, recalling—

—the way Erasistratus of Cos cured Aristotle's nephew.

Indeed, Mr. Goethe. However Saint-Simon sees in this the proof of the superiority of Egyptian morality over Christian ethics. How absurd! The truth is, Seleucus was simply generous. Generosity, not morality, is the answer. But why are some generous, others not? It all depends on how much we treasure ourselves, how little the others. Therefore the polarity between egoism and altruism cannot be bridged with equality or emancipation. The real secret of life and love is the ability to give oneself up. Alas, this ability will decrease, not increase, with the growth of individual freedom. Women's liberation, a historical necessity, will not help to replace failure with happiness. Nor will marriage laws accomplish that. Raised as the more altruistic sex, in the past, which is still with us, women suffered from their own softness. Must they harden themselves? Yes. But in consequence generosity will diminish in the world.

Unless their softness is passed to men.

Absolutely, Ms. Goethe. So you'll agree with me and Saint-Simon: the female voice must go public. Here's what he says: Our entire aim at this moment is to give women a sense of their strength and dignity, so that they can make all their sufferings and desires known without shame. Jesus brought women a first degree of emancipation. Feeling himself moved by a tender compassion for those who had sinned against the ancient law of oppression, he challenged the world to throw the first stone. We will do something a little bit greater. We will give every woman the power to hurl a challenge not only at her persecutors but at those who judge her. Come then, let the woman step forth who has the power to speak! Who has the power to write! Whether she imprisoned her life in Christian chastity, or whether she rolled in the mud, for her emancipated voice, gentlemen, I will enforce silence.

End of quote. Do I hear embarrassed silence? Yes, the stuff is antiquated—the sin of most *Normaliens*. But in the crux of the matter Saint-Simon isn't wrong. The silence isn't yet enforced. Women know it, so they chatter. Why am I an exception in the choir of singing sirens? Is it because I went to Spain, starved myself? Has the legend of my life added weight to my texts?

It has. But they have weight by themselves.

Thank you, Svevo.

I don't pay you a compliment, Simone. You play the right game. Leaving men out, you make them stand *hab' Acht*. An immaculate intellect—menstruation, pregnancy, menopause never enter your discourse, correct?—you converse with men's holy spirits. Bravo, Weil! You turned around Constantine's paradox demonstrating that a woman's purse is only filled with gold when it's empty.

Ms. Simone, do you always play a male?

Always, Ms. Goethe. But I would prefer to be a kangaroo.

WHILE WEIL LECTURES IN SEXTUS'S STUDIO, Mandelshtam, his wife, and Ann Kar drink tea in the kitchen. I can't stand Simone, Osip confesses, and I wanted to talk to you about your text, Ann. On the one hand I'm impressed with it, on the other hand I'm confused and irritated. I also mix genres, cross over, combine vignettes, dream of the time machine. But I check myself, and don't adopt the tone of the global village. But the way you repeat events, attribute them to different people appeals to me. The sense of déjà vu provides catharsis. Still, you absorb too much, my girl, and in the end all the crosscultural tricks may cancel each other.

You object to Euergetes being likened to Stalin?

Yes, and to Propertius falling in love with a mythological figure. But I approve of your assembling us all in Rome.

Aren't you happy to be resurrected in order to choose once again between Nadia and Ola?

Sort of, Ann. I even like the thought of being a Siberian woodchuck housed in the underwood together with my mistress, a bullfinch, and my wife, a turtledove.

But before I could change you into a pretty little beast, I had to find you, Osia. And so I did. On my way back from a disastrous party I recalled your lines about Venice just as I was passing a garbage bin at Broadway and 116th. A *Slavic Review*, buried under a morose slice of pizza, caught my gaze. I rescued the smelly thing, opened it haphazardly on page 689, and went red. Here you were, addressing me in the manner of a Soviet Homer:

O artist, cherish and guard the warrior: the forest of mankind follows him thronging, the future itself is the retinue of the sage. And ever more often, more boldly is he heeded. By Stalin's eyes is the mountain put sunder, and the plain peered into the distance. Like the sea without wrinkles. Like tomorrow out of yesterday. Furrows made by the giant plow reach to the sun. He smiles the smile of the harvester of handshakes in a conversation which has begun and continues without end in the six-oaths expanse. And every threshing floor and every hay shock is strong, close-packed, clever—living wealth—the peoples' miracle! Let life be big. Happiness is turning on its axis.

My "Ode to Stalin." What a gulag of a poem. I, a manic-depressive late riser, how could I write *let life be big?* Nadia, was I out of my mind? Was it I who composed this fucking epitaph for my own grave in the Sahara? It had a dreadful ending, but God the merciful let me forget it. Can you remind me of it, Ann?

The mounds of human heads recede into the distance: I am there diminished, I'll not be noticed any longer, but in gentle books and in children's games I shall be resurrected to say the sun is shining.

The sun is shining, pfui, pfui, pfui.

Don't get overexcited, Osia. The sun is shining, Stalinski is dead, and you're OK. Do you know, Ann, how he worked on this baboon in verse? In our room we had a square dining table which served us for absolutely everything. When Osia decided to write the ode, he took possession of the table. Normally, he wrote in bed, half awake, biting furiously on his invalid of a pencil. But from then on everything changed. He sharpened at least four pencils, spread out papers, occupied almost the entire table, and we had to eat on one little corner of it or even on the windowsill. Every morning Osia jumped out of bed, shouting *no cakes without work,* devoured a piece of bread, gulped down a cup of corn coffee, and seated himself at the table—pencil in hand.

You see, Ann, what a saint Nadia was.

Not a saint, a spouse. After sitting for half an hour in the poet's pose, Osia would suddenly start running around and berating himself for his lack of skill: now Aragon, there's a craftsman, he'd fondle his Elsa and get it down right off. Then, calming down, he would lie down on the bed, ask for tea, jump up, feed sugar to the neighbor's dog through the *fortochka*, pace the room. Brightening up, he would begin to mutter his own rhymes and forget about the ode. But then something would bring back the thought of it, and he would cry out: Nadia, I can't do it. All I see in front of me are his cockroach mustaches, his wormlike fingers, and mounds of heads. Why does he sever so many of them? Finally, one afternoon, Osia sat down and began: *With an avid hand—to catch only the axis of resemblance—I shall crumble the charcoal, searching for his likeness. I learn from him not to spare myself.*

That's the lesson Stalin taught to everybody, even to a Polish kid. I remember the day news of his death reached Warsaw. A first-grader, I stood guard at his huge photo—it was mounted on board and attired with a black ribbon—and thought of his good warm hands. He'd lift me, a small but serious pioneer, give me candy, send me to Artek. Were you ever there, Osia?

No, but Nadia knew a teenager who had caught typhoid in that camp.

A camp? To us Artek was a paradise where tots ran their own railroads, flew airplanes, drove combines, and increased productivity. Saluting Stalin's portrait, I worried that without Him Artek might cease to exist. Won't the Kulaks take it over, now that He's dead? What will happen to me? Can I become a tractorist in Polish People's Republic, an inferior non-Soviet state? Indoctrination makes kids not only fanatic but opportunist as well. I knew that I was expected to cry. In despair, I recalled the effect an onion, chopped, had on my mom's eyes. Had I one, I mused, I could run to the toilet, cut it with the red pocketknife Dad gave me for my birthday, and come out in tears, making an excellent impression.

What a hypocritical little fox you were!

Yes, ready to join the Politburo of Artek. But meanwhile, I felt an urge to piss and scratch myself. At this strategic instant our Russian teacher appeared—weeping and tearing apart her black silk dress. Seeing it so senselessly destroyed, I broke out in tears. She rushed to me, led me to the bathroom, washed my face, and whispered: He isn't dead. Next summer you'll be included in the Artek delegation. No, the Kulaks won't invade us. We love Him and He loves us. Yes, He saw us cry.

O NCE UPON A TIME THERE WAS LIFE, now it's only talking, Lotte sighs. Then, reaching for a cushion to support her achy back, she says: Dear friends. It's an honor to introduce to you on this Tuesday evening, our last before Christmas, one of our great contemporaries who, I'm happy to announce, yesterday accepted our invitation and joined the Institute. Moses Maimonides, a distinguished scholar of perplexity, will speak tonight about the evils of carnality which, according to him, can be avoided. In Rome, the hothouse of Neronian delights, your talk, dear Moses, will undoubtedly provoke a strong response. Confronted with your seemingly controversial approach I, for my part, experience a cathartic shock and regain my substance. Your faith, based on purity of reflection and language, maintains balance and integrity. Archaic yet curiously modern, you give me hope, Moses, that not everything is lost. Please welcome Professor Maimonides, a man with qualities, in our modest salon.

Thank you, Lotte. Please forgive me for boring you with an unfashionable subject, the Hebrew language. A good language, I believe, since it opts for omissions and protects certain spheres in order not to vulgarize them with words. To give you an example, Hebrew has no special name for the organ of generation in females or males, nor for the act of generation itself, nor for the semen, nor for secretion. It refuses to express these things and only describes them in figurative speech, or by way of hints, indicating thereby that we ought to be silent about them. When, nevertheless, we are compelled to mention them, we must employ for that purpose some suitable terms. Thus the organ of generation in males is called in Hebrew *gid,* a figurative reminder of the phrase "and thy neck is an iron sinew," or *shupka,* "pouring out"—on account of its function. The female organ, *kobah,* comes from *keboh,* "stomach." *Rehem*—"womb"—is the inner organ in which the fetus develops. *Zoah,* "refuse," is derived from the verb *yaza*—"he went out." For urine the phrase *meme raglyim,* "the water of the feet," is used. Semen, *shkbat zera,* means "a layer of seed." For the act of generation there is no word whatever, and so it is described by *ba'al,* "he was master," *shakab,* "he lay," *lakah,* "he took," and *gillah'ervah,* "he uncovered nakedness." Don't be misled by *yishgalennah*—it doesn't denote that act itself. *Shegal* signifies a female ready for cohabitation, and *yishgalennah*—"he will take the female for the purpose of cohabitation."

May I throw in a few ideas that occurred to me while you spoke? Naturally, Henryk.

Am I right to discover in your precious little treatise the roots of

Freud's interpretation of dreams and his thoughts on how sexual matters are censored? Or is it the other way around? Have you been influenced by Sigmund?

It's hard to tell who influenced whom, but I suppose Freud represents in every respect the mainstream of Hebrew philosophy. The camouflage of our language taught him how to analyze repression in figurative speech. It's never the penis you dream of. It's always a cock at dawn, announcing that Peter betrayed his Lord.

But I see connections to Wittgenstein as well. Isn't his idea of silencing the inconveniences of metaphysics a replication of what you just explained?

Certainly. But Ludwig never gave credit to anybody, kept his mouth shut, and thus impressed the Cambridge philosophical bears of little brains. But, clearly, his rejection of metaphysics was grounded on my recognition that the corporeal element in man is a large partition that prevents him from perfectly perceiving abstractions. However great the exertion of our mind may be to comprehend divinity or the ideal, we find a screen between Him and ourselves. The prophets frequently suggest the existence of a veil between heaven and earth. They say He is concealed from us in vapor, in darkness, in mist, or use similar figures to express that on account of our bodies we are unable to grasp His essence. This is the meaning of the words "clouds and darkness are round about Him," and of the passage "He made darkness His secret place." Every prophetic vision contains some lesson by means of allegory. God's revelation in a thick cloud did not take place without any purpose. He caused us to comprehend that He is hidden on account of the dark body that surrounds us. A tradition is current among our people that the day of the revelation on Mount Sinai was misty and a little rainy.

A little rainy! That's perfect, Goethe exclaims. Is truth revealed on cloudy days only?

Sunshine blinds, Johann. The mist, like the absence of words for generation, is to protect us through an assumed negativity. The mist stands for the imperfect corporeal element which is the source of death and all evils, but which is likewise good for the continuation of everything—as one thing departs, the other succeeds. All the great evils that men inflict on each other because of certain intentions, desires, opinions, or principles, are likewise due to nonexistence. They originate in ignorance, which is the absence of wisdom. Men frequently assume that in this world evils outdo the good things, and mourn this tragedy in poems and songs. But that is an error whose origin is found in the circumstance that an ignorant man judges the whole universe by examining one single person—himself. If, therefore, anything happens to him contrary to his expectation, he at once concludes that the whole universe is evil.

BUT WHAT ABOUT TREBLINKA? Henryk hears himself shouting, as he wakes up. Again, he dreamt about Rome and the last happy period of his life. On the day Maimonides lectured at the Institute, he became engaged to Silvana—and the seed of evil was planted. At their wedding he took her name and was transformed from Kowalski into Bonafiducci. A week later his wife suggested he change his first name as well—to Bel. From that moment on everything went downhill. A young academic couple, they left for the States, settled in New Jersey, got a mortgage, bought a house.

Going over the dream, Bel hears himself repeat: What about Treblinka? It's not one man to whom it happened, millions were destroyed. You cannot expect, Henryk, Moses calmly replies, to see the living beings, formed from the blood of menstruous women and the virile semen, who would not torment each other. But in spite of Treblinka, life is good. The tiniest grain of charity makes it worth living, and you're a symbol of how good triumphs over evil. Were you not saved by a Polish peasant? Aren't you in good health? A handsome, talented young man whom friends call Winnie the Pooh, and are right. You regard this world as the best of all possible worlds, and realize: when a pot is broken, honey doesn't disappear from the universe. After Auschwitz some of my zealous colleagues—right, Wolf, the Frankfurt crowd with Adorno up front—proclaimed the end of culture. No more Goethe. No more poems. Yet soon words were rhymed in German again—about Margaret's golden locks and her boyfriend's ashes—by a Jew from Bukovina. Culture continues, Henio, and we continue. The numerous evils to which we are exposed are due to defects existing in us. We suffer from what we, by our own free will, inflict on ourselves. Complaining, we seek relief from our own faults and errors. One day you may find out that Treblinka was not the worst life had in store for you. It provided you with living proof that goodness exists. Still, a trivial evil may defeat you.

It's a November Tuesday and Goethe sits at the window of Propertius's studio. Suffering from a light flu, he's wrapped all over in a woolen plaid and wears his old angora gloves, as he enters events into his diary. On the desk to his right there is a small note, cut from the *Manhattan Times:* Professor Bel Bonafiducci, America's foremost specialist in suicide, died yesterday on his way back from a bike trip along the Princeton canal. Sick with a severe depression, Bonafiducci jumped into the canal at the sight of his wife approaching him in a car. Dean of the Psychology Department as well as author of several bestselling books on Amateurish Suicidal Artists, Professor Bonafiducci, a survivor of the Holocaust, is survived by his wife Silvana, Ph.D. in Pathopsychology, and two daughters, Pola, 11, and Henrietta, 5.

A new record, Goethe mumbles to himself, six deaths in a month. In London Simone starved herself, in Suffolk Lowry drank himself to death. In Oslo, Olga put a bullet into her side. Karenina didn't listen to her best friend Florence and, instead of waiting for the publication of her novel, threw herself under a freight train in Siena's suburbs. On the Upper West Side Ann Kar's stepsister drowned in the Hudson, and three weeks later Henryk chose Carnegie Lake to accomplish the same. We approach winter with ever speedier steps. Nevertheless, we will gather tonight and do business as usual. I'll have Conrad read the text Malcolm prepared for tonight, which after his death Ernestine humidified with her tears before mailing to us.

The evening is chilly and everybody looks twice as old as usual. Not one black hair has been preserved on Svevo's scalp, while Ann's curls glow with the artificial red of Abigail henna. Seeing how the secretary of the Institute rolls her corpulent body through the door, Goethe remarks to himself: Lotte should go on a diet. Perceiving Conrad, whose skin resembles a bathing suit that has lost its stretch, Lotte murmurs to herself: Joseph should have an overall body-lift, and forces her fat ass into the new easy chair Wolf recently bought for her.

My dear penguins, Goethe addresses the small audience. Since the number of our dear dead exceeds common decency and we're all ready to join them, I'm not going to assume a mournful expression. Instead, I plan to send a plea to the Almighty to have our Institute for Global Vain Egos transferred to heaven, so that we can continue in eternity, generously supported by a grant from Saint Paul's Fund for Angelic Propaganda and Saint Peter's Longevity Study Group. Immortals are best at declining the irregular verb *mourir,* and even better at discussing death—the goal of everybody else.

To die was the favorite verb of our co-Fellow Malcolm, whom I asked to speak tonight. No, he is no more. But Ernestine sent us her best regards and the alcohol-soaked pages he intended to read to us. No one is irreplaceable, and in a few minutes Lowry will be replaced by Conrad. But before I pass the chair to you, Joseph, I would like to focus on a topic that Ann, Osip, and Nadia want us to consider—Afghanistan, an invaded country I personally know little about. Its ex-king lives in exile in Rome and is with us tonight. A shy, soft-spoken monarch, he will help us to free ourselves from old-age pettiness. We must be drawn again to larger questions, regain the altruism of our youth.

I hope, my dear king, that the text of our friend Lowry won't upset you too much. He was a metaphysical sailor, not specialized in courtly speech and not equipped with the elephantine skin of a *Geheimrat*. A drunkard, he crossed and cursed oceans of the cheapest vodka, and sank to the bottom. But let me stop here and yield the floor to Joseph Conrad Korzeniowski, originally a Pole, later an acclaimed English author, whom Lowry liked to tease by calling him *Korytowski*—a not quite kosher joke death turns into a charming anecdote.

Dear king, beloved friends. Lowry's text, an unfinished sketch, was kept in an envelope addressed to Joseph Conrad Korytowski. Ernestine numbered the loose pages and I'm going to keep to that sequence, although it may have nothing to do with the way Malcolm wanted us to hear his, I guess, testament. But judge for yourself.

Joseph the good. Sorry I haven't written. I'm a bit *herausgeschmissen*. I don't eat any food and in my bed I have twice geshitten. I'm living here in a comparative state of mundial fear. Also give my love to Goethe, the bailor, Liz Taylor, and Anna Karenina Kar, the author of *The Woman with Qualities* and *A Woman Grows Old, and Other Short Stories in Verse*. This I write on the night of November first, a soulless Mexican man in a *La Mordilla* cave.

November second. Tonight I have leaped out of bed and raced for Ernestine's room where I tried once more to strangle her. But the guard awoke and subdued me, although not without a great deal of difficulty.

November third. For the last year I had averaged at least two and a half to three liters of red wine a day, to say nothing of other drinks at bars, and during my last two months in Paris this had increased to about two liters of rum per day. Even if it ended up by addling me completely I would not move or think without vast quantities of alc, without which even a few hours were an unimaginable torture. Double whiskeys.

Sonoryl. Cocktails. Liquor. That's what my mind is all about. If Ernestine could turn into cognac, I would notice her. Otherwise she's an empty glass.

November fourth. I want to ask you, my male and female, first-, second-, and third-rate co-Fellows, if it's possible to compose a novel by the simple process of writing a series of short stories, complete in themselves, with the same characters, interrelated, correlated, good if held up to the light, watertight if held upside down, but full of effects and dissonances that are impossible in a short story. A novel with a purity of form that can only be achieved by a Conrad I'm not.

November fifth. The voyage that never ends is about to end. Untitled scrimshaws are given titles. My orphans, I baptize you. Disperse in the world, fish for readers. *Lunar Caustic,* my sweet son, if you cannot find a moon-girl, fuck your youngest sister, the wild *Under the Volcano.* The grave isn't dark, and my friend isn't laid therein. *Eridanus* and *La Mordida,* the oldest twins, assist me in my ordeal. A solid slice of *Scheisse,* I'm ready to sail, but the sea has dried out. Konradowski, do you see a bloody *Ultramarine* on the horizon? That's me.

November sixth. On with the work! Over those falls! Through those weeds. Enter her! Push! Penetrate the Holy Grail. Curse Archangel Karenin at the Moscow terminal. Die in Annette's arms. By the way, something must be wrong with her, I dream of Count Dolsdoy every day. Cable: Anny all right. In love with Leo Brodsky. Ready to join Malcolm Trotsky in Acapulco. Oh, Ann, the great love of every guy, liberate me from Ernestine and the bitter pills this witch presses into my mouth. Oh, *miła, miła Pani* Karenina, assist me!

I study, study, study the verb I know by heart. *Partir c'est mourir un peu, mourir c'est partir un peu, un peu partir, un peu mourir, un peu, un tout petit peu.* Why aren't you here, in *questo ospedaletto per il genio e la folia, per la bottiglia e la madonna? Perche no?* Josepho. Josephino. Josephetto. Are you in Egypt? Has brother Sextus sold you to the cannibal *ante portas?* Are you combing my queen's golden locks?

My eyes are so bloodshot that I can't see Ernestine. But I hear her crying. Poor disoriented creature. Soon your torture will be over. The verb will become flesh, as worms prefer it: rotten to the bone, not soaked in spirit. Adieu, Korytowski old chap. You're a great writer. I'm dying from admiration. No *Ultramarine* without the *Nigger* of your *Narcissus.* No *Ferry to Gabriola* without your peregrinations. But you had it so much easier! You lucky Pole. You stranger to my tongue. I hit you hard, but I did it out of too much love.

Good-bye midsummer nights in a cut cherry orchard! I kick and kiss the old familiar asses of the Vanity VIPs. Hungarian exiles, go ahead, deflower Ann's stepsister. Egyptian millionaires, come on, pay for our drinks. My bloody eye sees all the way to the stars where on the bedsheet of the night, entangled in Berenice's hair, Propertius snores away. Svevo, young man, have you finally grown senile? And you, Jewish Princess Liz Taylor Ann, is your head inflamed with intelligence and henna? Are you all there, digesting my words? Simone, are you with them? Hurry, my saint, you must end your *Hungerkünstler* career five minutes before the exit of *moi,* a gin angel.

Tra-ta-ta-ta. Dick up! I ride my Moby Dick back to Australia. Charlotte, meet your Werther in Sidney! We shall swim to Tasmania, keeping our heads under *Stolichnaya. C'est la fin.* Dick down! Bad boy go home. *Arrivederci Roma.* I am off to *lontano da dove.*

Just as Conrad terminates his reading, a young man slips in. Slim and dark-skinned, he looks tired, dark shadows engulf his large green eyes. Catching sight of him, Goethe gives him a sign, and the stranger hurries over to him. He puts an envelope into his hand, whispers a few words, and leaves. What is it? Lotte asks. For an instant her husband remains silent. Then he clears his throat, and mumbles: An Egyptian friend brought us an urgent message from Propertius. Do me a favor, read it, *meine Liebe.*

Berenice is dead. She expired in my presence at six in the morning, on November seventeenth. She remained unconscious all night but regained her spirits for a few instants, looked at me, and said: Put your hand on my forehead. Her skin was cold and covered with fine drops of sweat. She moved her lips, but she couldn't bring out a sound. Finally a murmur escaped from her mouth and she repeated the last words of Hostia: A burning fever eats me up. Wasps buzz in my lungs. A waterfall runs in my head. She paused, and I knew that now the text would change.

Sextus, she said, you loved me so much and I felt like in heaven. I had no breasts but you slept with me every night. Lotus flowers blossom in the Nile. I am dying. The fever consumes me. But don't go away. Let us talk until our voices turn into silvery bells. I want to tell you about my love for you. It all happened with such rapidity. The day you returned from Rome stands before me. Ever since my eye focused on your slight silhouette descending from the plane, I loved you, Sextus. I'll never stop loving you. Yesterday my urine was scrutinized and blood was found. My ultimate collapse is prompted by the loss of blood through all the openings of my body. I have no breasts, no weight, my mind is weaker than the brain of a newborn child. But still, I have you, Sextus, close at my side, and this makes my death a happy end. You have returned, the gods have presented me with an exceptional gift, my gratitude knows no words. So many poets prefer careers to women. But you left Rome for the provinces, so that I can touch you. The discourse of love is so monotonous, but I keep talking. The window is open and I face the sky of Egypt. Your devotion has reconciled me to this country, to life on earth. I have regained my faith, the tenderness of my youth. Do you remember our excursion on the Nile? *The Night of Cleopatra* you read to me? You're a cangia, sailing on the blue river of my mind. Other sailors are asleep, their heads dropped between their fists, but nothing can stop us.

Berenice's head dropped and her eyes closed. That was it. I remained seated at the edge of her bed and watched the film of my life unroll. Hostia's tiny white dog, the size of a mouse, jumped into my lap and began to lick Berenice's forehead. A black bird, the size of a moth, flew in singing as beautifully as the nightingale I once heard in my cherry orchard. I let it sit in my palm, even though I was scared that it might get infected with Berenice's bacilli. She died of pneumonia, and on the bird's black breast there was a white design that reminded me of her last X ray. The nightingale's eyes were golden and fire glittered in them. Now they seemed to converse, now they were silent. Do you remember Hostia, your first mistress? the bird inquired. Her lungs resembled Berenice's lungs. While she was drinking, a drop of blood trickled from her lips into the glass, and you recalled the Moroccan rosé wine you once drank together. Then she passed away, and you sat at the edge of her bed thinking about prostitutes in the Persian Gulf.

Goodness me! Again a talking blackbird, like in women's literature, I hear Goethe grumble. The cheapest of all cheap tricks. *Pfui, Teufel.* Malcolm, defend me! Shout that Sextus is no Faust, setting the entire universe in motion, but a sentimental fart—scraping the surface of his heart.

Where was I? I wanted to feed the bird with crumbs of the bread Berenice had eaten two days ago. But the bird refused to eat. The bread is too hard for me, I prefer ambrosia, it twittered, and I'm angry with you. Why do you call Hostia *Cynthia?* She isn't a Kowalski who needs a new name. And why don't you credit Marie de France from whom you inherited me, the black bird, your main metaphor? Who I am and what I mean? Don't ask me! A winged Amor, set free by the distress and death

◆ 145 ◆

of a caged Psyche? Oh, no, Sextus, it's a terrible verse.

I'm a talkative cat, a *gatto parlante,* the bird chatted, while I looked out the window. The sun, rising over the Nile, splashed water with blood. Cangias were floating by, young sailors were sleeping, heads dropped between fists. In Cairo's coffeehouses marble-topped tables dozed away. I had a headache. The tiny bat continued to lick Hostia's face, Berenice's eyelids. You should comb the queen's hair, it sang, before Euergetes has it cut and thrown away. Doves build nests in mulberry trees, but I keep you company.

Do you remember the house where you had Hostia the first time?

A villa with a wooden veranda?

Yes, and a wooden bed.

Did it happen in November?

On All Souls' Day. She was twelve and a half, but pretended to be fourteen—and an experienced girl.

She fooled me. I didn't realize she was a virgin. A bit scared, I sprayed away, and offered her cherries in chocolate. She declined, and I inspected the sheets. No blood, what a relief.

Then she caressed you with her child's hands and you felt embarrassed.

Yes, but I didn't reject her. I took her into my arms.

Convinced that you should get out of bed, not into her. Not again.

Well, our carnal standpoints were diverging, and so I said to myself: *Achtung,* in this affair, as in experimental prose, surprises are awaiting us. There will be exaggerated blossoms of sentiment. Decayed ideals of love. Pristine images. Tints of many books. Suicidal moods—tying things together.

Were you afraid the agony of this girl might infect you?

Yes, and it did, but I didn't know it. Not until—long, long after her death. My Berenice affair was about not repeating the same error. I slept with her to undo my past, to return Hostia's love.

I remember you, Sextus. Seated at the window of her room in a Roman brothel, you were writing *Cynthia,* a non–best-seller for battered wives. But it's the Hostia-Berenice tangle that touches me more than your rhymes. That vain replay of eros lost and regained—it has a Proustian quality. Here Egyptian totality—there hallucinations of smell, delusions of hearing, bromide and potassium and Valium.

Remain where you are, Propertius. I, your nightbird, I'll be kind to you. Together we'll fight your nausea, overcome the aroma of death, witness the start of a new day in the Sahara. The sun has risen and in the afternoon Berenice will be buried. But nothing can stop Euergetes's crimes. Here—see?—he's floating down the Nile where a row of temporary brothels has been erected along the shore, with the flower of Egyptian aristocracy performing as madams, their lingerie imported from Paris. This season the pharaoh is into boys. First castration, of course, then a mock wedding. Watch him, the old syphilitic, in his pink bridal dress, his silk crimson veil. The bleeding brides are carried into the marriage chapel on white sheets. Their screams arouse him—and speed up their end. At 8:00 P.M. the last bits of their flesh disappear between the teeth of the imperial beasts.

Forgive me for interrupting you, my bird. But there's one big secret and, perhaps, you can enlighten me. Why did Euergetes spare me and Berenice? We seem to be the only two white mice the cat didn't want to taste.

This mystery will keep future historians busy. He didn't kill you, he never spied on you. No one knocked at the door of his wife's bedroom when you slept with her. The moment you arrived in Egypt, he left her in peace. Is there a grain of goodness in every monster's heart? I doubt it. More likely, he considers you, a Latin poet translated into Egyptian, his only alibi on the day of judgment, which is at hand. The country is in ruin, no Roman money fund will raise it from the ground, and the pharaoh is a living corpse. He may not survive another summer. But even if he does, he's totally bankrupt. No, he can't pay his guards. Right, they'll assassinate him, soon. But you're free, Sextus. A messenger from heaven, I discharge you from your heavy duty. No, you don't have to record his last kicking. I'll do it, while you return home. Svevo cannot wait to have you back, and Ann's platonic love for you increases every day. Throw a last glance at your poor queen. Now it's time, go back to Rome.

Lotte stops, and hears Ann whisper: Thank God, he's coming home, the old family reunited.

Suddenly the room is filled with sighs. So Wolfgang gets up, and almost shouts: We promised ourselves not to indulge in mourning and self-pity! Well, Berenice is dead, but we're all happy about Propertius's return, and tonight our dear king is with us. Yes, this will be an unusually long evening, my sleepwalkers, but we must focus on *res politicae* again. The Afghan report was completed last week, and I don't want you, Shali, to wait until next Tuesday.

Why Afghanistan—out of all places? Isn't the sovereignty of small nations destroyed everywhere? May I remind you of my *Heart of Darkness?*

You may, Conrad, another day. Life is about coincidence. The Afghan affair has become Ann's personal nightmare, and later mine too. Why? Well, Ann, will you allow me to disclose the itching of our respective national skins? You will. Fine. Because of her background, Dr. Kar has perceived in the extermination of the Kashmir Sunnites—the plan of the late Soviets we want to abort—an analogy to the holocaust of the Polish Jews. Her reports from Peshawar touched me deeply. You may not be aware of it, Shali, but her compatriots were gassed in German ovens, so her equation worked for me too. Listening to Ann's list of horrors, I linked the tragic destiny of her and your people, King—poor, backward, remote—to the fate of Philemon and Baucis in my new play. The innocent ancient couple and their home, an old olive grove, are sacrificed on the altar of progress—killed by Mephisto in the name of a brave new world. But was the comparison correct? In our first talk about the Afghans, I asked Ann: A modern woman, how will you come to terms with the macho warriors of a wild land? Her answer, I must say, impressed me: When bloodhounds hunt my neighbor, Wolfgang, I have to forget that, as a matter of fact, he's an ass. In normal life I may prefer some people to others—vis-à-vis annihilation I can't. The life of an Abraham is worth as much as the life of an Ahmed. As it happened, the very same day I heard about the Afghan king-in-exile living a few streets away from our Institute. A week later I got in touch with you, Shali. We liked each other and soon became friends. One coincidence was helped by another. Fortune took our side. Mind you, our modest protests won't change history. But, perhaps, the worst isn't pain. It's much worse when suffering goes unnoticed. When we're hurt, we scream—in order to be heard. When we die, we want a stone with our name. Anonymity is the most terrible punishment. A silenced crime breaks our hope. On this note, my king, the floor is yours.

Ladies and gentlemen. It's an honor to be invited to a place where great minds debate the course of the world. Afghanistan is indeed a distant place, but it's not as primitive and barbaric as you may imagine it. Before I start with the sad tale of the Soviet invasion, I would like to give you a glimpse of my country by telling you a simple personal story. It happened around 1309 or 1310 our time. I suffered from arthritis and decided to get medical treatment in England. A day or two before my departure I visited the Industrial High School in Kabul. My joints were hurting and I walked around with difficulty. Soon I sat down in one of the studios and watched the pupils working. As Johann Wolfgang von Goethe hinted before, in Afghanistan women are and were discriminated against. From the Roman perspective I see that very clearly. But then it didn't occur to me that no girls attended the school. Today I find this obvious blindness on my part very strange, since one of my daughters is artistically very gifted. The peacock tails she paints are exquisite Oriental dreams. But let me not digress any further. As I said before, I sat in the studio without asking myself: Why are no girls here? A grave error. I should have improved the image of my country a long time ago.

Why have I not done this? Out of superstition and weakness. I counted myself among the enlightened Moslem intelligentsia, a small elite presiding over the uneducated masses. On the one hand I wanted to reform, on the other hand I was caught in the inertia to which the ruling class in the fourth world often succumbs. I tried to accommodate too many opposing interests, avoid antagonizing parties, keep the status quo. Of course, I didn't see it that way as long as I was in power. Then my weakness was combined with ruthlessness. To understand what I'm saying, you must remember that the old man I am now isn't the man I was then. After a quarter of a century in exile, I feel like an immortal talking to other immortals. Nothing matters anymore, we are gathered in limbo, and I can finally speak the truth. Under my rule Afghanistan was plagued by poverty and social injustice. There is no point in hiding this in your distinguished company. But at least my people lived in a splendid country of their own. Primitive, lazy, illiterate—they were a beautiful savage lot.

I am an old fool, I meander too much. Let me go back to the studio I mentioned before. There I was drawn to one boy in particular. Tiny and very dark, he was as agile as a young cat. His pencil was flying over the cheap brownish paper, the least expensive kind that I had distributed to art schools for free. Curious to see the boy's work, I wanted to get up and walk over to him. But the pain in my left foot made me stay where I was. However, the young teacher caught my glance and asked: Would you like to see Assudin's drawing?

Is that the name of the small boy with the enormous black eyes?

Yes. He's my most talented pupil. Quick as a mountain squirrel. Always the first. A slightly too agitated child. But what an eye for detail and color! Come here, Assudin.

The boy approached, holding his drawing. Not shy at all, he handed me the paper and watched me quietly. To my great surprise I discovered that the sketch represented myself. My back was bent, my left foot found itself in an awkward position as the tip of the sandal was resting on the right ankle. The likeness was striking, but what pleased me even more was the fact that he didn't flatter me. He depicted me tense and tired, with half-closed eyes. Each line of my face was distorted by pain, the curves of my body were drooping.

It's a remarkable drawing, Assudin. You managed to capture my arthritis.

What's that? he asked in a matter-of-fact voice.

An old-men illness. Could I buy your drawing? For a hundred gold coins?

Assudin didn't answer, and I saw that he was thinking. After a pause he replied: You can have it, I did it in five minutes. I have better drawings at home, but that's a quick one.

I thanked him, and proceeded to leave. But at the doorstep an idea came to my mind, and I said to the teacher: I would like you to commemorate the episode. Please arrange a ceremony, invite good pupils from other schools, and I'll have my son present Assudin with a hundred gold coins, to return the present he made me. Or I'll have the Minister of Culture give him the award.

After my return from Europe I inquired about Assudin's background and learned that his father was director of the Kabul museum, his mother a distinguished miniaturist specializing in flowers and birds. I asked her to be my daughter's private tutor, and she gladly accepted. Later, I helped the excellent lady to open a small private school of her own, the first art academy to be run by a woman. She and my wife became close friends, and a private channel of information on young Assudin was opened. Meanwhile he finished school but couldn't make a living as an artist, and I helped him to get the post of an assistant teacher in his own old school. When his father became sick, Assudin was assigned the job of museum deputy. I suggested it but soon realized that it was a shame to have him there. The work went against his vivacious temperament, and took too much of his time. In those days he developed a passion for the theater and started a small experimental · group in the suburbs of Kabul. This strange, surrealist place, mediating between the Moslem tradition and the European avant-garde, was our first modern stage. When foreigners visited Kabul, I told them about Assudin's theater, and everyone who attended his performances was amazed to find fresh, contemporary ideas in our city—beyond the limits of the civilized world. I had the Ministry of Culture back the small stage with grants, and it flourished. But once the theater established itself, Assudin got bored with it and moved on to other things. First I was disappointed, then I understood that he was an artist exploding with ideas, someone to start new ventures, not to cherish success. When I hinted at my disenchantment, he sent me a long letter. A single theater, he explained, wasn't enough in a country as enormous as ours. He wanted to start a grass-roots theatrical movement—educational theater, as he called it—organize groups all over Afghanistan, in schools and among workers, exploit a medium with great cultural potential. The stage, Assudin wrote, is a mirror. It helps us to see the world from a distance, to gain perspective, to overcome prejudice. It was a courageous letter, and I felt flattered by its tone. This excellent young artist trusted me—the ancient head of a torn country.

Soon Assudin's educational theater was on everybody's lips and the movement was spreading rapidly. But once the train was rolling, he jumped off. Inspired by an idea of mine, he traveled to Kandahar to paint historical sites and teach in two local art schools. When he returned and I saw his paintings, I wanted to buy them on the spot for my private collection. He smiled, and said: Buy all but one. Choose the picture you like best, and I am going to make you a gift of it. That's how our friendship started, that's how it should continue.

The money he got from me did not stay long with Assudin. A man with holes in his pockets, he was soon without a penny again, and had to take a job at the Post and Telecommunication Ministry. For three years he designed stamps. You may remember his most famous series, a set of twenty-four mountain plants and beasts shown against the sky. Yes, he engraved them all. But later he started to have problems with his eyes. My wife learned about it, and without asking me engaged him as our children's private art teacher. I wouldn't have dared to propose anything that humble to the great artist. But apparently she understood Assudin better than I did. Because of his chronic retinitis, a terrible ailment for a painter, he looked for *eine ruhige Kugel,* as Johann Wolfgang von Goethe would put it, not for a snowballing career. He accepted my wife's proposition and became the darling of our kids. But as soon as his eyesight improved I persuaded him to return to public life. It would have been a sin to keep our greatest artist for myself. The government appointed him principal of the school where he had graduated. A mistake. By then he had trouble with his heart and had to retire. For almost two years he couldn't work at all. Later he opened his own private school, a small venture, and taught a studio class at Kabul University.

Why am I telling you the life story of an Afghan artist? To bring my country a little bit closer to your hearts. Even distinguished scholars often have a distorted picture of our culture. They imagine us as wild tribes living in caves and huts, as religious fanatics fighting each other. All this exists, but other things exist as well. Under my rule we were a backwater with a very small intelligentsia. Yet modern minds were not completely absent from my land. There are Sunni and Sunni, as there are Catholics and Catholics. All religions are based on irrational faith, but you can either harden or soften the edges of your belief. Besides, each religion is also a way of life, and when times are good, it amounts to little more than a local tradition. I and my wife, we considered ourselves moderates—attached to the past, yet ready to move forward. Such attitudes were not widespread, but slowly they were gaining ground. Besides, I didn't believe in rushing things too much. Perhaps I was wrong. A weak, inefficient monarch, I was terrified by speeding up. The quicker you rush, the sooner you find yourself in the arms of death. Alas, the same may happen when you slow down, especially when a strong neighbor spins intrigues behind your back. While I reformed my country bit by bit, the Soviets invaded it.

In no time rationality collapsed, fervor surfaced, and soon we relapsed into savagery—for bad and good. Please see the paradox. Had my people been less archaic, there would have been less bloodshed—but more cowardliness and treason. In other countries the Soviets had more collaborators than in Afghanistan. Why? Simpleminded, my countrymen weren't familiar with the language of compromise so many intellectuals spoke fluently—in East Berlin or Prague. *Kein Nachteil, der nicht zum Vorteil werden kann,* you're absolutely right, Johann Wolfgang von Goethe. Under normal circumstances civilization is a big advantage, but in a state of siege—not at all. In the industrialized Czechoslovakia more people supported the Soviets than in the rural Poland, or in the wilderness of Afghanistan. The old concepts of faith and honor can work miracles.

But let me return to Assudin. In the fourth year of my exile, he escaped to Pakistan with his wife and two children, and joined me in Rome. He had changed so much that I hardly recognized him. We embraced, sat down, and couldn't utter a word for a long time. Then he began telling me what he had been through on his way from Kabul. He started in the late afternoon, stopped after sunrise—his voice almost inaudible by then. No, I don't want to burden you with the horrors he shared with me that night, but there's something I must mention. Antipersonnel mines, destined to attract children, and which come down from the sky in the shape of a kid's dream: a red plastic pen, a small blue truck, a doll, a miniature airplane. As the toys are picked up, tiny hands and arms are blown off.

No, most children aren't killed on the spot. Suffering from atrocious pain, they keep crying for days. With hardly any medication available, they perish slowly from gangrene, staphylococcus, the gram-negative septicemia. Their pain breaks people's hearts and fills them with unspeakable hatred. Who can bear to see one's offspring die that way? And think of the survivors, the girls and boys without feet, fingers, toes, noses. They are the living monuments to inhumanity.

I must beg your pardon for mentioning children. It's a cynical device politicians like to use. If you want to demonize your enemy, you accuse him of harming kids. It's a dirty trick to play this card, but you must help me to stop the crime. One day the war will come to an end, but the mass of cripples will remain. How will they earn their living? Who will take care of them? It's better to be dead than to survive such a terrible experiment.

Our children's *via crucis* takes away my sleep. You may consider this a sign of dwindling intelligence. But Johann Wolfgang von Goethe invited me here to make you understand what's going on not only in my country, but in the whole world. Small backward nations are endangered everywhere. We're the Indians of today. We're Philemon and Baucis. Our humble abodes are set on fire by new Fausts, and with us plants and animals go up in flames. If you don't protest, tomorrow Afghanistan will be processed into a missile site, the Pashtuns will become an extinct race.

For many days I talked over with myself the contents of this lecture. But the death of Malcolm Lowry, such a promising author, the end of the queen of Egypt, a lady famous even in heaven, and the shattering letter from Propertius, the greatest Roman poet, all this confused me. So I abandoned the prepared text in favor of personal recollections, and recalled Assudin. Then, troubled by my incompetence, I felt obliged to address general questions, but remembered our children. Finally my thoughts jumped to *Faust,* the greatest tragedy of modern times. Now I beg you: forgive me my incoherence. In a few days there will be another anniversary of Afghanistan's invasion. Action is needed. Ladies and gentlemen! Hear the appeal of a feebleminded king who lost the text of his speech—and his kingdom.

THE DEATH OF BERENICE releases a flood. Poems tumble from Sextus's pen, fall onto papyrus, sprout. Love lyrics mix with epitaphs for Hostia, Berenice, Karenina. An elegy describes how, returning late from a revel, he watches Cynthia and the queen of Egypt sleep in the same bed. A sonnet apostrophizes his regret for having rashly parted from his mistresses to start a voyage full of sadness. A stornello epitomizes the grace of love in solitude. Elaborate rhymes reflect the kaleidoscopic changes of Sextus's moods and make me realize that only a genuine lover can be a great erotic poet, Svevo remarks to Ann.

It's good he's back with us, and less depressed than usual. His affection for Berenice washed away the guilt he had suffered since Hostia's death.

Yes, he behaved admirably towards the queen.

Who had no breasts and was married to a monster. But isn't their sex life just legend, sponsored in part by our sympathy for the fabulous couple? Did Sextus really sleep with Berenice?

No one was present at the remarkable event, but he confirmed it in a conversation we had after his return from Egypt. Why should he lie?

To come close to his intention at least in words. To convince himself that he wasn't put off by the decrepitude of her flesh. Wouldn't we all like to be cured of physical revulsion vis-à-vis the beautiful souls we adore? To have a crush on them—rather than on a suntanned jogger, a big-bosomed goose? I suspect that Sextus may be telling us what he would prefer to be the truth—and what we prefer to hear too.

But there are also hints in Berenice's letters.

She had even more reason to mislead herself—and the world. Sextus's return to Egypt proved how much she counted in his life. And in her life no man counted more than Propertius. Each of them wished to accommodate the other. Yet he confessed to me that he had problems with his libido—while Berenice burnt for him with menopausal passion. Not the best combination, you must admit, for accomplishing something in sex. My doubts, Italo, come from personal experience. I once agonized for a man who honestly tried to respond to my fire. But in the end he was extinguished by it.

Didn't Sextus write: Strong love overleaps the very shores of doom?

In *Dichtung*—perhaps. In *Wahrheit*—no, my friend. I recall how I could never go to bed with a certain breed of men—brilliant, witty, affectionate. Yet their sagging bellies, fat behinds, and flat feet assumed a greater presence than all their virtues together. Their inner splendor lost against my physical disgust. Love is difficult, but sex is the final test. The tiniest chemical imbalance disturbs the fragile instant of coincidence. But let me not question anymore Sextus's last affair. Even if he didn't succeed in it, his poems to Berenice are a triumph. Last night, before falling asleep, I reread them.

We sleep with men?

We sleep with many women. Bodies are close, and lips, they are at hand. But words leave us, and reveries, they end. In dust and death, in bones turning to sand. If I die before you, Italo, I oblige you to have these lines engraved on my stele.

I want on mine: *See, crowned with flowers my bark has gained the port. The shifting sands are crossed, the anchor cast. Tired with long tossing I revive at last.*

That's more appropriate for a sailor, a Conrad or Lowry. For you, Italo, I have something better: *So now with tears among the dead the wounds of love and life we heal: and—leaving, ah, how much unsaid!—thy treacheries I conceal.*

The treacheries of Angiolina.

And other women as well. Eros is the only subject that never tires you. Any pretext is good enough to pay lip service to it.

Add death to it, Ann. Apropos, what did you think of the Afghan king's appearance?

It confused me. The rulers of the third world—we never quite trust them. But I watched him closely, and he seemed fairly sincere. Of course, the kids brought tears to my eyes. I wonder: is Afghanistan a lost cause?

For him—yes. He's so frail. Anyhow, no political solution can resurrect the dead, restore his country's savage serenity. Do you think there's a grain of truth in this story of his protégé, the painter? Or was it invented to prove that Afghanistan had been a civilized place?

Oh, no, it's true. Didn't I tell you about my encounter with Assudin? A remarkable character! I even reported about him in the *Manhattan Man*. The king, I think, is basically decent. He can't win or lose anything anymore.

Something else, Ann. All these days I have been gathering my guts to talk to you about Carol.

My poor crazy, what about her?

Goethe should pull himself together and do something for Carol. Arrange for an exhibit, dedicate an evening to her readings. We want her work to survive, don't we? Once he backs her with his authority, *Signora Eternità* will gladly embrace your genius stepsister.

She has been on my mind too, Italo. She and her failures. Her gift for pursuing too many things at once, and selecting the most unsuitable objects of desire. She wasn't satisfied with the schizophrenia of being bilingual, she had to become trilingual and compose her testament in American, a tongue she had acquired two seconds before her death. Her mind reminds me of an exclusive sanatorium where nobody answers the phone, but the phone keeps ringing. Her body is a wasted estate, a cherry orchard awaiting the cutters. Her psyche—a pack of lies. The more she fooled other people, the more she was getting out of her own hand.

Lies replace the terrors of existence.

But her drive to improve life through fiction spoilt everything. She opened strange vistas to middle-road types, and they judged her mad. Her ability to be seduced by a Leonardesque smile of some mustached guy was a serious sickness. Even her health was ruled by the need for grand effects. Whenever she had a common cold, it had to turn into a pathetic pneumonia. She dramatized the meaningless, overlooked the grave, panicked about the banal, and revealed what nobody ever wants to see: subtleties of soul, spells of metaphysical dizziness, tachycardia of eroticism. Fighting all conventions, she threw herself into the worst stereotype, her own mania, a little bit like Simone.

Did they know each other?

No, thank God. Imagine how Carol and Simone would have gotten on each other's nerves.

You're getting harder and harder on your sister, Ann. As if you couldn't forgive that she killed herself.

Suicide cannot be forgiven, and I'm angry because I keep blaming myself. There was a side to Carol that I should have cultivated—cheerfulness. Perhaps it would have saved her. She could be sweet as a cherub, expected no return for her affection.

Yes, she was a rare plant. No greed in her soul.

How do you know? You never met Carol.

I'm about to reveal a secret, Ann. I did meet her.

Where? You never went to America. Carol never came to Italy.

She did—to see Eglizer at the Algebra Center in Trieste.

To see Karl?

She must have been in despair, although then I didn't realize it, in need of advice and consolation. She came to Trieste a month before her death.

You amaze me, Italo.

Believe me, Ann, I'm still amazed myself. The *Blitzkrieg* of it all. She phoned me at my office, and said: I copied your number from my sister's address book. My name is Carol Kar, tomorrow I fly back to New York. Would you like to have dinner with me? I was engaged, but something in her voice compelled me to say: I'd be delighted, as if I had sensed that it's tonight—or never.

Where did you meet?

At the Pizzeria Magris in the Via Poliphilo. We shared a calzone, and afterwards I invited her for a cappuccino at the Mito Absburgico, opposite the railroad station. During dinner she didn't say a word, just looked at me with a curious smile. It rendered her mouth asymmetrical, and made me remark: Unlike Ann, you aren't a *gatto parlante,* Carol. Are you a sphinx? No, she replied, I'm a kangaroo, and your Australian isn't good enough. I laughed, and my eyes encountered hers. She relaxed, and began to talk: Now I'll imitate Ann, Italo, chat about God and the world, and ask you a question: Do you know why I'm here? Without waiting for my reply, she whispered: Because Trieste is the nearest place to the *lontano da dove* to which all Jews are on their way. I didn't understand, but didn't dare to inquire either. And I still have no idea what she meant.

The old Polish joke about two Jews meeting in Paris. Where are you emigrating? one asks. To Uruguay, the other replies. That far! Far from where? Ha, ha, ha, ha. But I'm dying to hear what happened after the coffee. Did you guys end up in bed?

We did. Don't you see how my ears turn red? What a night! It cannot be compared to anything I have experienced so far. Perhaps only someone ready to die can make love without any ulterior motive. All my life I have been allergic to the way women open accounts with men, the investment banker's attitude they assume in sex affairs, their subtle hints that they take a risk—and expect to earn interest. Sure, they act out of an instinct for self-preservation, which I couldn't detect in Carol. This both delighted and frightened me. Because of my own residue of selflessness, I revere such characters as your sister. But more in theory than in reality. Had I not known about her imminent departure, I would have been scared to death by her giving herself to me—a stranger—with such passion. In the morning I drove her to the airport and, like a true hypocrite, pretended to regret her going away. But Carol must have known better. She didn't respond to my assurances, her lips were sealed all the way to Marco Polo. There wasn't much traffic on the road and we arrived too early, only to learn that the flight wouldn't take off until the late afternoon. Do you want to see Venice?

I asked Carol. She smiled: Aren't you busy, Italo? No, I lied, for you I have always time. *Non vero,* but well said. Oh you Italians, the constant *cavalieri.* Since you offer, let's go. After all it's my first visit to the Queen of the Sea—and my last.

Why last? My voice must have sounded alarmed. Never mind, Carol replied, it's just a figure of speech. I like oppositions and play with them all the time.

In this case we should visit the *ghetto nuovo*—the oldest ghetto of Venice and Europe.

Are you Jewish, Italo?

Wie es das gnädige Fräulein wünschen. I'm either Italo *der Schwabe,* or Ettore Schmitz, *Italiano.*

Hector Svabenius sounds best, Carol smiled and kissed me on my neck. A little kiss, and yet a climax. There's so much cheap glitter in the world, Ann, but in Carol's eyes there was fire. Her mouth was hot and dry, the hand she pressed into my palm was ice, and her words—a complete surprise: I'm glad we met, Italo, but I'm equally glad we part tonight. I'm too tired to test your feelings for me, my feelings for you. Today's enchantment will dissolve into tomorrow's regret. But until the afternoon we will stick together and pretend to be a perfect pair of Jewish honeymooners. Yes, we have eaten bread from many ovens, and know that the taste depends on the state of the stomach. When you're starving, the bread is always good. On this note, Italo, lead your eighteen-hour-old love to the New Ghetto, and wed her—under the gaze of our absent God—in an empty synagogue.

Carol paused, and the fire in her eyes burnt out. In an instant her pupils lost their brilliance, became dumb and flat. She fantasizes, flashed through my mind, but why shouldn't she? She pays no attention to her changing exterior. Beautiful women, Ann, have a tendency to carry themselves as if they were shop windows, and we—their clients. In your twin there wasn't a trace of that.

She wasn't beautiful.

That morning I found her a Garbo. Her gray eyes occupied half of her face, her skin glowed, her auburn curls shone like copper.

Like me, Carol applied henna to her scalp.

Still, Ann, I was totally taken with her. Animated, light, rapid, she transcended the territory of femaleness by ignoring the rules of exchange men and women have imposed on themselves. All eagerness and speed, she didn't calculate anything.

What a eulogy! You crush Carol with praise. It's good you spent only one night and half a day with her. I assure you, Italo, a healthy portion of egoism was stashed away behind her exquisite façade. In spite of her vulnerability, she managed to survive for quite a while, having an apartment, money, men who took care of her, and a few friends dedicated to her as to a saint. You depict her as a young girl, but when you met, she was middle-aged. And so were you, Italo.

Believe me, Ann, that day we were youngsters again. We married each other in the oldest synagogue in the New Ghetto, ate *pasta Alfredo* and *gelato al cioccolato e pistacchio,* embraced at every corner. When at 4:45 I brought Carol to the airport, your sister said: *Svabianus Svetonius Tranquillus,* see you next year! Not in Jerusalem. In heaven!

Why didn't you prevent her from returning to New York? Had she stayed with you, she would be still alive!

I told you, Ann, I was in ecstasy, but afraid at the same time. You know the *Angsthase* I am. Carol seemed like an exotic bird. And who was I? An author so unsuccessful that he had gone into banking. The failure of an *amante.* A man given over to growing old. I had nothing to offer to a distinguished New York artist, a striking woman full of life.

You should have listened to Carol's suggestions.

I assumed she was just depressed, like myself, like you, like most people in the world.

Did she mention to you the man who rejected her?

No, but at the end of our mock marriage, she murmured something that sounded like a Slavic name.

Myloslav?

Perhaps. She said: God accept me as the spouse of the Italian nobleman *Tranquillus Hector Suetonius Svevo,* and added in a whisper: *Miloslavus.*

What *pech,* Italo! You really should have married her. Instead you let her return to a man she should never have met. At the brink of impotence, he inflamed my stubborn sister by assigning her one night a week—and falling off her straight into snoring. When she first told me the story, I imagined him plump and sallow, I hated him. Well, he ruined my sister's life without even realizing it.

Did he really? Then he must have possessed some appeal. My own experience with Carol makes me think that she was a specialist in scaring away ordinary guys. A stodgy bulldog wouldn't have been able to attract—and kill her.

You're right, Italo, I transfer to him my own guilt.

What guilt, Ann?

I deserted her when she needed me most, came to Rome when she was about to slip, and let her fall. When I recall it, my heart breaks—and indicates Myloslav. But he isn't much of a suspect. Only hints can be found between Carol's lines, and she mentioned only once that she fell in love with a man who didn't return her feelings—in a letter from the Public Library. Want to listen to it? I know it by heart.

Dear Ann, I'm researching for you the Christ-Veronica relationship, our mutual venture, but it's a man who occupies my mind on a twenty-four-hour basis, a man who doesn't even grant me the pleasure of calling him *lover,* and who refers to me as his *erotic friend*—one of his many females, not his mistress. Imagine, he has divided us into three groups: erotic, ex-erotic, non-erotic, and keeps the sword dangling over our heads. First thing in the morning I ask myself: Are you still in the first division, or have you been downgraded to the second? I presume he isn't even aware of his cruelty. He just intends to prevent me from assuming the special role I desire to play in his life. So he makes me a number he can cross out any time.

Poor Carol! How could she put up with him?

Worse. The less the guy cared for her, the more Carol longed for him. Finding no release, her passion grew into a disease, and a nervous fever began to consume her.

I need neither food nor sleep anymore, Carol continued in her letter. I run through Manhattan, a madwoman ready to be run down by a car. The pride I used to treasure so much in the past has evaporated. My entire being is reduced to a single wish: to see him, touch him. I cannot describe the high-pitched pain that tortures me. No word to render the penultimate states of my inner dissolution. Every cell hurts. Nothing provides consolation. I'm at once inside and outside of myself. A sparrow trembling in his hand, I'm hungry and thirsty, yet he fails to feed me properly. My senses are confused, and I'm split in two. While Anna throws herself under a train, Simone watches her end in slow motion. Every day the shores of the Hudson attract us more and more. Waves whisper promises. Oh Ann, help me unify again, clarify my mind, tell me to relax, explain to me that Myloslav is just a man whom I should abandon. Sister, stop the annihilation of my brain! I cannot eat, cannot sleep, I burn. For God's sake, Ann, keep the endless succession of accidents away from me. Don't you see? Your twin's body is covered with dotted lines and arrows—indicating where I'll be cut and sewn. Soon.

I can't bear it, Ann. Had I known, I would have made every effort to keep her in Trieste. But what role did Eglizer play in all that?

He was Carol's first lover—and her best friend. His dedication wasn't of this world. For twenty years he phoned her every day, wrote to her daily. She must have flown to Trieste to seek his advice, but I doubt if she was able to confess her trouble. She was so proud, and she would have hated to hurt Karl.

What a tangle of a life! What a trap! A few days after her departure Carol sent me *Explorations,* a Chicago magazine, with a brief note saying: Look for my contribution. It will provide you with more information about the fool you married in the *ghetto nuovo.* Read it carefully, and don't regret her absence. Isn't it strange? Yesterday I found a Xerox copy of her text, and put it into my pocket. Today I wanted to read it to you at the very beginning, but our conversation developed away from it.

Read it now.

Shall I? No, it has no title. Out of breath, I run through Central Park to his place, run against a rock, a tree trunk, a balustrade. My body is bruised all over. Yesterday I fell from the staircase. Before yesterday I cut my finger. But don't mention it, I admonish myself, prepare for the split second he's ready to share with you. Soon you'll sit on the couch, touch his skin, kiss his knees. But you must be inconspicuous. He's going out. Let him take a shower, wait for the moment he comes out of the bathroom, naked. Look at him, multiplying every second. Have time dissolve on your tongue. As long as you're alive, not everything is lost. People fall in and out of love. Pray to God to make him go for you one day. But right now don't disturb him. Let your eyes glide about the ordinary surface of a body that delights you so much. He's growing old and fat. Look and remember. He puts on black corduroy pants, a white designer shirt, violet socks. Soak in the familiar colors and forms. Savor the texture. Next year, when the birthday club meets to celebrate his fiftieth birthday, you'll toast angels and laugh with them about the low life you led on earth.

Shall I go on, Ann?

Yes. It's the story of a cockroach motel: you check in, but don't check out.

I watch him, and the spasm subsides. If I could fix my eyes on him permanently, I would suffer less. But the painkiller of his presence will be withdrawn from me in three minutes. He's getting ready for a cocktail party or a business dinner, a ball or a date. Whatever. It's his imminent absence that is a mortal threat. Still, I have enough common sense to recognize that my agony means to him less than a drink. If he had to choose between a glass of champagne and my life, he would sip from the glass. There is no better armor than indifference! A gift from heaven, it fuels my hell. We descend the staircase of his brownstone together, but he keeps at a safe distance and avoids touching me—in order to get rid of me as quickly as possible. When he's in good spirits, he may treat me as a queen. But right now I'm just a pawn, one of ten, and the first to be sacrificed. He is silent, but his eyes tell me: in this city of gays, girls aren't in short supply. When I'm tired of one, I drop her for another. So don't bore me, Carol. Hi. He hits hard and heads for the subway, while a bell rings in my head: shallow is the grave wherein you'll be laid.

CROSSING FROM AVENTINE TO PALATINE, ITALO AND ANN stop to contemplate the hills that support Rome, masses of tufa and conglomerated sand and ash thrown by neighboring volcanoes, now extinct but active until the very recent past. How crystalline the contours of the Alban hills are, Svevo remarks, pressing Ann's hand. Apparently traces of human life were found under the great flood of lava that had issued from the Alban hills and flowed towards the site of Rome, stopping only about three miles short of it, near the tomb of Cecilia Metella. Last Sunday Wolfgang and Lotte went there on an archeological hike, looking for broken pottery and bronze implements, but she strained her Achilles tendon and he had to pay three peasants to carry his corpulent companion to the carriage.

Unverbesserlicher Wolf, interested in everything, and Lotte pays the bills.

I love the sight of the hills in late fall, when outlines are diffused by haze. The old volcanoes rise like islands from a red sea of leaves. No, he isn't discouraged by Lotte's accident, but plans to explore, as soon as she is recovered, the remains of an ancient sea beach, conspicuous in part by its fine golden sand and its deposits of white potter's clay. Because of its yellow sand the Janiculan was once known as the Golden Mount, a name which survives in the church we visited last week.

San Pietro in Montorio?

Yes. Do you remember how beautifully it's situated? On hard lime-stone rock, at the edge of a crater. The old capital is a collection of volcanoes pulsating in our blood. A bunch of crazy authors, we were right to select Rome for our sojourn.

Perhaps, but it's a little sad. We sift through prehistoric dust, walk on water-worn pebbles, discuss chips of limestone rock that have formed a conglomeration bound together by volcanic ash, a sort of natural cement, or the shower of red-hot ashes that fell on a thickly growing forest and converted the burning wood, partly smothered by heat, into charcoal, or the charm of the tufa rock.

Apropos: in the valley I explored with Simone some years ago, the charred branches of trees, their forms well preserved, could be easily distinguished. Do you recall how I took her pictures there?

Yes, we begged her to stand on the wall of Romulus and to remove her glasses. While she was wiping them, the serenity of her unmasked face was suddenly revealed. She smiled at us, and shouted: It's tufa mixed with charred wood. Meanwhile I picked a piece of olive branch and gave it to her. She began to examine it, and you shot a whole roll of film, some of the best photos of her. On the way back we let her talk about the physical changes in the site of Rome since the first dawn of history, do you recall? The Forum Romanum, the Valbrum, the great Campus Martius and other valleys were once impassable marshes and pools of water, Simone lectured. Gradually they were drained by means of the great *cloacae,* the earliest architectural works of Rome.

Apropos, Carol's last lover was an architect.

Here we go! Now I understand better. Every profession deforms the body and the soul. Dentists suffer from stiff necks and dream of the *vaginae dentatae.* Architects confuse the foundations of a house with the fountain of life, interior decoration with essence, craftsmanship with inspiration. They suffer from the force of gravity, adore solidity, are obsessed with the concrete—the pure carbonate of lime which cannot be penetrated, as it prevents water from running through it. Their homes imitate igloos and are conceived as frozen snowshells, to shelter and cool the soft hot core of desire and regret. Oh the architects, a species in itself! How they mistrust the transient brilliance of quicksilver, whistle tunes, but forget the composers' names. Like beavers, they barricade themselves against the river of time, cement veins, block bloodstreams with mortar, stop flux with heaps of stone. Fearing the ephemeral, they dispute the existence of eruptions and earthquakes, disbelieve that the self resembles a volcano, refuse to read Lowry. Their efforts to line the aqueducts of nerves with pounded brick are proverbial. They reinforce skin with three to four coats of stucco, surround the heart with a balustrade of artificial marble, adjust the moldings of the lungs. At night, sleepless architects count bones and wall off the soul in ever tighter niches of plaster or porphyry, the red basalt that abounds in the vicinity of Berenice. Oh, the architects! They respond to deliria with descriptions of pavements, pacify eros, drive sex into a terra-cotta statuette of a putto they suspend from a nail, prefer meatballs and beer to ambrosia and elixir, divide the mind into closets and shelves, separate surfaces and cells, seal off the vacuum they wish to fill. Still, I'm taken with their down-to-earth charm as gourmets, good dancers, sonny boys, womanizers. More, I'm delighted by the way they react to metaphysical subjects. Heaven is high, I say, and they ask: How many floors up? Evil is deep. Indeed, how many wine cellars down? They dismiss what cannot be measured and depict themselves as middle-of-the-road blocks, fitting smoothly everywhere. But they remain in between, fit nowhere, bypass one haven after another, suffer from their own brand of schizophrenia, turn sour.

Miss the affection of a Carol—again and again.

I MADE THE WRONG IMPRESSION, the Afghan ex-king keeps repeating. I shouldn't have strayed from the prepared text you helped me compose. I should have avoided all sentimental rubbish. A nuisance, a senile fool, how can I negotiate a solution? I don't have my brains together, I have grown too old, Assudin. An idiot of a monarch, I lose control of myself, confess my grief to strangers, ask them to pity me, to mourn with me. Instead of requesting that they press for political settlement, I cry in front of Europe's crème de la crème like a widowed cock.

Clouds part and a sunray penetrates Assudin's studio. Calm down, Shali, the painter says. Goethe phoned me yesterday. He was very impressed with your talk. Really, he wept while you spoke, spent a sleepless night. Yes, he'll raise the Afghan issue all over the world, organize an American lecture tour for Voronskoy, the ex-KGB—better known as the ex-lover of Karenina, yes, he changed his name after her death—who has just arrived in Rome via Pakistan, with his own tale of horror and guilt. Calm down, Shali, stop moving your head. I have to study your nose for a minute. In the late November light your face looks exquisite, all the beauty of our race is subsumed in it. It was an excellent idea to have your portrait painted against the vista of Peshawar. The night you talked at the Institute, I finished the background—the horseshoe ring of hills, their contours softened by the foggy October air. I sketched the city from memory, as I saw it the morning we arrived on the outskirts of Peshawar, after our long march from Kabul. We were completely worn out, but at the same time, exhilarated. The children sang: We made it! we made it! And I hallucinated, catching before me a fata morgana of the city as it had looked on my first visit there. When I was six my uncle—the last *povindah* in our family, a splendid man of thirty-five, his profile as fine as that of a mountain bird—stopped with his caravan at our home in Kabul on his way from Samarkand. He headed for the fall market in Peshawar, transporting innumerable treasures, gold threads and glass pearls, carpets, silks, embroideries. A sack of gems was unloaded, and he allowed me to take a handful. Each stone shimmered with another hue, and I ordered them on the floor according to size and color, starting with the largest and brightest ones. Unable to part with the jewels, all day I rearranged them into ever-new patterns. My parents didn't intervene, but in the evening Father came in, and asked: Would you like to accompany your uncle to Peshawar? He's leaving tomorrow morning and wouldn't mind taking you with him.

I couldn't utter a word, but happiness illuminated my face. Pack your things and go to bed, Father said. I nodded, and rushed to my room. That's how that memorable autumn of my life began. A small basket was attached to the side of my uncle's camel, and I, wrapped in a woolen blanket, was inserted into it. During the journey I felt slightly seasick. The world moved up and down, like a wave crossing an ocean.

Oh, the peculiar feeling a kid has on top of a camel, a sort of a walking mountain. No, it's even more pronounced. My first trip, at three—I'll never forget it—was like traveling in the sky, flying above the Himalayas on an enchanted carpet.

Before reaching Peshawar we stopped at several smaller markets, each packed with people and goods. Everywhere tea with milk was boiled in huge caldrons, and I drank it out of my own silver cup, attached to my embroidered belt. What a pleasure to sip slowly a hot, sweet drink, warming the palms, trying not to burn one's tongue. The youngest of all the traveling merchants, I was greeted everywhere as an honorary *povindah* and allowed to touch the finest silks, play with ornamented silver knives. While the crowd buzzed around, I overheard conversations in which the word *British* frequently occurred, and I asked my uncle what it meant. Foreigners, he replied, they have occupied our country. But we will regain it. The *povindahs* spoke of crossroads, China, silk routes, and other things I didn't understand. They mentioned the emperor Alexander who climbed the mountains with his caravan a long time ago, leaving behind a greater distance than that between Kabul and Peshawar.

How long were you on the road?

I couldn't tell. But we arrived at the outskirts of the city on an early October morning. The sun was rising, the air was misty and moist. Suddenly the fog parted, like a curtain, and the necks of minarets, the white and golden domes appeared in front of us. It's Peshawar, Uncle said, let us stop and look. He took me out of my basket and put me on his lap. I had awakened only a few minutes earlier and was blinded by the sun. As it ascended, colors intensified. Am I dreaming? I asked. No, you're awake, Uncle replied. We have reached the most exquisite town on earth, the goal of our journey. Peshawar lies within a ring of hills that have the form of a horseshoe, Uncle said, smoothing my hair. See the mosques? Don't they shine like white and golden eggs in a large basket? Silent and serious, I bowed my head, like an adult, and he shouted: Let's move, the heat is increasing. We descended to the city, a huddle of flat-roofed houses and dusty streets. Don't fiddle with your feet, Shali, I want to finish your silhouette.

You should have painted yourself, a six-year-old, seated on a camel. You were such a beautiful boy, with huge black eyes. Eyes like stars. My wrinkled face isn't worth the time of our greatest living artist. If you don't want to portray yourself, paint compositions like the one you presented me with last week. It's hanging in front of my bed, and I can see it before falling asleep and after awakening. It's the most significant picture you have ever done, a masterwork epitomizing our tragedy. The dirty page from the Koran, the vase of flowers, the apparition of a face made from parts of a plant, cracks in the wall—everything conveys the sense of condensed mourning that transcends the ugly melancholia to which we humans succumb. Your painting will appeal to people unaware of the Afghan war a thousand years from now. It's strong, very strong, even though it goes against our tradition of ornaments and words. No, I don't pay you compliments, I quote. Yesterday Moses Maimonides visited me. An old Jewish scholar, trained in abstraction, he isn't particularly interested in realist art. But your picture touched him, and he inquired: Who's the artist? It's an old master, that much I can see.

Assudin.

Assudin, Moses repeated, took a notebook out of his pocket, and wrote down your name in Arabic. Seeing that he's as fluent in our language as he is in Hebrew, I congratulated him. But he replied:

Congratulate Assudin. Art isn't my cup of tea, but I'm drawn to this canvas—with its strange suspense of light and time. It reminds me of a Dutch painter of women with letters in their hands, pearls around their necks. Sad and a little sick, they're stuck in their existence, a drama in yellow and blue.

M Y DEARS, GOETHE ADDRESSES THE INSTITUTE, another Tuesday, another death. Shall we rename our place the Exit? You have a better word, Svevo?
STGM? What's that?
Sic transit gloria mundi.
Excellent. We should have new stationery printed, with STGM on top, followed by our ex-co-Fellows' initials and crosses.
Stop it, Wolf, I cannot bear your jokes.
Dein Wunsch ist mir Befehl, Lotte. I'm going to start with the letter from Nadia, smuggled out of Leningrad, and then proceed to Osia's epistle, exported in violation of the customs laws from Woodchuck Penal Colony, Vladivostok District.
Wouldn't it be better if I read Nadia's letter?
You wish, I obey. Go ahead.
Mandelshtam is dead. Maybe Rome can write a requiem for him. I can't. The best minds of my generation go down the drain, and I wonder: how can I recover the memory of friends whose integrity was stronger than their sense of fear, who could live through horror without giving themselves away? There is nothing more beautiful than speaking with the dead whose words we know by heart, whose texts we admire. It's like going to a sanatorium where nothing is expected of us but to get better, or with old friends to the south—in order to acknowledge the perfect proportions of the Greek temples in Agrigento.
Today an unknown man brought me Osia's left glove and the unconfirmed news that my husband is dead. I asked him about the right glove but he didn't answer. He suggested Osia might have lost it while chopping wood. Now the man has left, and Osia's right hand has turned blue. I must confess that it's not his death but that business with the glove that makes me ill. The cold will damage his right hand and he won't be able to hold a pencil. That might interrupt our communication.
Anyhow, Mandelshtam is dead, enveloped in a warm snow-shroud, a clean swaddling cloth. Crows kiss him with their beaks and the wind

rocks him to sleep. But Osia is prevented from a sound rest by an avalanche of images. He dreams of you, his beloved vain co-Fellows, and of women: the Hebrew widow in Lausanne, Olga in Rome, and Karenina, with whom he apparently had a tête-à-tête on the eve of World War I. They sailed together to Byzantium and on his way Osip wrote ten sonnets to her as *Santa Sofia,* but entrusted them to me. He crossed so many black and red female seas—to fall asleep all by himself in an ice ocean. The snow is heavy with lice, and Mandelshtam scratches himself all the time, his frozen skin turning inside out. In the pine trees phones ring, the Underwood types, and crows, our faithful comrades, carry the napkin imprinted with Osia's right hand to a Central Committee plenary meeting. Aha, now his rightist deviation is certified.

Hallo, it's five o'clock, here's Nadia. May I lie at your side, touch you? No, I'm not your mistress, I'm your wife. You don't have to pay attention to me. No, I won't disturb you, I know my place. I'm the ironing board in the corner, but my lungs breathe. I'm still alive. No, I'm not an Aphrodite, but my mouth is shaped into the smile of a Mona Lisa. We are in Florence, Osia, and my pretty left hand balances a rose you bought for me but passed over to Olga. No, I don't mind. What a lovely woodchuck you are, Osia! Your tail forms a third of your body, your back is overgrown with brownish black fur. Your nose, chin, cheeks, and throat are whitish, and the underparts glow like a chestnut. An *arcotyms monax,* you're a real monk and a burrower, hidden in the deepest hole. Today you chop trees, tomorrow I chop corpses, but on *shabbos,* when the air tastes like vanilla ice, we stuff ourselves with heavy cream at the Odessa embankment. *Schlagobers, bitte sehr,* says the *Obers,* a Volga German of Austrian descent. The sun is black, your *panta rei* poems swim better than swordfish, and we chat about Propertius and Hostia, boating on the Yangtze. A boy releases a Chinese kite, my henna-colored hair falls out. Cha, cha, cha.

You have gone with Olga to Hawaii, you dance with her at a beach café. And at night, well, at night you make love to her. But the fan, my dear, your gift to her, has returned to my right hand, and I balance it now, while the fingers of my left are hurt by the rose you plucked in Florence or somewhere else, for somebody else. It's over, Osia. Stop scratching yourself! You're Russia's greatest poet and I, your unattractive widow, am alive. The hole they dig for you is the right size. You'll fit into it just fine. Now go to sleep. Snore and hibernate. Hibernate and snore. Everything you wrote was smuggled out. Nothing was lost, with the exception of your life. I can't tell you how happy I am that we won. What? A glove, plus a fur coat. Now that you're dead and I'm alive, I wear both. Adieu.

Lotte's hands shake in the silent room. In the orchard the *Ostwind* embraces naked cherry trees. Sextus takes the letter from her, clears his throat, and mumbles to Goethe: Why don't you go down and make tea for our Institute's secretary, while I continue with the letter from Osia.

Distinguished Vanity Members. I'm dead and hope this good news will reach you soon. In respect to my postmortem career I rely in particular on Jossif, our youngest guard. There is a chance that he'll smuggle out my last will, since he adores the Holy Virgin more than Godfather Joseph. Before my death a few disasters occurred. I lost my right glove and, in consequence, my hand was damaged and I couldn't write. But it's all forgotten. Now I'm pure spirit and don't need hands, pencils, papers. What I invent in my middle-aged head is immediately impressed on ethereal membranes. It's almost too easy, and the verses I turn out in limbo aren't great. In fact, they are fairly banal. I seem to suffer from an aftershock and rhyme trees with corpses, corpses with Agrigento, Agrigento with snow, snow with black sea. Am I just a parody of a poet? Maybe, but I'm not going to worry about this. I have Nadia to care for my reputation, and I count on you, Lotte. Wolf may mess up the scraps of paper covered with my scribble. But you'll transcribe my traces into an Apple Plus, save the juice of my life in a diamond disk, bury the ashes at the Poets Pantheon in Sydney See.

Please, don't censor anything. Leave all the repetitions. The whole monotony of it, even the boring echo of *I slept with a ton of lice over my belly.* I did, and they increased my capacity for sexual dreams. So I went through the whole lot prescribed by Sigismund the Great: birds and beaks, ice cucumbers and cannons, Niagara Falls and cones. The effect was reinforced, as in Sextus's studio on certain Tuesday evenings, by the *kleine* snore-music of my co-prisoners and the musings of our guards, Eros and Thanatos. Inspired by them, at midnight common thieves addressed their prayers to various Venuses, Misia and Mila from Minsk, Tola from Omsk. Around one o'clock black marketeers hula-hooped around huge hips, sighing and sweating. After two the founders of forbidden sects, Judaism, Christianity, and Islam, sucked at Persephone's fragile tits, while naked Psyches buzzed around their pricks. Finally around 4:00 A.M. all of us, including myself and another scribe, shrank to the size of newborn Tannhäusers and slipped for an hour into the cave, tepid and pulsating, of Madonna Laura, our most familiar lady. Imagine! Pushkin's first translation of Petrarch found its way into our prison library, otherwise overstuffed with the Red Classics. A slim booklet, bound in turquoise leather, it must have been confiscated from a Saint Petersburg home, or placed on our shelf by God's hand. While I read aloud, some masturbated, others wept, and a young kulak hung himself.

The sense of symmetry and measure was so strong in our camp! I told them about Michelangelo, and they taught me how to avoid mines. But you know how clumsy I am, especially without Nadia. First I lost my right glove. Then, turning back to find it, I stepped on a mine. Goodbye, Wolfi, and here's my last advice: don't finish *Faust*. Only the tragically incomplete excites posterity. Propertius, don't grow too old! It's all right for Svevo, but for an erotic poet—no. When you live as long as Picasso, everybody wishes you dead. Of course, it's too late to copy perfection, a Schubert or a Trakl. Those Austrians really had a sense of timing, no German can outdo them. Goethe, do me a favor: stop being immortal. If your heart refuses to cease, consider using your own hand. By the way, Olga, have you killed yourself in Helsinki? Or are you still hesitant about the weapon? A Browning, *chérie,* fits your image best. Take it out of the top drawer in my desk and don't delay your departure any longer. I'm cold and damned lonely here.

That's it. *Vive Staline!* I toast you, Nikita Sergeyevich Aragon. My ode to Dzugashvili cannot compete with the elegies you conceived through Him and your Soviet wife, and I congratulate you from the depth of my heart. It must be wonderful to fall in love with the colossal Steel-and-Hide. Contemplating his sexy mustache, I too tried to arouse myself, but I couldn't get it up. Now in my second life as a woodchuck I make up for that. I apply His linguistics in my verse and the result is great. Simone, greet Paris for me, *auguri* to Sartre and Simone de B. Essence precedes existence. Nothing outlives matter. Sincerely, Osip Emilevich Mandelshtam. Chuck. Wood. Chuck.

W OLF IS IN BED WITH THE FLU, Italo cannot move because of the arthritis in his knee, but our king and Assudin, whose pictures we all adore, are here. I expected Moses to arrive any minute, but he just called to excuse himself for being late and asking me to begin. I open our *soir fixe* and retire to my easy chair. Sextus, kindly replace me at the table and start with your most interesting talk.

Thank you, Charlotte. But I would rather sit at the small mahogany desk, our most recent acquisition, where I can be near the lamp. My left eyelid has been giving me trouble. I'm about to develop a tic and see as through haze. My memory isn't working either, so I need to look at my notes. I have prepared for you a critical discussion of the late writings of Anna Karenina, our ex-co-Fellow and an author I value highly. It pains me to witness how she's being dismissed as a female writer, ghettoized. The study of sexual agony and our escape from it into death is as serious a subject as political economy. Everything originates from within, I swear. Wars and holocausts are caused by frustrated passions. If we could reform our souls, the world would be better. To improve itself, humanity has to compare the text of a woman with the text of a man.

Tonight I want to draw your attention to Anna's lesser-known writings, her sketches on Simone, our obscenely difficult ex-co-Fellow, and the persuasive beauty of her metaphors. For instance, while Weil starves herself to death, a black bird eats crumbs out of her palm. Furthermore, and here the real mystery begins, talking to Simone about Cynthia and myself seated at the edge of her deathbed, the bird suggests that my first mistress committed suicide because of me. When I first read Karenina's text this obvious falsification infuriated me. Cynthia died of pneumonia, and not by her own hand, the *Britannica* of 1910 tells me. But with time I have become convinced that the bird and the Russian author are right, while I and the Brits are wrong. My past dissolves like a layer of mist and, gaining clarity, I see the bird as a figure of speech signifying myself. Indeed, I'm the nightingale, alighting at female breakfast plates and picking up crumbs of bread.

I'm glad Wolfgang is sound asleep. He'd consider my words to be using too much poetical license, as the *Schein* I try to sell instead of the nauseating *Wahrheit*. No doubt, I'd get on his nerves. I'm also not insensitive to the shadows of disapproval on your well-behaved face, Lotte. But tonight, dearest secretary, you must bear with me. Please don't whisper to Assudin about the results of the test I had last Saturday. It's public knowledge that cancer is devouring my prostate, that my urine consists mostly of blood, that my male hormones have been entirely wiped out by whom, I wonder: Comrade Krebs or Doc Cholesterol?

Don't transfix me with your eyes, Lotte. I agree that my general loss of blood combined with the arteriosclerosis may be the reason why I identify with the bird. But since I do, kindly tolerate what I have to say. Svevo shouldn't monopolize the subject of age. I too grow old and want to share with you my senility. So where was I? In pursuit of Karenina's black bird that understood me better than all of you taken together.

Simultaneously with the Simone essay, Anna wrote a diary that contains many surprising details. The new gas oven she had installed a week before her suicide. The dinner party with Lowry and Conrad. The first drank vodka, the second looked out the window and wondered if ships were moving up or down the Hudson River. That particular evening Weil played Antigone, a difficult role if we take into account the existence of André, a brother you cannot bury in a sacred sepulcher. Proust didn't attend because of an asthma attack. Somebody was attacked on the subway. No one had a Mercedes Benz, but Manhattan protected them from the brown iron fists. Yes, *liebster Wolfi,* from the SS-misfits who would have liked to catch them. Miss U.S. offered them food and shelter, but her affection was a hundredth of what they desired. So they felt depressed. When equal love there cannot be, let the more loving one be me. It sounds good, Auden, even when I misquote you, but it's easier said than done. Anyhow, a bunch of immigrants, they drowned their sadness in scotch and Sophocles.

Am I drugged or drunk? How insensitive you are, German muse. I have some vitamin C in my veins, some Valium, a glass of Beaujolais. *C'est tout.* Not enough to silence me in my own villa. Especially as I have to tell you about the super Zurbarán painting Anna discovered in a Bronx SOR.

What's a SOR, Sextus?

A single occupancy room, Italo, a specialty of the richest island in the world. Unable to force Voronskoy to pursue her, Anna was roaming the streets—day and night. At dawn, it happened late in August at a rundown downtown bar, she made the acquaintance of Annie, an old black bitch living in a SOR. Annie's boyfriend—he worked as a guard at the Metropolitan—fell in love with the masterpiece I mentioned before, turned into a burglar, and escaped with it to the Bronx. No, not to the ZOO, to the SOR. A fascinating story, Lotte, I'm sure you want to know it all.

Annie, a compassionate creature, realized Anna's abominable condition and put her up on a spare foam mattress. Upon awakening in the SOR, Karenina saw the Zurbarán—and couldn't believe her eyes. There was a table in the middle of the painting, and its drawer was open. It revealed nothing, but she knew the meaning. There is something in store for me, Anna thought, and rushed out to take her life. So *ist das,* dearest Lotte, death is in store for us. Every drawer is a coffin, and even though you're seated at the side of an immortal—absent right now—*Tod* tiptoes around. Welcome, Signor Mors, I like the way you slide into my studio, silent as a sea lion. Please study death with me! *Ecco,* you're accompanied by your wife. *Buona sera,* Signora Mortadella, I like your pink dress with white holes. Hostia hid them in her lungs, Berenice in her breasts, while I have the honor of housing them in my honorable prostate.

It's almost midnight but my Roman villa isn't lit. It's mid-May but my cherry orchard doesn't blossom. In the setting moon the ring on your finger, Lotte, the silver jewel Goethe gave you in order not to marry you, glitters and dissolves in blackness. *Mehr Licht!* Even in the *Sterbestunde* I imitate your would-be husband. I, the ancient Propertius, repeat the words of a modern *Dichter,* while a blood vessel bursts in my brain. But it's nothing, Lotte, don't cry. Look, I'm a black nightingale. Now I'll fly out of the window, singing: *Au revoir, arrivederci Roma. Adieu. Adieu. Adieu. Sic transit gloria mundi. Mundi gloria. Transit. Port Authority. Transit. Wear your ring until you arrive in the last harbor, at the Mortadella Isle of Alabaster. Wear your ring! It's a talisman. It prevents death's access to . . .*

S LOWLY THE SMALL CONDUIT moves up the Scalae Caci, a long, sloping ascent cut through the rock from the side of the Circus Maximus and framed by the remains of early walls. The stairs connect the Nova Via with the Clivius Victoriae, a hill on top of which Propertius wished to be buried.

He played us a last trick, Goethe whispers to Charlotte, and chose for his tomb a place you reach by the single steepest staircase in Rome, and one that is in the worst condition. Once basalt-paved, the path has been exposed to too much bad weather. It's good you wear your old Bally shoes. Nevertheless, don't hesitate to take my arm whenever it feels slippery. Does your Achilles tendon trouble you? Not too much? That's good. I'm completely out of breath. In the future I shall refrain from expeditions to burial sites. Wasn't there once a gate here? Yes, you're right, the Vetus Porta Palatii. Livy mentions it. Remind me, and I'll find for you the quote. Through it Romans fled when defeated by the Sabines. Now I realize what Sextus really was. A snob. That's why he wanted to repose in the core around which, by a series of expansions, the historical city was built. I hoped he would agree to have his tomb in his beloved cherry orchard. We could have topped it with a nice Greek stele and visited him daily, or even twice a day. It would have made life so much easier. But never was he practical. He preferred extremes, either courtesans or queens, nothing in between, and of course outlived them all. I wonder who's going to climb up so many steps to pay him compliments at that pretentious peak of a grave.

Well, the view from here is wonderful.

My child, you seem to forget that his eyes are closed. But you're right. The saddle between the Palatine and Esquiline outlines itself magnificently in the chilly winter air. However, that's not enough of a reason to pilgrim to this platform. I hope you won't catch a cold, Lotte. I expect more wind at the top.

I can't forget how Sextus got on my nerves that last evening, and I'm ashamed of myself.

No reason to be ashamed. A premortal nuisance, he's a nuisance postmortem as well. What an idea to have his tomb covered with soft tufa blocks. They'll simply melt away, like ice cubes in a glass of whiskey. Really, he had the mentality of a go-go poet, a bloody Slav, a Russophile Pole. By the way, what do you think about this Czech from Manhattan who got some prize for something?

Teofil Pyscek? He got five Oscars for his terribly boring documentary on Smetana.

A big shot he isn't, but sufficiently pleasant and handsome, and only in his forties. Isn't he good material for a Junior Fellow? We desperately need fresh blood, and some entertainment. I didn't found the Institute to become a grave digger. It was a big mistake to collect so many potential corpses. Suicidal women, drunkards, womanizers with prostate cancer, menopausal queens, senile ex-kings. I suppose Svevo should be blamed for that bad turn of affairs. You can't applaud old age and get away with it. We should change our admission policy. No more ancient celebrities, we're sufficiently senile. Since Sextus's death Ann has become so aggressive, and Moses' chutzpah increases every day.

What about ourselves? Just recall how old I'll turn tomorrow.

That I want to forget. Besides, we're monuments. It's going to be very refreshing to have Pyscek join us, and hear him talk about the newest stars and stripes, rather than Afghanistan.

You want to drop Shali?

No, nobody will be dropped, but we need a more *abwechslungsreiche Kost*. I'm sick and tired of our death ballet—how glad I was to miss Sextus's last performance—and of Karenina's texts. Why do I dislike her so ardently? Well, she's worse than Pearl Buck, totally incoherent. Here, take my arm. We'll reach the top in a minute. Where's my funeral speech? In your bag? Or have I packed it into my backpack?

No, it's in the pocket of your coat.

Fine. I'm obliged to you for having me wear my old but warm Weimar *Pelz,* a perfect outfit for today.

Its shabbiness plays down your preposterousness.

What a *spitzes Zünglein* you have, Löttchen. Apply it to Pyscek, so that he knows his place. But don't discourage him too much.

Shall I invite him for next Tuesday?

Yes. And let him prepare a small talk on the idols of New York. I long for new cuisine. Lighter. Watercress with garlic. No more eggs in mayonnaise. Now let me read the text with as little solemnity as possible.

Carissimi amici! Our little band disbands. *Herr Tod,* a true terrorist, kidnaps one colleague after another. We have climbed all the way up to the top to bury Propertius, and from what I see around me, the place should suit him. A big crowd of shepherd's purses, the annual herb of the mustard family, bravely resists the freezing blows of a Siberian wind.

Life is about dying, but death isn't the end. *Panta rei,* one thing changes into another, nothing perishes, mourning makes no sense. The slight corpse of our co-poet will nourish the white silky lining of the shepherd's purse, a delicate female plant that will penetrate him now—reversing the clumsy pattern of nature. Really, everything is relative. We should have offered membership to the untidy Albert E. from Princeton.

Anyhow, now it's going to be the other way round. The tiny and soft shepherdess will enter the remains of our favorite erotic pet, push through Sheol, and succeed—where earthly femininity tends to fail. She'll force Sextus to sleep with her not once or twice, I mean not once or twice a week, or according to some other rhythm every Propertius prescribes for his many girlfriends. Here a plant plays the absolute empress, a famous man is a grain of sand. Each date is fixed by her, and he obeys. The shepherd's purse requests constant sex—from sunrise to sunset—and since he cannot escape, her wish will be fulfilled. I'm sorry to say, but you're trapped, Sextus. The sex you refused to Cynthia and Berenice, Roman courtesans and Persian prostitutes, Egyptian sub-teens and middle-aged Poles—you'll grant it to a plant. Flowers don't menstruate, they won't give you even that short break. Until the end of

Saturn's rule, your sperm will flow into one purse after another—inseminating your great-granddaughters. Propertius, you have what you wanted, a last abode carved in a fertile ground. Had you agreed to stay in your own cherry orchard, you would have been spared. Charlotte keeps the place clean. But since you wished to become the poetic nucleus of New Rome, here you go—right into a sweet-smelling sepulcher. Incest is best, according to Seneca and myself. Once erect—always erect. Sleep well. Don't die of eternal sex.

I TALO, HAVE YOU READ Moses' open letter to Wolfgang?
    Concerning Wolf's new protégé, a certain Termidor or Teodoric Pyscek?
Teofil.
Im Gottes Namen, Teofil. What a name!
Pyscek is even better, at least for a Pole. It sounds like *pyszczek,* a small snout or muzzle. A diminutive from *pysk.*
His mug is pretty big. Is that what Maimonides objects to? The discrepancy between name and object?
Moses isn't drawn to Pyscek's physiognomy, but he mainly objects to his being an asshole. Here, read, his attack is vitriolic:
Dear *Direktor!* Do you want to ruin our reputation and have the Institute descend to the level of an American Society for the Futility of Scholarship, where critical inquiry is replaced with twenty-five simultaneous slide shows, discourse with blurb, and intelligence with self-advertisement? Are you striving, my cool colleague, for the humanist universality of public TV? If that's what you intend, you should change your name from Johann Wolfgang von Goethe to J. W. Got, Ph.D., and start a freshman senior citizen career at the Coca Moca University in Jerusalem, North Dakota. They indeed need International Vanity and may even consider offering you a double appointment. In addition to being employed as the Institute's executive director, you'd teach creative poetry workshops at the Weimar School of Verse, turn a second Nabokov, and beat the first one with an unexpected weapon—your age. While he had an English governess, you'd learn American from a Czech at eighty-eight, produce your first *Lolita* at ninety, and receive the National Book Award at ninety-four. Is that what rustles in your head, Wolf? What you need Mr. Snouty for? Do you plan, my *Geheimrat,* a secret reincarnation? Do you have a girlfriend across the

ocean? No? So you want to invest green-paper gold on Wall *Gasse?* Open and close your monumental mouth on CBS news?

Whatever your intentions are, Goethe, before taking off for New York you should consult me, an old Jew, rather than Dr. Pyscek whose mug, I beg your pardon, reminds me of a behind with two holes instead of one. It won't look good at your side, Johann. If you need a companion, take Lotte with you, but make her slim down first. In the States they prefer plastic blondes to overweight muses—and other folks to Germans. Don't ignore this simple fact—and supplement your new name with a new descent. Why not claim that J. W. Got goes back not to Johann Wolfgang von Goethe—who's that, anyway?—but to Josek Wladimirovich Gottesschwanz, whose herring stand was the pride of the Odessa fishmarket? Or Janciel Wolfek Goptak, who dealt in ladies' panties in Drohobycz? Or, *tout court,* Wojta Gopčatek, the glory of Frydek Místek, in whose *Gospoda* the best pre-Communist *Sauerkraut-knödel* of our *Mitteleuropa* were washed down with a real *Pilsner?*

Now take my helping hand and spice your humble Jewishness with a sprinkle of a very special Oriental saga. In the land of unlimited opportunity people like to have it both ways—to eat the cake and to have the cake earn interest. How they do it? A genius like yourself will soon find out. But meanwhile I'll whisper into your ear what my Bronx relatives whispered into mine. First you must show how hard it was to climb all the way from the *Schweinedreck* of Grójec to the suburbs of Boulder, Colorado. Then, as the first part of your prime-time talk show approaches its end, you hint at your origin's sublimity, hidden beneath a Himalaya of herringheads, push aside a mount of freshly chopped onions, and dig out from the massgrave of your mind a great-great-great-grandpa who, a true wandering Jew, walked all the way to Odessa, Drohobycz, Frydek Místek. Where from? From the cherry orchards of Cordova where he was born on March 20, the eve of Passover, in the year 1135, and spent his childhood playing with his brother David and sister Esther, an aspiring Jewish princess with auburn curls and the eyes of an inquisitive cherub. Yes, my foxy Wolf, the moment has come to lift the veil of mystery. But don't be too profound. You're present not *in vivo,* but *in vitro.*

Cordova has just passed the zenith of its glory. The Arab rulers foster the development of science and art. So you indulge in the Jewish hunger for learning and cite the manifold influences that shaped the education of your Spanish ancestor—without neglecting the boy's *sechster Sinn* for business. His father, besides training him in all branches of Hebrew knowledge, implanted in his son a sound dose of the secular. This you sketch in simple terms and proceed to stress that, unlike his rust-colored sister, he's a very dark child. His hair is so black that it looks almost blue, his eyelashes are long and thick, his wrists veined and fine. The insignificances of physiology appeal to everybody and help wash down the irrelevancies of geography and history. No one in the audience knows if Cordova is a shtetl in Bohemia or Galicia, and why in 1148 the city was taken from the last Fatimite caliph by the victorious Almohades, spreading over Spain from North Africa. No, it's not easy to introduce militant revivalists, reestablishing Islam in what they considered its true design, to Alabama housewives. So it's time to bring back the familiar, the auburn hair of sister Esther—or is her name Margaret?—and remember that by now the female TV majority can be kept in front of the screen only by a detailed account of her charm. Otherwise attention will dwindle and the sound of disaster become audible: the peculiar noise of munched popcorn, the crackling of potato chips. Now move on quickly, Got, or it's going to be your last prime-time oh-ho! Drop the revivalists—obsessed with the unity of God, tolerating neither schism within the faith nor dissent without— and don't lose a word on how the position of Jews has become increasingly delicate. Throw yourself straight into the subject of persecution, and go full speed. Call the hardship a holocaust, bla-bla-bla about escape and immigration—that will ring a bell—describe how brave the kids are—brother David and sister Carmelita—crossing borders and seas with their tiny feet, and never complaining. By the way: how are they dressed? What about toys? Is Rachel carrying in her arms a Barbie doll? Is Aron robbed of his beloved Mauss by a Moravian pervert? If yes, the brute's name must be Shveyk, and it's best to suggest that he rapes the Auschwitz animal-survivor in a clover field. Be prepared for a phone call from Santa Agatha, Mississippi, informing you that Mauss has survived the attack—an extra-miracle helps—and is getting in touch with her lawyer.

Alas, good times are over and you enter an unsettling territory, the city of Fez where you face an avalanche of problems. How can your ancestors become friendly with Abdul Arab ibn-Muisha, a Muslim theologian? It contradicts what people just saw. Who'll believe your words, when images show that Arabs throw rocks at Jews, not drink tea with them. To have your pussycats swallow the bitter pill, you have to dilute history with gossip. Wasn't Abdul ibn-Arab particularly good-looking? Or gay? Or an illegitimate child of your ancestor's cousin on his mom's side? At this point the human touch is urgently needed, otherwise nobody will believe that Muisha Abal stimulated religious feelings in your grandpa. None of this is sexy to begin with and must be cut short. Now, Wolf, hurry directly to Cairo, the new home of the dark little boy who has grown up and achieved prominence at court and in the Jewish community.

Cairo suits you, Got. Exaggerate the elegance of the palace, the splendor of the Hebrew salons. The more cheap glitter, the better. Bring in Cleopatra, and the Hollywood tresses of Liz Taylor. Contrast Berenice's blonde locks with Esther's chestnut tone. A true Jewish princess in Gucci shoes, she's about to fall in love with an Egyptian prince and contract a marriage in Camp David. He's enormously rich but—*c'est la vie*—a dwarf with a harelip. In spite of this she has a crush on him—a frog, if I may say so, with an exquisite soul—while you, fox, reach the climax of your show by painting the poem of a first encounter between the rose of Sharon and the mini-monster. Brushing back her golden mane and bending over, she kisses the imperial harelip—and ecstasy erupts. The touch of her lipstick turns the toad into a pharaoh, a miracle even in Iowa. As her mouth's rosebud opens and sucks in the prince's hairy protrusion, moms hold their breath, teenagers gasp. In this instant a million female hearts recall their first boyfriend's acne—and everything else. In an orgy of mass coincidence, one single question is asked: Had I kissed Bobby's filthy mug, would an Apollo have jumped out of his pants? I did kiss him but, because of his foul teeth, with little conviction. Maybe that's why it didn't work. See, Got, how little it takes to make females feel guilty for their inability to change a beast into a man?

Anyway, this cheapest of all tricks hits hardest. But you aren't yet at the happy ending. Like every TV magician, you still keep a final rabbit in your tweed pocket. Your grandpa's brother David, with whom he carries on a trade in diamonds, is shipwrecked in the Indian Ocean. As the female majority dozes away in an Egyptian reverie, you address the male minority. Last week Dow Jones tried to commit suicide, and even the faintest sign of bankruptcy makes the breadwinners' ears prick up. Like an ex-save-and-loan guy, Grandpa goes to medical school and graduates with honors. Immediately he's appointed to King Saladin and becomes so attached to him that when another king—Richard I, name him *en passant* to avoid confusing your audience with too many royalties at once—approaches him from Ascalon, offering the same position but a better salary, your ancestor refuses. A smartie, you refute the Jews-for-money prejudice, and pause.

Pause? You can't do that, co-Fellow, you aren't in Rome! A short pause on TV, and you're gone—replaced by the next-in-line prof. Instead of stopping, push for another pinnacle, my friend: your ancestor's marriage to the sister of Ibn al-Amli, one of the royal secretaries. Digress and explain why at Saladin's court they were all male. Blame it on the lack of affirmative action, it's time to emerge from the mists of the past. Grandpa's wife resembles Esther in her younger years, only her hair has a darker shade. Since the weak gender is still caught in the harelip-prince dream, appeal to males, chat about his flourishing business and prepare the final effect. Now shape your lips into a pathetic pair and reveal the real name of your ancestor in a voice pregnant with pride. It's now or never, Got! Disclose the true origins of your blood and brain. Say it, man: Moses Maimonides.

Isn't that great! You aren't related only to a bunch of Jewish paupers. You also descend from Rabbi Moses ben Maimon, alias Maimonides! You're my cousin as well. Oh let me embrace you, my dearest kin. Stripped from all herringness and *Knödelheit,* you're beamed all over the globe, your face splendid as the sky over Salamanca. Past and future fuse, the vulgar and sublime unite, the German proletariat hugs the Hebrew intelligentsia. Here it's *getan,* the *ewig weibliche Television* takes you into her arms, presses a purse—stuffed with green gold that buys it all—into your sweaty palm. Here you go, Goethe-Got-Moses. You didn't sell your soul to Mephisto, you sold it to a snout from New York.

Toll! Poor Pyscek managed to infuriate Moses a lot.

As they grow old, Goethe and Maimonides are increasingly on each other's nerves. The appearance of the American ass was just the last straw. Moses hates hype, Wolf wants to join the Big Apple. The conflict between them is inevitable. How was Pyscek's Tuesday talk?

A slice of shit. What made you miss it?

A trip with Karl to Frascati. We walked in the vineyards, watched clusters of black grapes being cut. In the afternoon we had a couple of glasses of a slightly too fermented grape juice—and our stomachs upset. A true October excursion, it reminded Karl of his youth in Vienna and me of his home in the wine-hills, at the edge of the *Wienerwald.* Before we started to slip from one exile into another, we lived there for a while. Now it seems to me as though it were in another life. But tell me more about Snouty's lecture.

Forget it! A spectacle in asinine self-publicity. Next to this idiot's chutzpah, our egos shrink to the size of buttons. I thought Maimonides would collapse, while Goethe looked refreshed and amused, obviously enjoying Pyscek's mindless pomposity.

What was his topic?

He glorified his boss, a New York real-estate baron, a Bump or Grump, who's married to Pyscek's compatriot, the ice-hockey star, Zdenka Podsadlová.

Is Pyscek Polish or Czech?

He claims to be half and half, to be related on his father's side to the Polish owners of the Pysk hotdog chain, and on his mother's side to the leading zillionaire of Czech descent—what's her name?

The famous Funfanson?

Exactly. Wasn't her husband in shoelaces?

Laces and shoeshine. Each footcover we wear perpetuates her empire.

So we should patent the Kar-Svevo suede shoes with zippers and make Funfanson tumble.

What's her first name?

Franka. But her estate in Ohio is called the Ann Karenina Ranch.

Aha, I read about her in the *Gondola di Venezia*. Right, the tabloid financed by the Mafia. The ranch has a castle she designed herself. Forty-four boudoirs decorated with Van Gogh's sunflowers or Monet's water lilies.

Forty-four?

Yes. Why not?

For Poles it's a mystical number. One of our Petrarchs prophesied that *his name would be forty and four.*

Whose name?

Who knows. Perhaps Funfanson's. Maybe Adam Mickiewicz . . .

The dissident?

No, the poet. The one into protest is Adam Michnik. Well, perhaps Mickiewicz meant that in the brave new world—supervised by the Polish pope whose career, as a matter of fact, was foretold by Słowacki, another of our senior bards—a shoelace giant's widow would subdivide her property into forty-four bedrooms, twenty-two yellow, to harmonize with the *słoneczniki*, and the rest pink, to go with the water lilies.

Didn't Funfanson buy *The Girl with Auburn Hair,* the last Michelangelo pastel that was still in Rome?

Yes, now it's in her bathroom, framed in blue-veined Mastroiani marble. The rarest stone is carved into a shell and inlaid with mother-of-pearl.

Her taste is famous! Karenina wanted once to visit the love nest that carries her name, and asked Funfanson for an audience.

And?

No answer. But, on the other hand, Pyscek told us that his boss's wife, this Zdenka or Benka Bump, acquired a special jet-copter in order to attend Funfanson's famous zoological garden parties.

Coming from where?

From her residence in Bambuti Bigbeach, New Caledonia, or World Disneyland Ten which is being built after a plan she produced together with her four-year-old son, Grump Maximus, Junior. Every weekend Zdenka lands on Ann Karenina's main meadow—where industrialists and real-estate sharks walk Funfanson's baby lions and giraffes on leashes—and rushes to the silver basin, to feed fresh Portuguese sardines to her darling, the white baby seal saved by Brigitte B.

You relate Pyscek's lecture?

More or less. This Grump is really megalomania incarnate. He wants to rename Manhattan.

To Bumphattan?

No, to Grumpcenter, and the earth to Grumpglobe. He has also schemes to crown the poor old head of our planet with Grumpton, a skyscraper in the shape of a bowler hat—a thousand times higher than the World Trade Center. No wonder Moses went up the wall. But did Wolf really fancy his talk?

He loves the colossal, and so he was taken with it, like a kid. Don't you think America is the country for him? There Wolf could really spread his wings, and run the World Vanity, first—and then for president of the United States of Earth. When Pyscek announced that the Grumpton will be fifty-five miles high, Goethe asked: Is it feasible, from the point of view of statics, to extend it to five hundred miles?

And what did *Pysk* reply?

Why not? Let's go for five, prof.

But the force of gravity?

Why be bothered with it?

At this point Maimonides rushed out, bumping into the glass door. But Goethe was so fascinated with Pyscek's fairy tale that he didn't notice our perplexed master's ostentatious exit. In fact, by then Wolf's own perplexity exceeded all common sense. Drunk with the spirit of unlimited progress Teofil was pouring into his ears, he jumped up shouting *Bravo, bravo,* and had to be subdued by Charlotte. She took her husband by the hand and led him out of Sextus's studio, murmuring *senilità, senilità.*

Italo and Ann laugh. It's early afternoon and they visit together the Museo delle Terme—to see the picture on which Propertius based his last poem. Svevo found it at the back of the top drawer in Sextus's small desk, and as they enter the oval hall where the mosaic is displayed, he begins to read:

> Monotony. Monotony. Monotony.
> The landscape fades. Niles are
> flowing away. The sky is high
> and crocodiles, my dear, dream us
> away and let papyrus scrolls
> fall to the ground. Pompeii is here.
> And here is Palestrina. The poem of
> my life is written on your skin.
> Hippopotamus drops his head and dreams.
> Egypt is distant. Egypt drifts away.

Our sentimental Sextus wrote the poem on a piece of papyrus he cut from a large scroll. At the bottom he noted the date and below his source of inspiration: mosaic pavement, discovered on the Aventine, preserved at the Museo delle Terme.

So here we are, searching for Sextus. His death closed a chapter in our collective Roman romance. Now our lives deteriorate.

Yes, he had us retrace our own erotic episodes, wrestle with fate, rebel against the agony of aging, learn how to grow old without reaching the shores of idiocy, how to remain intact. His mind was a quicksilver vessel. It took him an instant to decide about returning to Berenice, a woman he didn't love.

If he didn't love her, *amor* is an empty word. He dedicated to her a whole decade of his existence, sacrificed his career.

We have discussed it before, Italo. No one knows the details of his Egyptian affair.

But it's a fact that, setting out for a breastless woman's side, he missed the Pan Poetical Competition he could have easily won. He of all people! A poet of prostitutes with big boobs, as Lucretius put it, who in his diary mentions that as a four-year-old he was so curious about his mother's breasts that he asked her to uncover them every day, first thing in the morning.

By midlife he began to change—from a *Sexus* into a *Fidelio,* from an absentminded Casanova into Berenice's step-husband. In retrospect his life resembles an erotic *speculum exemplare,* with the physical catching onto the spirit.

Still, his final portrait is an ambiguous image. An impressionistic soulscape, it looks different every day.

Yes. On Monday I find him an erotic hero, on Tuesday—an eternal *Salonlöwe,* elegant to the very end. On Saturday he plays the sex idol of old age. That's why we reread his poems, outline the shadow of his silhouette, revisit the shores of Egypt, dream of his hands caressing Berenice's hair. Reality discourages us from believing in perfect love, Sextus's story makes us gain hope. But look at the mosaic. Obviously, the landscape is taken from the banks of the Nile, and the geometrical guilloches, with their still-life motifs and scenic masks, resemble the floor in Berenice's bedroom. The hippopotamus on the left has a humorous expression, the crocodile smiles at the rose bouquet between his paws. The style brings to mind the celebrated pavement at Palestrina and the mosaics at Pompeii—with a bird's-eye view of a river.

Indeed, not only Roman poets but also mosaic workers owe a lot to Alexandrian models. Sextus once told me that the finest pieces—he referred to them as snapshots, but in fact they are called emblemata— were small scenes and portraits transported all over the world, from the great centers of production to distant provinces where pavements were prepared for their reception.

Isn't *Plato's Academy* we passed on our way one of them?

Yes, and so is the mosaic Propertius brought from Africa. Do you remember? The one he discovered at Hadrumetum during his trip to Tunis—their last journey together.

Who could forget it! Somebody told Sextus about a remarkable tablinum at a Hadrumetum villa, and he decided to show it to Berenice. Extremely weak and light as a feather, she couldn't walk anymore. But he wouldn't have servants lift the queen, and he carried her himself.

Yes. They drove out to the deserted place, and he deposited her in the middle of the ruin's central hall, on a thin cotton sheet and pillows. Adjusting one of them under her head, he heaped up some loose gray clay, and encountered a smooth hard surface, a mosaic representing Virgil and himself. The artist depicted them in an empty whitewashed room, papyrus scrolls on their knees. That of Virgil was inscribed with a verse from the *Aeneid,* that of Propertius with his second elegy to Cynthia. The first was flanked by Clio and Aphrodite, the second by Cupid and Pan. Sextus swept away more dust, and the satyr's hooves appeared close to Berenice's locks. In the adjacent remains of a nymphaeum he found another mosaic—the parting of Aeneas from Dido. When the queen's eyes caught a glimpse of it, she whispered into his ear: Soon, we're going to part as well, dearest, but we're together still, and I'm happier than Dido, whom no man carried in his arms. While she spoke, Sextus detected a gloomy picture of the underworld, with Hades raping Prosperine. Afraid that it might remind her of Euergetes, he hid the painting from Berenice by spreading a blanket in front of it, and then said to the queen: Let me carry you back to the carriage. She put her arms around his neck and closed her eyes, but opened them just before he walked out of the ruin. At the gate a half-effaced fresco of Cupid and Psyche, kissing, glowed in the sunset, and she begged: Let us stop for a second. Sextus lowered the queen onto a marble bench, sat next to her, and put her head in his lap. They remained in the villa until dusk, in spite of Berenice's fever and incoherent speech. She kept repeating: My departure is imminent, but how can I ever be separated from you, Sextus? Tunisian gods, have pity on us! Preserve us both in the stones of a mosaic, let the dead sea rock us to sleep.

HI, IT'S TERRIFIC TO SEE YOU.
A loud voice interrupts Ann. Turning in surprise, Svevo and Kar catch the sight of Teofil Pyscek entering the hall, press hands, exchange glances, and finally, backed by their civilized selves, greet the creep: How are you today?

Great, Pyscek replies. It's a terrific city and I enjoy myself tremendously. We have masses of super pictures at the Met, but the one downstairs is simply great. My boss is furnishing his Mammoth Motel with the best we can find, and the stuff downstairs is just right. The *Academy of Plapo*—could you spell his name for me—we're buying it. Guess why? The chum to Plafo's right, what's his name? Socrates, thanks, he looks like Grump's dad. Weird, isn't it? The same potato-shaped nose, the same sort of beard. I had a good look at him, and that's how he looks. Get the point? No? Boss fell in love with this piece of mosque because Sofrates looks like Grump Senior. Get the point? No? Once the South Bronx slums are replaced with the Grand-Grum Condos, Dad has to go. But before he's out, we're going to put up the *Plapo Academia* in the middle of the lobby. What I'm speaking about? The Grumpton, what else? The tallest skyscraper on earth, the Farum Romanum of our century twenty-first. Ha, ha. The finest craftsmen in

Rome handcarve twenty-seven thousand solid alabaster columns for us. Yesterday Grumpy rang to tell me that the first two couples had gotten in, and are real posh, posh as Czech blondes. Get the point? Grumpy's spouse is Slovak, and ever since we're all into Czecho-Slovak squeeze, pardon me, madam. I'm going to repeat to you, word for word, what Grumpy said on the phone: I can afford the finest workmanship and I figure, why spare the expense? I want the best, whatever it takes. Isn't that great! Why spare the expense?

If I understand you correctly, Mr. Pyscek, Ann says in a low voice, you have come here with the purpose of negotiating the purchase of the *Academy of Plato,* Rome's most valuable mosaic.

You said it, madam. Only the best is good enough for us, and I'm a guy who puts himself directly on the line. *Si, si, si.* I'm here to make a deal. What deal? What line? The bottom line. Grumpy relies on me. First thing in the morning, I'm immediately put through to him. You try to call him, then you'll see what I'm talking about. Incredible perks! I live like a king. The Scrompates business isn't the only venture we have here. I'm after Mr. Goethe also. Grump wants him to cut the ribbon when the Casino Complex in Zdenka di Lido is opened to the public. It would be great to have the old man fly over just for that. Grumpy would send his private jumbo jet for him, although selling the Boeing and buying a rocket is the first thing on his agenda. The plane is a dream. It can seat up to twenty thousand, but can be reconfigured for just two, in this case Mr. Goethe and his spouse. But personally I would advise him to go by himself. He looks fine. Very lean, very cute. But Mrs. Charlotte, no. Why doesn't she exercise, go on a diet? I admire people who put themselves directly on the line. Mr. Goethe, he does that. But Mrs. Charlotte, no, far from it. Get it? Mrs. Grump's such a sports person, she won't be happy to see Mrs. Goethe arrive at the Grump International Airport. Publicity is money, money is publicity. We're ready to invest in Mr. Goethe, but in Mrs. Charlotte there's no return. She's not just overweight. She knows nothing about ice hockey, and doesn't give a damn about real estate. Life isn't about throwing money out the window, unless there is a big crowd downstairs, and five channels to tape it. Get it? Grumpy's spouse is an accomplished person, she is an athlete, and her taste is great. If she were less busy she could do without architects. Do every project, inside and out, all by herself. But she's in big business too, and pushing Grumpy when he slides back even an inch. Are you free for drinks?

Oh, I see. What about tomorrow, Mr. Svevo? By the way, I bought your book *Man Is Growing Young.* Fabulous, I saw it in the window, and knew: that's what I need. In big business, Grumpy says, we don't grow old, we grow young. Isn't it super? The more money you make, the more there is to it. You have zillions of tons of wet concrete poured from truck after truck into huge rinks, and that puts you into mint condition. Life is a hotline. You go around in a $3000 suit and feel young. You're driven to the heliport in time to catch a copter for our famous 5:30 cocktails at Ann Karenina, and you feel even younger. You accomplish a lot, you run ahead of time. That's it! You run ahead of time. Time can't catch up with you! So you stay young and grow younger. Mr. Svevo, Ms. Kar, it was terrific talking to you, and do me a favor. Tell Mrs. Goethe that the sort of climate we have in Manhattan wouldn't agree with her. Mr. Wolf is a bear, but Mrs. Goethe should reconsider and spend the winter in Rome.

T HE POPULATION OF POMPEII at the time of its destruction cannot be fixed with certainty, Italo reads from the guidebook, as he and his two companions, Ann and her old friend Karl Eglizer, enter a narrow street leading to the Forum. It was of a mixed character, he continues, as both Oscan and Greek inscriptions are found up to the last. Although there is no trace of Christianity, evidences of the presence of Jews are not lacking. A wall painting in the Strada dell'Abbondanza represents the Judgment of Solomon, and next to it an inscription reads *Sodoma, Gomorrha.*

The two words were also scratched on the wall of our Warsaw house, and when I asked my mom what it meant, she replied: The end of the world.

Oh, your mother, Eglizer exclaims in his high, almost girlish voice, and takes Ann's arm as if he wanted to direct her away from her remembrances. Your *mamerle!* A victim who keeps excavating her old Pompeii in order to make a new one out of our lives. A survivor who perceives the entire earth as her very own graveyard, and brushes aside other claims to suffering. Forget her, and let me inform you about the proper Pompeii—a relatively minor destruction site which has captured our imagination. Only about two thousand people perished here, as has been estimated from the number of skeletons. But as a second-rate provincial city ceased to exist, the phantom of a town was born from the ashes. Vesuvius raised Pompeii to the stars, immortalized its common nobodies: a butcher cutting lamb chops at the *macellum,* a housewife sifting through silk at the cloth exchange. A couple was cast in lava while eating lunch, a teenager became a statue as she plucked a flower. A young woman stroking her lover's neck was turned into a charming relief. What an exquisite death! In one split sec all of them transformed into art objects.

Stop philosophizing, Karl.

All right, Ann. Read on, Italo.

As at Rome itself, Pompeii's forum was surrounded on all sides by public buildings of a commanding character, and its pavement, composed of broad flags of travertine, was intended only for foot passengers. At the north side stood the imposing temple of Jupiter which, however, was evidently overthrown by the earthquake of 63, and is now simply a ruin.

I beg your pardon, Italo, throws in Karl, but I wonder if you're aware that Goethe's colossal head of Juno is said to have come from this temple. It has been the subject of some controversy, but Wolfgang believes that he indeed possesses the *caput* of the Juno Pompeiana. Yes, that's his main argument against Moses who claims that a tiny gem has better chances of survival than a pyramid and that, accordingly, the miniature has to be regarded as superior to the gigantic. A typical quarrel of two old *Herrn* stepping on each other's toes. Now, of course, Moses is worried about Wolf in the States, all by himself. But I keep telling him: he has more robustness than the rest of us, and is swimming like a fish in that ocean of progress. I must say, I admire his courage. He discovers a new continent, while we barricade ourselves in an ebony tower, go on sentimental pilgrimages, decipher palimpsests in a hundred dead tongues, lament the extinction of people and animals, foresee the extermination of everything, hold on to the past, while the present overruns us. People to whom Plato means nothing purchase his *Academy,* and we, who know by heart the conversation he had with Socrates on August 5, 1945, interpret this as the end of culture, and lament.

Please, Karl, don't get upset about Pyscek's intrusion into our quiet Roman existence. Naturally, he's at the center, we're at the periphery— which has always been more dedicated to the past. Dinosaurs? I, personally, don't mind being one. What Grump deconstructs, I am willing to reconstruct.

You have read too much Derrida, Italo. What's the matter with you guys? Your sophomoric tongues are good for nothing, and I may consider cutting them. No more prattle. Let's walk around the small temple of Isis, and listen to Italo's guide.

Not remarkable in point of architecture, the Isis temple is interesting as the only sanctuary in Pompeii dedicated to the Egyptian goddess Queen Berenice established as a leading deity. The stucco is somewhat gaudy, but the plan is curious. It deviates from the ordinary type in order to accommodate the peculiar rites of Isis. Here once stood the statue of the goddess, bearing upon her head either the hieroglyph of her name, or the horns of a cow. And from over there the veil—it was drawn aside for her mysteries—was suspended. An escort of lamenting women carried the corpse of Osiris and deposited it at the feet of the statue. Then the chief priest displayed around it small objects that had been imported from Egypt, to be dedicated to the worship of Isis: fruits, shells, lotus petals, crocodile teeth. A moon-earth goddess, she absorbed the attributes of all local female deities of sea and soil, of healing and magic as well as the universal love-death features of a *magna mater,* and had a great vogue throughout the western world from the time of Vespasian onwards. Nursing her Horus baby, she played the Madonna, mourning Osiris's death—the *mater dolorosa* of the pre-Christian world. Standing at the side of the resurrected sun god, she embodied the triumph of good over evil.

No wonder Berenice identified with Isis, and pictured herself and Propertius as the sacred pair, Karl begins to inject, but is interrupted by Ann: Rooms and ruins, architecture and archeology, the legend of Pompeii. Isn't it strange? In order to understand the principle of building, we contemplate destruction. In order to grasp the idea of love, we reflect on its lack. But can presence be really deduced from absence?

From what else? Bread tastes best when you're starving. Eros is a *rex*—in the wake of rejection. Ruins speak most eloquently about the whole, and every sparrow on the roof knows why our Ann is obsessed with architecture.

And our Karl not. So what! Architecture is about civilization. An artificial shell, it shelters the adolescent souls of adults.

Indeed, my guide agrees with you, Ann. Just listen: Architecture didn't spring into existence at an early period of history. The concepts of symmetry and proportion could not be evolved until at least a moderate degree of civilization had been attained. Primitive man was a master of illusionist painting that captured the magic of being born and dying, the hope of being a good hunter, and his guilt of killing others. A gifted sculptor, he found the breadth of female hips in a stone, intuited the roundness of female breasts in the curve of a bone. He needed art, but could do without architecture. The cave sufficed him.

Sure, and that's where artists still are. Bums in the grotto. Upstairs architects wine and dine.

Allergic to them, Ann?

Sort of, Karl. No more architecture! I want to see the obscene frescoes we were talking about at breakfast.

Yes, it's something for us—*hors de combat.* At our age one succeeds best in one's brain. Oh the unparalleled vigor of our imaginary attacks! The feverish search for young epidermis and sperm—in the left hemisphere.

I warn you, Karl. Your organ of speech is in danger.

Have it, Ann, but spare my silent one. Perhaps there is still hope. I mean, when I look around, I begin to disagree with my own words. This place is filled with middle-aged unisex couples, and so is India and Sri Lanka. They travel, ski, jog *à deux.* They communicate all day, share evening classes in ceramics and basket-weaving.

But at night her clitoris, Karl, cannot bear the sheer sight of his prick, and his cock falls at the mere thought of visiting her cave. But, in principle, each of them is a sucker for sex.

Karl and Ann, Italo exclaims, you should open a sex office. For Him—the door to the right, For Her—the door to the left. Together you'd finally harden men, melt women, and earn a few *soldi,* right here, in Pompeii.

D O I DISTURB YOU? asks the older colleague entering the room of the young moon scholar. I heard new material was brought from the Earth, and was curious to get your opinion. Besides, I cherish every pretext that allows me to come and talk to you. The older I am, the more our lunar procrastination gets on my nerves. Facts are accumulated, but you're the only one who interprets them in a sensible way.

I imagine scholarship on Earth must have been very different from what we pursue here.

Naturally. There life was based on the challenge between the inside and outside, the indoors and outdoors—between architecture and landscape. But the moon, a desert of dust, had to be made into a global motel in order to accommodate us—humans escaping from Earth.

Inside of our steel-and-plastic ziggurat we recreated the Earth, with its forests and gardens, hills, lakes and rivers, huts hidden in dark under-woods and castles rising on mountain slopes. We imported gazelles from the African savannah and alligators from the Nile, robins from Siberia and grasshoppers from Burma, and managed to have them multiply here. But in spite of all our efforts, the moon has remained a giant incubator. If we want to get outdoors, we have to board a space-ship. Ours is a postterrestrial interior civilization. We carry on like animals in a zoo, plants in a hothouse.

Our existence reminds me of the fairy tales narrated in some Earth texts, the stories of people who penetrate into the stomachs of monsters and find in them miniature replicas of the world they left behind. Our moon is such a space within. A paradise of the womb, it's protected overall, well-tempered. We are aware of what exists outside, but this awareness is an abstraction. Our sky is just a screen with endless facets, depending on the shade of the glass and the way it's cut and polished. Locked inside, we lack the daily experience of transition, and this devitalizes us. Forever enshrouded and ensiled, we cannot evolve and unfold. We're stuck in a status quo. Therefore things that could be achieved on Earth cannot be accomplished here. Entelechy is absent from our lunar bodies and minds. A utopia realized, the lunar condition excludes all hope for utopia.

What do you mean by utopia?

The desire to travel to the outskirts of ourselves.

At least we can go to the Earth.

Yes. Without the prospect of this journey our life would equal entombment. Born from a groin, we graze away in a translucent lunar grotto. Perfect inner emigrants, we are so tame that even the horror of being completely within doesn't turn us on. Hermetically enclosed in the moon egg, we have been changed from humans to lunatics, impotent and sad. Instead of fighting, losing and winning—we interiorize all conflicts.

What else can we do here—where even the eyes of the castrated grizzly bears are filled with tears as they present bluebells to lonely wanderers?

The poor civilized bears! They remind me of a book that was un-earthed last year in the vicinity of London, in a small place identified as Cambrigia. It's entitled *Winnie the Pooh.* When you came in, I was just pondering this strange little text. I don't know what to make of it. Is it meant to be satirical? Or is it a philosophical treatise, disguised as a children's book? Is it a novel about somebody in particular, a person camouflaged as a bear with very little intelligence? At some point this booklet was enormously popular on Earth. Last week the Middle Europe Excavation Team found a small stone relief showing Winnie the Pooh and his companion Piglet.

Where did they discover it?

In the ruins of Warsowa, a third-rate provincial city of that region. The picture is inscribed in the native tongue of the local population. Since they used the Latin alphabet, it's going to be easy to decipher the text. However, I'm baffled by the fact that no other document in this script has survived.

Do you have any idea what it says?

It's short and I presume it's either a simple description of who Pooh and Piglet are or a quote from the book, something like: I could spend a happy morning seeing Roo, a kangaroo friend of Pooh, or: I could spend a happy afternoon being Pooh.

But let me ask you about something else. That piece of a mosaic that was found in Manhattan. Were you able to determine what it depicts?

More or less. I'm collaborating on it with the Greek and Roman Department.

But Manhattan was neither a Greek nor a Roman colony.

No. But apparently Manhattanites were big collectors. They sent expeditions all over the world and hoarded valuable remains of other cultures on their tiny island. They kept them in a huge museum complex, the Museum Mile, stretching along one of the main avenues. It consisted of skyscrapers and underground vaults filled with treasures. The Greek Antiquity Team tells me that this excellently preserved piece of mosaic comes from an Athenian workshop. It was established by a philosopher who went sour and metamorphosed into a mosaicist. The picture represents himself in the company of his colleagues of whom we know two: Plato and Socrates. Since the darkroom is occupied now, I cannot show you the holographs of the icon. But you can study sketches I have executed after them. They retrace contours and complete the blurred areas of the mosaic.

Yes, I can distinguish the outlines of two men, one old, crooked, with a big belly and a bushy beard, the other slender, taller.

That's Plato.

Why is the breast of the older man covered with letters? What do they mean?

Grump, an American word. It could mean anything—a city, plant,

animal—it could be an adjective or verb in the local slang, a curse or acronym. But most likely it's a name scratched on the mosaic by a visitor to
the Museum Mile. Whatever, I couldn't find it in Earth Names Register,
and we shouldn't attach any importance to it. Wouldn't you like a drink?
This is the time I take my milkshake and watch the sky turn purple.

The new laser plant has added astonishing variations to our celestial
roof.

Yes. The effects help me visualize sunsets on Earth, as they are
described in the terrestrial mythology books and lyrical texts. Recently
I have been studying the fragment of a poem by Sextus, a Roman
author. It's dedicated to the memory of his friend, a man by the name of
Svevius or Svevo, and entitled "A Man Grows Old." Shall I read it to
you?

> The flames of setting suns
> inflame your cheeks.
> We gaze at shores and trees
> but hands turn cold.
> The air is clear and waves of gratitude
> inspire dying lips. Are you here, Italo?
> A great monotony enshrouds the path
> I take. I hear my queen, and many other women.
> They come and go, they tiptoe through
> my house.
> Where—to the left—Hostia
> carries a dog. An ibis follows—to the right—in the queen's
> footsteps. A glowing fruit descends into the Nile.
> A yellow dress. A cangia. Berenice.

Beautiful! So simple, and full of suspense. Who's Italo?

Perhaps the friend to whom the verses are dedicated, or an allusion
to things Italian. When I read the poem aloud, my cheeks turn red, my
hands shiver. On the moon there are no great poets. Why not?

There are no great emotions. No sunsets, no Niles. No outer wilderness to be contrasted with inner monotony. No transitions from one
state to another. We are jailed in architecture, trapped in the ultimate
freedom of choice. No taboos or social barriers prevent us from falling
in love with a man or woman. On the moon the sources of the erotic have
dried out. We date each other, engage in sex—a tiresome obligation—
drift apart. What was accidental on Earth—here it's institutionalized.
No birthday is fêted in a spontaneous way. Everything is sane and comfortable, but nothing matters, nothing moves our hearts.

Occasionally someone's nerves give out, and he ends his life.

But on the moon suicide has a touch of unpleasantness. Unlike on Earth, a self-chosen death isn't a social act. It takes revenge not on society, but only on a person. The scope of a lunar suicide is limited and banal. It's about a man who wants to punish a woman because of her being late for dinner or slow in bed. It's about a woman who asks her lover for cherries and never receives them. On the moon suicide remains without consequence, although it happens all the time.

Every day. It happens so often because life tastes like paper. Going downhill on artificial snow in artificial mountains isn't about skiing. It's about being quick. On the moon speed replaces passion—men's only excitement. Therefore the lunar climate is even worse for women, as their nature enjoys rapidity less than ours. That's why they are so disturbed. Speeding up, we expand our ziggurat. But women are all into academia. Pale sterile orchids, they research the Earth and waste away.

Either architecture or academia. The rest makes no sense. Literature, art, theater, music, dance, and what have you is just garbage, noisy and pretentious. When one cannot refer to anything outside, words drop dead within the soul's four walls. Without the filter of the open air, color degenerates to paint. With no birds fluttering between sky and land, the music of the heavenly spheres cannot reach the lunar instruments. The richness and subtlety of terrestrial art cannot be reproduced on the moon. Our masters succeed neither in sonatas nor triptychs. None of us can ascend to the garden of true art. Why?

It's because we fail in transcending sex. I cannot tell you how sad I am after my weekly squeeze sessions! Coming out of my current female, I feel like disappearing forever into the black moon dust.

I don't date women anymore. Before falling asleep I try to think of the sun setting over the banks of the Nile, and of the mysterious terrestrials immortalized in poems: Hostias, Berenices.

You must be the last moon scholar who pursues Earth poetry after working hours.

Perhaps, but that's the best part of my life. Poetry, reverie, solitude—and a few hours with you, my only friend on the moon. But what an error our ancestors committed! They should have rather perished than escaped to this lunar asylum!

Don't despair, my dear young friend. Sooner or later you'll be sent to the Earth. A confrontation with that nuclear wasteland will cure you of terrestrial nostalgia.

But that's the only thing worth living for.

Other things may emerge from the depths of your dreams. Don't despair. You may be able to reform our sterile culture with your intense sensitivity of an Earth child. Be well. I'll drop in next week.

After the older colleague's exit, the young moon scholar fetches a thick notebook from behind his desk, opens it in the middle, and begins to write in the imperceptible ink he invented to guard his privacy. It shows only after the plastic sheets have been subjected to sub-red radiation.

There is no innovation without a crisis, the moon scholar scribbles. A mental malady made me abandon electro-processors—the way they compose sentences out of the chaotic bits of information our brains project onto the screen terrifies me—and return to handwriting. What a relief! For the first time in my life I seem to be in touch with my body, to communicate directly with my own centers of intelligence, to tap the galvanizing sources of inspiration—the charades of my innermost being. I listen to my voice transporting the linguistic atoms through the labyrinth of my organism, and feel at once petrified and shattered. An apparatus charged with expectation and music, I attune vocals and consonants to the symphonic sound of preprogrammed scores.

At the beginning, handwriting seemed impossible. Trained to express myself in symbols and formulas, to deal with isolated concepts and signs, I could not make my mind and hand obey the complex syntax of the classical Earth English I have opted for, a language a hundred times more sublime than the Moon-American we use here. At first I wasn't sound-sensitive enough to catch on to the Anglo tone, and I began to lose hope. But then intuition told me that in order to assimilate myself to any Earth language I had to change my lunar way. And, step by step, I did. I tore myself away from the propelling pulse the moon lasers dictate and started to imitate terrestrial slowness. Slowly I began to regain the Earth roots of my race.

Every day I worked for many hours in the Earth Manuscripts Library, studying signatures, copying the aggregate of distinctive qualities characteristic for each type of handwriting. Slowly I acquired features I had lacked before, and slipped into a more expressive entity. I slimmed down, my eyes widened, my pupils enlarged, and I realized that once I had been just an anonymous moon-monad without aspects. Slowly I learned to assess my own mental state and moral disposition by analyzing how the unique traits of a particular handwriting affected me. Slowly I shaped my own style by diving into the magical emblem of the I—a category of being, a cipher of sentiment, and a graphic device. Slowly I outgrew the unfocused sketch of a *homo lunaticus* and formed myself according to the distinct script of an Earth man. What had once resembled a scrawl slowly transformed into a proper drawing. Seeing myself for the first time so clearly outlined, I felt a sudden desire to be fully defined by the character of my writing. For this I strove, and today each of my words vibrates with the verve of my letters. My *b* has a female swing, my *i* a male poise. Although I am not yet completely free from the moon rhythm, it no longer possesses me. Neither control systems nor failures of negligence frighten me anymore. I'm my own medium and my own message.

For hours I sit back, relax, dream, exercise my hand in doodles. I wait patiently, breaking the main rules of the moon routine: to rush, progress, advance. Indeed, what shall I hurry for? In the misty future death alone awaits me. Slowly I have learned to induce upon myself visions and hallucinations, and to forget about the opaque perspective of the lunar cage. Numbers and statistics no longer fascinate me. I refrain from making a career. Instead, tearing paper to bits and playing with them, I distract myself, freeing my mind from the futile moon meditation. I let go, let the entire gray mass of brain cells succumb to chorea, the rare Earth disease of men and dogs that liberates limbs from coordinated movement and makes them slip into spasms, rise to the divine fury of a Greek chorus. Every day I suffer from chorea attacks. They strengthen my chorion, the embryonic membrane which encloses the archaic core of the self and makes it resist the degrading terms of the moon existence—its solitary solidity, its strangulating stress.

But still, intuition whispers in the guttural voice of the moon scholar's mother, you have a long way to go, baby. You have to unteach yourself the boredom ordinary moon-men succumb to. Read Earth chronicles, son. You must become an expert in chronology, recapture days and months. No one on the moon could ever put his finger into Time—an open wound. But on Earth at least one author succeeded in regaining seconds. I read you the sixth volume of his French novel before you went to sleep—remember?—and following my advice you wrote your dissertation on *Tempus fugit,* the fear of seeing Time flee and eat us like a mouse. You must reread Marcel's book now. He was a good friend of Sextus, your beloved Roman poet, and his text, more precise and reliable than memory itself, will serve you as a chronoscope and a chrysalis, the defenseless pupa of a butterfly species which your step-father saved from terrestrial extinction and bred at the foot of the

Moonomalaya. You too may emerge one day from the pupa of an ephemeral moon-insect and rewrite lunar history from the point of view of the Earth at its most precarious moment, just before the final collapse. In order to achieve your goal, you must abandon moon indoctrination, son. Once you were a scholar who busied himself interpreting fragments recovered from our mother planet. Later you imposed on yourself the lost discipline of handwriting. Now you have to prepare yourself, my consolation, for your life's decisive action. You must rescue the last sparks of the Earth spirit that still linger in the stuffy moon atmosphere by engaging in erotic ecstasy. To be ready for it, go into hibernation, blood of my blood, and dream about passion and love as they occurred on Earth.

I obey you, mother, the young moon scholar coos, the seemingly blank notebook in his lap. May my imperceptible handwriting be the passport to the paradise lost of the spoilt *Terra Dolorosa*. My reverie is initiated by the five remaining pages and the half-burnt cover of an American book. It's bound in raw cloth, and when I inspect it closely, I decipher *Memory*, printed in ornamental red script, and the photographic picture—torn to pieces and glued to the cover's back—of a middle-aged man. His face strikes me as extraordinarily kind, and he wears an outfit similar to the models depicted in the late-twentieth-century chapter of Earth Fashion, the most detailed and inaccurate section of the *Great Terrencyclopedia*. The photo's background consists of brush where, something tells me, Time hides. Once in a while it winks at me, and yet I see nothing. Stupidly, I mumbled to myself: Perhaps I can date it. My boss overheard me. Now he has me scan the snapshot back and forth. My peace is gone. My journey to the Earth is put off. Oh, how bored I am, a bundle of nerves. I gulp tranquilizers, and groan: Earth gods, reveal the date! Rescue me from that damned lab.

Hip, hip, hooray! Time has come out of the brush. Scrutinized by the Super Laser Eye, the dark mass has opened up. Between the leaves of an unknown tree I have detected a plaque inscribed *Century 21*. The photo is dated. Hip hip hooray! Now they'll give me a vacation.

Stretched out on a mossy lawn in the Luna Park, I muse on how my literary relic is related to the man in a light blue coat lined with yellow, an olive green felt hat, and anthracite-colored trousers. His coat's top button is open, disclosing a black sweater and a white collar. The book was unearthed in the outskirts of Roma, but—intuition tells me—the picture was taken in the suburbs of Manhattan. Its somber aura makes me think of mist and fall, my favorite season, often lauded in poems.

It could be November, the ninth month of the Roman year, which begins with March.

In college the Earth-calendar class was taught by a plump instructor with pimples and a predilection for Latin quotes: *Nota bene,* boys, November 11th marked the beginning of winter. On the 13th *Epulum Jovis,* the sacred banquet, was celebrated, and on the 14th the Roman senate decided to have the month renamed in honor of Tiberius, whose birthday occurred on the 16th. But the emperor declined, saying: What will you do, my honorable lickspittles and conscript assholes, if you have thirteen Caesars? My own birthday, the young moon scholar murmurs to himself, corresponds to November 29th. But why did it all pop up? Why are November days embracing each other in the foggy tunnels of my brain? Why can I not take my eyes off that man's face? Why do I search for his photographer around New York, while all evidence points to Rome?

A wild dove rests on a cement rock. Instead of clarifying my thoughts, I turn increasingly restless. On fire. Does it mean that my journey back to Earth is about to start? Can I, a forty-two-year-old lunatic who wants to escape from the moon, write a book on century 21 on Earth? Become a terrestrial author? Jump out of myself right into the silhouette of the bearded fellow, smiling at me from the picture? He may be a couple of years older than myself, but this doesn't concern me. I'm ready to sacrifice my younger moon age for his older Earth skin. To be his twin. Identical. To be him.

I gaze at my terrestrial double and, burning with desire to give him a name that would indicate my moonness, open the Earth Names Register under M. *Michael, Michelangelo, Mozart*—none of them reflects my meek nature and does justice to his blue-coated cheerfulness. I need something more aloof. What about *Martin,* the saint of Tours? At ten he became catechumen, at fifteen entered the army. While stationed in Amiens he divided his coat and gave half to a beggar, and on the following night had a vision of Christ making this act of charity known to angels. On a visit home he converted his mother to Christianity, but his zeal in fighting the Arians aroused persecution against him. An ascetic, he lived on the deserted island Gallinaria, near Genoa. Ordained to the humble office of an exorcist by Hilary of Poitiers, he was chosen bishop in his later years, wrote his confessions, and was commemorated by the church on November 11th.

In the Roman calendar only eighteen days divide his festival from my birthday. Although I'm instinctively attracted to *Martin,* I sense trouble as well. The saint's c.v., the suburban snapshot, and the image I have of myself don't fit together. From the self-assured joviality the stranger's moonlike face conveys, a charitable impulse cannot easily be deduced. No, this man wouldn't divide his coat with a Manhattan bum, and generosity isn't my strong suit either. Two healthy egoists, he and myself, we don't deserve the name of *Martin de Tours.* Myself? Wait a second. A Slavic sound, suggestive of *Myself,* surfaces from the swamp of my mind. Aha. From now on my second half will be called *Myloslav,* the cross of a name suitable for someone who's supposed to share my exile. But while I'm about to escape from the moon, where has he emigrated from? A quick decision has to be made, and I make it. Myloslav belongs to the crowd from CentEura, the sub-Asian archipelago Propertius derides in his *Bread-and-Puppet Circus,* a novella based on the *Odyssey* that ends in Manhattan. Yes, I recall the first sentence: Prone to melodrama initiated on the imperial stage of Vindobona, suspended between the bridges of Praga, and resolved in the ruins of Varsova, this third-class land is neither flat nor hilly, and it has very limited opportunities.

The *Moon Atlas of the Earth* refers to CentEura as Boho-Ungaro-Ponia, but I prefer the acronym *Unbopo,* and revel in the fact that the names of the two main rivers, which once crossed this backwater, start with *Vel-* and *Vis-* respectively. So far Frydek Místek remains the only city that has been excavated there, although—at least according to the Moon Equippe chief—this hole in the ground should have never been unearthed. But since there are no other archeological sites, Frydek Místek shines like a star in their sky, and I fancy the city—Myloslav's birthplace—as dull and dusty, and ask myself: was Cekopolk or Poloboh spoken there, or something else still? Did Myloslav, the secret sharer of mine, talk in a Pan Slav Politongue or a local form? Friend, help me! Speak!

The dove spreads its wings, and I listen. Is it the wind? No, I hear his voice, and rejoice. Myloslav is fluent in English, and proclaims: I'm an architect—unaware of the effect his words have on me, a moon-man trapped in the lunatic panurbium. An architect, he repeats, arrogant and proud. But I push him aside, and cry out: Don't poke fun at me! Born into a moon-scraper, raised under the translucent roof of an extraterrestrial planetarium, I hate the idea of transforming the open space into an interior. I loathe architecture, yet nothing attracts me more than architecture. Therefore, Myloslav, I'll wed you, my earthly Ego, not to Eve, whose lips turn carmine when she desires you, but to

Madame Architectura, a calculating *belle.* Instead of rewarding you for your dedication to her, she'll inflame your senses but remain frigid, lock her wine cellar and lobby. Unwilling to grant you either small or big metropolitan favors, she'll banish you to suburban *petites,* make you tickle their delicatessen toes, kiss the chimneys of their house additions. A schemer, she'll prevent the Myloslav & Myself Associates from erecting the seven wonders of century 21. Our brainchild, the Grump Grandyosnoy Hotel in Saint Petersburg, and the Gru-Mao-Chu in Wuhan will go down the well. She'll undermine our plan for the Pangramphos in Athens, sabotage the Kanga Grampa in Sydney, steal the blueprint for the Grumpo Grande in Caracas, and announce: You have built your life on a total error, Myloslav. You have fallen in love with someone for whom you're a nil.

Nihilum, nic, nichts. The *Grump Duck* you want to carve from the ice in Dicelandia has a beak, but no wings. The Earth will cease to exist. But there's Eve. Her effort will save the face of a Myloslav from Frydek Místek, and in due time it will find its way to the moon—and into my hands. On a foggy November day on which, as always, you disappointed her, she'll frame you against the site of the future Saint-Martin-Half-Coat Church, develop the film, print the picture, and hand Myself a ticket to Earth.

Dark dust clouds gather above the lunar roof, and the moon scholar's sleepy gaze abandons the blue-coated architect and begins to research the space opposite him. Invisible, the creator of the photo reminds him of *Las Meninas,* a lost oil-on-canvas by an anonymous Spanish painter. He is mentioned in a small fragment of what's classified as a Sort of French Discourse on God and the Rest whose unknown author argues that the invisible is more interesting than the visible. Indeed, I must admit, the moon-man whispers, that it's not the architect I'm after. My eyes seek the photographer he sees while his picture is being taken. Oh mother, help me penetrate to the invisible other side.

A hot lunar evening knocks me out. I fall into lethargic sleep and meet large, blue-grayish eyes appearing, as if in a mirror, in front of me. Fine red veins cut through the mercurial whiteness of the eyeballs and make me recall a curious shell on display in the Earth Museum. Its outer surface is covered with script, while the inside, lined with raw cotton, carries a bloodred drawing of a face. What purpose did it serve? The dream meanders and leads me on. On page 139 of my Roman remnant of a book a similar shell is reproduced in a feminine-looking palm. It bears no writing, but someone is portrayed in it too. Who? For whom?

A moon detective, I remember and compare, hold on, wait for things to click into place. Saint Martin divided his coat in Tours. Someone in Manhattan divided cotton, drew on it, glued it into shells. To marry the impermanent to the solid? To settle the soul of plants in the ex-shelters of snails? Am I mad to find a thin veil of coincidence between the contours in the shell and the face of the architect? Can they be one and the same? How is the photo related to the shell, the book to the man, the copy to the original? The air smells of hidden links. The Earth, from which humanity has been now absent for over a millennium, needs a sensitive moon-man to select from the few surviving fibers of its lost fabric what's really worth preserving. Intuition, assist me!

Follow me, son, the moon scholar's mooma replies. I'll tell you where to go. Freezing, chilly, still cold, warmer, warm, hot, very hot, boiling. You have arrived at your destination, child, the terrestrial spot where a gray-eyed female is photographing Myloslav. Slight, intense, she's your age—and the one you have always wanted to have opposite yourself. Her hair is highlighted with henna, the secret substance of Earth courtesans—Nile mud mixed with the purple seed of puffins, the purpure of purse crabs?—which cannot be obtained on the moon. The woman's skin, pale and oily, reminds me of water chestnuts, aged ebony, unbleached cotton. Her features strike me as southern, but not beautiful. Very thin, she seems to be bent with pain. But, perhaps, it's just the smile. Hovering around her face, it hints at death. Like a lady from the Medium-Age Space I visit every Sunday, she could have a sandglass in her hands, an ermelin at her breast. Yes, it's she whom I have loved since my birth.

Finally you meet your mistress, inspiration whispers, but it's too late. She's infatuated with Myloslav who doesn't give a damn about her, and you see at first sight that they aren't suited to each other. She stands opposite—an opposite of that man in every respect. Her vulnerability is exposed to the vulgar ways of his robustness, and I cry out: Go away! Build a stable for another mare! Don't ruin her.

Shy and solitary, the woman watches Myloslav from a few steps away. But she's absent from the picture, and I know why. Whenever he, a social cat, dashes in, she steps out, although it should be the other way around. Her memory is excellent, while he's a sclerotic. Were life on Earth as logical as lunar romance, the man with the clogged arteries would shoot her, in order to retain what he'll otherwise forget: her silver-striped scarf, her asymmetrical mouth, her curls. The woman, she doesn't need any aides. Hers is a photo-memory, etched with the best sketch of that instant.

The snapshot establishes Myloslav's presence, documents the woman's absence, and demonstrates how the first is indebted to the second. A copy is created, but the creator is lost. A heap of paradoxes, with me, the greatest nonsense. I, the yet unborn moon-man, will be the moving spirit of Myloslav's affair with her—my beloved. I'll grieve for the pain he'll cause her, and wonder: why does it never work out? It could be just like a light summer canvas imprinted with the outlines of two people in embrace. As the wind blows, the fabric is folded into an erotic sculpture, at once soft and solid, as you have never seen it before. The material is provided by Myloslav, the woman supplies the drawing, and I, the hot lunar breeze, I stage the love-and-death melodrama in outer space. But meanwhile tell me, mother: What on Earth brought those two together?

Contraries, son. Eros on Earth wasn't suffused with the common sense of which there is too much on the moon. Myloslav collected females, the woman was aroused by how he touched her the first evening. Without passion.

Without passion?

The promise of passion is locked into a lack of passion. She was inspired by the hope of inflaming him. But her seduction backfired, and she only set herself on fire.

I'm divided between them, mother. My female nature yearns for her sensitive skin, my virility wants to jump into Myloslav's pants. I'm this woman's lover, standing behind her and inspecting her frame with my hands, and I'm her, saying about myself with a little laugh: skin and bones. A man in the moon, I circulate between him, her, and myself. Now I'm Myloslav, smelling her hair on the way to the subway, now I'm myself again, sighing: she's my unfulfilled fate, and longing to spend with her November 29th, my Roman birthday, which in that particular year of century 21—very much towards the end of the last Earth era—falls on a Sunday. Oh terrestrial demons, have Eve travel with me to the suburbs of Manhattan. I may be a lunatic, but still I'm a better Adam for her than the architect.

At last! She faces myself—and not Myloslav. The significance of her switch escapes the builder. An anti-hero, he adjusts in his head the design of shelves where tomato soup cans and frozen bluefish will be displayed to their greatest advantage, and he composes a modest prayer: Christ! Am I sick and tired of the bathroom adjustments. Jesus! Let me put my hands on the Half-Coat-Saint-Martin Church. To influence God's decision and to polish his own image, at mid-Sunday

Myloslav attends Mass in the company of the woman. When it's over, he introduces her—my associate, Father—to the gay parish priest and begins to measure the parking lot—here the nave will hit the cross. Playing her role as well as she can, the woman notes his measurements and reflects on the absurdity of her attachment. That's the moment I enter the stage, the young moon scholar whispers into the apparition of his dead mooma's ear. Changing the course of events, I'll spare her tons of despair and turn this lame-duck duet into a vigorous triangle, a geometrical figure that highly intrigued the Earth philosopher Weil. She valued it higher than the cube and the circle, although she didn't practice it in life. But we'll practice it, since our respective aims complement each other so well. I wish to return to Earth, the woman to escape from it, while Myloslav just wants to moonlight. The result is a cubist drama to be filmed with three cameras: hers, his, and mine.

Ancient Earth gods, provide me with traces of this woman's biography! The amount of data on terrestrial femininity is so limited, and I'm particularly handicapped. I lost my father at an early age, and since then I have been more attracted to older men than to younger women. Only the remembrance of my mother's milk-filled breasts has brought me closer to the other sex. Like myself, she was an Earth addict. Her enthusiasm inspired my dream to descend to Earth and complement my male moon-self with a terrestrial soul. I would like her to resemble my favorite heroines, Anna Karenina and Effi Briest, share certain features with Hostia and Berenice, and have the brains of Saint Simone who tops the Women of Intelligence Register. Myloslav's mistress is my ideal, but I know nothing about her. Does her stepping out of the picture hint at her suicidal character? Was she ready to starve herself to death? Did she give herself to the architect as quickly as Karenina to Vronsky? Why did she choose a lover of booze, sun-dried tomatoes, and chocolate truffles?

Had I in my hands Myloslav's calendar with the names of his dates, would I be able to fish her out? Or would I find on November 29th of each consecutive year another female first name? My intuition tells me that the latter would be true. A Pooh, he emptied women like honey pots, labeled the empty containers ex-erotics, and organized them into a club, slightly reminiscent of what we have here. More humane than the terrestrials, on the moon we don't murder people sentenced to death. Instead, we submit them to a mock execution and then make them join the Post-Execution Band. A social fact, and not just a night-mare, it degrades its members to total irrelevance, and thus prevents

further crime. A civilized institution, it brainwashes the moon population more effectively than the electronic chair. Using similar devices,
we are about to eliminate sexual infatuation. An animal passion, on Earth
it could flee into the open and evaporate. But in the claustrophobic
lunar setting love is an antipersonnel mine exploding the psyche.

My problems are not only with the woman but also with slipping
into Myloslav's skin. A restrained lunatic, how can I cope with his
promiscuity, how can I even understand it? Why did he have to disappoint so many females? To maintain distance by means of large
numbers? To avoid responsibility? Did they get rid of him, did he drop
them? Was he easily bored? Were fresh impulses his only weapon
against impotence? Did he have them line up for their turn, compete
for more than one night a week? A terrestrial womanizer, Myloslav
eludes me. Yet he's my own soul I must catch.

In my moon-text the woman will remain nameless. But I, her lunatic
lover, will nickname her after an Australian bag-animal and whisper
Kangaroo into her ear—something Myloslav never did. He considered
her a PTS, a Part-Time Squeeze, and that's how I'll call her officially in
my *Century 21: A Moon Memoir*. It starts with PTS's and Myloslav's first
trip together in a rented red Chrysler S, the model for our Space
Speeder. The architect has carefully planned every instant, in order to
exclude from their short November ride even the slightest chance of
the adventure PTS still hopes for. The schedule is so tight that not even
a small something at a mysterious McDonald's, hidden in the fog that is
creeping up from the Hudson, can be squeezed in. Eroticism is safely
locked out, as on the moon. In the afternoon the couple will have tea,
but intimacy will be given no chance at the suburban home of Myloslav's
compatriots, whom she wishes to ignore. A travelogue is being shut
before it has been opened. Myloslav, do you realize your meanness?
No. Neither does PTS. Her amor is blind, yet she's aware of colors and
interprets their vehicle's redness as a good omen. Purple, she murmurs,
isn't that a nice surprise? Myloslav doesn't reply.

Mooma, why is he so unkind?

Their brain currents don't coincide, son. He's preoccupied with
architecture, she tries to save their outing from being a complete
disaster. In vain. The seasonless view her eye meets as they roll through
the suburbs brings to her mind the changing landscapes he explored
not with her. A reservoir they pass on the right reminds her of an Aruba
beach he visited with a wealthy businesswoman, a pond they pass on the
left of the Central Park Lake she desires to cross with him in a rented

boat. But he drives on, silent and even more down-to-earth than usual, dreaming about the roof tiles of his would-be Half-Coat Church.

Poor PTS, the moon scholar sighs. Like a cockroach drawn by a sweet-smelling poison into a mortal motel, she suppresses the sight of street signs signaling Small Stopomouck where in a barrack—to be replaced by Myloslav's masterpiece—they are to attend Christian rites. A Hebrew, PTS looks to the Mass with as much pleasure as one can derive from a moon-tax memorandum. In fact, they act as a reminder. Myloslav, a weak believer in the God for whom he wants to build, is here because he hasn't yet received his contract and first check. *O weh!* Such is the light artillery I and PTS must annihilate before we can break out of his business circle—into the erotic. But we unite our forces and abduct the stubborn architect. Turned into a hearty helicopter, his city car is forced to land in Hawaii. Rushing down a stony road, it transforms into a pink jeep and proceeds to the vast reef where the ancient Kilauea volcano slopes into the Pacific.

Now hurry, my son! Replace Myloslav in the paradise of the Sandwich Islands where the guano deposits outdo the shark fishing grounds, corals abound, and the cider and tufa cones grow out of the ground.

No, mooma. Myloslav and PTS must go there together. You and I, we shall follow them. Look! They approach pit-craters that enlarge gradually, as their walls break and fall, and the discharged lava flows with comparatively little violence. Like Lowry, the author of the best under-earth novel, they're on their way to the engulfment of volcanoes erupting with subterranean energy. They face denudation, deep ravines, valleys and tall cliffs eroded on the mountain sides, and the soil from disintegrated rocks. They find their way through the incredible variety of vegetation to Mauna Loa, the biggest boiling belly, and Amuna Kea, the White Top, so named from the snow on its summit, and Manua Hualali, rising abruptly from the extreme northwest shore, and the enormous gorges of Waipio and Waimanu, with nearly perpendicular walls, and Halemaumau, liquid and lofty. They enter the grand spectacle of Hawaiian nights when glowing cracks run across the crust, the crust breaks into cakes, the cakes plunge down, and lava-lakes are created over whose surface fire-fountains play. At dawn they arrive at the bed of volcanic sand, framed by the spongelike pumice and ashes, supple and soft with promise. In front of them a sculpture park extends. Here lava has been shaped into floral spirals and rusty bats, there into a stiff group of Soviet colonels trapped by a creased curtain and a wrinkled cheek.

The *Great Encyclopedia of Earth Geography* mentions, the moon scholar mumbles to himself, that the natives referred to the quiet and regular eruptions of Mauna Loa as her menstruations, since they consisted mainly of the red-colored lava, the Aa. Once it had cooled down, they made holes in it and planted banana shoots and sweet-potato cuttings. Although the holes were simply filled with stones or fern leaves, the plants grew and in due time were productive.

Come, son! The couple has reached its destination, the fertile womb of Amuna Loa, the alchemic cave created by the escape of lava over which a crust formed. Far away from the barren suburbs of Manhattan Myloslav and PTS press against each other, with only a last thin slice of unconsummated desire preventing them from completion, at the side of a small channel with steam cracks on a sheet of verdure, a rug of tropical pasturage in the middle of a garden island, well-watered on all sides by large mountain springs and enclosed by salt lagoons. Finally, they have come out of what's counted and discounted, of the petty and part-time. A Honolulu hamster has shredded Saint Martin's half-coat into a nest. In the distinctly tropical forest of Hawaii nothing has to be divided, nakedness is shared. Sleeping under an *olea sandwicensis* two turn into one and a true sandwich is born—with four hands, four feet, two heads, but one mind.

Oh, ah, aha, a pua-owl cries. Myloslav's embrace tightens around PTS, but there's a but. At the pinnacle of passion, *Pan Architekt* turns soft, and asks me to enter the stage. Otherwise PTS will be hurt, die from unreturned zeal. It's time for the moon-man to come in! So I squeeze myself into Myloslav's unresponsive skin and on the wings of her wind fly to our midsummer night's adventure. I come! She comes! A geyser of blue gum erupts, a cork goes up like a rocket. The lean leaves of the *erytherina monosperma* brush our eyelids, sandalwood sings, and naio, the bastard sandalwood, licks our lips. I carve small ebony idols out of her childlike breasts. She's a fruit-bearing strawberry my tongue tests and tastes. I, a lunatic scholar, grow into the ohelo berry in the lava of her underbelly. A wild shrub, I drink the hot redness of her discharge, and get wilder and wilder with each up and down. Now she's a litchi, the white Chinese pear, and I'm *persea gratissima,* the alligator spear. But it takes her one second to change into an Indian tamarind, while I acquire the appearance of a cantaloupe, granadilla, and guava. I touch her cervix and she's introduced to me as papaya and kauila and *alphitonia ponderosa* and vaccinia and fragaria, while I'm sharpened into a sapodillo and loquat and mesplus, the violet plum ripening in the moisture of dense orange forests, and tamarindus, the pointed paddle of a kayak, cutting rivers into hot shivers.

Entangled in the fibers of her flesh, enmeshed in her hair, I, a moonbeam, become PTS's hetropogon consort, and penetrate her, my *poa annua*, in my capacity of her *cyndon dactylon*. Our union is perfect, but we choose to repeat it again and again. Oh my *bohemia stipularis!* Oh my *colcassia antiquarum!* Copulating with you in the koa forest, I'm as profuse as the mamake and *pipturus albidus*. You're the shaft, I'm the bark. You're my blood, I'm your hide. Oh my kalo, I cultivate you from dawn to daybreak. Our coincidence restores fire to the sun, dew to the moon. Oh my Hawaiian gallinule, my mongoose, my moongoose, my monogose. You're my habitat, I'm your bird. You're my snake, I'm your gecko. You're my earth, I'm your sputnik. We feed on nectar, stroll on a smoking carpet at midnight, and in the morning sizzle into the sea. From Labor Day to July 4th we breed in our cinder cave. Then we ascend to the stars.

Planets come and go. Moons are made, unmade, remade. But nothing disturbs us. You repose in my arms and I'm clothed in you, my wool, my cotton, my silk, my mauna kea. You're my experiment with life, I'm your guinea pig. I'm your shepherd, you're my sheep. God alone keeps track of our many names. Some say we shouldn't have met. Before our encounter, alarm sounded on earth and moon, voices warned us we were sterile waterless gardens, not suitable for cohabitation. From both a distant past and a distant future red lights announced the end of our affair. But we went ahead, unafraid of hazards, and found each other on this archipelago of the northern Pacific, at this volcano. Pale moon creatures, we took off our Manhattanite outfits and were reborn as aboriginal Kanakas whose reddish skin has been compared to lava. Our auburn hair is curly, our eyes blue and expressive. The yum, the arum, and the sweet potato are our chief articles of food. This vegetable diet renders us a bit pneumatic. But a certain stoutness is part of our uncivilized charm. We address each other in diminutives, acronyms, alliterations, and rhymes imitative of the Song of Solomon. We wear sandalwood sandals and a strip of silk around the loins. The last Earth savages, we are also the last lunatic pair that has escaped extinction. Grateful for our good luck, we dance the hula. We dance the hula together in the blue hoop of our doomed universe.

I T'S THE FIRST DAY OF ADVENT, waves run white manes and fog rises along the horizon. The temperature falls, and a promise of snow seeps through the air. Malcolm is on my mind, Conrad says to Eglizer, that fiend of mine who was my best friend. My twin, my secret sharer, he doesn't leave me. I learn his texts by heart and they mix with my own stuff. Since his death I'm blocked, not a thought comes to me, as if everything had been dictated by him. When I wake up in the morning, I catch a glimpse of him in the mirror, shaving. Later I hear him in the kitchen, opening a bottle. I close my eyes under the impression that we live together in a southern country, amidst hills and lagoons. Our shack, old and limp, stands on an inlet, mild air softens our features. Days are uneventful but full of suspense, the moonless evenings are bathed in dark blue. A fishing boat comes round the point, and Malcolm murmurs: Doesn't it resemble a cream-colored giraffe? It's a giraffe, I reply, swift and stately, followed by a scalloped rim of wake. We inspect the horizon, spot the wash of an unseen ship. Turning to me, Malcolm says: It must be a whale. I put my hand on his shoulder and reply: It's Moby Dick whirling across the bay.

You think I've turned gay, Karl? A decrepit sailor at the brink of death discovering a liking for jack-in-the-pulpits? But so what! I'm in love with Malcolm, and my current writing amounts to a cheap imitation of his style. I even copy his way of insulting people, and I dream his dreams—of Edens and salmonberries and thimbleberries and wild blackberry bushes, and of the dogwood behind our shack. It blossoms in April, and its pink, pointed petals remind me at once of penises and female breasts. Womanlike, Malcolm furnishes our place with bright blankets and carpets, their Oriental patterns indicating the cycles of life. When my hands touch the ornaments, I feel relieved and no longer ask the *cui bono* of it all. Finally we're together. Two chums, we sit on a bench, smiling at the sea. Two tough loners, we work on our respective Odysseys—one and the same text in two translations.

Malcolm has taken his residence in the center of me. Right here, behind my backbone. No, he doesn't drink so much anymore; I mean he isn't drunk from dawn to midnight. But he does bang his fists against my defective disks and scream: Joseph, your heart of darkness is unbelievable crap! Why didn't you sail to Hawaii instead of going to the Congo? How could you dare to indulge in blackness, you who're so terribly white! You never understood anything about savages, neither in Africa nor anywhere else. You hadn't the slightest clue as to why they tame darkness by means of some beastly cult—their only way of being civilized. That you failed to grasp because you're a moralistic ass. Afraid of your own wildness, you masquerade your soul, clothe yourself in serious symbols—and pretend not to care about being serialized in the tabloids. *Pan Polak,* you have always been too proud of your Polish prick, red and white but not sufficiently hard. Since it couldn't penetrate the heart of darkness, you had to propose to it. If you weren't impotent, you would have proposed to my spouse instead, and mixed her rich black menstruum with the whiteness of your own thin sperm. Oh the verbosity of your sea silence—it really puts me to sleep! Your English, a Pole-made eng, is so slow, so *eng.* Really, it feels less comfortable than a marsupial bag. On the other hand, what sheer pleasure it is to spy on your struggle against the innermost Polishness of your talent, as it talks you into tackling top topics only—from *Macbeth Polonius* to *Ube, Pole Rex*—or into composing humanist cookbooks the Swedish dynamite of a jury prefers and the united global mediocrity likes best. Yes, sell them the middle road of an obliging author who admits that the world is bad but promises to improve its state by means of his sound but dumb scribble.

Before falling asleep I often feel myself snatched off by him, then suddenly dropped. He is gone, but I hear his voice: *Pan Jósef,* take my arm and let's *polak* together to the tune of a polka, wash down the *polnische Wirtschaft* with a splash of vodka, toast the Lumumba heart of a Congo night, save a couple of savages—since we cannot rescue even a single Pole—and get killed in a preposterous protest staged by one of your patriots. Sweet Joe, you picture yourself a cosmopolitan, but you belong to Bydgoszcz city. And so it is. Malcolm alone understood the difficulty of entering the heart of anything if you're from the provinces. The damned *Minderwertigkeitskomplex* that makes you whisper *vivat Polonia* into the salty ear of a Hong Kong go-go girl, ask a Texas tramp *connaissez-vous Chopin?,* explain to a Jew that your poor *Polen* is the Christ of nations, invent a pitcher with an ear inside. Once Lowry inquired: Why have you crossed so many seas and continents, Joseph? Escaped into a foreign language? I didn't answer him then, but I'll tell you now: to unpolish myself.

I don't buy that, Conrad. He loved to tease you. And you enjoyed his jokes.

No, Karl. He had come to know the hell of me before I came to know myself. He turned me in and out and grasped the invisible agony of someone who has set his heart on the impossible—to become an English writer.

But you are one, Joe. You aren't Gombrowicz chasing his Polish pants in the gay bars of the Retiro.

It's an illusion, Karl. I'm still bilingual, and what would I be without Florence, my faithful editor? My last opus will be dedicated exclusively to her and finally dispel the myth of my being fluent in English.

In the exaggeration you prove to be a Pole! But what really prompted you to switch tongues?

It's not what, it's who. Lowry! It was his idea—a booze fume, as he called it later. That's why he kept poking fun at me. That night I walked him home, put him to bed, and was about to say good-bye when Malcolm cried out: For the sake of your Black Madonna and my salvation, stop rhyming on the white eagle being fucked by everyone. Stop playing the persecuted pussy. Stop meowing about the *lux ex oriente,* while stuffing yourself with the *luxus in occidente.* Stop pole-poting, *Pan.* Check it out, scream: Ice cream, you scream, we scream for a smoke in an American asshole, *elohssa nacirema na ni ekoms a rof.*

Astonishing!

Yes, Karl. I obeyed Malcolm, and failed.

Come on, Joe. You're the pride of the entire globe.

Spare me your sarcasm, Karl.

I'm sincere, dear chap.

You don't have to pay me compliments, Eglizer. I took Malcolm's advice and went further than any other Pole—but not far enough. I should have dwelt a little less on the mysterious symmetry of love and death.

And glorified Lowry a little less as the super-Shakespeare speaking out of you, a simpleminded Słowacki. You diminish yourself to please your vanity and forget some dreadful writing he did. What about *The angelic wings of the seagulls circling over the treetops shone very white against the black sky.* Want to throw up? But I agree. The best and the worst in you and him is symmetry: the search for the lost twin. You both spark with genius, but on the whole, thank God, you lack his volcanic depth. But say, Korzeniowski, what glued you guys together?

Narcissism, negritude, and the gays within ourselves. We understood nothing about women, and so you have them in our books: alter egos with boobs, guardian angels, pretty psyches, sour shadows. Sailors, Karl, don't need mistresses. They have ships, sunsets, and the sea, a serene, sinister siren.

And the bottle.

The sweetest representative of the opposite sex—Malcolm's words.

Whenever I hit the waves, he poured spirit into himself. But it could have been the other way around.

No question. Lowry would have been perfect in the martyr-savior role of a drunk *pisarz polonais.*

You know what I regret, Karl? That he and I never globe-trotted together, never sailed the same boat. We could have served as the living test of the eternal duality of existence—of nature's delight in twins. Most people fear duplication, but we were above such pettiness. I could have been cast into the role of the blond female brother, a beam of light, welcoming his dark male sister in the thicket and leading her on. Oh, Karl, we were leading each other, and misleading each other all the time. Malcolm always first, I always second. If he was Adam, I must have been Eve.

No, he performed the snake and tempted you with *Anglia,* the apple of his eye. But let him rest in his grave. As a matter of fact I wanted to talk to you about another mad genius, Carol Kar, at whose side I had the privilege and displeasure of spending most of my life. Her work needs some pushing. I'm looking for ways to get her Veronica venture published, and for money to commission the man, yes the architect who ruined her life, so to speak, to build a house for her House of Time.

Is Veronica that monster of a text in which Mechtild of Magdeburg meets Nero's mother, while the Greek Church Fathers discuss iconoclasm?

Quite. There was nothing she couldn't combine. Have you ever seen her mile-long cotton scrolls? For a quarter century she applied red paint to unbleached cotton, the symbol of her skin. Shortly before her suicide she switched to a lapis lazuli sort of blue and to silk—her sky and sea from then on—out of which strange things emerge.

I understand little about art, Karl. But Ann once tried to explain to me the meaning of Carol's work. How it reflects the mobility and flux of the contemporary life, fuses psychology and aesthetics, converts the personal into the universal. Alas, my conservative eyes aren't convinced of her greatness.

You're wrong, Conrad. Carol's drawing resembles nobody else's drawing, but her line—folding and unfolding, making and unmaking itself—captures everybody's agony. You look at her cloths and recall your own destiny. I admit, she's high-pitched. When you see her things for the first time, they get on your nerves. What a hysteric, you think. What an exaggeration. How often did I say to her: Lower your tone, Carol. Why expose your cunt with such vehemence? Be quiet, girl. But whenever disaster threw me off my feet, I caught up with her intensity. She really knew how to put her finger on the cracks in the human nut.

You loved her, Karl?

That's beside the point, Conrad. Don't suspect me of being just an erotic opportunist.

OK, OK. Wasn't she terribly erudite, your Carol? A bit too much?

Perhaps, and on top of it, she confused both Veronica and Christ with herself.

And it was you, Karl, you of all men, a specialist in cybernetics, a connoisseur of champagne, who fell for this weirdo?

Shame on me, Joseph. Ours was an alchemical union, with sulphur biting copper, and it mostly consisted of strolls through the Vienna Woods or in Riverside Park. In motion, we invented the miracles Jesus was to perform on his way to Caparnaum, psychoanalyzed the water in which Pilate was to wash his hands. While boating in Central Park we discussed the Children's Crusade, or the cannibalism of cynics.

Forgive me for interrupting you, Karl. But I don't want you to miss that lonely sailing boat. It cuts through the fog as through a milky glass. A misty Venetian afternoon comes to mind, Carpaccio's paintings at the Accademia.

I and Carol, we went many times to Venice. The damp air made her hair curl. Once, when we were on our way to Afghanistan . . .

I thought you traveled there alone?

I've been to Afghanistan three times—once alone, once with Carol, and the last time with Ann.

The two sisters had little in common, I have been told.

They were identical twins, but totally dissimilar. Carol suffered from permanent depression, while Ann, as you know, is always hyper. One wanted to jump out the window every day, the other is a survivor.

May I ask: Were you involved with both of them?

You may. Yes, but not at the same time. In my youth I took care of Carol, later I played the platonic double of Ann. With her I climbed up Stromboli, biked in Nanking, explored the slums of Peshawar. It's getting chilly, Conrad. Couldn't we continue our chat indoors?

We could have tea with Moses. Yesterday he phoned me, and complained of feeling rather lonely. From his windows the sea is as clearly visible as from here, so we won't lose our source of inspiration.

His violent attack on Goethe has alienated him from both Wolf and Charlotte.

And from Italo too. And what about you, Karl?

My heart is with Moses, but I envy Wolf's vitality. He plunged right into the complot of the New World—a *Geheimnis* even to a *Geheimrat*.

I admire him too! While we took to Pompeii, Goethe toured atomic plants, attended seminars on nuclear winters, participated in the plenary sessions of the New York Club, debated our chances on other planets.

In his striving against Wolfgang, Moses keeps reducing himself to a relic—an Alexandrian alabaster phial filled with the pure spirit of the past.

He reminds me more of an old-fashioned shoemaker shocked by the sight of a plastic sandal *made in Pakistan*. But, of course, he's right to point out that Pyscek plus Grump amount to zero minus. What a comic-strip couple! A black dwarf riding atop a giant white camel. Yet they are thrashing the earth, and Wolf takes them into account.

T EA, OR DO YOU YEARN FOR SOMETHING STRONGER, HERR KARL?
To begin with, a *Hagebutentee* with a drop of rum will do, Moses. Then I may want to visit your cellar.

And you, Conrad? *Wyborowa* on the rocks?

Wrong. Earl Grey with a splash of milk.

So what brings you here, besides deep affection for me?

The freezing sea breeze unsettling our achy bones. We walked for hours along the shore, unable to tear ourselves away from our dear deceased, first Malcolm, Joe's twin brother, then Carol, Ann's Siamese sister.

Her stepsister, Karl.

In fact you're right, Moses, but in theory you're wrong. Stepsisterhood has no sex appeal. Believe me, it's much better for us—and for the future generations—to believe that they were twins.

You prefer mythology to truth, Karl. When will you grow up?

In my grave, the ideal place to attain adulthood. There I intend to enjoy together what was separated on earth: the body of Carol and the spirit of Ann. Or perhaps the other way around.

I never met Carol, and I regret it to this day. I could have asked Ann to introduce her to me when we were together in Manhattan. But somehow I never did. Maybe it was better so, since I disapprove of people who take their own lives. A suicide inflicts so much hardship on others.

Carol didn't kill herself in order to punish anyone, Moses. If she had, I would be the first to complain about it. No one knew her better. No one. She wasn't made for life. The temperature of her soul was never right. She found herself either in the tropics or in Siberia. Childlike in appearance, she was a pack of dynamite. I mourn her suicide, but I don't resent it.

I don't want to pass judgment on Carol. But suicide is a symptom of arrogance.

Arrogance?

Yes, a thousand times yes. It's the total refusal to comply with what fate has in store for us. But let me not argue against Ann's sister. Did I ever tell you how we met—Ann and I? It was in a Spanish seaside spa. I'll never forget our first stroll on the beach. The landscape looked like a cubist picture by Juan Gris, who was really so much better than Picasso. We conversed about the names of God—something one cares about only when one is very young. I was then twenty-three and pre-occupied with two things: the definition of the tetragrammaton and my love for Ann. Oh how clearly I remember that afternoon, mild and pale, permeated with the late summer's autumnal aroma. Visibility was excellent, and the crystal-clear sea reflected two clouds. To her eyes one resembled a crocodile, the other a porcupine, and so I recalled that in his last letter to me Shakespeare compared clouds, spread out across his native sky, to sheets in a simple room where you wake up at the side of your beloved.

Se non è vero, è ben trovato.

Don't interrupt him, Eglizer. I know no better topic than love. Go on, Moses.

I was so immature then, so terribly shy. Ann was menstruating and her scent drove me crazy. That's why I communicated to her with such ardor the mystery of the tetragrammaton. To convince her of my academic potential. Oh how I wished to be a Kant, Schopenhauer, or Nietzsche—distinguished and old—who could impress the woman of my dreams not with words but with fat printed volumes. In the morning Ann mentioned Wittgenstein to me, whom she had met in Cambridge a week earlier. She remarked that he was good-looking, but failed to inform me about his gayness. Jealous, I attacked poor Ludwig vehemently, making a fool of myself.

You never make a fool of yourself, Moses. You're too smart for that.

You shouldn't tease an old man, Joseph. Anyhow, what an after-noon! With incredible speed the sea turned from silver to flames, and I was picturing myself as a drop of golden rain falling between the auburn thighs of my soft-spoken Danae. She, however, was a Salome— in love with her John.

A construction-business dope.

Or a would-be Corbusier. But I still cherished the hope of seducing her away from the architect. All I needed, so at least it seemed to me then, was time. Therefore I addressed a silent prayer to Saturn, and asked him to cooperate. Forget about *fugit,* I begged, stay with me, *Tempus.* Don't move! But you know what sort of a runner Time is. He refused to stop even for one second, and was already outrunning us. What a nightmare to see the last day turn to night and not be able to arrest it. What injustice! Horrified by the vision of Ann departing for New York, I talked about time and the necessity to repudiate it. In my despair I declared: We have to fill time with eternal truth and love, but I meant: I am a Niagara Falls ready to fill you up. Ann laughed, but my words must have touched a secret nerve of hers, and after a short silence she said: Leave eternity alone, Moses. It's the instant that counts. Do you believe in love at first sight? I shivered, since it had just happened to me. I fell in love with her in the first five minutes of our first talk. When she asked the question, the tone of her voice rose, and I knew immediately that she was thinking about another man. My heart hurt, and I wanted to cry out: Forget him, Ann, stay with me! No one has ever loved you more. Instead I sighed: No, I don't believe in love at first sight. It's sheer madness. Worse, it's false. Even worse, it's metaphysically impossible.

I was convinced you never lie! What a consolation! Maimonides is as human as the rest of us.

Yes, I heaped one lie on top of another, all against my better judgment. I called love at first sight a disease, a brain tumor. While I jabbered, my soul shuddered, and admonished me: leave her alone. This young female fancies somebody else. Don't torture me, I shouted back, don't cut me away from hope. I'm also young, younger than Ann. There must be some future for us.

But there was none.

No, Conrad, there was none. She, a jewel of femaleness, chose to ignore me, the rising star of Hebrew philosophy, and threw herself away, on a nobody. Oh, how I hated the man! I wanted to call him names—a raccoon, a puffin—but I managed to control myself. Modeling my face after a baby weasel snout, I tried to sway Ann by means of body language. In vain. She remained a *bel ange sans merci.* Meanwhile dusk crept in and my arguments flickered in the air like a swarm of fireflies setting fire to my rival's brownstone. I wished the man consumed by flames, since his presence on earth made me into an absence. I boiled with affection, but didn't dare to even touch Ann's hand. Nothing could make her love me—my mind accepted the fact, but my spirit rebelled against it. Meanwhile Ann complained about her cement block of a lover. Last summer, she whispered, I wanted him to go with me to the beach, but he backed out at the slightest suggestion of an outing. Her voice broke at *outing,* and pain pierced my chest. Ann, my heart implored her, don't let him do this to you! But pride kept my lips sealed, and Ann continued: The desire to go with him to the sea really overwhelmed me, Moses, and I went as far as to buy a black cotton bikini, and to put it on one night. A sort of joke. I smiled, but he grew tense, didn't take the hint. To relax him, I chatted: It was so cheap. Black isn't in fashion this season. The textile merchant, a Jew from Lvov, sold it to me for half price. The top is so small. It fits only someone as underdeveloped as your Ann.

How cruel of her! To tell you all that.

Not cruel, Karl. Oblivious. She forgot about me, and I tried to extract a grain of hope from her confession. At least she trusts me, I told myself, lets me see through her affair. But why was the *Baumeister* upset by her wearing the black bikini in bed? God knows. Anyhow, he refused to make love to Ann and she spent the night on the floor next door. Not disturbed by her absence, he had a good rest in her bed and left in the morning—without a word. Ashamed of her story, Ann had turned all red in her face. And I stuttered: Perhaps that's the way he is—reserved.

Reserved!

An idiotic comment, yet it provided her with immediate consolation. She glanced at me with gratitude, her gray eyes lighting up, and put her hand into my hot palm. My heart jumped and prompted me to propose. And I proposed—to have dinner together—and praised lobster and oysters to the first and last great love of my life. A nervous wreck, I pretended to be a bon vivant, a connoisseur of shellfish and wine. By the time we had arrived at the Sarcástica Seductora—I selected the restaurant for its name—I found myself in a dazed state. I prayed to God to make her love me and, afraid that He might be offended by my immodest wish, thanked Him for having granted me the privilege of dining with Ann. Isn't life strange? She never returned my feelings, and I still consider myself a lucky man. God prevented the architect from extending his hand to her. She abandoned Manhattan and arrived in Rome the very day Goethe appointed me a Vanity Fellow and her—my consolation. Now we are such old friends, we see each other every week. Ann is admirable, and she hasn't aged a bit. The same passionate girl I remember from Spain. After Carol's death a few fine lines appeared on her face, and she lost weight. But she's so brave, so learned, so compassionate! Will she ever be attracted to me as a man? Hardly a night goes by without me dreaming of the black bikini—which she puts on to go with me to the beach, and takes off to throw herself into my arms. I watch her undress through the golden veil of that afternoon in Salamanca, a cubist canvas bathed in her blood. Every time her hand touches mine, I melt. She inflamed me then, and I'm still burning.

What stubbornness—the two of you.

It may have something to do with the peculiarity of our Hebrew natures. Take menstruation, Karl. We confessed to each other that nothing excites us more than the fantasy of blood exchanged with semen. Alas, Ann had no desire to be fused with me.

Never? But what happened that evening? After the Sarcástica Seductora?

Nothing. We just talked and around midnight I walked Ann home—tears in my throat. I was close to falling on my knees, and begging her: Don't go back to this man! He doesn't deserve you. Stay with me! I'll be dust at your feet. A sheet, I'll wrap around your skin. But I knew this would only embarrass her, and so I did and said nothing. We strolled on the promenade, watched the moon rising against a maze of masts and sails, and recalled you, Conrad. Who can smell the sea without thinking of your sunlit mist and the lonely pyramids of ships escaping into the self's distant gloom?

That's what I told Joe: you're the greatest sea author.

Absolutely. Superior even to Lowry. Profound he was, but too captivated by the bottle. You, Conrad, you lead us on. Your texts sparkle, and when I read them aloud I want to be buried in your lines. You leave no room for doubt, and I wish I were a mouse in the food locker of your ship and could sink with it. You're such a good night-fellow. Ann and I mention your books all the time. You, Italo, Simone, and Propertius are the stars in our firmament. By the way, is Goethe still in the States?

Yes, in New York.

How could he traduce us like that? Desert intellect, sell out to trivia and kitsch, replace soul with soap, go mainstream?

You exaggerate, Moses.

No, I don't. He has betrayed our ideals, stopped pursuing truth. I do not understand anything anymore, and Ann is terribly troubled too. Which way will it all go now? Will our lives simply spill away? For my part, I am not ready to give up. I too want to join the modern way, but not like that! It's not the surface that interests me, Karl. We must grasp the core of the subatomic structure, the deep pattern of subconsciousness.

D ECEMBER CREEPS THROUGH MY BONES, says Charlotte to Ann, and I wonder how Wolf is bearing the biting cold of New York?

Don't worry! He's a geyser. Forget him for a while, profit from his tour. For years I have been wanting to talk to you, but he always stood between us. And you were so withdrawn.

It's because he assigned me a ridiculous role. I play his muse and platonic mistress—a B-movie parody of Gretchen and Helena combined. But everybody knows that I'm just a housewife, and only half human. Like an old dog assuming the appearance of his master, every day I resemble Wolf more. I wonder what's next? Will I grow a beard? A tail? Oh, Ann, it's hard to live with a giant. One's dignity evaporates. Every night he fucks another *Weib* and in the morning, upon returning from her, he calls me his *Seele,* while I butter his *Kaisersämmel,* stir his hot chocolate. The world is his harem, but does he feel an erotic obligation toward me? Not at all. Virgin Lot, he shouts, where's the *Jause?*— meaning: hurry up, I'm getting ready for the night cruise. I bring him the coffee, he licks the cream off the spoon. His eyes turn dreamy, his prick stands *hab acht.* For five more minutes he chats me up, jokes about Mandelshtam. When six o'clock strikes, he starts to transmit a hundred perfidious signals, bite his nails. At *Punkt* ten past he kisses me goodbye and runs out, whistling the Venusberg aria.

Yes, that he has been doing to me since our first meeting in Weimar two centuries ago. Of course, then I was too naive to see through him, blinded by respect and hope. Now, Ann, I often feel like killing him, or myself, or both of us. Really, I should explode. Instead I retreat into my shell, store my pain. That's why I'm so fat. But I won't become a garbage bag. No way. Already a first step has been made. To gain perspective, I let Wolf go to America alone. Our first separation in God knows how many years. What will come out of it? So far I like it. No one is dragging me to archeological sites. No one gets on my nerves. But I must confess, Ann, his absence renders me sad and restless. At night I agonize for him, as I did once—before my menopause. You should have seen me then! I was a Karenina obsessed by a single thought: if he won't make love to me, I'll finish myself off.

And did he make love to you, Lotte?

No. At the pinnacle of my passion, he screwed a Hebrew widow, only a year or two younger than myself, who gave him lessons in the art of aquarelle. It happened in Lausanne, Ann, late in November. The wind was deflowering lemon blossoms, and she wore a silk blouse, the color of vanilla, open at the top. Goose-flesh, pink with voluptuousness, was disclosed, and I couldn't take my eyes off it, while he brushed across paper with the eagerness of a sophomore. It took him two hours to seduce her, Eckermann reported in a note to me. My sight was glued to her skin, and I kept repeating: two, two, two. You let him travel alone, now take it.

Imagine, Ann. He told me to stay in Weimar, and there I waited—for his letters. But nothing came for an entire week. Finally on Monday a young postman delivered the note. Even before I had finished it, my entire face was covered with a rash, as if I had scarlet fever. That night I didn't undress, didn't go to bed. In the morning I sent Wolf a cable announcing my arrival in Lausanne. In three days. No, he didn't fetch me from the coach station. He waited on the widow's wooden veranda, and greeted me with the words: She's a modest watercolorist who doesn't deprive you of anything, *mein Kind.* I admit that she isn't completely indifferent to me, but you are my *alles,* Lotte.

A fox!

Yes, a fox addressing a hen. That's why I consider him my custodian. While we stood on the porch, the widow's head appeared in the window. Seeing her, Wolf bowed his head, and said: Promise me to refrain from intervention. In return I promise you: Soon it will be all over. The last words must have reached the poor artist's ears, as even from a distance I could see them turn red. The wind carried away lemon petals, and I felt sick and ashamed of myself. Wolf, on the other hand, preserved his perfect composure, and continued: In the second half of November the mildness of a May day doesn't last long. Short are the daydreams of late autumn, Lotte. We are still enraptured by the season's golden glitter. But soon the spirit of winter will cool and enlighten us.

Oh, those guys! How they divide us: to the left the sweet girls who take care of their flesh, to the right the obedient servants of their souls.

The first, of course, can be declassified in no time. You go to bed a mistress, you wake up a *Dienstboten.*

Absolutely, Lotte. You remind me of such a change. Worried about the growing coldness of my lover—no, nothing recent, it happened many years ago—I wrote him a letter asking for a little more affection. If by affection you mean sex, he replied, the answer is: there has been not a drop of it from the very outset. I praise the day we met, consider myself a lucky fellow to know you, a remarkable person, and hope that you'll stay in my life forever. My feelings are warm, even tender. But sex, God forbid. This less than a year after my abortion—of his future kid.

Did you leave him then?

Not yet. We kept seeing each other for another year. But his words echoed in me night and day. So I had to discontinue the affair.

That's what I should have done a century ago, Ann. But in my younger days German females feared sex. This Wolf encouraged. He called me his *anima,* and derided *amor.*

But after all, Lotte, you have become a mythical couple. It's a pity you don't have offspring.

Can you imagine being Goethe's son? A poor little sufferer dwarfed by his grand papa?

But a daughter, an Angelica Kauffmann type of a girl? Very talented, but not a genius. Wolf would adore her. A precocious child, she would rapidly acquire several languages, show marked talent as a musician, play chess, and make the greatest progress in painting. At twelve she would be a notable, with bishops and princes competing to be her sitters. Wolf would travel with her to Italy, and visit every single museum he dragged you to, Lotte. Everywhere she would be fêted, as much for her gifts as for her charms. She would execute portraits of his famous friends—and of her dad, in every possible costume and setting—pursue engraving and etching, speak Italian and Greek fluently, express herself with facility in French. From Count Panin she would pick up some Russian, from Mickiewicz some Lithuanian. A flirt in Rijeka would teach her *tail* in Serbo-Croatian, while from her first lover, a native of Budapest, she would learn an ill-fated proverb: It takes two Poles to produce a Hungarian. However, Angelica would be most accomplished in English and make a fortune painting Brits in Italy. In Venice she would be introduced to Lady Chatterley and accompany her to London. Well received by the royal family, she would become a firm friend of Sir Joshua Reynolds, appear in his notebooks as Miss Engel, and return the compliment by including an idealized portrait of the great man in her grisaille *Et in arcadia ego.* There Reynolds would appear as the angel of death inscribing a stele with *Fräulein Angelica Goethe, the First German Paintress.*

Before you continue, Ann, I just want to refresh your memory. Wolf never slept with me. Not once. And God failed to infuse into me his sacred sperm.

He still may. Nothing can stop me from depicting Angelica's excellent career. Wolf would, of course, prevent her entrapment in a clandestine marriage with an adventurer passing as the Swedish Count de Horn. Instead he would introduce her to innumerable classical subjects and have her paint Leonardo, flanked by Goethe and Dante, expiring in the arms of Schiller. Employing his genius for intrigue, Wolf would bring about Angelica's election to every single European academy of fine arts and manipulate the Holy See into commissioning her with the re-decoration of the Vatican. Thus she would overpaint the loggiae with her own version of Raphael's life, end it—this most daring of all her fresco cycles—with his entombment in Urbino, and represent herself with pennons as *Angela Raphaella,* his soul.

Alas, Wolf, an immortal, would survive his child and talk curators into buying her art. After Dresden, Saint Petersburg, and Munich, he would bombard the Louvre and the Getty, get her face on the cover of *Vanity Stress,* videotape her paintings, popularize her technique—the infusion of silica that secures permanence—promote her, the only woman on earth of whom he wouldn't be jealous, more than himself, explain her singularity within the female sex, claim that in her alone intuition was married successfully to intellect, transform his daughter into an honorary man and refer to her as my Angelo Goethe.

You're insane!

You see, Charlotte. My nonsense makes you smile and for a second your sad face, flattened out by superfluous fat, gives way to a young woman's animated likeness.

Who knows, Ann, perhaps we should have had a daughter. Focusing on her, Wolf would have been less crazy about subteens—his newest disease—less of a ladies' man. Every night I dream of him sleeping his way through the States. His horny fingertips inspect plastic blondes, and although it takes him a while to erect his cock, he still cherishes the idea of colonizing Venus.

There's something imperial in Wolf's vitality. In his will to drill the earth. He embodies the male chauvinist pig all emancipated women hate—and want in bed. No, I don't speak of myself. But, then, I'm not a proper female, Lotte. At sixty I look like a boy. My biological clock must have stopped at puberty. A hormonal deficiency saved me from becoming a *Frau*. Men pet me as if I were an exotic animal, or the infant survivor of an extinct race. All I want from them is sex. I am appalled by the idea of building a nest. But since men always suspect women of wanting safety, my affairs are marked by a basic disjunction. Men either believe that I don't give a damn about them, or they don't give a damn about me.

The quantity of your flings contradicts your complaint, Ann, and for Maimonides you're the only woman on earth.

Poor Moses! Really, there's no justice. So good-looking, so terribly bright, so devoted to me. And all I could come up with was to spend one night with him, and tell him at the end of it that I didn't love him.

So there was something between the two of you?

A long time ago. In Salamanca. I'd had too much wine, and found myself in a strange state of suspense, floating between exhilaration and despair. Moses sniffed around me, and I was indeed a bitch in heat. A bottle of Mocero increased my menstrual flow. We walked along the shore, more and more aroused by the sight of the full moon, but—to play it safe—conducted a conversation on Conrad. Yet Moses couldn't help alluding to his affection for me. He spoke about the wish to be a mouse living in the food closet of the *Nigger,* and sinking together with the ship. Since that evening I had revealed to him my nickname—Kangaroo—I knew what he meant: my pouch. His face burnt, he kept licking his lips, and I had a good look at him. In the sky a red Mars pulsated, and I decided to be generous. When we arrived at the porch of my little hotel, Moses asked me if next morning he could take me to the airport. I said no, thanked him for the dinner and, seeing that he was about to fall into bottomless sadness, put my left hand into his right palm, and said: Come up. A typical Jew, always ready for misfortune but unprepared for good luck, Moses froze into a column of salt, and whispered: What did you say, Ann? Come up, I repeated. Let's go to bed together, and tomorrow you can drive me to the *aeroporto.*

And?

Moses was great! He kissed every square inch of my skin at least twice, came a hundred times. He was profuse and profound. While I couldn't help thinking about my no-good Manhattan man, Maimonides melted in my arms, outlined my cunt with the tip of his tongue, called me his sweet kangaroo, and implored me to let him stay inside of me forever. I, on the other hand, soon became tired of his caresses. The room was hot and stuffy, and I whispered: I'm short of air, Moses, please open the window, let me rest before my transcontinental flight. A flat lie. I saved my emotion for someone else, and dozed away at Moses' side knowing that he wouldn't close his eyes. Afraid of disturbing me, he either held back his breath or tried to adjust it to my breathing. But at the same time he couldn't refrain from humming into my ear: Ann, Ann, Ann. On fire, he was a Karenina, I—a bored Vronsky.

Oh could I only be young again, Ann! Today I don't even dream of adventures anymore, I just worry. While Wolf is grabbing the New World, I feel left behind, nonexistent. How does he cope with the New York winter? Is he after U.S. virgins? A nervous wreck of a sterile muse, I spend sleepless nights regretting that I didn't pack his old Weimar coat, that he may catch a cold. But I'm not yet a stone. While you described your night in Salamanca, I recalled the day I met Wolf in Weimar.

G AZING AT THE GOLDEN THREAD OF THE SETTING SUN as it bridges the shores of Manhattan and New Jersey, Goethe writes: A shipwreck may also take place on dry land. It's fine and praiseworthy to recover from an accident and put oneself right as quickly as possible. Life is only calculated in terms of profit and loss. But what if a shipwreck happens to the whole world and the earth cannot recover from it? This is the question I have to address in the last act of *Faust II*—and the reason why I visit the New World. I have come here to perceive in a new light the old Rome that seems to be with us still, but isn't with us anymore. My journey wasn't calculated in terms of profit, how could Moses accuse me of that? I want to understand how much of our culture can be lost without uprooting humanity entirely, and to what extent our relations can become casual without undermining the individual self and destroying the collective psyche. But does a world soul exist? In my youth I believed in it. Now I suspect that psychology may be identical with culture.

In *Elective Affinities,* my best book, I noted that a life without love is only a *comédie à tiroir,* a poor episodic play. One pulls open one drawer after another and shuts it again, hurrying on to the next one. Anything that is good or important only hangs together in a haphazard manner. One must be starting again from the beginning and would be glad to end anywhere. But in the New World there seems to be little affection and closeness. Life appears hectic and fragmented. My metaphor of the *tiroir* comes true. Nothing is permanent, everything falls apart, is glued back together, collapses again. In principle flux appeals to me, but I'm surprised to see that the entire individual life and the whole society can be reduced to sheer busyness. Experiencing constant movement, I become afraid of the spiritual chaos that may result from it.

In order not to deviate from my old habits, I'm after fresh females whom I want to cleanse my corroded shell. But the impersonal way they do it here upsets me. All my life I have believed in sex as a commodity. But compared to how they deal with it in America, I feel like an incorrigible romantic. I cannot accept that the terms of each intercourse are set in advance, and that every detail is openly discussed. When I ask a blonde to sit in my lap, she returns my request with a long list of her own requirements: the exact duration of every single copulation, the number of them, the exclusion or inclusion of oral sex, the type of birth control we're going to use, and ultimately: who comes first. But the way women look and behave astonishes me even more than their interest in technicalities. Only a hardly perceptible *je ne sais quoi* hints at age differences and I have real trouble deciding if a certain lean and supple female part belongs to a twenty- or to a forty-year-old. Finally, I'm shattered by the freedom with which they approach me. For the first time not women but I am a sex object. Focusing on my tiny mirror image in their pupils, I ask myself: how much pleasure can you still supply?—a question they ask themselves at the same time.

Running her artificial nails over my decrepit but not entirely broken vessel, a woman declares: I like to do it with a great granddaddy. Another sniffs at my armpits, and exclaims: I'm dying for an old man's sweat. A third covers my eyes with her palms, and whispers: I go for celebrities. Neither shy nor guilt-ridden, the women here embarrass me by their sincerity. They state things in a matter-of-fact way, don't restrain themselves. Verbally—and otherwise—they are more liberated than I am. Educated, with careers of their own, they don't fish for promises and compliments, and aren't drawn to me the way women were in Europe. In theory I approve of that, but in reality I'm scared. Admirable in itself, in sex this emancipation turns not only against men—it turns against women too. When all taboos fall, erotic encounters resemble operations—with each partner worried about his or her ratings. Am I first-, second-, third-class? Or just a useless ass?

After an American *coitus* I'm not a *triste* animal. I'm a nervous wreck preoccupied with: Am I still OK? Or will she answer my shy *May I call you tomorrow?* with *No, don't call me, I'll call you,* a deadly phrase. Yes, it has come to that: what the wolf did to innumerable redhoods in the European underwoods—here it's done to him. No widows to teach me how to master watercolor, no silk blouses to open discreetly at the top, no necks pink with desire. In New York I attend workshops on free lovemaking, seminars on equal sex. Women of the Charlotte type don't exist here. No one would agree to stay at my side for the sake of providing me with intimacy and permanence. Lotte, she did more than that. She bore silently the bitter knowledge that I wasn't inspired by her constancy.

Indeed, my imagination is kindled by short-lived pleasure, not by eternal presence. Poor Lotte! Her soul must be poisoned with resentment. I had her lead the existence of a married nun, made her grow as fat as an abbess. Was it all in vain, or can a secret meaning be extracted from her devotion to me? At any rate I have been wrong to assume that our platonic union might be regarded as a model for future relations between men and women. The future is here, but women have changed in a way I could never have foreseen. In the Old World they were created out of my dreams, here they subject me to their own reveries. In principle I'm against slavery and rejoice at the sight of female autonomy. But it won't improve the quality of sex. When each side pursues its own fantasy, one cannot achieve coincidence.

Aren't my notes totally irrelevant in this electronically processed place? I consider words concrete traces—of blood or ink—on parchment or paper. But here letters flicker on and off a lighted screen. Brief flashes, gone in a split second, they offer no shelter, and I feel completely alienated. In Manhattan my only compatriots are trees, blades of grass, and squirrels, performing their acrobatics in Riverside Park. I have only two old friends here, the river and the sky. When the sun sets, I discern in its gold the locks of my many Margarets. Throughout my life I have experienced an inquisitive urge for curiosities. But I find depressing the marvels which mix and melt here. I know that no one can walk unpunished under palm trees, and that one's opinions must change when one moves to a land of elephants and tigers. But it may be too late for me to adjust to the *nunc et hic.*

An artist-scientist, once I looked forward to being transported to the center of the twenty-first century. But amidst laser printers and beams, I'm ashamed of my soul's obscurity—a mummy contemplating itself in the looking glass. It may be an achievement to have arrived here. But I suffer from too many disturbing sensations. Thank God Charlotte isn't with me. She would be mortified with shame, drop dead during my TV talk shows on prime time. *Prime time,* a concept no Maimonides could have ever invented. Prime, secondary, tertiary time! Not even the sequence of day and night is left alone. Your scroll, Saturn, is made of bank notes. The stream of time isn't blue, it's dollar green.

The sun has set, the night is punctured by shafts of light. Electricity dematerializes the bulk of the World Trade Center. Why am I so terrified by progress? It seems to flourish excellently, it conforms to human needs. Why do I flee avenues of concrete and glass, evoke alleys of lime trees and cherry orchards? Drenched with nostalgia, I must admit that I'm less of a giant than I assumed. I'm just an old man at the verge of delirium. My inner directions are gone. Moving on and on, time overtakes me. My old-fashioned attitudes equal prejudices, my arguments are taken as seriously as a child's fantasies. Yesterday I overheard the director of the Goethe Institute remark to his wife: *Der alte Herr ist nicht mehr klar im Kopf.*

I long to talk to Italo in Italian, to Moses in Hebrew, to Simone in her sternly sophisticated French. The castrated American of Grump and *consortes* intimidates me, and so does the metaphysics of a civilization I cannot grasp. I should have asked Eglizer to accompany me. He could have helped me assimilate the modern miracles of cybernetics, conquer the fear of robotic machines. My lonely journey is speeding up the process of aging. I'm not myself anymore. I falter, vacillate, I cannot respond to challenges. Separated from my friends and Charlotte, I'm going deaf and blind. My entire energy is channeled into creating the impression of vigor, but I'm a relic. I work hard on my speeches, fill them with witticisms, learn the jokes by heart, play tricks with myself in order to distinguish between people. This one has a wart on the top of his nose, and his name starts with a *W.* Don't confuse him with the president of Mainstream Banking who has a *Warze* on his lip, and whose name is Weinsting. But every public appearance is a torture. I'm sick with anxiety that in the middle of a sentence I may forget who I am.

In the past I pictured myself as a permanent resident of the *Abendland.* What silliness! Nothing is eternal. Our proudest products turn to traps, disintegrate to graves. Before I pass away, I'm taught that even the universe won't last. Big bangs come and go, and no one gives a damn about a Goethe—with the exception of *Herr Tod.* He tiptoes, and tiptoes, and tiptoes around my bed, drawing ever smaller circles, while *Frau Sorge,* the old gray widow I betrayed in Lausanne, sits on the sofa, smiles at me, and whispers: I have returned, Wolf, you won't escape from me anymore. Come on, I have built a paper theater for us. You'll play Faust, I'll play Gretchen and Helena.

With her at my side I, who have never worried about anything, I'm constantly *besorgt.* I worry about my dawning dementia and our Institute's doom, about my wife being overweight and the earth being reduced to a wasteland. But mostly I worry about my end. Kindred by choice to no one and condemned to die far away from Lotte, I watch myself falling to the ground—a snowflake of a *neige d'antan.*

Panta rei. The Hudson flows, Carol's corpse floats by, and I'm tempted to jump into the waves. Polluted and poisoned, yet they are sirens, singing of my last fling: before they bury you, Johann Wolfgang, in this city's cement, you'll break apart and finally fall for your wife.

Lotte, this is my last message to you: I have always loved thee. Remember what Freud told us when we visited him in Vienna? Sex requires distance. If a man admires a woman too much, he's bored by her cunt. If a woman is too close to a man, she's disgusted by his tail. It's fun to brush by a stranger in the park. It's hard labor to insert one's prick into a spouse of two hundred years. I confess, this has really been impossible for me, a man suffering from an ailment which Sigmund termed—after me!—the wolf complex. Do you recall his words? The wolf is a male whose cock keeps saluting streetwalkers but refuses to greet a lady. Why? Because he doesn't want her caress—he wishes to devour her. Going for the lowest is just a compromise—a civilized way out for wolves who dream of tearing flesh apart. Cannibals, the more they love a lamb, the more they're afraid of touching her—even with the tips of their tongues. I ruined the lives of who knows how many sheep, but I wasn't unaware of my terrible character. The evening we met for the first time I prayed to God to guard me from harming you, the little redhood of my heart, and asked for guidance. Consider her sacrosanct. Don't ever touch her! The Almighty answered.

But I wish to procreate with Lotte, I exclaimed. Will you then infuse the Holy Spirit into her? Make her pregnant with a daughter? I want an exact copy of Lotte, and have already a name for her: Angelica. I'll educate her myself in languages and the visual arts, turn her into the best woman painter of all times. Oh, God! Grant me the favor. No way, Wolf, he groaned. The earth is already overpopulated with your illegitimate offspring. If you intend to stay at Lotte's side, you must refrain from rubbing her. This is my last word. Don't bother me again.

A sleepless night followed. I took Faust on a leash and walked him around Weimar. When I heard the first rooster, I looked into my poodle's dark blue eyes and sighed: What shall we do? Shall I kill myself, desert Lotte, try to forget her? Wau, wau, Faust replied. It's impossible to obliterate my *Frauli,* and you aren't enough of a sadist to make her a widow. Wau, wau. There is only one way out. Beg madam to become your Mnemosyne.

What a genius you are! But is it going to work?

With God's help it will, I give you the word of a dog.

To show my gratitude for your advice, I'll call the masterpiece of my life *Faust.*

I couldn't care less, Wolf. Dogs read whodunits, not tragedies, and it's in the nature of things that those who inspire texts only skim them, or are even illiterate. Personally, I am not an analphabet, but I am not a bookworm either. I prefer smelling trees—sprinkled with the sweet piss of Weimar's prominent bitches—to reflecting on men's vanity.

Do you remember, Lotte? I rang your bell at eight in the morning and you opened the door still wearing your nightgown.

Wau, wau, Faust jumped up and down. You lifted him up with a comically troubled expression in your eyes, and asked: What do you say, my dog? What brings *Fausterl* and his *Herrli* so early to my house?

I examined Faust's snout in your enlarged pupils, took in your stout but well-proportioned figure, was charmed by your lithe smile, and announced: This night Faust and I have decided to propose to you. We want to appoint Saint Lotte of Weimar to the rank of the eternal muse at our modest court.

Come in, Wolf. First let's have breakfast together. Would you be interested in warm milk, Faust?

Wau, wau, cold milk and a piece of pâté, *s'il vous plait.*

And you, Wolf? Coffee or tea?

Tea for two, with a splash of milk. And at least five *Butterbrote.*

Don't imprint your paws on my gown, Faust. Lie down. Marmalade or honey?

Honey for three, Faust loves to lick spoons.

Wau, wau.

Now tell me more about your offer, Wolf. Does the position of a royal muse pay?

It depends on the general state of the treasury. Right now it's not an

American salary. But who knows what the future has in store for us? *Che sarà, sarà.* Besides, we have Faust. I'm going to make him the hero of a very big melodrama.

Wau, wau. The royalties from *Faust* will flow into your purse until the end of time.

Isn't your dog slightly too proud?

He may be, but in principle he's right. We are after an immortal business. Give us your yes.

Wau, wau, the contract has to be signed. Put your fingers into the cherry jam, Lotte, and impress it on Wolf's napkin. *So. Gut. Es ist getan.* Wau, wau.

C ARS STREAM ALONG RIVERSIDE DRIVE, trees swing, skyscrapers throw shadows onto water and asphalt. The moon travels above the roof. While my last night on earth comes to an end, I recall the enchantment of our first evening in Weimar. Wrapped in a familiar fabric, we recognized that we were twins. Aren't we hatched out of Helen's egg, Lotte? I asked, and you replied: This is Weimar, not Troy, Johann.

However, you're a certified Miss Universe, Lotte.

You laughed and I knew that you had a crush on me, but you also rendered me so shy. I, the first man to pass his hand under a female skirt, I didn't dare to kiss your wrist. Your hands were the color of mother-of-pearl and opened up like two shells on your blue dress. A train sped along the river and its fury had me postulate: Let's never part from each other.

My voice trembled, and for a second your eyes lit up. Then a shadow passed over your face, and you whispered: I'm outside of myself. I stand in front of my house and observe its moonlit façade.

Don't be afraid, Lotte, come into the house. The impossible will be real. *Partir c'est mourir.* Let us never part from each other. While I was saying it, it occurred to me that fairly soon I'll be going to Strasbourg. You asked if I'd take you with me. I responded that this time I had to be by myself—and did not perceive this as a contradiction. But you did. Hurt and confused, you committed a fundamental error. Instead of uncovering my hypocrisy, you forgave me—and made yourself vulnerable to future assault. But you also saw through the fox you were about to accept as the future guardian of your chicken soul, and hesitated:

Give me time, Johann.

For what, Lotte?

Give me time till tomorrow, Wolf.

In an instant *Johann* was dropped, *Wolf* was adopted. But Faust alone caught the crux of the switch, and coughed: Wau, wau. Amen.

You asked: What do you say, dog? He jumped up, licked your finger-tips, and lied: Wau, wau. I congratulate my old *Frauli Goethe,* and greet my new *Herrli Wolf.*

Oh, Lotte! I have always blamed my perverted nature for preventing your defloration. But I might have exaggerated my own fault. Perhaps you weren't completely without guilt. No street has ever been paved with charity. Why didn't you have more common sense, sweetie? Instead of excusing my falsity, you should have objected to my male perfidy, and said: Don't you see the big-bosomed female I am? I'm overflowing with juice. I'm given to erotic musings. I'm a sensuous, ripe pear, ready to be plucked. Love me or leave me, Johann.

Your mouth was moist and red, and I asked: Do you paint your lips, Lotte? You should have replied: Yes, Johann, but only for men who want to kiss them. Had you said this, you would have turned me on, and nothing could have stopped me from disregarding God's secret plan. You know how brave I am, especially when Faust is at my feet. And he was with us—his snout wet, his tongue perfectly pink, his pupils fixed on yours. But you, Lotte, you behaved like a hermetically locked virgin, dropped the curtain of your eyelids, and uttered: Tomorrow, Wolf. Tomorrow I'll paint my lips.

And sure enough, the next morning the tomorrow of our life together was sealed. But it would have been another tomorrow, had you offered me that night your underbelly, and not a cup of Red Zinger. That evening everything was still possible. Later—no more. I took your reluctance as a sign from God. But that evening he was absent, you were present. Oh how drunk I was with the thick, sour smell of your flesh! I hallucinated about your heavy tits, the undulating contours of your hips, your milky skin, your shockingly blonde hair. All humans are animals. That night you should have encouraged the wolf in me.

Forgive me, Lotte. My talk doesn't make sense. Nor does our existence on earth. Today I confess: Finally I have fallen in love with you. What do I mean? No, not that I could sleep with you. You're terribly fat, and I, quite opulent myself, I like slim girls. No, it's something else. In all these years I kept repeating, you are *mein alles,* Lotte—

just for your sake. But now, before expiring in Manhattan, I begin to believe in my words. I would have been nothing without you, Lotte, you would have been less without me. My persistence and your patience are saturated with sterility. But even sterility may be sublimated into a sensible substance. Terrible as it was, our marriage has contributed to our victory over many other misfortunes. Yes, I wrote the *Elective Affinities* to penetrate the impossibility that imprisoned us. But when the book was finished, I was still in the dark. There is nothing more ambiguous than solutions to the most elementary problems. The selectiveness of sex, like the alchemy of life itself, is governed by enzymes. But love is pure abstraction.

The pain in my chest announces a cardiac attack which will be followed by arrest. In an hour or so I'll be a piece of garbage. Therefore let me show that I'm still a Goethe—capable of strolling away from his personal decay. I shall amuse you with an account of the latest folly of this computerized state, a proof, perhaps, that progress brings back obscurantism. This most advanced society on earth suffers from the crudest prejudice, revels in animism, cultivates a belief in reincarnation. A few days ago I was introduced to an investment banker who pretended to be possessed by spirits, to two *Hochstaplers* who assumed themselves to be under the tutelage of spectral beings, to three brokers who consult crystals before buying stock, to four vice presidents and a president of vice who indulge in Indian magic, and to a self-proclaimed priestess of the new stone age. A former actress, she wore sweatpants and sneakers, sold colored pipe-water as the elixir of longevity, and preached outdoors. A guru with security guards, she baptized her followers with acid rain, bathed in a bloodred stream at sunset, performed the dance of Salome—the plastic scalp of John on top of her head—and led close to a million people on a *postmodern crusade.* Isn't it strange, Lotte? Unable to cope with our own inventions, we may regress to the level of savages. Unable to confront unhappiness, we prefer to behave like donkeys. *Plus ça change, plus c'est la même chose.* You can illuminate the mind—and still make it darker.

Like our old dog—how could we abandon him in Weimar?—I'm going to die alone. No, that's incorrect. Out of the stalagmite grotto of this manmade island, Mrs. Sorge has ascended—to blind me. But she has made me see—the beauty of our life together. In the penultimate moment, *in dem vorletzten Augenblick,* my thoughts come to rest at your side, Lotte. My fingers are too stiff to open the ring in which your miniature is set. But I see clearly in front of me that August Sunday when you were portrayed by Angelica Kauffmann. You sat opposite me under a tall pine tree by a rustic table, outside the artist's summer studio. Before arriving in her secluded abode, we walked for hours on a narrow and exposed mountain track where you followed me unhesitatingly and with easy steps from rock to rock. The little-used path was so overgrown with ferns that at some point it almost disappeared, and we were lost in the thick undergrowth, amidst the moss-covered stones. Then we discovered a bridge and from it we saw in the valley a wooden church with a curiously shaped tower, partly overshadowed by steep cliffs. The whole day I didn't take my eyes off your face, kissed your hands, pressed into them bluebells I had picked at your feet. Lotte, you must not be embittered! Try to forgive me, remember all we did together. The rivers we crossed, the hills we climbed, the vineyards where I picked grapes for you, our boating expeditions, bike rides to old castles. I'm dying swaddled in memories of our days together, our uphills, our downhills. I clasp you in my arms, squeeze my mouth into your palm, and beg: *Verzeih, verzeih mir, Lotte.*

It's a terrible punishment to die in an empty suite of the Manhattan Plaza. Instead of waiting for the final clogging of my arteries, I would prefer to cut my veins. But I cannot find my Swiss pocketknife and the carpet is white. No, I don't want to mess it up, even though I should commit suicide. My last statement, it would diffuse all doubt. How could Moses believe I was in love with money and power!

Were you here, Lotte, you would carry your old companion to dry land, hold him tight. You wouldn't let me disembark all by myself, on the dark shores of a continent that isn't mine. It's awful to stagger alone. The air is stiff with sadness, my heart leaks. No Charon to conduct me to New Jersey. The wind wrinkles lightly my skin, the boat circles. It's getting late, I'm in a hurry, I should go straight. But I meander, fall, stand up, sink, speak, see, sink. Stars gleam, city lights glitter, Manhattan becomes a ghostly apparition. Am I taken far off, cast away, left behind—like Faust?

After our long life together, how can you let me die alone, Lotte? Aren't you my ferrywoman, my helmsnymph, my gentle old girl, my indulgent muse, my anabatic absence, my eternal presence? Talk to me, Lottchen. Don't you have words for your departing friend?

Oh, it's coming, like an orgasm, like a storm! In a second I'll be stopped with splendor. Endurance slips out of my mind. And yes! Yes! Yes! I hear your footsteps. You arrive, you're here. No, you don't have to say it. I know what you mean. I love your hands. I love your neck.

I die, but you hold me tight. Now! Come, Lotte! Close my eyes. Let me kiss your skin covered with my handwriting.

M RS. CHARLOTTE GOETHE?
Yes, my child.
Djuna Barnes. I hope I don't disturb you.
Welcome, but you have to bear with me. I'll be with you in a second.
Is this Goethe's grave?
Yes, I buried him last week. The place was originally reserved for another poet.
For whom, if I may ask?
Propertius. But Sextus selected for himself a more impressive residence, while Wolfgang expected to be immortal, and so neglected the whole business. When they brought him back, I decided to simplify our new life and kept him at my side—in our Institute's cherry orchard. So here he rests, and I'm planting daisies. They'll grow into a nice flowery cover and provide his last bed with a feminine touch—something he will appreciate even after death. Were you one of his overseas girlfriends, Ms. Barnes?
No, Mrs. Goethe, I intended to become one, but I was too late. When I entered his suite—under the pretext of conducting an interview for the *Manhattan Man*—your husband was choking on the couch. His eyes were closed, but when he heard me, his lips parted as if he wanted to say a word. I took his hand in order to check his pulse. But the instant I touched him, all activity ceased. His temples, low and square, receded, his skin lost color. An involuntary witness, I found his death painful, and yet a happiness. A small smile gave his mouth an infantile appearance, and while I watched, his short hair began to grow on his forehead and rendered it narrow. He reminded me of an aged Anteros, whose statue at the Acropolis I once admired. It was explained to me that in Athens Anteros didn't symbolize the pain of unrequited love, but was the god of good weather—modeled after a local hero, a man who proclaimed the sky his roof.
I have always admired the stylist in you, Ms. Barnes. Have you been working on any new *Nightwood*s lately?
No, Mrs. Goethe. Nowadays death is my business. Stricken with an incurable malady, I have removed myself from the New York vanity scene to the more familiar futility of Rome. My last days will be dedicated to

the melancholy of European easy chairs and to the silky nocturnal serenades of Italy. It's so much easier to expire in an old-fashioned setting. One needs the stature of a Goethe to pass away on the Upper West Side. Death is a trifle. But when it concerns us we want it to be a monument. And in the provinces everything appears more meaningful than in the center, don't you agree? I would like to end my life in a Roman museum, with my fingers aroused not by flesh and skin, but by marble and paint. No, that's not the reason why I surprise you in the nakedness of this winter garden. I have taken the first available cheap charter and come here in order to reassure you. I may not be a typical woman, Frau Goethe, but I know how to console another woman's heart. At your husband's dead feet I found loose sheets of legal-size computer paper scattered on the floor. I gathered them—they were numbered—and read the beginning and the end. So I learned that on his deathbed Johann Wolfgang von Goethe had written to—and for—you.

Let us go inside, Ms. Barnes. Would you like to have a bite? *Das Leben ist ewig, aber darin liegt seine Schönheit nicht.*

Are the clipped hedges the oeuvre of your hands?

They are a Sextus masterpiece.

They may look good in the heat of an August afternoon. Do you want to be buried here also, Mrs. Goethe?

No, Ms. Barnes. I don't want this orchard to become a tin of sardines. I have too much fat to rot away here. A solid piece of junk, I should dissolve in the air. Is it true that Wolf's exit occurred on the fifty-fifth floor?

More or less.

Was the window open?

At that height no window can be opened. But the air conditioner was on.

And conditioned Wolf to death?

More by apparel than by destiny. Your husband's head was thrown back against an embossed cushion. His dead hands seemed somehow wiser than the body. Standing at his bedside I reflected on how a flux of fact and fancy had been ended. Death had excommunicated the *Schein* and the *Wahrheit,* had changed existence to the pure essence of memory.

Will you have coffee or tea?

Tea is fine with me.

And a *Butterbrot,* to line your stomach. You have to eat in order to overcome jet lag.

Yes. Transcontinental flights are a horror.

So you arrived for a flirt, and stayed for a night watch?

Yes. Fate appointed me the guardian angel of your dead man. I assembled the papers, stuffed them into my backpack, took the elevator to the lobby, and had the *Nachtportier* call the nightshift of the Metropolitan Police. By the time I had returned home, your dead husband's visage was being beamed out around the globe. Had I not stolen his text, it would by then have been heard by a trillion TV addicts.

I understand, Ms. Djuna, and I'm obliged to you. You saved us from the media sharks. I would rather die than have his last letter to me read on TV. Here is your *Butterbrot*. Shall I pour some warm milk into your tea? Eat, eat, my child, you're so thin. And what's that blood doing on your ankle? Did you hurt yourself?

Every four hours I have to inject myself with interferon. Soon I'll have to do it again. May I do it here?

Of course. But meanwhile, *essen Sie, mein Kind.* How is life in Manhattan, do you like it over there? Another *Butterbrot?* What do you think of the old German oak table we sit at? I inherited it from my parents, and brought it all the way down from Weimar.

That's where you met your husband?

Indeed. The stormy December evening Wolf paid us the first visit my father was in bed with a flu. Johann arrived late, wrapped in a black velvet coat with a hood—very much *à la bohème*—and had about himself an aura of promise and arrogance. His mouth was shaped into an ironic smile. He entered, and mumbled: Am I your only guest?

Yes, I replied, Father is sick, and the wild weather has kept everybody else at home.

Can you receive a solitary guest?

No, but can I let you go out into the cold?

I guess you could, he answered, looking fixedly into my eyes. But why should you? I swear that you'll be perfectly safe with me, Fräulein Lotte.

Is that so? asked I. Aren't you a *Frauenheld?* And thought: he has the skin of a baby, smooth as porcelain.

That I am, come with me.

I laughed, and a strange intimacy developed between us, as if our bodies were relentlessly moving toward each other. I felt slightly faint, Johann's presence diminished and enlarged me at once, shivers crept up my backbone. I tried to diffuse the uneasiness and disengage myself from him by means of humor. But while I joked, curious visions were invading my brain. I saw myself as a warm sea and as an alchemical vessel. I felt as if he were a ship crossing me—on his journey to the south. Have you noticed how archaic the imagery of sex is? For us females it's all about cavity and moisture—the primordial watery grotto ready to receive men. We played music, first Wagner and Bruckner, later Chopin and Palestrina. I watched Johann, and thought: his mind has the brilliance of a mirror. Why do I want to tarnish its quicksilver with my blood?

It's an Aristotelian metaphor, Mrs. Goethe.

Is that so, Ms. Barnes? I wasn't aware of it. But it's an archetype too, and women, methinks, go after different archetypes than men. In your *Nightwood* I have always felt more at home than Wolf. He didn't like your book very much, but he adored your photo on the cover, the one in which you wear a white silk scarf with large pink dots—or are they strawberries?—and a small straw hat. One day, when I was reading your book, he took it out of my hands, outlined your face with his index finger, and said: I would prefer meeting this girl to reading her. What a pity you met only after he had passed away! *Essen Sie, mein Kind.* You're so thin. There's no equilibrium in nature. I'm eighty pounds overweight, you're at least twenty pounds underweight. Your erotic dreams must be different from mine.

I usually dream of corks pushed into the bottle of my body.

Here you go. I dream of steamers at sunset, moving slowly through the red sea of my blood. By the way, we need fresh blood, as Wolf used to say. Wouldn't you like to join our Institute? The director is dead, but I'm still around. I'll get rid of an imbecile by the name of Pyscek. Why don't you replace him, Ms. Barnes?

I have AIDS, Mrs. Goethe.

So what? We all must die of something. Your illness strikes me as a good metaphor for the terminal stage our Institute has entered. No, Ms. Barnes, you don't have to go to the bathroom. You can do it right here. Rest your arm on my Weimar oak table. Do you need any help? Yes, let me hold your hand. After the injection you have to lie down? I understand, it's a shock, I have read about the side effects of this medication. If AIDS won't finish you off, interferon will. Oh, Karl. I asked you not to come into the kitchen without knocking at the door. But since you're here, let me introduce you. Ms. Djuna Barnes from New York, the author of *Nightwood*—Herr Doktor Karl Eglizer from Vienna, a scientist and the author of a privately published collection of miniatures, *Eine kleine Nachtmusik und andere Nacht- und Todtexte.*

Ich begrüsse Sie, Fräulein Barnes. My congratulations, Lotte. Wolfgang's grave has made a lot of progress.

I do what I can, Karl. I have removed all the laurels and ribbons and planted some daisies.

Is February the right month to plant flowers? It's freezing. I would have waited until the end of March. And what's your opinion, Fräulein Djuna?

Leave her in peace, Karl. She's recovering from an overdose of interferon. It's supposed to save her, but I presume it will kill her.

AIDS?

Yes, Mr. Eglizer.

Oh splendid! I hope you'll keep us company until the very end—the first co-Fellow to aid away at this venerable institution! With you at Charlotte's side we're going to steer into the remotest backwaters of the blackest night-oceans.

I proposed that to Ms. Djuna before you arrived, Karl.

And have you accepted, Fräulein Barnes? You must! We'll make you into a living stele. Do you still have your scarf with pink strawberries? Oh, please, wear it at the election ceremony. Next Tuesday.

Don't rush her, Karl, wait.

Wait? What for? Isn't Frau Barnes dying? You could have waited with the daisies, Lotte, but Djuna's cooption has to be a *Blitzkrieg.* She has waited long enough to be recognized as a great stylist. You can't make her wait for anything any longer. Will you join us?

You don't have to answer now, Djuna dear. Rest. Do you need an extra cushion? A glass of water?

I'll be going now, Charlotte. I don't want to disturb our new member. You flew in from Manhattan? Do you still have your flat in the Washington Square Mews? Svevo once told me that you shared your studio with a famous Hungarian photographer, Géza was his name. As a student I lived in Washington Square Village and liked to stroll back and forth on Christopher Street. It was so gay then. Gayness incarnate! Now, with AIDS taking its toll, it must be a place mortified with melancholy. Oh, you must tell me more about the Village. Next time. We'll talk. In Rome, waiting for our lives to end, we do nothing but talk. An endless festival of eloquence, a *Sprachfest.* Do you still wear that small straw hat Goethe fancied so much? And so did everybody else, with the exception of you, Lotte, who didn't like it then. Now you may like it better. Djuna and Lotte are going to take to each other, let me tell you that, my beauties.

Don't talk so much, Karl.

All right, Lotte, and *küss die Hand,* Fräulein Barnes. If you agree I would like to read from your *Nightwood,* once the official part of the election ceremony is over. I'm the only one to get the theatrical tone of your prose right. Conrad and Moses can only spoil it. Don't let them impose their tenderness on you. Hold on to Karl! I can explain to you what happens when atoms split, and how solid states dissolve into nothingness. Once again, all my best, Ms. Djuna. See you soon, Lottchen.

L IFE ISN'T ABOUT PARADISE LOST and paradise regained, as our ex-Fellow Malcolm believed. Life is about the equilibrium we regain when we find an explanation. Each loss is a shock, and there are shocks that we don't survive. Johann Wolfgang von Goethe, the majestic founder of this vain association, lost his equilibrium at the sight of the New World. He looked forward to seeing it, but could not bear what he saw. Who could blame him?

Stop being sentimental, Karl. Johann has departed for the Isles of the Immortals, but his female reincarnations will soon be with us. I have planted daisies. They will feed on his rotting flesh and by the end of April cheer us up with their pretty yellow hearts. Meanwhile an attractive young woman has arrived in Rome and joined us. Her name is Djuna Barnes, she's seated to my right, and will divert us tonight with her account of Wolf's terminal hours—and other New York gossip. Djuna intended to take Johann into her arms, but his sudden expiration frustrated her plan. Am I right?

Yes. It happened on a crisp January evening. Washington Square was covered with fresh snow, snobs were about to gather at Sally Saturday's table at the Apollo Diner, and the George Washington Bridge hung in the air like a cobweb of lights.

Djuna Barnes has been kind enough to come to us from the moist New York underwoods. A dark flower we're all familiar with, she doesn't need an introduction. But I would like you to realize that she represents also an apocalyptic plant. Her head is bent over a glass, her auburn hair shines, but under her skin a deadly disease resides. Therefore let us greet Djuna with a small ovation, let us encourage her to speak to us.

You must excuse me, Lotte, I won't be able to speak. I'm drunk. Never mind, Djuna. Better drunk than dead. Start, I beg you.

At Kennedy Airport journalists asked me, Ms. Barnes, why are you flying to Rome? I didn't answer, but here I'll give you an answer. At every point of history there is one city in the world to which everybody is driven. Babylon of the Sodomites, Jerusalem of Jesus, Rome of Nero, Florence of the Medici, Vienna of Wittgenstein, Paris of Picasso, Manhattan of Man Ray. Right now Rome is again the capital of the international intelligentsia in exile. Today everybody heads for Rome, with the exception of Djuna Barnes who has come here on a private mission. But I beg your pardon. I'm not strong enough to continue speaking. My head spins, reflections outrun each other. Interferon often provokes sudden allergic reactions. I have to withdraw. But before I go, I want to thank you for appointing me to this honorable position. It may—or may not—scare away my imminent death. Tonight Dr. Eglizer wanted to read from my *Nightwood*. But I would like to discourage this idea, Karl. Why should you be bored with that old stuff? Instead, read from *La Somnambule*, a work in progress, and a bijou of intellect.

Before you start reading, Karl, please let me ask you a few business questions. Do you want me to remain the secretary of the Institute? You raise your hands with a speed that contradicts our senility. Thank you for your faith in me. Here are my suggestions. Since everybody burns with desire to be buried in Propertius's cherry orchard, we have to limit the number of our Fellows to those who are present here tonight. I have allowed myself to formally exclude Pyscek—his absence will prolong our lives—and asked Karl to act as my assistant. Nobody wants to assume the responsibility of the director, and thus everything rests on my shoulders. I need help. From now on living women will represent a minority at our gatherings, but I plan to promote dead femininity. Simone's translation into Latin is long overdue. We have to proceed with a critical edition of Karenina's diaries and dissertations. But nothing haunts me more than Carol Kar's work, as it slips into oblivion. Your sister, Ann, wasn't our member, but we remember her vividly, and we'll engage in massive lobbying on her behalf. Isn't the Colosseum the best spot for a summer installation of Carol's shrouds? Shouldn't we try to sell her Veronica project to the city of Jerusalem? To Jews for Jesus? Yes, Italo, go ahead. You have been trying to interrupt me for a long time.

The Afghan king is dying, and Assudin also is in the hospital. Cancer of the lungs. Both want to be reassured that we won't drop their cause.

We won't drop it. We should have been involved in many other honorable causes, but we were too lazy. Tomorrow I'll go to see both of them.

Are we done with the business?

I guess so, Karl.

Let me then drop all the whale shit, to use Djuna's delightful expression, to the bottom of the night-ocean, and proceed to *La Somnambule*.

L OVE BECOMES THE DEPOSIT OF THE HEART, analogous in all degrees to the findings in a tomb, Djuna says to Ann, as they ascend the Scalae Caci.

Don't talk so much while we climb. You'll exhaust yourself.

Exhaustion animates me. It runs toward me like a catastrophe, magnetizing my mind. What is this staircase made from?

Polygonal blocks of lava, neatly fitted together and laid on a carefully prepared bed, similar to that used for a mosaic paving. It's a true *via strata*, a good specimen of Roman roadmaking, in which the blocks are fitted together with utmost accuracy. Here *la strada* is bordered with a massive travertine curb. How well did you know my stepsister, Djuna?

Not very well, but an intaglio of her identity lies in my heart. It wasn't easy to be a friend of Carol's. I used to be very irritable, and she contradicted me all the time, or kept discussing things I wasn't interested in. Are these stones the remains of fortifications?

Yes, they show how the natural strength of the cliff was increased by artificial means. The walls were set neither at the top nor at the foot of the hill but more than halfway up, and a level terrace was cut in the rock on which the base of the wall stood. Above that the hill was shaped into a cliff, not quite perpendicular but slightly battering inwards, to give greater stability to the wall, which was built against it, like a retaining wall, reaching to the top of the cliff, or a few feet higher.

Is it lava again?

No, it's soft tufa of a different shade. The brown is warmer in tone, and full of charred wood. The spooning out of the steep cliff must have supplied the material for the wall. Over there you can see ancient quarries, used as reservoirs for water. The heaps of stones to the left are the remains of the temple of Jupiter Victor, and to the right is a rock-cut cistern with vertical shafts.

What's their age?

Goethe tried to determine it, but his rather amateurish research didn't yield much. He maintained that they resemble the Servian wall—especially in the system of headers and stretchers and the dimensions of the blocks. Apparently the chief technical difference lies in the open vertical joints found in some cases. But at the western angle of the hill there are remains of an earlier fortification, constructed with blocks of gray-green tufa, smaller in size than those of the main wall. There the technique is primitive, as the blocks are of irregular size and not laid in courses of headers and stretchers. The nearest parallel is supplied by the foundations of the temple of Jupiter Capitolinus. Have you ever read Delbrück?

Der Apollotempel auf dem Marsfelde. Yes, years ago.

Do you remember his spectacular drawings of the Palatine, the Scalae Caci, and all the rest we're passing on our way?

Vaguely.

Wolfgang presented me with the first edition, printed in Weimar and hand-colored by Charlotte. I'll show it to you at home.

How far is it still to Sextus's grave?

Not far, but the path gets narrower and steeper. Shouldn't we sit down for a minute? You're out of breath.

All right. Rome is a tomb within a tomb within a tomb. A ruin within a ruin. A Warsaw survivor, you must feel at home here.

Here everybody feels at home.

Was the earliest settlement, bearing the name Roma, situated on the Palatine?

Yes, the hill was both easy to defend and possessed means of communication with its neighbors. It's roughly square in outline and the Roman antiquarians sometimes apply the name *Roma quadrata* to it.

What did *Roma* mean?

Perhaps a river, but it's uncertain.

Can one trace the boundaries of the original city?

More or less. They passed along the foot of the hill, *per ima montis palatini,* and the angle-points were given by the *ara maxima* in the *forum boarium,* the *ara consi* in the *circus maximus,* the *curiae veteres,* near the arch of the Constantine, and the *sacellum larum,* at the north angle.

Your sister would have liked Rome. Why didn't you bring Carol here?

It was too late. She killed herself a month after my arrival. But you're right, Djuna, I should never have left her behind. This relic of a city could have become Carol's paradise regained. As if to remind myself of that, she jumped into the Hudson on December 11th, when the *septimontium*, the festival of seven hills, is celebrated here. Instead of suicide, she could have gone for a walk—from Palatium to Cermalus, the second summit of the Palatine, and along the saddle between the Palatine and Esquiline to Velia. Then across the two westernmost spurs of the Esquiline, Oppius and Cispius, to Fagutal, the extreme crest of Oppius, and to Sucusa, often confused with Subura, the eastern spur of Caelian. Can you explain Carol's death, Djuna? Recently, I met with the man she agonized for, an ordinary fellow, good-natured, phlegmatic, low-key. So I'm less inclined to believe that she did it out of unrequited love.

You have mythologized Carol to such an incredible extent, Ann. She was pretty ordinary herself. A New York artist with a third-rate career whose stuff didn't sell, she was as unsuccessful as the man. Both lacked glamour, and for a while that glued them together. She was better known abroad, he had more money, but in Manhattan neither of them had a name. Their feasts consisted of pasta with pesto, they laughed a lot, and at the beginning their relationship was completely devoid of drama. I agree, his appearance was slightly too solid, but it hinted at hidden dimensions. He was no donkey, and with time his attachment to your sister grew stronger. Alas, his sexual appetite decreased. She hoped to arouse it by separating from him. A miscalculation, it backfired on her.

Perhaps you're right. A few days after my arrival in Rome I received a copy of Carol's letter to the man together with a brief note saying that she had left him. She sounded relieved, on her way up, clear, rational. No bitterness, no resentment, no despair. This last communication from my sister hasn't stopped puzzling me. Maybe you can interpret it, Djuna.

I'll try.

Dear M. The future is out, the past is in. I dwell on instants we spent together, each of them a pebble nestling in my palm, and on dreams. So light, they weigh nothing but outline themselves with great distinctness. Do you remember the two dreams I described to you last summer? In the first I was directing a play, and had you, my leading actor, dance on an empty stage. In the second it occurred to me that it was you whom I seeked, while searching for my brother. After I had stumbled through ruined corridors, fallen from many staircases, I emerged on a square topped with a white church, and approached a woman to ask if she had not seen you. But before I opened my mouth, she shouted: Are you also an architect?

No, I'm not an architect, and you aren't my leading actor, maybe that's what's wrong with us.

Wait, Ann. Didn't she stage some sort of a parody of Chekhov—an estate, a husband, a wife, two daughters, a lover—at that time? By this strange writer who committed suicide when the Soviets invaded Poland. What's his name?

Witkacy. The play is a persiflage of *The Cherry Orchard* mixed with a ghost story for kitchen maids. A husband shoots his wife as she betrays him with her cousin, a penniless poet and a student of philosophy who never managed to graduate. But the dead woman dislikes it in the other world, and returns to her little manor to discuss her ex-sex life and poison her two little girls.

Yes, the theater overlooked the Hudson, the phantom's husband was a sixty-year-old Jew, the poet—a gay Irish-Italian boy, the estate overseer—a muscular black guy from Brooklyn with a cocker spaniel. One girl was white, the other black. This made a joke of the dead woman's assurances that she had both teens by her husband.

But continue with Carol's letter, Ann. It's fun, deadly fun.

When we were together I often dreamt of you, M, but my dreams didn't provide me with joy. They were always about a role you refused to play. Since I left your bed, I sleep soundly, but my nights are blank. Has separation affected the chemistry of my brain? Be well. I'm all right, don't worry. You must understand that I had to discontinue our affair. It was the only way to spare ourselves. I have a small office at the theater, and see the sun set, a sailboat pass. What a soothing sight. Now my equilibrium will be restored. Farewell, dearest. I'll write to you soon.

A week later Carol's body floated down the Hudson. The closeness of the river must have pushed her. Or the theater did it. She had the dead woman come out of the ground—covered with dirt. For herself she chose water—to stay clean.

Or to be washed clean. At the outset of her affair Carol confessed to the physical attraction she felt for this man. Every fiber of my flesh, she said, has been saturated with his sweat. I smell his sperm in my hair, I taste it in my tears.

Tasteless rubbish!

That's how she put it herself: I'm disgusted by my drowning in his fluids, sister. I desire to be myself again. To be cleansed of his dirt.

I can't stand it, Ann, her madness once again—amidst broken tufa, pozzolana, and lime. Enough is enough! I want us to reach Propertius's platform around midday. Come, help me up, let's take the last flight of steps. The geese sail north, but the afternoons are still quite short—and freezing.

Look, Djuna. As the sun moves up, the tufa rocks light up, and the hill seems transformed into natural architecture. But it's not natural at all. Over there the large temple of Juno Moneta stood once—the goddess of money and wisdom who should have enlightened Carol.

Get away from her. Don't let her blackmail you with her suicide. Oh, that twin of yours, as incongruous as a piece of white marble veined with red.

I'm so grateful, Djuna, that you brought with you her *House of Time*. Isn't it a minor miracle—with its afterimages of people, plants, and animals sketched on the silvery gauze?

Not at all! It's monumental and at the same time inappropriately delicate. An effeminate detour. As usual, Carol indulges in the sentimentality of loss. Is that Sextus's tomb?

Yes, under the oval tufa block.

What a windy spot. And there's a curious odor in the air. Rather sweet. The smell of his atoms? But for me it's time. The crystalline drug has to interfere with my sick substance. Can you hold my bag, Ann, while I sit behind the stone, fish out the needle, find the right vein, sacrifice a drop of red. What a splendid view Propertius has chosen for himself.

THE SHIFTING SANDS are crossed, the anchor is cast, Italo writes. Since Wolfgang's sudden death Charlotte has softened, opened up. She narrates the first days of their relationship with the trepidation of a young girl, and I revel in the Weimar phrases she throws in. The letter Djuna brought from New York reconciled Lotte to her own past—and to the world. Finally, she has accepted Wolfgang as her husband, and this posthumous marriage animates her routine. When I see Lotte busying herself at Goethe's grave, I think of a newly wed woman, changing the sheets, preparing breakfast for her man. As long as he was alive, she couldn't lose an ounce. But in the four weeks that have passed since his death fifteen pounds have gone. She doesn't hold anything back anymore, defrosts herself, grows new limbs. When I wake up at night, I see her strolling in the garden or standing at the window—her face moist with excitement. She stopped being the intolerable locomotive we all joked about, and she doesn't avoid our eyes anymore. A proud old lady, she walks with a raised head, beaming with anticipation. I feared that Wolfgang's death would knock her off her feet, instead her life's end meets the beginning, Rome and Weimar touch. Wolf's confession has taken over Lotte's imagination. The knowledge that he died with her name on his lips has healed her. How vain we humans are! Thirsty to have words confirm what facts deny. Eager to feed on the lies of our beloved ones.

I'm worried about Djuna, Italo, cries Ann, rushing in. She broke down on our way back from Propertius's grave, and hasn't been well since then. Her speech is incoherent, and her notes make me fear the worst. Here, read:

The Odyssey of yesterday is the Pompeii of today, the earth—an archaeo-logical site. After having accomplished the round-the-world-flight, I dream of going to Riverside Park, or to the movies, or perhaps to the Jewish cemetery in Prague—with someone who would be close to my heart. The sun is about to set, little time is left, but the man I love is good for nothing. In the morning, while I'm still asleep, he opens my fist, clutched around his wrist, and closes it around *The Death of Virgil.*

Once it was possible to return to Ithaca. It was a long way to go, baby, one sailed for years. But the Concorde, *chérie,* takes just a day. Effortless, the return doesn't make any sense. It's enough to have eyes travel up the walls, cross the ocean of old paint. To move one's ass is an anachronism, saint. But if the mind wants to globe-trot, let it go. Aiding away, I may become a tourist myself. A blind searchlight, I comb the periphery of the nightwood, while a caged Ulysses, the dummy of Penelope in his arms, splashes in the bathtub. A blonde plastic doll, I watch him tiptoe on my hot front, dot my holographic pupils. Oh God! What an unpardonable error has been caused by your lack of affec-tion. You, who created me, come on! Share my suffering. Bear the holocausts canceling each other out in the mousemeat of my brain. Pain roams through the corrupt cells of that damned camp, my body, breaks into that bloody gold mind—a jail.

The phone rings, Italo lifts the receiver, and says: Yes, it's me, Djuna, don't overexcite yourself. Ann is here, we read your notes. Yes, I understand. You can't put up with it anymore. The pain. Not any longer. Yes, I do understand. Your mind spins. No, no, you don't abuse us. No, it's all right. Still, Djuna, isn't the world an interesting sight? Your kitchen window overlooks the Forum. Aha, you're in bed. You see only a ruined wall. You do find it framed in a certain beauty? Good, my girl. You're still fond of air and water? Of me, Ann, and Lotte? That's good. That's very good. I'll be with you in fifteen minutes. Wait with the injection. Yes, I have the key. Don't come to the door. Just wait. Yes, Ann will come with me. Stay where you are, Djuna. Don't move. We'll be with you in a moment.

OUR RUBBER BOAT FLOATS toward Serapium, the indecisive light of early spring envelops our aching bodies, and I recall Sextus and his love of caves and women, shades and sacred rites, Maimonides says to Conrad. His canvas bag stretched over his knees, Joseph looks up and encounters Moses' face—the contour of his head droops sideways in a boyish way—and his half-naked hairy chest. Lines of a poem he cannot identify emerge from his memory—tell me in what grotto did you spin the fine thread of your song? With what step did you enter? From what sacred fountain did you drink?—and he excuses himself: Sorry, old chap. I'm not paying attention to you. But the sheer presence of water, even here in Tivoli, makes my mind buzz away. Looking at timbrels hanging from the hollowed stones, walls lined with pebbles and shells, at all the aquatine spontaneity tamed by the decorative bric-a-brac, I see China in front of me: the Yellow Sea during the season of the typhoons, when the air is thick, the surface resembles an undulating piece of silk, and the sun, pale and without rays, pours down leaden heat. Soot rains over the deck and I smell sulphur.

I forgive you, Joseph. Somebody else should keep you company here—not I, a *Landvogel* of a Jew, in whom water evokes the desire for dryness. However, Hadrian's grotto fascinates me too. Hollow and fluid, it feels so female! Turned on, I become a bridled dolphin, eager to enter a secret underworld, cool and salty—as Ann's skin.

Leave her in peace, Moses. We have come here to commemorate men—not your never-more mistress. In his younger days Hadrian used to meet in the cave with Callimachus, Josephus Flavius, and our Propertius. With the first he had a brief affair, the second he despised, the third he treasured. Yes, it was Sextus who urged the emperor to invite *the historical traitor,* as he called Josephus. Why? To study the mentality of a collaborator.

Rather, the character of a swine who can never waste enough words on his brother's butcher. The Roman sword—it shines in Flavius's prose. The victims are mere mosquitoes—a nuisance around a sleeper's ear. Their courage is lacking in realism, their heroism equals hysteria.

You hate the man, Moses. But Josephus isn't a bad writer at all. After his return from Egypt even Propertius began to defend him, arguing that the anonymous authors of the papyruses he admired might have been pigs too. Easily.

I disagree. Josephus wasn't only immoral, he was totally corrupt. You may defend him, Joseph, but I cannot forget who he was and what he did. He descended from one of the noblest priestly families, studied jurisprudence. At the age of nineteen he was familiar with the Judaism of the Pharisees and Sadducees. Remember! He spent three years in the desert with the hermit Banus, the great Essene—before coming here. Why he came? Out of noblesse oblige: to intercede on behalf of priests punished by the procurator Felix for some minor offense.

I keep reflecting on his first visit to Rome, Moses. Keep imagining him. At twenty-seven Josephus was a virgin and a puritan—his mind immersed in the Bible, his body strong and lean, his dress severe and simple. A striking young Jew in Nero's capital—he must have suffered a split. A Dr. Jekyll, he encountered Flavius, his Mr. Hyde, in a Roman whorehouse.

Wrong, Joe, in a theater. But otherwise you're right. There was a Hyde. Alityrus was his name. An actor of Jewish descent and a favorite of Nero, he introduced Josephus to the empress Poppea. Extremely impressed with the handsome Israelite, this hyena helped him. With his mission a success, Josephus headed home—a changed man. Rome's ruthlessness convinced him of the empire's omnipotence and undermined his faith in Palestine. Back in Jerusalem, he expostulated with the revolutionary Jews. But they refused to listen to him and he was dragged into their rebellion. Then—his first step to treason—he tried to persuade them to lay down their arms and return to their *legal alliance,* his words. While they fought for their lives, he first sweated over letters to Roman aristocrats begging them to have patience with *his ill-affected brothers,* later organized his own law-and-order pro-imperial force. Outraged, John of Giscala incited the Galileans to kill the future Flavius. But no one succeeded in cutting his throat. Bad luck!

Or good luck, Moses. His death wouldn't have changed the course of history. But who else would have reported that Christ was crucified not with thieves, but with rebels.

I would rather see him dead than a Roman journalist. First he played dice with his brothers' lives—then the emperor's lapdog and parrot.

Remember Judith, his beautiful young wife? He abandoned her for another woman when she was nine months pregnant.

But when Jerusalem was stormed, he saved the lives of quite a few distinguished Jews, prevented the burning of sacred books.

And repaired to Rome where he was the first one to receive a state pension, twice as high as that of Pliny the Elder.

A masterpiece of imperial diplomacy, yet a stupidity. From that point on everybody's hatred focused on Josephus.

But nobody dared to attack the scribe, with the exception of Justus of Tiberias, a real hero. He accused Flavius of having been a Roman agent—and the real cause of the Jewish rebellion.

Yet to everybody's amazement, in his defense Josephus departed from the facts, as they are narrated in his own *Jewish Wars,* and described himself as a partisan of Rome—and a traitor to his own people—from the very outset. That I call guts.

I call it cynicism. Even then he wanted to show his eternal belief in the empire, his lifelong mistrust of Israel.

But perhaps he indeed doubted his people. Remember his favorite saying? What is life about? Cold blood. But look at my ex-brothers. A word, and they turn red. What a boiled lobster of a nation.

A traitor's bon mot! Flavius considered himself the only Hebrew—Hebrew, mind you, not a Jew!—who was up to the Roman standard. The moral norm of Madame Poppea and her sweet husband.

There was something a historian could learn from them, Moses. That total power corrupts totally. That empires rise from a sea of blood.

Ay ay, but only for a while, dear Joe. Then they fall. Aren't we both fond of the grass overgrowing the Golden Palace? Flavius, he was not only my people's gravedigger, he was also a fool. Who else would have set his heart on a Neronian joke of a Rome? Believe that it would last!

He didn't believe it for a minute, Moses. He just pretended to. But you're right. The man was spilling with self-hatred. Sextus told me once about Josephus's extraordinary fit—of satisfaction. Let me recall it. Oh yes, he saw a caricature of Jesus, as an ass fixed to the cross. It had been scratched into the wall of a house he was passing with Propertius, probably by some local pagans making fun of their Christian neighbors. Gracious me, Flavius exclaimed, stopped in the middle of the street, and delivered a whole speech on Jews being obsessed with crazy martyrs. A nation of assholes, he shouted, presided over by a donkey. What a great drawing. It renders the essence of their latest epidemic: the cult of a crucified beast excreted by the *mens ebriosa hebraea.*

This from a guy who defended Nero's mental health.

To keep his head on top of his neck. Don't forget, Moses, Josephus's patron—Epaphroditus, I think, was his name—earned his bread as the emperor's eye. You know what comes to my mind? Perhaps the oration against our Lord was meant for the ears in the wall?

No, Joe, it was part of his ongoing public program. Hallo, hallo, here Radio Nero. From the foot of the Invincible Sun Statue of Our Caesar, hallo, hallo. Flavius speaking. *Urbi et orbis,* dear Romans. In addition every Saturday afternoon he read to Poppea from *Nunc,* the top secret bulletin compiled by him for the exclusive use of the imperial half-wit.

Josephus's elegant silhouette moving along the corridors of the Domus Aurea haunts me. Daily, blood was spilt there, and at least once he slipped on it. Yes, I have it from Suetonius. He met Flavius at the door to Nero's private chambers—the historian's hands covering his ears—that very instant the emperor had his youngest lover, a ten-year-old, castrated. The boy's cries were echoing through the vaults. It was the only time anybody witnessed Josephus lose his composure. But, as always, he had the good luck of meeting Tranquillus. Another courtier would have surely denounced him.

Indeed. Performing one *salto mortale* after another, Flavius earned his pretty estate in Jerusalem you should visit, Joe. It lies on the right bank of the Cedron amidst olive groves.

Did he really enjoy it, Moses? I heard that in his last years he suffered from chronic sleeplessness, moved constantly, developed a number of tics, couldn't control his bladder. His hands trembled and mimicked, even in sleep, a ceremonial washing. A psychosomatic response to the symbolic blood on them, don't you think? Pilatus had a similar problem. He washed his hands fifty times a day, with perfumed soaps imported from all over the globe. He used to jump up in the middle of a sentence, his palms at his nose, and run to the loo, or to produce out of his pocket a bottle of rose oil—and rub it in, in front of his guests. Fate has its own subtle ways of punishment.

Alas, subtlety is reserved for criminals. Fortune loves to approach them with gloved finesse, while the victims are treated with a boxer's fist.

But in the end Josephus protested the misrepresentation of Jews in *Against Apion.*

Apion? The Roman ambassador at Alexandria who opposed Philo and his companions?

Yes, the ones who petitioned Caligula—and his horse—on behalf of the Egyptian Jews. Apion tried to kill their cause.

Give me a break, Conrad. Enough of that scoundrel. By the way, Egypt brings to mind our finances. The Institute's deficit is so huge that it may outrun us before we reach the common ground of Propertius's cherry orchard.

Indeed, and there's some very bad new gossip. Apparently Mezoros is shifting from grain export, a fairly solid branch of commerce, to USE bonds. Yes, it's Pyscek who persuaded him to invest on Wall Street. And you know what happened last week?

Dow Jones crashed, I noted it with great satisfaction, Joe. May it be the last blow to Grump and *consortes.*

They'll survive, but our existence is at stake. Mezoros played too high—and lost a lot. No, he isn't bankrupt yet, but we aren't his priority either.

What an interesting development!

I'm sure it makes you feel good, Moses. You were the first to call Pyscek our angel of destruction. Oh I remember the scene! When you threw it into his face, Lotte laughed. But Wolf stood up, and shouted: Don't perform a burning bush, Moses.

Now, thanks to the Czech undertaker, our German genius is feeding Charlotte's daisies. And what's in store for the rest of us, Joseph? With my physique and white beard, I would make an excellent Wandering Jew. And you, I presume, can get two hot meals a day at the Sailors' Soup Kitchen. No, we won't commit collective suicide. Let's rather become engaged to Ms. Reality. I mean, you, the youngest, should buy her a bridal ring and pay compliments every day. We must prevent her from having Lotte do dishes in a pizza parlor.

Don't dramatize, Maimonides. We still possess a few things.

Like what?

Sextus's villa, to begin with.

Aha, my Joe wants to make a luxury condo out of it? A *condominium poeticum*—with the garden turned into a golf course. What a fabulous idea. Goethe's grave could act as the chief mound, while Propertius's mosaics would embellish the sauna. But isn't the real estate market rather depressed?

Your perplexed way of talking won't solve anything.

Oh no, Joe! It's your *polnische Wirtschaft* I'm counting on. Why not sell the crown of your eagle for the mustache of your leading electrician?—and make a gold mine of rubles. *Noch ist Rom nicht verlor'n.*

Nor is Manhattan, Maimonides. It swims in money.

Sure! So let's found the Non-Advanced Scholars Research Center at the East Side Young Jewish Men's Association, Korzeniowski. There you'll be responsible for the Apple Talk class, while I'll redo my stuff: replace tetragrammaton with president of Palestine, *et* so on. Of course, why not succumb to the very reverie that brought the fall of our *Grosswolf?* Still, isn't it comical that we have become dependent on Berenice's slave, whom our darling Sextus smuggled out of Alexandria and freed in front of us on a stormy Tuesday evening? In January. Some fifteen years ago.

Yes, it's ironic—and engraved in my memory. A nervous boy of sixteen, Mezoros was fiddling with his ear, biting his nails like a hamster. I sort of liked him—and watched him grow into a financial giant with awe and disbelief. Slowly he became the center of our orbit, a mythical beast holding in his fists the key to our physical well-being. Really, Sextus had an eye for the queer and smart. And since Berenice loved Mezoros with maternal ardor, he came to regard the boy as a token of her affection.

Yes, he sheltered him as much as he could from Rome's perversions. But the youngster must have had some substance of his own. Remember how handsome he was, a sweet cookie to be devoured by this city.

Well, he came here from the Egypt of Euergetes. Outwardly an insecure adolescent, inwardly he was a mature man who had eaten bread—and crap—from many ovens. When Mezoros told me about his parents—he had lost them at an early age—he stated the bare facts. Later I learned from Sextus that his father had disappeared in the gold mines of Berenice, his mother died in the desert camp. The five-year-old was found by a female relative. The rest sounds like a fairy tale, but may even be true. The old woman helped out in the imperial kitchen and used to take Mezoros—if that's his true name—to the palace with her. The childless queen heard about the undernourished but fair infant and became interested in him. She adopted the boy, but hid him from her husband. When Sextus appeared on the stage, she begged him to smuggle her son to Rome. Delighted to fulfill her wish, he came up with a Hollywood screenplay. Mezoros was carried out of the palace in a golden cage wrapped in black silk, while Propertius stood on the terrace and told Euergetes that Berenice had presented him with a cub allergic to light, that he planned to convert his Roman estate into a safari, and that he'd name the lion Euergetes the Greatest.

While Moses breaks out in laughter, Joseph begins to unpack the lunch box prepared by Lotte. Provolone on pumpernickel for myself, and for you, my philosophers' egg? Lox on a veil of cream cheese and a bagel-bed, I guess. Go ahead, bite in, Maimonides, while I keep reminiscing for a few more minutes. Shortly after Mezoros's arrival in Rome I took the boy for an excursion, and—believe it or not—we paddled around here in a rubber dinghy, as we do today. He had visited the museum of Alexandria with the queen, and so I wanted him to see the Serapeum. Unfortunately, our outing provided him with more pain than pleasure. The sight of the grotto and the memory of the Sunday spent with Berenice—to whom he referred as *my sweet mother*—brought tears to his eyes. But he suppressed them and repeated, word for word, her tale of poets and priests seeking inspiration in the bowels of the earth. In caves and dark groves watered with perennial springs. In the underworld, as it's reflected in the wonderful verses of *your uncle Sextus*. At sunset Mezoros became even sadder and gave me an account of the muse Calliope, drawing water from the fountain and sprinkling men's feverish lips. No doubt, he identified her with Berenice.

So he must have loved Sextus.

Yes and no. The three of them were a sentimental tangle. First Mezoros was terribly fond of Propertius. But when he grew older, and started to compete for Berenice's favors, jealousy spoilt his affection.

That's why they never lived together?

No, Sextus wanted the boy out of Nero's reach. So he put him up at his aunt's estate, just outside of Urbino. But Mezoros didn't like it there, and arranged for himself an apprenticeship with a wheat merchant at Ravenna. Three years later he became the junior partner, five years later inherited the business. Soon he was number one in the international grain market and this further strained his relationship with Sextus.

But in spite of the conflict he offered to sponsor the Institute. How generous.

Yes. Initially Sextus refused to take even a penny from his adopted son. It was Wolf who persuaded him to accept Mezoros's money for a noble end: to create, I quote Goethe, a hideout for the semi-extinct international intelligentsia. So an endowment was set up but never properly supervised. Now it turns out that Mezoros didn't put aside enough funds. Everything was tied to his income. Since it has suddenly shrunk, we're in big trouble, Moses.

In this case let's swallow more sandwiches and feed the swans with the crumbs of what he's still spending on us. Or you eat, while I continue paddling to the statue of Antinoos. At sunset the veined marble is transformed into flesh and makes me shiver. Then, at dusk, we shall enter the Serapeum and imagine that we're at the spot where Antinoos drowned under mysterious circumstances.

Mysterious? Nonsense. He checked out Egyptian seahorse grass. Stoned, he dropped into the river with the grace of a sack. Poor Hadrian! Gay to the tips of his nails, he couldn't bear such a prosaic end and worked hard on his lover's romantic death. That's why the place of the little accident is called the entry to the underworld. There the emperor had a long valley cut into the tufa, an artificial grotto beautified with a hundred silens, each of them mounted on a fox or a carp. In its apse Antinoos is immortalized as a Narcissus-Echo in one. Seated on a whale, he holds a pen in his right, a nightingale in his left. Yes, there's one last *Lachsbrötchen* left, Maimonides. Sure, our Institute does resemble more and more a kindergarten. *Diggen sie* in, *mein Kind.* Kant is dead, picnics are in, and so are the big boobs of Diana of Ephesus. Blood shot into my ears when I saw my teacher and spiritual guide press his lips to her moss-covered nipples.

It's all in the eye of the beholder, Conrad.

You Hebrew hypocrite! Every sparrow on the roof is well informed about what men of a certain age prefer. Just remember how Goethe offended Ann by proclaiming: Now that I'm fifty, I can't be bothered with underdeveloped fronts.

Oh, yes. He did it on his 251st birthday, and in the presence of several not very well-endowed females. But tell me, Joe, why do so many talented women resemble ironing boards? During Simone's lectures I couldn't help contemplating her flatness and comparing it to Lotte's pneumatic nature. Perhaps Wolf wanted to pay his wife a compliment, rather than offend our ladies of intellect. Anyway, you can't accuse me of sexism. Just take Ann. She's pretty flat, yet I have always been attracted to her.

Exactly! That's why I'm so upset. Why my heart is bleeding. Moses Maimonides kissing wet marble tits!

Men must regress before the earth can receive them, Joe. *Homo est humus.* My second childhood, which I'm about to enter, is a breath away from my final collapse. Four centuries ago no one could have forced me to spend an entire day in a rubber dinghy, no waterworks would have seduced me from my desk. But today my mind's clarity recedes, so I retreat into cool springs concealed in the ruins, revel in aquatic plays. Aren't they sexy, the sparkling jets, the silent fish basins? You're right, I'm an old impotent cat. Yet I cannot stop *chercher la femme* in the shadowy caves, in the white, scintillating flesh of oysters.

The world turns rotten and we, what do we do, Moses? We skip the morning session on the homeless in Manhattan and the afternoon talk on Afghanistan. While the world goes down, we float around Hadrian's erotic grotto.

Because we're an impractical joke of a perplexed God. *Gesundheit*, Joe!

R EMEMBER MAY IN NANKING, FORTY YEARS AGO?
Yes, Ann. First lovers in the parks, first signs of felicity, first refusals to wear uniforms, first silk blouses embroidered with dragonflies. Mao's portraits come down. A pupil of Matisse returns from the rice fields. Hand-painted posters advertise a Chinese-looking Gérard Philipe.

Balancing chopsticks between the three remaining fingers of his mutilated hand, the dean of the science division discusses solid state physics with Dr. Eglizer, a foreign expert. And the doves, the holocaust survivors, make a nest in the middle of the campus.

We saw more of them in the imperial garden. They fluttered around a class of school kids, painting pink peonies. That day we biked through the suburbs to a ruined temple, discovered an alley of stone elephants. You took pictures, Ann, and years later they reappeared in Carol's *House of Time.* Meanwhile China is omnipresent, and flooding us with its beauty and trash. This must be the tenth exhibition we have seen in the last two years.

But the first to include Chou's scroll with doves, and that's what we have been waiting for. The contours of dry leaves, how fresh they look in the diffuse sunlight. It moves my heart to recall how the weak overcame the strong, the soft overruled the hard. As soon as the revolution was over, Tao returned.

I wonder: how did Chou manage to paint this scroll? Without a proper studio, with only a dwarf of a desk. Could he do it in the small pagoda that had been transformed into a teahouse? He liked to sit there, a notebook in his lap. Where did he get silk?

From the silk shirt, your birthday gift. Don't you recognize the fabric? Cut and reinforced with cotton. The brush he made from the hair in his ears. He improvised, yet there's nothing tentative about his picture.

But at the same time it's so strange. The disquieting background of peaks and deep ravines seems to shine through, as if Chou overpainted a palimpsest. A painting is a voiceless poem, he kept repeating during our last visit. Chinese art has an idealist quality. It mistrusts the material, tries to render the essence. The scroll is dedicated to *Matisse, my Teacher.*

If he was indeed Chou's teacher—and not just a legend.

Does it really matter? His wish to be his pupil made him one. When he recounted his meeting with Matisse, his eyes glowed, his voice broke. Imaginary or not, the friendship with Henri helped Chou believe in his art. That it was accepted by *tout le monde,* including the arrogant Parisian crowd.

Oh, the miracle of acceptance. Perhaps it's more central than the miracle of love. The short *yes* for which Kafka has invented the metaphor of the theater in Oklahoma—which rejects no one.

Yes, it's a key to the happiness of humans—and animals as well, at least according to the famous experiment performed on rats by our friend Claudino Schwarz. Assuming that their lives could be extended by little food and a lot of exercise, he divided them into two groups. Those with less to eat and more jogging developed musculature and shiny fur. But one of the hungry runners outdid the rest—and the whole lab was puzzled. A big male with white ears and a white tail—named Białek, I think—he inspired speculation on the link between his mint condition and color. But the secret was revealed by a videotape—of a Polish cleaning lady with the whitish rat in her lap. Interrogated by Dr. Schwarz, she admitted her fondness of *Białouszek, a fine little man,* whose belly, ears and tail she caressed after work. That was the beginning of Claudino's international career. Changing her words to gold, he coined a new scientific motto: Better Being through Benevolence. But coming back to Chou's scroll. Do you recall the impression it made on Pound?

Sure. He particularly liked Chou's palm, holding the broken eggs, predicted that the picture would become a classic, and promised to immortalize it in a poem. But in the end he presented Chou with some incoherent lines, suggesting misfortune or mourning. My memory is dim.

So is mine. The past is all mixed up, but the scroll revives it. Leaning against the mulberry tree, the old painter contemplates his fate without bitterness. The sun is rising and the moon, its faithful companion, is following in its steps. The splendor of the world unfolds in the haze of late summer. Torrents plunge, mountains watch the flight of the wild geese, fishermen's boats glide down the Yellow River, dive under the pink phantom of the Nanking bridge. Everything is at once solemn and casual, as in the best paintings of Matisse.

Chou seems to greet Henri, his distant master, with his right hand. Even though it's deformed by arthritis, he placed it in the middle of the picture. So it forms its axis and creates a miniature landscape, shimmering with gold.

He used chromium yellow, with a drop of minia red, for his veins. Serene, the artist falls asleep and all creation enshrouds him. Colors and lines unite in his pupil. Ready to die, Chou reflects himself in our eyes—as though in a mirror.

Let's go now, Ann. My back is beginning to hurt. Once we went to China, now we escape to Chinese exhibitions to forget our present life, a bill we can't pay.

No, a check Mezoros refuses to mail. Where are the days when we could afford to bury Propertius on top of Rome! Today Lotte is begging the city council to donate oil for the coming winter.

And you're dying for a part-time job at Roma Locuta.

It's the biggest World-and-Word Processing firm, Karl. You should be proud of me. They'll teach me how to package my texts more attractively, and make us rich and famous. Meanwhile, instead of behaving like two dinosaurs under stress, let's go home and see if Djuna is still alive.

She is. All night I listened to her arguing with the man I'm allergic to. Yes, Carol's nemesis. Now it's the other way round. It's Myloslav who's talking Djuna into killing him. I heard her repeat at least twenty times: No, I'll never go to bed with you. Never. If you want to wreck yourself, fuck another AIDS case.

And?

He insisted that sleeping with her is his priority and provoked Djuna to deliver a whole lecture on condoms. That they don't work vis-à-vis a terminal patient. Furious, she shouted: I'm not a mantis and you aren't a kamikaze, Myloslav. No, no, no, I won't allow you to lie down on the cushion of my hair. It's reserved for retroviruses, not men. Refrain from touching my skin, a dirty sheet. No! We aren't heading for intimacy. On the contrary, we opt for distance—the safe in-between you specialized in when you were with Carol.

Oh the bitch!

Djuna isn't bitchy, she just cannot help remembering. So she cried:

Why haven't you jumped after my friend into the Hudson? That's much cleaner than dying from AIDS. Your suicidal mania is distasteful. Pfui, stop licking my knee! No, I won't mix my saliva with your sperm. No! Keep your tongue to yourself.

A long pause followed, then he whispered in a lovesick voice: Your hand, Djuna, is older and wiser than your body. It's so light and cool. If you don't want me to touch you, let your hand glide over me. No, she hissed, there's blood all over it. Every four hours my poor hide is punctured by a needle. Still, the spring is here. Today the first daisy has opened on Wolf's grave. It's so pretty.

Yes, Djuna. But I don't want to see it. I hate this place. Let's go away—the two of us. To some islands. To the south. To Hawaii.

That's where Carol wanted to go with you, guy. It was mid-May, she phoned me, and sighed: Djuna, I want him to go with me to the sea. Just for a day. A weekend would be bliss, but I'm too proud to press for it. Pride is my chronic disease.

Djuna, please.

If you want to stay with me, Myloslav, close your eyes and listen to your ex-mistress talking to me: At four I suffered from chronic depression and looked forward to very few things, Djuna dear. One of them was going with Mom to the Rosetip Bazaar, a huge Warsaw market. A prewar relic and a reminder of the Orient, it was so different from the state-owned shops, with their bread loaves from before yesterday, their blocks of beetroot marmalade. At the Rosetip goods welcomed the eye. Eggs—large and small, white, brown and with spots—rose in pyramids or reposed in straw. Bread smelled from far away. Butter was shaped into mounds and topped with a radish. While a pint of fresh sour cream was poured into Mom's glass, the smell of rosemary penetrated my nose. The abundance made me fall into a stupor, but an even greater delight awaited me—perhaps. I hoped to return home in a droshky covered with a heavy hood. Inside semi-obscurity ruled. The air smelled of oats and horse shit, and I felt secure: no ruins, no Germans, no radio-active rain, no parents who'd die or abandon me. The droshky saved me from myself, yet I rarely returned in it from the Rosetip Bazaar. Why? Too proud, I never asked my mom for it.

All this Djuna told Myloslav?

Yes, and more. So you see, she continued, Carol was incapable of begging you to go with her to the sea. But she bought a black bikini and put it on one evening, before going to bed. Too bad you didn't get the message.

I did, Djuna, I did!

And failed to fulfill your mistress's modest dream?

Carol wasn't my mistress. She was an erotic friend, one of many, and I didn't want to lead her on. But you, Djuna, you would be my mistress, my all and only.

Stop it!

It's the truth, Djuna. From the beginning to the end of my affair with Carol I was in the passenger's seat. I slept with her out of respect and a dose of inertia. After all: why not? I had a lot of warm feelings for her, but she never turned me on.

What about generosity? You could have rewarded her with a trip to the beach. Didn't you know how grateful she was for the smallest sign of attention?

Don't torture me, dearest. How could I go to the sea and never tell her what I tell you every minute? I was too indifferent, perhaps. But not cruel. Anyway, her suicide has blown up our little romance, given it meaning it never possessed, made me a scapegoat.

I insist: you should have taken her to the beach—at least once. Carol knew you'd never fall in love with her. So she dreamt of a ride in a droshky—in your arms.

Sentimental rubbish!

Not at all. Had you gone with her to the sea that summer, perhaps she wouldn't have taken her life. Only a small gesture was required.

Were we on the same wavelength, I could have done something right! But we weren't. Carol often laughed at me, saying: No Czech can descend into the well of a Polish heart. Perhaps. Who wants to go there in the first place? But this much I can tell you, Djuna. I saw her suffering and prayed to God—I was a believer, she not—to have her cured of her crush on me, an ordinary guy turning fifty. A nobody with an ebbing libido. Her senseless passion embarrassed me. Why was she so keen to open the top button of my shirt and caress my neck—at the very spot where it was overgrown with warts? Why was she so taken with my protruding belly, for God's sake? Her ecstasy made me uneasy in my own skin. It itched under her gaze, and I had to jump up and run to the mirror, shouting: I hate every inch of myself, a rotten bag with almost no hair, and no juice left for you, my thirsty angel. Oh, Djuna, there's nothing more suffocating than one-sided affection. It traps you like a rabbit. Sure! Had I been able to catch Carol's fire, we would have been in heaven. Alas, she burnt on the equator, I froze north of Copenhagen.

No, I couldn't warm up. No way. In sex, as in roulette, trying is no good. Remember Rose Selavy in Monte Carlo, with her Mona Lisa mustache? She tried for a month, but won nothing and turned all pale. She had figured out a million strategies to make it work, and I don't have to tell you, Djuna, that no one had better brains than Selavy. As it happened, I was spending a dirty weekend in the Casino Hotel and walked into the den with my *petite* Erose, her gray matter the size of a peanut, who had never before tried her luck at roulette. Realizing Rose's agony, I encouraged her: assist Mlle C'est-la-Vie in her struggle with chance, while I have a scotch next door. Half an hour later I found the two women in contrasting moods. Erose played once—the first and the last time in her uneventful life dedicated solely to eros—and won, while Rose lost her last penny—and finally felt inclined to depart for New York. I offered to buy her a ticket for the *Bride & Bachelors,* the new electric submarine that was to take off from Duchamp the following Monday. But Rose declined and suggested that I buy a lock of her immortal hair—she was almost bald by then—for the exact amount of the fare. I agreed and we took farewell of each other. That night I impregnated Erose—whom her success in roulette had rendered even more sexy. This was our last union. On Tuesday midday I took the TGV to Switzerland, she continued on to Paris. Nine months later she gave birth to our son Marcel, whom I have never encountered but refer to as *Eros-c'est-la-vie.*

In Lausanne I met my fate—in the usual disguise of my mother. An art freak, the next morning she dragged me to the Musée des Beaux Arts where a rather awful textile show was on. Of course, her eye fell on Carol's three wooden chairs covered with white cotton, or was it silk? They didn't appeal to me in the least, so I wouldn't have noticed them. But *mama* exclaimed: Fascinating, and forced the catalog upon me. Boring me to death, she read aloud the artist's biography and outlined Carol's face with her finger. I intended to toss the photo away, but it caught my attention. Had I seen her before? At a Manhattan cocktail party? Examining the mediocre portrait, I mused: I'm through with Erose. Why not look up this one upon my return from Europe?

She gave me another version of it. But go on, Myloslav.

I phoned Carol and said: I'd be honored to have you for dinner, even though I didn't care much for your Swiss stuff. Carol laughed and replied: I can't resist your charm. In the *Great Polish Encyclopedia* my dad edited, it went under *Bohemian bonhommie,* or how to approach a lady not on a white horse but on a skate board. Today's Friday the thirteenth, it couldn't be an unluckier date. Besides, it's my Czech day. Last week Selavy founded the Central European Dance Committee, and five minutes ago he asked me to a soirée of Capek-polkas in the East Village. At Christmas he'll stage some of your religious patriotism, the Holy Hus History or the Secrets of Saint Schweik.

So Carol came?

Yes, but she was late. A pupil of Mondrian redid her place. Burning the old paint off the window frame, he set her flat on fire and she helped him extinguish it. Then she fed the artist, got rid of him, forgot my address but recalled my number, rang me from the subway station, and arrived half past nine—in black pants, stained with white paint, and a black sweater. Later her uniform used to get on my nerves, but that evening it appealed to me. It rendered her so thin, and I thought: a bird. Does she feel like one too? Curious, I put my hands on Carol when she turned her back to me, to study my drawings. A sudden impulse—not sexual at all. I traced her backbone and ribs, avoided her breasts and belly. Mistaking my examination for eros, she smiled and whispered: skin and bones. After a pause she added: I'll be going. No, I wasn't disappointed, I was relieved. A mass of chestnut hair curled around her head. While walking her to the subway, I kissed it and said: I recognize the brand of your shampoo. Really? I don't believe you. It's blue, I announced, and she burst into laughter: True, it's blue, I have underestimated you. You have won first prize, a flight for two to Hawaii—where I went a year later, but not with Carol.

Was it love at first sight, Myloslav? Did she ring you next day, first thing in the morning?

Not at all. Had I not called her a few days later, I'm sure she would have forgotten me.

Why did you ring her again?

I needed company, Djuna, and I liked Carol. I liked her well enough to go to bed with her. The next time we had dinner at her place. After I had finished the dessert, raspberries with *crème fraiche,* I asked her to sit in my lap.

That's rather explicit.

It's how she must have considered it. But I swear to you, Djuna, I didn't mean it. I just wanted to feel the bird in my arms—not to fuck it.

Did you enlighten Carol of your intention?

No, it was too late. To my "sit in my lap," she burst into laughter: A Czech euphemism for screwing? Her eyes shone with eagerness, and I remarked to myself: well, it may hurt her less than saying: No, Carol,

I just want to hold you for a sec. A serious mistake. Worse, the first step to her tragedy. This evening, and on many nights to come, I made love to Carol. Rather unsuccessfully. I knew it and she knew it too. Soon I became convinced that we couldn't make it, but with her it had gone the other way. My insufficiency kindled her ambition—to arouse me one day. Were I more adequate, she would have desired me less. It's life.

It's death.

That I realized only later. The idea that a woman of Carol's stature could jump into the Hudson because of a guy like myself—it wouldn't have occurred to me in my worst nightmare. At the beginning she depicted herself as a totally liberated female, a believer in promiscuity who would never become infatuated with a single male. When I dared to doubt her words, she derided me. In those days she was so exuberant— I, a sentimental ass. The first summer, before her departure for Europe, I confessed that I'd miss her terribly. It was true. I didn't love her, but I had become used to her. But she burst into laughter. Later I saw her waiting for a kind word—then she wouldn't have laughed anymore— but couldn't utter it. Here was a woman whom I had once admired for being above the conventions. Now she was succumbing to them, full speed. While I tried to get an erection, she whispered into my ear: Do you love me a little? Plump, answered my plumule, and went down. Plump. See the two of us, Djuna Barnes? A dead cat with a singing bird.

Yes, I know, Myloslav. Why run against the wall, Carol? I asked her more than once. Because I must, she replied. Fate is playing a terrible game with me. It's not myself, it's my skin that longs for him. Pity me, Djuna. I can't fall asleep without a pillow in my arms. Holding on to it, I imagine it's my man. Take him away, and I'll die by my own hand—my hand being wiser than my body. Nonsense, I shouted, nonsense! Help me dismantle your madness, or transfer it to me, Djuna Barnes, a supreme stylist. For years I have been after your affection, and I'm still ready to grab you, dear. Come! Let me seduce you away from a mediocre Central European! Elope with me to the sea! I'll be your sister and mistress, your husband and wife. Come! I promise you a moon full of honey, a wedding gown of sheer delight. Come with me! We'll cross the Elysian Fields, arrive at the gate of gayness, slip right into it. Look into the mirror, Carol. Flat and fine, aren't you a camouflaged page? My boy—not his girl? I swear, I'll be in seventh heaven doing what he refuses to do. I'll lick your earlobes, suck your nipples, inspect your crevices with the tip of my tongue.

Don't go on, Djuna.

That's where I stopped anyhow, Myloslav. I shut up, and a long silence awaited me. Finally Carol sighed and mumbled: Thank you, darling, it would be the final solution, but I can't accept it. You're into life, Djuna—I'm into death. Our paths part. Don't ask me to drag you into my abyss. I'm not a dragon, and I'm not really gay. Neither fowl nor fish, I don't fit into Myloslav's down-to-earth design. But can I ever fit into your serenades? Soon I'll swim, while you, our man in the land of femaleness, you fly. On Saturday you wear a billycock and a corked mustache, tight trousers, a red waistcoat—and go out with Gertrude Stein, hiding her date from Alice B. Toklas. But Sunday night you steal out of the house in a strawberry-colored bra, a miniskirt and no panties, and proceed to the Saint Christopher port where until dawn you fondle several Dadaists plus the cock of Joyce, whose delicate hands you direct to we all know where. What kind of gayness is that? A brief eye contact with a man, even a Czech, and he ejaculates.

You're a fool, Carol, I objected. Myloslav hasn't paid me the slightest due.

So he will. Soon he'll discover Djuna and fall for her. I predict: you'll free him from his phobias and fears—the peculiar interest in his toilet seat, the horror of contracting something through sex. The desire to drink you up will transform my *Schlappschwanz* into a ferocious chipmunk. He, so infinitely slow in raising his palm to my cheek, he'll consume you in one go.

So Carol knew it before I knew it!

I won't let her prophecy come true. No, Myloslav, the gate to my graveyard is locked.

Grant me the favor, let me die in your tomb. I loathed Carol's suicide, but meanwhile death has caught up with me. My wish to become a second Corbusier has faded away, I have time for a sick wife. Rejecting me, Djuna, you'll duplicate bad luck. But if you accept me, we'll make some sense out of our triple nonsense. Once I had a calendar filled with women's names. But I could recall neither their figures nor their faces, neither the color of their eyes nor the shade of their locks. My indifference was such that twice I got involved with cripples, but realized it only after the end of my romances. Before I met you, Djuna, I had loved no one.

Your mom?

Each year we spent the summer vacation together, and each year I brought tears to her eyes. Oh, dear, I was so bottled up in my own joviality. Carol had to kill herself to shake me out of it. The shock smashed the glass. Water flooded her lungs, and my soul was set free. So here I am—a changed man. Softer, more generous, I'm ready to return what she has planted in me. A seed has grown into a tree. It will provide shade for both of us, my girl. Let's board the Transsiberian, sail away. Every four hours, while you inject yourself with interferon, I'll hold your hand. Give it to me, Djuna. Don't protest.

You wish to be married to my foul flesh?

Yes. Carol wanted to sleep with me while she menstruated, when I had a flu. The exchange of our fluids—a motion picture in white and red—it's shown again and again. Before falling asleep, I watch her adjust a fresh napkin between her thighs, smeared with sperm and blood, and smile. She strokes my prick, a dirty little thing, and smiles back. How could I be afraid of your blood, Djuna? The mortal threat? Carol searched for me, the blind Amor, in the depths of the Hudson. But she missed me. You, my princess, you find me at your feet—without lifting a finger. *C'est la vie.*

No, *c'est la mort.* You may be a mad dog, but I'm not a Salome. No, not one kiss. I reject your proposition to be infected with AIDS—for nothing.

Not for nothing, dearest. For a change. Let me evolve back into a lower species, be a fish feeding happily on your bacilli. Overexcited by your terminal disease, I want to dive into your sick-sea, fuse with it. Or do you prefer me to be an Indian widow throwing herself into the flames that burn her husband? Oh, don't repulse me, Djuna. Let's engage in a sex deluge. Be a red robin to a white-haired dove. A stubborn old fart? Fine. I'll be one. Nothing can break my persistence. I'll be after you, Djuna, day and night. Once a mere *lew salonowy,* now I'll roar like a king of the Sahara, storm your nightwood. If you're my thanatos, I must be your eros. If you make my day, you must be my night. *Mylanoc,* does it not sound right? Come, together we'll prove that there's no light at the end of the tunnel.

Calm yourself, my Czech pigeon in heat. No, I'm not your bride, I'm a New York writer. But right here, in the mulberry tree that grows in front of my window, there's a dove. Coo, coo, my boy, and soon she'll agree to build a nest with you.

My Czecho-Slovak self flew away and left me a lunatic: a Pole on a white horse. So I'll oppose the German tank you pretend to be.

Enough, Myloslav. The Institute is about to fall apart. Ann is glued to her Apple Plus. Moses has applied for the distinguished emeritus status at Kyoto University. Lotte toils away in the capacity of the Prop

& Goth Condo superintendent. Conrad considers a last cruise around the world. Eglizer dabbles in reincarnation. Digging a grave for his former solid-state, he hopes to be reborn as a sex-cat of robotics.

Why should we then wait any longer? Let's aid away while facing other faces. No, better no faces at all. Burmese beasts, the monkeys of Macao. What else?

The Khmer Rouge extermination camps.

T HE END IS THE END IS THE END.
   Don't be such a Gertrude Stein, Assudin admonishes the Afghan ex-king. Don't add an end to each sentence.

What else? Exit? No, I'm too old to return to Afghanistan and supervise the formation of an interim government the Polish pope offers to mediate—between the wolf and the sheep the wolf has devoured. Yet I'm too young to retire to the New School for Senior Sovereigns at Baton Rouge, with its swamps and alligators.

It will be like in the Nile delta. On clear winter nights you'll busy yourself with discovering in the sky the Hair of Berenice. No, you're right. There no one knows about her affair with Sextus, even though ibises and crocodiles may have heard from their African relatives about the lovers' last trip on the Nile—in a swift, swift cangia. But will the Americans pay for me, Shali, your court painter?

That's beside the point, Assudin. The stipends for monarchs are enormous. We can both survive on one. Two old men, what do we need? Our children are grown up, our wives dead. Yes, it pains me to leave them behind, rotting away alone. The least I expected was to be buried here, close to our great friends. Lately I dreamt of Charlotte planting a cherry tree on my tomb.

I too dream of similar silliness—an eternal senior-citizen place where we can hold hands, listen to nightingales, reminisce. But the money that makes the world go round has run out. And soon we'll be rushed into yet another diaspora. Oh, God, it has happened so rapidly. The death of Sextus, the distant expiration of Wolf. Then Ms. Barnes arrived and soon departed with the Czech, what's his name? He had a kind face, kind and sad.

But caused the suicide of Ann's stepsister.

That's what Charlotte told me. But who's without guilt in that sphere? Love—no one can do it right. Didn't Ms. Barnes refuse to take him up, initially?

Yes, but his mind was set on her. His adoration was not of this world. Where did it spring from? Physical attraction plus a deep sense of shame. A sinner, he tried to exorcise his body of an old fiend.

The devil of a lifelong indifference. But who are we to judge him? An army of women may pay for the pain our first love has inflicted on us. His first wife was pretty awful, I heard.

Yet we keep falling in love with the original type. If our first beloved was called Eve, we're likely to choose for our last fling another Eve. On the surface, the old-age affair will appear as the opposite of the youthful infatuation. But, in fact, it will be a reaction to our first romance. If the first Eve was a frigid bitch, we will be cold towards the second Eve.

Yes, a man may reward with warmth women lacking in affection, punish with coldness those who care for him. Where Eve 1 hit him, he'll return the blow to Eve 2.

Yes, what an irony! In bed with E2—melting at his side—he'll assume the role of E1—and be as responsive as a brick. Psyche is such a symmetrical thing.

It's shameful and sad, but remember what Goethe used to say: It's no good blaming ourselves for the chemistry of sentiments. Yes, it spoils our better selves, but so what. In sex we prefer challenge to devotion, suspense to certitude. I once had a mistress who clung to me like a child. While we strolled, she wanted to hold my hand. At night she held me in a tight embrace. And I? Was I grateful? No, I was bored, and dreamt about whores. Two years went by. Then, to my greatest surprise, one night she opened her arms and simply walked out of my bed. Just a little annoyed, I went back to sleep, mumbling to myself: a small piece of theater, she'll be back tomorrow. But I never saw her again. At the beginning I didn't mind. But as time passed, her absence turned into a slight but permanent pain. A sort of discomfort a dead tooth gives you. Only then I realized that her affection had been like a warm blanket— between myself and the world.

Myloslav once used the same phrase. There was a tragic touch to this man.

He was a little mad. Once I invited him to the Indian Café. Five minutes after we had walked in, a black sailor put a quarter into a music box. A man's voice began to sing "Memphis in June," and a strange monologue came out of Myloslav. No, he wasn't drunk. We had a martini or two at home, that's all. What he did? He spoke to a mirror.

First he asked it in his own voice: Why do you tremble, my bird? Myloslav, I whispered, and put my hand on his shoulder. But he didn't pay any attention to me, and replied in a different, high-pitched tone: Because I'm an idiot, because I'm not fit for life. When I heard him producing this absurdity, I raised my voice: Come on, old chum. But I couldn't interrupt him. Immersed in his thoughts, he continued: Your fragility is robustness—in disguise. You're charming and funny. I'm always amused when I watch you jump around, alight gracefully at the edge of my palm, pick up crumbs, chant a small hi-ho, hide your misfortune, wave your tiny flag of good luck, fool me. You're a special bird —swift, gay, and marsupial. I beg you: stay away from the Hudson.

The sailor threw in another coin. "Memphis in June" returned, and so did Myloslav's female voice: Let me reside in the pocket of your pants, and I'll stay away from the river. The rest I barely recall. Another change of tone, something about his pocket being already overcrowded, and the coffin of his heart. I paid and tried to lead him out. But at the door he escaped me, ran back to the mirror, and cried: *Dadada, ja, tak.* A simple salty *yes*, and the bird won't change into a fish.

Oh my! Now the guy is globe-trotting with Ms. Barnes. The older one gets, the more life resembles a duet Mohammed plays with Beethoven.

G INKAKU-JI-MAE. A taped voice is switched on, and Djuna asks Myloslav: Isn't that our destination?

It sounds right, but there should be a canal to our left. Here it is. Moses is supposed to wait for us in front of a small coffeeshop across the street.

If I know him, he's waiting at the bus stop to make sure we don't miss each other.

Ginkaku-ji-mae.

And there's Moses' bent back at the lamppost.

Welcome, my dearest! I was afraid your Japanese might not be good enough to understand the synthetic voice that announces the stops—I can hardly understand it myself. So for the last half hour I have been inspecting one bus after another. Finally we're reunited, the three of us. How's your health, Djuna? Any better? Oh, it's improved? No kidding! No interferon anymore? Just pills. But that's wonderful! You've done it, Myloslav. Love heals everything.

And you, Moses?

I'm fine. Alienated like a man on the moon, or a guinea pig undergoing an experiment with philosophers: they're removed from their respective homes, parachuted all over the globe, and closely watched from above and below—to determine who can adjust and who cannot. How long can a Kant stand it in Kamchatka? Can Descartes cogitate in North Carolina? Will Pascal pursue God in Polynesia? And Moses Maimonides: will he mellow down in Kyoto, and finally get rid of his perplexity?

And the outcome, Moses?

No definite results as yet, Myloslav. However, Kant may prove tougher than myself, with his *Sternenhimmel* without and his moral principle within. He's teaching forms of intuition to the weary clouds fleeing the Soviet sky, while I, more depressed than perplexed, grope around temples and gardens, and reread old books. Tonight I spent a few sleepless hours in your nightwood, Djuna, and was struck by your unpredictable style. Your prose contradicts the very concept of fiction. Like life itself, it doesn't get anybody anywhere, and tiptoes out, leaving us oblivious of God—that transparent veil with which we blindfold ourselves. Do you know what I'm after right now? I relativize my own opus. Karl presented me with a Macintosh Plus, and I use the easiest of his programs to process my *Guide*. I erase sentences, rearrange paragraphs, replace Hebrew words with citations from Yiddish or Basque. Watching my thoughts flicker on the screen, I doubt that they really belong to me, and if yes, whether they're adequate to reflect on the tetragrammaton. Once I wrote that the corporeal element in man is a large partition which prevents him from perceiving abstract ideas perfectly. I put this on paper way back, the evening Ann left for New York, and every cell of my body ached and longed for her. Collecting my thoughts, I recalled—step by step—our stroll on the beach. My heart was bursting, and I whispered to myself: Let it burst, let the flesh be drained to the last drop. Physical desire is nothing. The corporeal is just a screen hiding the truth. But what was the truth? That I was young, terribly sick with love, and in need of consolation. To transcend the suffering her indifference inflicted on me, I had to elevate myself above it. So I thought with adolescent solemnity: the corporeal element in man is a screen. Oh, were it that simple! The mental is as much a partition as the physical, and the more we neglect the corporeal, the more traps the mind sets for us. Men given to abstraction are sleepwalkers, losing sense not only of what's right and wrong but, more importantly, of what's right or wrong with them.

Is this the right way, Moses?

Yes, Myloslav, we continue along the canal. What I wrote down in Salamanca has been canceled out by what I have experienced ever since. It's not the corporeal that is vapor and darkness. The abstract envelops us in an even thicker mist. While we focus on the mind, squeezing out of it ever new similes and equations, our unattended body begins to revolt. The coordination between the physical and mental breaks down, the chemistry is upset, allergies surface. Then our essence starts receding to the subconscious, and our life's fabric disintegrates.

Do you transform your *Guide* into the Apocalypse of Moses? I hope not. You aren't an evangelist, and this isn't Patmos. But I agree with you. Too much illumination obscures the brain. Cutting ourselves off from our dirty flesh, we aren't getting any wiser. Reason proves to be as much of a prison as was prejudice. Too much sublimation spoils the blood, and so we grow increasingly infantile and fearful.

I'm afraid, Djuna, that once disturbed, natural balance may be lost forever.

But what's natural, Moses? Has there ever been a proper equilibrium? No, equilibria come and go. Perhaps we're about to witness the birth of a new harmony—to be established between an individual and the lit screen. Perhaps the silent face of a friendly machine will force itself upon us, reach all the way down to the subconscious, rescue our essence, regenerate our substance.

Well, Djuna, maybe it's happening already. Chapter 9 of my *New Guide* starts with the sentence: The abstract element in man is a partition that prevents him from perfectly perceiving the lifesaving mechanisms of his physical well-being. The mind isn't necessarily clear. It can be as opaque as the body. But let me not bore you any longer with my philosophizing. After all, we aren't in Kamchatka but in Kyoto, charming and archaic, with a past as extraordinary as the Rome of Nero. It's good you have arrived here at the beginning of December, when details are hidden under snow but bigger entities are revealed by it. In its distinct beauty the winter surpasses all other seasons. Leaving my footprints on the white ways and frozen canals, I feel like a Buddhist monk walking out of a Japanese woodcut. The road we follow was used for daily strolls by the philosopher Nishida Kitaro. It then changes into a narrow path winding along the Sakura-bashi canal, which can be crossed back and forth. Between here and Reikan-ji, the Notre Dame convent we're going to visit, there are eleven stone bridges, each of them a small masterpiece, with posts modeled after bundled children. Our first stop is the tomb of the sixty-third emperor. Hypochondria prevented him from attending his own coronation, and he remained a sick frog throughout his life. Everybody expected him to die young, but he reached the age of sixty-one. The humid coldness of his hands and feet made his concubines call him Reizei—a cold spring—and avoid his caresses.

Hence the phrase *to go to bed with a reizei?* Does it mean to make love to a reptile?

How erudite you are, my girl, and how well you say it. A reptile, yes, and one with an insatiable appetite for fresh young females—as if he hoped to warm himself inside of them. A steady number of virgins was kept at the court, some of whom were his own daughters from the imperial harem. His ex-concubines told the frightened teens to take a long hot bath—before and after—and to never open their eyes. It's going to feel like making love to a snail, they warned, but at least you don't have to do anything. He'll creep in between your lips, slowly eject his icy phlegm. Its melting in your mouth is the worst part of it. Since he can't deflower you with his too soft prick, he'll insert his thumb, fiddle around for a while, lick the blood from his palm.

For God's sake, Moses! Myloslav's modest soul turns red.

I'll be finished in a moment, Djuna. Reizei doesn't expect you, the concubines continue, to remain all night at his side. Once he has cleaned you out, slip out of his bed. It's not likely he'll want to use you again, unless something catches his attention. Therefore be as silent as a carp, and dead to his touch. Open as much as you can, but don't moan or cry, and you'll be rewarded with a gold piece. He'll deposit it in your bleeding purse, a good hiding place, so don't object—and don't take it out until you're back. No, the coin won't fall out. Blood will glue it to your skin. You're tight, small and tight. It will stay in all right.

You render me speechless.

I'm growing old, Myloslav, and I'm in Japan. Here no one has a clue to my former existence, and I find it too tiresome to explain my roots. So I invent stories and dive into their classics, of which many are pretty erotic. Here sex isn't constrained. Jewish taboos, Platonic ideals, Roman virtues, Christian guilt—it's all Esperanto to the Japanese. Pleasure is pleasure, a piece of flesh, not a veil one fears to tear.

In the subway Myloslav found a sex-comics booklet and—my poor puritan!—almost threw up. But, on the other hand, you aren't aware, Moses, of the metamorphosis he's about to complete at my serpentine side. All these months he has been shedding his dove gray coat, growing blue feathers.

I can't see them, but my eyes have deteriorated. Does the change manifest itself also in other ways?

Myloslav doesn't start his days with: There are no cakes without work.

Now I exclaim: *Vive l'amour—vive la mort!*

Good. You're maturing into a respectable old boy. But do you know how I begin my mornings?

Not in the company of the tetragrammaton.

No, I prefer *Genji monogatari,* and daydreaming. Like a suburban spouse, I portray myself as an attractive individual straying from one adventure to another. Today I depict myself as the emperor Suzuki, tomorrow as his mistress. Here everything is equally foreign to me, so I have stopped distinguishing between reality and illusion. As a matter of fact, fancy is the only way to absorb Kyoto. In addition, I have developed a taste for theater, and see myself performing in plays redesigned by me. Lately I have been rehearsing the role of Lotte in *Werther.*

Apropos, Moses: in spite of her protests, last month all the cherries were cut and the condo board transferred Wolf's remains to the right corner of the garden—in order to accommodate an underground garage.

Oh, my God! Poor Lotte.

Poor but brave. The last guardian of our vanishing world, she refuses to abandon Propertius's villa.

Yes, I know. Recently she wrote to me: As long as I'm here, not everything is lost.

And that's so. She transformed Sextus's old studio into an archive of us all. No, not by herself, she got unexpected help from Wanda Grau, Carol's old friend and vice president of More Money Bank. A satanically smart person nicknamed the President of Vice, she presented Lotte with the most advanced Superplus Minus, a rocket of a computer. And the ex-editor of Karenina and Conrad—the source of their success—joined the venture.

Is it the famous Florence, the top secret agent of the literary world? Nobody has ever seen her, but they chat about her even at our tea parties.

The very same, a short woman who doesn't lack one ingredient indispensable for greatness. One, she suffers from asthma. Two, she can gulp down more Bloody Marys than Lowry and still come up with a good joke. Three, she edits every text to the bone.

In English?

Mostly, but not exclusively. She's married to a linguist. A compatriot of Conrad, he's a world authority on nouns of motion, verbs of emotion, and adjectives of locomotion. He conquered her heart on a beach at sunset—after they had discussed the question of accents since 10:00 A.M. Still, it wasn't an easy task. Young Florence was as popular with guys as Karenina. But so was he with girls. A very good-looking couple, they produced two kids. But in her middle years Florence met Weil and emancipated herself. At fifty-eight she traveled through Egypt on camelback, visited Berenice, and saved some of the queen's latest papyruses together with Sextus's last sonnet. Now she's finally arrived in Rome.

Excellent. I hope she'll put her hand to Wolf's collected works. A little editing would do them a lot of good. Even *Faust* wouldn't suffer from a bit of word-processing.

You can rest assured, Moses. In the whole world there's no better editor than Florence. She relies solely on her ear, instinct, and common sense. If she feels like crossing out *aurea prima,* no Ovid can stop her. When she has set her mind on replacing *to be or not to be* with *oh damn it*—no English gentleman can prevent her from carrying out her plan. If integrity exists, its name is Florence. The Medici employed her, but she quit her post at Petrarch's. With such an editor at her side, Lotte may succeed in preserving world literature for the distant future on Venus or Mars. Florence will compress our excretions into a single text, transfer the text to a single hard disk, replicate the original, and bury the copies everywhere—in the ruins of Manhattan and under the snows of Siberia.

I don't doubt her energy. But what about funds?

Florence's husband has a pal at the Kanga Roo University in Sydney, the last educational institution on earth that hasn't devoured its endowment. Feeling provincial, the Kanga wants to build the world's biggest manuscript library. Lotte has already a name for it: *Globook.* It has enchanted the Australians, so they may invite Mrs. Goethe and the editor to a small island, off the southern coast, where the International Vanity archives could find a home one day.

Lotte in Sydney! The epilogue of our era.

What an old-fashioned phrase, Moses! Why not call it the final deconstruction of postmodernity—and please Derrida.

So oder so—time is coming to an end. Inside a pyramid a Japanese garden is spreading out. Inside the garden an American disco is hidden. Inside the disco a Roman atrium treasures two frescoes: one of Donald

Duck waltzing with Propertius, the other of Berenice—her husband's head atop her stupendous hair.

You dislike our dear little age, Moses.

No, Djuna, I revel in it. Everything is with us, as long as the electricity is on, the disk in. My Kyoto acquaintances report that computers have replaced their relatives and friends. People sleep with the screens on, wake up when there's a blackout. But I switch off the machine before I go to bed—to be what I am: a lonely, a very lonely old man.

You switch off the machine because you're brave. Not afraid to fall back on your own personal nothingness. But most of us stand in front of the dark mirror, waiting in vain for a meaningful image. The machine is the lonely bachelor's bride flashing her lights at him, turning him on. But the moment you turn her off, it's over. And you find yourself in the blackest Black Forest.

You flatter me, Djuna, and I drink your words. They fête me here, but the communication comes to zero. I'm confused by their peculiar pronunciation, they don't understand my Jewish Japanese. But it's no good complaining about destiny. Let's cross here. The building on the other side of the river is the Reikan-ji, a nunnery established for the tenth daughter of the Emperor Go-Mizu-no-o. It's famous because of a relic that is preserved here, a sacred mirror—the *reikan*. As in Platonism, the sense that all reality is a mere reflection of another world resides at the heart of Japanese philosophy, and I catch myself using their religious metaphors while meditating on the endless chain of mirrorings in mystical Judaism—on the Shechinah transmitting the light of God from above to below.

I don't feel like visiting the convent, Moses. Yes, I'm slightly short of breath. Couldn't we just walk around the complex?

Of course, Djuna. Reikan-ji is furnished with an extraordinary inner garden arranged on two levels. The lower part is celebrated for the endless variety of its mosses. Now they're mostly covered with snow, but here and there you'll be able to compare their different shades. Above we have a real park with bushes and small trees, their trunks and branches strangely twisted. It's a perfect day to contemplate their naked contours, outlining themselves clearly against the white ground and the pale sky. The dwarf cherries, planted in circles, remind me of baby apes. You'll like them, Djuna dear, and Myloslav will appreciate the path I have chosen. A corridor between two wings, it will lead us to yet another section of the garden. There we shall examine the architectural structure of the two principal buildings, the Sho-in and, east of it, the Hon-do. Then, taking a slight detour to the west, we'll pass two tombs and reach the temple of Anraku.

It's surprisingly mild.

Yes, it's an exceptionally warm day, Myloslav. Seeing my shoe-prints in the snow, I remember the afternoon I walked with Ann along the sea. Do you know where she is? She stopped writing to me. Can you imagine? After all those years. Not a word. Lotte mentioned that she returned to Manhattan. Together with Karl. Is that so? You don't know? You aren't in touch with her either. Terrible! The closest friend I have in the world—and I don't even know where she is. Old ships, we drift apart instead of heading for a common haven. In November I Xeroxed for Ann an ancient Japanese legend about two lovers, the lord Naku Samu and the younger lady of Ajè, and sent the copy to her, c/o Signora Goethe. But yesterday the letter came back with a brief note from Lotte saying that she—the mama of us all!—doesn't have Ann's New York address. I'm so hurt, Djuna, and so worried! Something must have happened. She's either sick, or . . .

No, Moses, Ann isn't dead. If she were, every sparrow on the roof would mourn her. Remember her changing moods? Her sudden outbursts of despair? Her equally sudden returns to life? Soon you'll receive a note from her, I swear to you.

How kind of you, Myloslav. Yes, you may be right. Let's sit down here, the bench is sheltered by brush, the sun is getting stronger. Allow me to read aloud the story I copied for Ann. It has come down to us from prehistoric times, but I took a modern translation and revised it: Lord Naku Samu and the younger lady of Ajè, both of them fair to look upon, yearn after each other. After days and months they meet at a song-hedge, and the lad sings:

> Hanging cotton cloths on a young pine tree of Ajè,
> Lo, does it not seem
> Someone beckoneth to me?
> Ah, little Ajè, my isle!

Whereupon the girl replies:

> Although you may start when the tide is at flooding,
> Oh, my dearest one,
> Hidden by eighty islands, yet you did not take note of me!

They wish to converse but fear to be observed by others. So they flee from the merrymaking place and hide under a pine tree. There they hold each other's hands, draw knee to knee, confess each to each their yearning, and satisfy their longing with pleasures ever refreshed. It happens in a jewel-clear season of golden wind and clear moon, when passing cranes and the music of distant breezes are heard in the pine trees. They look up and see the wild geese flying east. Mountains are quiet, clouds lazy, and on the near hills colored leaves are scattered. The sound of waves, dashing on the rocks, puts their ears to sleep, and that night they enjoy unequaled happiness. Forgetting how late it is, they are surprised by cocks that suddenly begin to crow, barking dogs, and the sun growing bright in the sky. They are very young, it all has happened so rapidly, and they don't know what to do. They are ashamed to be seen by others, and don't want to return to the world. So they pray to be transformed into two trees. The boy is called Nami-pine, the damsel Kotsu-pine. Up to the present their names haven't been changed. The place of their first and last encounter, the Two-in-One Pine Forest, is not far from here.

Aren't you an old romantic! A Moses Philemon whispering into the ear of his dear Ann Baucis. Alas, she's no pine. She's a butterfly.

I wouldn't mind growing into a tree, Djuna, if you would only agree to be my damsel-pine.

You see what you have done, Moses. You have awakened Myloslav's Czech inspiration. But what about acid rain? Won't it destroy the damsel's dainty dress? If she isn't deadwood already. Well, I'm getting chilly. Let's go, guys. Give me your hand, Moses. Oh no, it's so cold, it trembles. Come on, Maimonides. Your pine will write, soon. But she won't fall in love with you. What cannot be—cannot be. You aren't two young trees. Far from it.

But she has been on my mind for over a century.

And you have been on hers, but other men were on it as well, including one who's present.

After a life of departures, why can't she return to me?

She is repulsed by your constancy, Moses. It's against the grain of life itself—an affair rotten to the bone. Take me, the aging and aiding away Djuna Barnes, that most unsuitable object of desire, and take Myloslav—that most unsuitable man to desire me. I can't detect one atom of affection for him in my sick soul. Nothing that would justify his adoration of me. Still, I have consented to become his mistress. Why? Because I'm a dying cynic whose best friend jumped into a river out of too much passion for him. Our relationship is sealed with sheer negativity. But two minuses produce a plus. Ah, amor plays with the cheapest matches.

But you ignore them, Moses. You believe in the crystal-clear quality of a *mens sana in corpore sano*. But how could it be? Aren't we abodes for retroviruses, trenches for defective chromosomes, meatballs? But enough of that. Look! On top of an ice-cake a duck floats down the canal. Give me one of the crackers you always keep in your coat pocket, Myloslav—I'll feed it.

Feed the duckling, Djuna, and stop torturing our perplexed guide and me. Here, have two crackers. Stuff one into your mouth.

Djuna hits hard.

You're telling me! Am I not a specialist in her killing subtlety!

A depressingly bright girl, she beats her head against her heart, and her heart against her head.

No, against me.

She doesn't mean a tenth of what she proclaims. Just look at her! In her strawberry-colored gloves and her little black hat, she reminds me of Karenina the day I fetched her from the Moscow railroad station. She wore a black coat with a silver-fox collar. A lock of her chestnut hair escaped from her hat and swept my cheek.

I too met Anna. Just once. She took her right hand out of her rabbit muff and gave it to me. It was so light, her hand, and my fingers brushed the fur. When we were in India, Peter Brook's *Mahabarata* played in Calcutta and we went. There's one scene I can never forget. You saw it too? Well, it's the one with the good king. He arrives—remember?—at the gates of paradise with a small dog in his arms, only to learn that dogs aren't admitted to heaven. Well, he replies, if the dog isn't allowed in, I won't enter either. For a long time I was all alone, and so was he. But now we're together and cannot part from each other—even if paradise is to be missed.

I see, I see. Anna's muff made you recall the dog, a little piece of fur in the actor's hands.

Listen, Moses. Djuna and I, we're like the king and the dog. She would never admit it, but I know the truth. Even if she were to be banned from paradise, she wouldn't abandon me. In the theater, upon hearing the king's answer, she gave me a long glance and a smile ran over her face. She said nothing, but she put her hand into mine and moved her lips. God, I knew what she wanted to say: We'll never part from each other, not even at that gate of heaven. Guess what provoked her outbreak today.

My legend of the two pine trees?

Yes. I observed Djuna very closely while you were reading. She went pale and for a split second looked at me. It may be true that I have gone for her because of Carol's suicide, and it's true that for a long time she rejected me. But now she accepts me, and not because of my persistence alone. Her feelings have changed under the pressure from her flesh. She isn't indifferent to me anymore.

It's curious what unites two people.

It's more than curious. It's extraordinary. What threw me into this affair? An image—of Djuna injecting herself with interferon. She was seated at Charlotte's oak table, her face calm, undisturbed by self-pity, girlishly aloof. A drop of blood dangled at the tip of the needle and she wiped it off with a Kleenex. When I saw the strained blue of her enlarged vein—something broke in me. A wall was shattered, a fluid was released. I felt helpless and embarrassed, like a kid, and faint with happiness.

Come here, old men! There's nothing in the world like a Japanese duck. Have you ever seen a more beautiful readymade? The snows of Kilimanjaro aren't whiter than its hood. Its coat is as black as the united reactionaries of the globe. And its coral beak burns like the blood of the proletariat.

O UR WALK HAS TIRED YOU OUT, Djuna. Tonight we should stay home.

We'll disappoint Moses. He wanted so much to take us out for dinner.

I'll call him and explain, and later you can call him yourself.

All right. I'll tell him that he has chosen us a room with the most splendid view. What's the name of the garden we're overlooking?

It's the garden of the Jakko-in, the Nunnery of Solitary Light. There is a description of it in our guidebook. Shall I read it to you?

Read it, Myloslav, and open the window a little.

Everything in the garden, with the exception of the iron lanterns, seems to be connected in some way with Go-Shirakawa's visit.

Who's Go-Shirakawa?

I'll look it up in the index. Here it is: "Go-Shirakawa, emperor, adopted as his daughter Kenrei-mon-in, the only survivor of the Taira clan which was annihilated by the Minamoto clan. Kenrei-mon-in became a nun, and when Go-Shirakawa retired as the emperor, he joined a monastery too, and one day came to visit his adopted child at the Jakko-in. All these events are recorded in the *Heike monogatari,* on pages 246-47 of the Sadler translation."

The Sadler translation? It's right here. Under the leg of the coffee-table. I asked you to put it there to straighten out this crooked little thing. Take it out, and use my notebook instead.

Page 246. This is how Jakko-in appeared to Go-Shirakawa when he arrived: "The pond and trees of the ancient garden were dignified; the young grass had grown thick, and the slender shoots of the willow were all hanging in confusion, while the floating waterplants on the pond might be mistaken for spread-out brocade. On the island the purple hue of the flowering wisteria mingled with the green of the pine tree, while the late blooming cherry among the green leaves was more rare than the early blossoms. From the eight-fold clouds of the kerria that was flowering in profusion on the bank came the call of the cuckoo, a note of welcome in honour of His Majesty's visit."

The pond is a virgin canvas, the island rises out of the fog like a phantom, and the willows strike me as almost kitschy in their winter disguise of old silver-haired women. Instead of a cuckoo I can see and hear several crows.

Why don't we stay here until the spring, Djuna? Then our view will match the text.

Oh, the spring. It's a millennium away from us, Myloslav. But read on, my dear.

"The garden extends between the Hon-do and Sho-in; the waterfall which Go-Shirakawa noted drops here in three stages to a small pond. Like the waterfalls of most hill gardens, it is recessed and, dropping in stages that are hidden in the hill, it attempts to give the same impression that one would get from a much larger fall seen on a distant mountain."

We must go to the waterfall one day. One cannot see it from here.

We can go tomorrow.

Or after tomorrow, or after after tomorrow. There is plenty of time. Look what the crows are doing. They are forming a cross on the lake, with perfect right angles. They must be pupils of Malevich. Now one of them flies away, and the masterpiece goes to pieces. Ephemeral constructivist art. Carol would have liked it. But I interrupted you, Myloslav. Continue.

I'm almost at the end: "The mood of the whole garden, in keeping with the tale of Kenrei-mon-in, is a melancholy one. The west gate leads to a path up the hill where there is a small abandoned Shinto shrine."

The goal for another excursion.

The guidebook also mentions that on the same hill as Jakko-in there is Kenrei-mon-in's tomb. It can be reached by a flight of stone steps east of the road to the nunnery. However, the present grave is not old, since the emperors were powerless in her time. It is unlikely that Kenrei-mon-in originally had any tomb at all.

It's much better not to have a tomb than to have one. Death isn't about acquiring stuff, it's about getting rid of it. Night is falling, but it's still so light. The moon illuminates the pond, the corpses of the willows are entangled in arabesques. A fin-de-siècle scenery, a set for the beheading of Salome.

There's a small spring under a shrub to the right of the Jakko-in path. Do you see it, Djuna, the black spot that looks like the earthly ending of a moonbeam?

Yes, what about it?

The guidebook says that on her way to Jakko-in, Kenrei-mon-in saw her face reflected in this pool by the moonlight, and thus called it Oboro-no-shimizu—clear water seen in the hazy moonlight. But *oboro* means vague and hazy only when it's applied to the moonlight in spring. Again, Djuna, we are reminded of our obligation to stay here at least till April.

I feel so strange, Myloslav. The whiteness of the garden reminds me of a winter in Vienna, a winter tailored in part for life and in part for death. I was pregnant and suffering from a laborious confusion of contradictory desires. I felt that the past I had left behind might mend a little if I bowed low enough, if I succumbed to physiology and gave birth—to the son or daughter of a man who wanted me to abort. Nausea plagued me, and at night the rapid beat of my heart prevented me from sleeping. I had an apartment on the top floor of a sickly looking *Gasse* which didn't know to what it should pay tribute: to the Franz Joseph Kaserne to its right, or to the Elisabethspital to its left. My bedroom emanated the spleen of an accidental headquarter from which a Bourbon had been carried to death, or of a cocotte's nest, cut to the poor woman's purse. A heavy coat of snow was about to slide from the roof of the opposite house, but lacked in ultimate courage and was suspended at the edge like a Chinese comforter. You should keep a valet and a cook, Djuna, I said to myself. Instead you search again for your particular comedy of manners—a comedy of adjusting your stomach to the surprises of a new situation. The first and most imminent question is: Will you throw up now? But then you have to ask yourself: Will you agree to give homage to your femaleness, or forget its claims and terminate what otherwise could become interminable? Will you duplicate yourself and—what's worse—the man in the semicircular stare of an infant who could be heavier than his dad and taller, have a stout oval face, a mouth pressed too intimately close to the bony structure of the teeth, and other features a little heavy too?

Were you then pregnant for the first time, Djuna?

No, for the second. Twenty solid years separated the first embarrassment from the second. When I was still in *Gymnasium,* I had a quickie with Karl Eglizer's twin brother. He was the only Austrian member of the tiny International Brigade, and fought and died in Afghanistan.

And?

No and. Just a grandiose asthma attack followed by an abortion and another asthma attack. Otto Eglizer, a good friend of Elephant and a *Dozent* at the University of Klagenfurt, specialized in the elective affinities. Thus upon returning from the hospital I cabled to him: Spirits kindred by choice don't survive. Our motto was Otto, but now Otto is *tot in toto.* Djuna disqualified for future breeding.

But not totally disqualified?

No, not totally. Twenty years later you could see me again in a state of potential maternity. Walking or driving alone through the Vienna Woods, dressed as if expecting to participate in some great event, wishing to be correct at any moment, I was tailored in part for death, in part for life. But in the crux of a thousand impossible situations, death's best tendency is to accumulate. It accumulated in the lower part of my body, and burst out one foggy, freezing morning. A flood poured out of me, making me address my flesh and bones in various tongues, and add to my dictionary of dolors a few new nouns imitating the malice of my inner fluidity. Stuck in a strawberry-colored soup, I rang Otto and moaned: Djuna Bourbon has to be carried to a women's doc, or else she'll be carried to death. I'm coming, Otto shouted, and twenty minutes later carried my messy person out of the bloody bedroom, repeating: You aren't a Bourbon, madam, you're Victoria, Queen Victoria in a cheaper material, and you'll make it.

Otto sounds like a hero.

He was the last hero of a decent old Europe that today is recalled in circumlocutions. With the fury of a fanatic, he hunted down his own decency, and died from it. Otto would have made it had he bowed a little lower. But he never liked to bow, even slightly, to someone who looked as if he might be someone. He should have been cut from a cheaper material, should have insinuated himself more deeply into the vanity-circus of our dear world. He could have. Conversant with history and heresy, taster of rare wines, thumber of rarer books and tales of men who become holy and of beasts that become damned, versed in all plans for castles and bridges, given pause by all graveyards on all roads, a pedant of baroque churches, his mind dimly and reverently reverberated to Karenina and Goethe, Maimonides and Jesus. An aspiring Jew and a Christian who kept undoing his Christianity, he could have traded his life for a commodity. Instead, he made it into a medium through which he received, at the appropriate time, the serum of his own past that he might offer it again as his blood. Curious and weak, yet he picked some divine fire from his brain and died not far from Peshawar. A sweat-stained spangled enigma, he brought himself to heel, and turned his fate from sniffing the decaying brocades of Graz to saying grace—in Afghanistan.

So you lost your child?

Yes, and like Duchamp's bride I was connected to several machines. They pumped new gasoline into me, while the youthful voice of an eager medical resident kept buzzing: *Ja! das ist ganz richtig.* I tried to figure out what was so very right, but my head didn't go along with my question and, not finding the truth, suggested a whole sequence of senseless answers: Yes! It's quite right that I'm interested in gynecology. Yes! It's quite right that I have driven around the world only to mis-carry in Vienna. Yes! It's quite right to keep the legend of my life unexpurgated. Yes! It's quite right that every woman with a sense of humor is a lost woman.

Would you like a little tea, Djuna?

A good idea. Have some too. In the closet above the stove there is a whole collection of teabags. Jasmine would suit me best. I feel so strange tonight, Myloslav. As if I were looking down at my life the way a man looks down the barrel of a gun to take aim. I put my hand on the poor bitch of my life—a waterfall, a red cascade tumbling down from Lahore where I was so sick, and you were so good to me. It tumbles down, my life, and it stands still in one spot. And that spot is Kyoto. I may be wallowing in hysteria, my dear, but I feel like I'll need a doctor. Soon. Fairly soon. Why don't you ring Moses and ask him the number of his doc or, even better, the number of the hospital.

I S IT OVER?

Almost. Djuna hasn't regained consciousness, or opened her eyes for a whole week. They have put her on I don't know how many machines. I begged them to switch them off, to let her die in peace. I begged one doctor after another. They all bowed their heads, but did nothing. Have you seen where they keep her? In a hermetically sealed glass box. No one can touch her, no one can breathe the air she's breathing. Moses, we must do something! She is completely naked, one medical class after another is brought in to see her, and on the front wall of her cage a student is indicating her internal organs with little dots and arrows. Moses, we have arrived at the gates of hell, my mistress and I! And dogs, Moses, dogs aren't allowed in! They say dogs cannot go to hell. But I must go with her! We must go together! Do something, for God's sake, Moses, do not let her die like that!

Calm down, my dear boy. Calm down, Myloslav. I have rung the hospital director and the surgeon general and the Minister of Health and the Commissioner on Humanitarianism and the Committee on Euthanasia. I have phoned everyone who's anyone in this country. I have tried to reach the emperor. But they are more afraid of AIDS than of the atomic bomb. And so they're ready to violate every single human right of Djuna Barnes in order to protect humanity from contact with her. But let us not despair. Let's return to the hospital and sit in front of the glass until it's over. Let's not leave her alone for one more second. Maybe she'll open her eyes and see us. Maybe she'll speak to us, and the monitor will transmit her voice. Since we cannot do what we want to do, let's do what we can do.

M YLOSLAV, LIFT YOUR EYES! Look at the screen! Your name has appeared. Djuna is speaking, the printer is printing out her words:

Myloslav, Myloslav, what's the matter? The matter of the guillotine? Do I have to supply my own knife? But I have no knife, I have only your razor. Can you supply it for me, dearest, so that I can bloom in my mouth, like Carmen? Like Carmen, a red carnation in her fingernails. Why glass? Why so much glass? Have I been turned into the incomplete Big Glass? No, you can't do this to me, Myloslav! You can't turn me over to Selavy! You know very well what she's capable of. She'll grind me in her chocolate machine, she'll sell me to her sadistic bachelors.

No, Myloslav, no, please! They'll slice me up, drive across me, they'll make my heart fail. Myloslav, they'll squeeze me in between the transparent sheets the impotent Selavy could never finish. They'll snow me in. They have already snowed me in. Frau Mann presses her face against the window and says: They have snowed in Djuna Barnes. And you, Myloslav, at her words you turn your coat collar up and repeat: *Ja! das ist ganz richtig.*

Moses, do something! Don't make me sit and listen to what she says. Help me! Let's smash the cage, let's free her. Look. There is nothing left. Only skin and bones, and a soul. She's a bird, Moses!

Myloslav, here, speak into the microphone. She'll hear you, speak to her.

Djuna, I'm here, I'm with you, I'll never leave you alone. We are at the gates of paradise, and we're going in together. Hand in hand, or rather you're holding me on a leash, since I'm your dog. Do you remember me? I'm the black poodle Myloslav, the reincarnated Faust. Wolf and Lotte left me in Weimar, but I ran down all the way south, all the way to Rome. To be with them again. It seemed that I arrived too late. Wolf was no more, and Lotte was planting daisies on his grave. But it wasn't too late! At our old oak table you were injecting yourself with interferon, and when I smelled you I knew that my old life had ended. In a split second one dog died, another dog was born. A nameless mongrel, older, much older, and yet a puppy. Wau, wau, said I, and you replied: Hallo, Myloslav. Is that my new name? I barked back. Yes, this minute you have been rebaptized, friend.

Oh, I feel great! You're right, Myloslav. I thought I was in hell, but we're heading for heaven. You're a puppy, and I'm a kid. An obedient girl, I drank poison. It tasted so good. Out of a thimblelike glass. A green poison. Green as grass. Greener than the Green Party. Greenest as the garden of paradise. Now I know where we are. We go down *unter den Linden,* and into the Musée de Cluny to see once more you, the unicorn, and me, the lady, to play with you, the rabbit, and me, the parrot. A doctor, a cigarette in his yellow hand, is taking me off the wall. A doc, suspecting that he has come upon his last erection, is bending over me. But it's nothing. It's passing. A mere shadow. A mere whisper. Speak to me, Myloslav.

Speak to her, Myloslav.

Djuna, I wanted to tell you about this new chum of mine. Another dog. No, not a Czech, a proper American. His name is Einstein, and unlike myself, he's a big reader. He has read all your books, and not once, not twice. He read them three times. And *Nightwood, Nightwood* he read four times, and is now teaching a course on the nightwood as *Nightwood* in the Kyoto School for the Creative Wood. He has a big photo album of his own, and everyone in it looks like a dog—even though they're dead.

Look, Myloslav, she smiles. Her eyes are closed, but her lips move and smile. I told you, everything will be all right. She doesn't mind being naked. She may even like to be naked in front of you. Yes, I'm certain she likes it. Why don't you tell her that it's hot here. It's the middle of summer, that's why she's naked in her bed, while you sit at the edge of it and look at her. Speak into the microphone, Myloslav.

It's midsummer, Djuna. It's August in Lahore. You're sick with a flu, you have a temperature and lie half asleep in your bed. You're naked, and my eyes are glued to your small breasts. Then they wander down, all the way down, and back again, back and forth. I burn with desire to touch you, but you're very ill, and I don't want to disturb you. The fever makes your skin glow, your nipples swell, but all I dare to touch are your curls, your sweaty chestnut curls. We have come a long way, Djuna baby. A very long way. I watch you. I watch over you. No one can harm you as long as I'm at your side. The most faithful watchdog on earth, I guard you. I make wau-wau, and scare away all the bad guys, all the cross-eyed guys who could hurt my Djuna.

She doesn't speak anymore.

No, but she smiles. The fine curve of her lips ascends.

Madam is dead.

Come now, Myloslav. It's over. You have walked through the gate together.

HERE YOU ARE. I have been looking for you all morning. So you have started to draw again?

It's not really serious drawing, Ann, I just sketch Kenrei-mon-in's tomb. Last night I dreamt of tears falling on my feet. I looked up and saw that the stone was weeping—a stele inscribed with the name of Kenrei-mon-in. So first thing in the morning I took my notebook and a red pencil, and climbed up here.

Carol told me that you never dream.

Once I never dreamt, it's true, and when I did it was either sex—women the size of butterflies chirping around my prick—or my job—

what color paint should I select for the toilet seat. But nowadays I, the walking antipoetics, dream of weeping rocks. Carol must inspire me, who else?

Even your sketch looks like one by her hand. It's hardly perceptible, and there's not one straight line. Astonishing. The drawings you did in the past were all cubes. You excelled in right angles and suppressed ovals and spirals—the slightest suggestion of a curve. Carol interpreted your style as the sign of an obsession with the squaring of the circle, and used to say: The sphere Myloslav cannot screw in life, he squares in art.

She was best at poking fun at me.

It was less personal than you think. You served her as a pretext to rebel against the Mondrian-Malevich-Machine-Malaise, her words, a puerile infatuation with the capital M, and the Meta-Manhood, a deadly trend in modern architecture. The M had defeated the female G—the grotesque *gaudium* of Gaudí—Carol complained. Now look at the results: Myloslav's designs, male exercises in monotony and vanity.

Had we gone along with her *gaudium*, the world would be a monster. No walls—just cotton curtains, silk veils, sick membranes. Sieves suggestive of shells—instead of roofs. Stalagmite-shaped columns, windows the size of a crack, doors in the form of an apple. Baobablike beds, tables made of sheets suspended between branches, opaque mirrors set against the sky. And lamps—endowed with the gift to obscure every space.

Not very functional, but who can forget her drawings? The one for Wanda's villa at Nun Tucket, remember? The façade had the shape of a sail.

Yes, Lowry fancied it, and even tried to persuade me to take it up. But it wasn't realistic. You can't pursue utopia, if you want to make a living. Still, it was simple compared to the studio she envisaged for Berenice and Propertius—an elephantine cave carved in black ebony— or the honeymoon boudoir for Karenina and Vronsky—a kangaroo's pouch in hematite and wool—or the igloo-sauna for you and Italo.

You still find her projects ludicrous?

Not ludicrous, intolerable. Architecture cannot imitate spontaneous growth and flux. It's indeed about the M: the mind moderating nature by means of measure and mathematics. Carol's grotesques hurt my sense of proportion, go against the grain of my character. Yet slowly I grow tired of squaring circles and come closer to her. Shell-shaped houses? After all, why not. There's more and more nostalgia for the organic in the world. Old age makes us discover nature—and the sphere. I could accommodate it in my cube, I admit. Mantegna did it in his house in Mantua. I could do it in the Sea of Japan. Do you happen to have an aspirin?

If it's a regular migraine, take two or three. You look as distressed as an owl tied up in a muffler.

No, not an owl, I don't fly out at dusk anymore. Nowadays I'm out at dawn. Djuna's death has changed my habits. I thought of myself as an evening man, but now I go to bed at ten, get up at four, leave the house at sunrise.

To do what?

To walk in the Jakko-in garden and imagine I am a retired emperor, who has turned monk, visiting a nun he loved once. She's an old crooked willow, but still the closest tree he has in the world. Seasons pass, a rainy autumn afternoon is followed by a spring morning. The mood of the whole garden is a melancholy one, and so is my own mood. The face of my mistress reminds me of parchment, and I remind her of a ruined statue. Corrosion consumes us both, but we're still together.

We are together, the last remnant of our little band of friends. Moses is here, and as I have come to visit him, I have found you too. In the past I never thought of you as my friend. There were times when all my rage against the world was centered on Myloslav. A grave error. To blame you for her suicide is like blaming the water that entered her lungs. Chance put you, a pebble, in her way.

Every day it's harder to bear her death. Why couldn't I get the better of myself and love her? Oh, God's bag of tricks! No end to them. Djuna said once that I was a tiny toy boat, meant to travel back and forth in a bottle of Beaujolais. Yet I have been thrown into the ocean, and now even the Pacific seems too small for my sorrow.

Don't talk like that, Myloslav. It doesn't sound right. You mustn't identify with the women you lost. Look at the lively line of the Hie Jinja and its three bridges crossing the stream.

Tomorrow I'll return to sketch the temple's gate. Surmounted by a pointed gable, it resembles a peak.

And the Japanese character for mountain.

The shrine's roof overhangs far in front, but is cut short in back, like a girl holding up her skirts.

Now I hear the old Myloslav, the *sukničkár*. I'm glad he hasn't lost himself completely.

No, not completely. Only 99 percent of myself has evaporated. Every time I look at the Hie Jinja, it occurs to me that I would like to visit it with Carol. It's not uncommon for Shinto shrines to claim certain beasts as their messenger animals. In the case of Hie this honor goes to the kangaroos. They keep a couple of them on the premises, and up under the eaves of the Ro-mon, at each of the four corners, perches a small, carefully carved marsupial.

Why don't you go there with me? In the company of her totemic sisters and brothers, we could finally become reconciled to each other.

Let us reconcile right here, Ann. You're so inextricably entwined in the history of my life that I'd better make sure you become my best friend before we part from each other.

Do you plan to leave?

No, I want to stay near Djuna's grave. So I may as well amuse myself with drawing roofs and gates, and bridges and stone lanterns—until the end of my days which, I hope, isn't that distant. But you're still alive with pleasure, Ann, and you have Karl. Yesterday I saw him with a bunch of maps under his arm. That's the surest sign that he plans escape. I only wonder where to? Hasn't he been everywhere?

There are still a few spots untouched by his soles. But right now he wants to morally support Charlotte and Florence, struggling in Sydney. I guess I should join him. Soon.

You should. There isn't a soul more dedicated to you than Karl, even though it took you a quarter of a century to realize it.

You said it! We have spent our life ridiculing the Philemon-and-Baucis sort of pair. Now comes the punishment: two bits of crummy wood, we wait to be made into a single bench—somewhere in the south. Meanwhile the Isles of the Immortals seem nearer at hand than the end of the world. Apocalypse, after all, is the business of the young. Like suicide, it requires energy. The young jump into a river. The old stroll along it, talking.

Turning the pages of their life. When Djuna died, my book was completed. But I cannot tear myself from it. From sunrise to sunset I leaf through it—an old fool in search of the truth. As long as it mattered, I wasn't even aware of it. Now the soufflé has collapsed, so I try to reheat it.

GOOD MORNING. I have been looking for you everywhere, Ann. So here you are, with our ex-architect and ex-*amant*.

Spare us your sarcasm, Karl. Myloslav has a headache, and I'm in an elegiac mood.

I had breakfast with Moses. He was elegiac too. I can't bear it: the elegy of senility. Nothing can stop him from reminiscing about Salamanca. The taste of the shellfish, the smell of Ann's period. Kyoto's moonlit pavilions don't do us any good. Action, friends.

Didn't I tell you, Ann? Karl's on the move again. Sailing off to Tasmania?

Perhaps. But meanwhile get up off your asses and let's sail to a sushi bar. Last week a new one opened downhill, in the former villa of the connoisseur So-ami.

The *crétin* who settled in Plastic Plain, Oregon?

Yes, and sold his place to a sushi chain from New Jersey. It's their first venture in Kyoto. Shall we go?

We may as well. The bar is beautifully situated. Next to a tiny waterfall, the Moon-Washing Fountain, a good example of the extreme refinement to which the aesthetes of the Muromachi period aspired. While fish dissolves on your tongue, your eyes feed on the ripples of the Brocade Mirror Pond and the neck of the White Crane Island where ducks and turtles sun themselves. Each rock that breaks the surface of the pond has a name.

Of course! Tiny White Pebble, Narrow River Pebble, Round Floating Pebble, Great Flat Pebble, Zen Meditation Pebble, Longevity Pebble.

That's the one we want. Let's go, kids. The spirit is a peripatetic.

THIS VALLEY IS SO PEACEFULLY RURAL, as if we were far away from Kyoto.

Soon we shall see the city. Higher up the road offers a splendid view of it, framed by the nearer hills and the tall umbrella trees. A bridle path leads to a small pagoda, a weatherworn bench stands in front of it. After the beach in Salamanca, that's my favorite spot in the entire universe. On a clear day one can catch a glimpse of Kiyomizu's homely roof.

Oh, what a charming miniature! So aged and fragile, and still so feminine.

I knew, Myloslav, that you'd fall in love with this pagoda. The giant Kiyomizu protects her from the distance like a man watching over a mistress he abandoned a long time ago but cannot forget. An after-image, she's asleep in the back of his eye but keeps waking up. Suddenly she pops up in his pupil, silhouettes herself sharply in the detail of a moment, glows away. When Ann was here, I asked her to accompany me to Kiyomizu. We arrived here at dusk. It was April, and the woods were quiet and empty, as they are only near the end of day. The sun had been down for some time and the city was outlined against a damp red sky. When we emerged from the forest, Ann first perceived the pagoda, then the Kiyomizu, and whispered: Look, Moses. A little boat, she encounters the battleship of her life—coming full steam. Tell me, Myloslav, were you the one for whom she bought the black bikini? The man who didn't want to go with her to the sea? Did you have an affair with her? Or was there another architect? A twin brother of yours?

No, Moses. There was nothing between me and Ann. But the twins shared their lives—and their romances. When Carol fell for me, the same must have happened to Ann.

You mean she hurried from Salamanca to Manhattan, leaving me in despair, not because your open arms awaited her? You suggest she wanted to serve as a screen onto which Carol would project her un-requited passion? You imply . . .

I don't imply anything, Moses. It's the truth. Why should I lie? My list of conquests is long, but Ann doesn't figure on it. Like the Kiyo-mizu and the pagoda, we have known each other forever but never intimately. Apart from short episodes, there has been only one man in Ann's life—Karl.

But the *Baumeister,* the accursed builder who inhabited her heart, smiled from her lips, descended from her pen onto paper?

It wasn't me, Moses, it wasn't Myloslav. It's a myth she has created and maintained throughout her life. Why? Perhaps in order to remain faithful to Karl. Or because of you. To keep you at a distance. People like Ann cannot do without legends. Existence suffocates them, fiction makes them breathe. Because of the twinship, hers was a double fiction: she invented her agony for me, and she invented her triumph over it. So she defeated both of us—me and her sister. Poor Carol! She manipulated reality too, but to her disadvantage.

Let's not dwell on the past. Forgive me, Myloslav, and follow me to the right. From this vantage Kiyomizu surges straight out of the cliffs, ready to head for the city, like a courtesan, her lips painted in bright evening colors. Aren't we a paradox, Myloslav? The two *M*s! One a womanizer, the other an ascetic.

An ex-womanizer and an ex-ascetic, Moses. While you steal out of the house at 10:00 P.M., I go to bed. When I get up at 5:00 A.M., you return—worn out, with bags under your eyes, and smelling of perfume. Dust gathers on your volumes of Pascal, and Schopenhauer is a true dust-orchard you should sell to Selavy. After decades dedicated to divine incorporeality, now you demonstrate physicality. I, however, converse with angels who—according to your juvenile writings—are intelligences without matter, and observe my reflections fly around— flying being the motion you once considered the most sublime movement of the brute creation. So I grow wings, you run after skirts. For this change may the Almighty be praised, whose design and wisdom cannot be fathomed. You laugh, Moses? Adding one profanity to another, you direct your mind to unkosher stuff.

Not so much my mind, Myloslav, as my *panim,* the Hebrew word for face, from *panah*—he turned.

You do turn, *Pan* Moses—*za paniami.* You won't be allowed into Eden, I'm afraid. Or you may turn into a column of salt.

No, Myloslav. I'll ascend to the Japanese hell where a man's hand doesn't dry when he puts it under a skirt. But there's something to what you say. Fate is angry with me. First, my application for permanent residence has been rejected. Second, the university is trying to terminate my distinguished emeritus position and induce me to teach Shalom-Zen to pale, bespectacled, and mostly male students. Third, Popoirier, that pretentious Parisian parrot we lunched with yesterday, got for himself what he plotted to get—an eighteen-year-old Japanese pet. Now he works at a new intrigue: the transfer of his class, a post-structuralist French disgrace, to me, Maimonides, who was lured here by the promise of total leisure. But there is a definite chill in the air. We should head back.

Wait! How can we abandon this view just as the moon is rising above Kiyomizu's black shoulder. Up in the sky the sight of the great temple— down here the ants, transporting the grasshopper to their hill, eager to feed on his death. Shall we stop at Djuna's tomb on our way back?

Yes, if you wish.

Last Saturday I finished working on it. Now the entire grave is covered with two kinds of moss. The darker contrasts with the lighter —and creates a cross.

Djuna wasn't a Christian.

Of course not. It shows two paths—hers and mine—crossing each other in Kyoto. If I happen to die before you, Moses, promise to bury me at her side. There's enough space for the two of us.

Nonsense, Myloslav. You're still a child. No, no, I don't refuse. Sure, I'll take care of your bodily remains.

In the twilight the pagoda looks so flat, like Djuna in the glass box. Permanent residence or not, nobody's going to remove you from here, Moses.

The same applies to you, young man. You're going to cruise through foggy mornings, I through feminine fragrances. In between we'll discover new shrines and ponds, waterfalls and graveyards. You realize it's a miracle the city has survived. Originally the good guys intended to bomb Kyoto, not Hiroshima.

Let me touch the pagoda for the last time. Her skin has retained the warmth of the day. But there are tiny drops of dew, so it feels sweaty, like Carol's skin—always eager to touch me.

Come on, my boy, or you'll catch a cold. It's too late to go to the cemetery. No, it's not a good idea to visit it every day. Really, I'd rather have you explore with me the local dens of sin.

I can't bear the sight of women anymore, Moses. Each of them reminds me of someone in the past. The punishment of a lifelong womanizer—a wax cabinet of faces, bellies, locks, lips. A collection of skins. Only at Djuna's tomb am I at peace with myself. I recall her and Carol, and the three of us fuse into one. At last the caresses are distributed evenly. My tenderness for Carol knows no limits, Djuna's affection for me knows no bounds. Everything falls into place. Desire and action coincide.

It's no good entering paradise while you're still alive. Come, we mustn't stay here any longer. I cannot see very well, give me your hand, my boy. Oh, it's so hot. What's the matter, Myloslav? You aren't falling sick? You're all right? You must be strong, you must support me, an old man. Don't even think of what you want to think about. You're transparent. I can read your thoughts. When I first met you, you were solid and opaque, and I hated your good looks and your bullish health. But today I would give a lot of money to have your robustness returned. You have lost so much weight, you don't joke anymore, don't laugh at your own jokes. But, really, it's your laugh, Myloslav, that everybody loved so much. I forgive him for everything when I hear him laugh, Ann used to say. His laugh and the appetite for life mirrored in his blue eyes when he wakes up in the morning. The appetite that made you waltz, gulp red wine, devour chocolate truffles—we all envied it. You tremble? Don't do this to me, my boy. Come, let's hurry. You need a hot drink. What an old idiot I am. How could I allow you to sit for hours in this damp forest!

Y OU FEEL BETTER? Oh, I'm so glad. I was dreadfully worried. Dreadfully. Ten days with such a high temperature, without consciousness. Myloslav, how could you do this to me? But it's passing? Yes, yes, everything will turn out fine, just fine. I can see that you're returning from the dead. You met there with everybody? With Karenina and Simone? Oh, yes. And with Djuna? Of course with her you spent the entire ten days. I understand, you deserted me, your old friend, to visit young women. As always, as always. Carol was with you too? Good, my boy, good. So now you have seen with your own eyes that we're still together. Nothing can separate us, a tightly knit band, a big family. No space, no time to get in our way.

No, I can't hear you. What is it you want to tell me? You must speak louder, my child. The text? What text? Oh, I see, our text. You have read it? No, of course, not the whole thing, parts of it. Fragments. What do you say? Death? There is a lot about death? In our text? Well, we were such an odd collection. We were more into death than into life. With the exception of you. You were all for life, you didn't belong with us, or so it seemed in the beginning. A healthy little rock, a tiny solid pebble, you didn't fit into our text. In fact, you never wrote a word. No, it's not true? You protest? You wrote, yes, what is it that you wrote, Myloslav? A letter to Carol which she incorporated into the text? What a surprise! Well, then you're part of it—part of us.

Your lips are dry. Want a drink? Drink, drink, my child. Yes, I know, you're too weak to hold the glass. Let me hold it for you. Slowly. Drink slowly, very slowly. It's good? Sweet? No, not juice. It's just water. You like it? It tastes good. And you want to try a piece of bread, from inside, the soft, the softest part? Slowly, eat it very slowly. Like a bird, crumb after crumb.

A narrow-lattice door of the sort one still sees in Kyoto.

A narrow-lattice door? What do you mean?

It was fixed so its place could be taken by an earthen door if fire threatened.

Don't excite yourself, my dear boy. No fire threatens us.

The entrance hall contains a wooden sign that is an old advertisement for an apothecary shop. There, there, on the shelf to the right is my medication. A little brown bottle with green liquid.

There is plenty of medication here, no need of more, my boy.

The flooring of the hallway has a built-in squeak to warn of intruders. Squeak. Squeak. Moses, the intruder has entered into the alcove. He sits under the painting of a seated man, which has raised contours and is inlaid with mother-of-pearl. Mother, mother, have you phoned her in Prague, Moses? It's so late. It has also some inlaid glass, and there is a wooden roof tile in the shelf of our chamber, an ancestor of the roof tiles used today.

I leave you now, my child, just for one second. I'll be back before you can turn around.

The cupboard over the shelf is decorated with a charcoal drawing and a relief by Ben Nicholson that Erose dropped in Teheran. The pulls on the cupboard doors are patterned to be abbreviated. To be abbreviated. The narrow-lattice door to the bridge in Prague. To the crest, to the house.

I'm back, my boy. Here, I need your arm. I need to find your vein, your bloody little vein. Here it is. No, I won't hurt you, no. You see, it's over. And you're better. I'm sure you're better.

The sliding screens on the east side of the room depict dogs. Wau, wau. Two dogs. One is Faust, and the other, the one who reads *Karenina,* his name is Einstein.

Don't speak so much, my child. You'll exhaust yourself. Want a drink? A drop of water?

The screens are fitted with flush locks and keys—for security. The dogs cannot escape. What shall we do, Moses? I must free them. They must go with me. The three of us, we must always remain together. Faust, Einstein, Myloslav. Pssst. These are pseudonyms. We work for the underground in Prague. We're conspirators. It's all about conspiracy. The decorative nail covers on the beams of our rooms are made of china rather than the usual metal. Why have you come with me, to this castle, this castello in Milano? *Mily Pan* Moses, why have you come all the way down to the south?

I need your hand again, my boy. No, no more pain. I'll just hold it. Just hold it. To hold hands—the best we can ever do in life—of those whom we love, and even of those whom we don't love.

The sheet paulownia-wood ceiling has a square hole in it—to be solely for access to the sky. The hole to the hidden, soundproof sky is a trap. The innocent sky is screwed to the skin of an ambling river.

I can't hear you, Myloslav. The roof? If the roof is sheated in sheet brass? I guess so. Why shouldn't it be? But why worry about the roof? A copper mirror? You want the copper mirror you gave to Djuna? It isn't here anymore, my boy. Don't you remember? You put it between her hands before she was buried. Yes, yes. She has it. Don't worry. She'll return it to you herself. The stones? The stones that cover her tomb? If they could be used as emergency weapons? I guess so. But against whom do you want to defend her, my dear? Please, don't excite yourself. There is no need, absolutely no need to defend Djuna. She's all right. Would I defend her? Of course I would. The doorway? What doorway? To her room. Yes, indeed, gold lacquer bats are painted above it. Yes, it's correct. Could I bring you Djuna's fan, the one you bought for her on the market, the one with the fish on it? Of course, but I would have to leave you for a minute to go into her room. Yes, you want me to do that. Bring you the fan with the fish. All right.

Moses, this tearoom is too crowded, I cannot breathe. Moses. Bamboo uprights, shelves, closets, someone hiding behind the back door. The ceiling, the natural grain of the ceiling. Bamboo uprights. Moses!

Here I am, my baby. And here's the fan. You like it? Yes. The fish is blue and beautiful. Do I know its name? I'm not sure, it may be a dragon-fish, or a frog-fish.

Vulnerable paper screens. Windows should be built narrower, to make them less vulnerable. Cicadas, how noisy they are.

Yes, it's June, my boy, cicadas are very noisy.

Another stair leads to the roof. You should go there with Mother. There is an eight-mat veranda for moon-viewing and tea.

You want some tea, my dear? That's a very good idea. Jasmine tea, green tea, Russian tea?

To make this compartment noiseless, its walls and screens were doubled and its floor specially insulated. Tea roses in the red-wall room, noiseless moon-viewing ceremony. Oh, Moses. Carol has come to my castle, but I have no hands to touch her. She has come, and I cannot reach over to her, and she goes away, she leaves me, her face wet, her body wet. *Pani,* don't go away, don't. I'm coming with you, wait, wait, I'm having my last sip of tea with Moses, and then, then I'll come. Don't go away, don't do this to me, Carol. Wait! No, no, I can't have tea with you, Moses. It's too late. Carol is here, she has come, she's waiting for me. For me and our two dogs, Einstein and Faust. Leave the book here, leave it here, Einstein. Karenina is waiting for us, she'll write you new books, many new books. No, no tea. Carol is here. I must hurry. Hurry, hurry! The room is built to resemble the belly of a boat. I must step down to enter it. Carol, wait, I'll help you to step into the boat. The room hangs out over the wall of the grounds and reaches to the pond. It's an emergency escape, and we escape through it. Yes, we're safe, Carol. No, you haven't slipped into the water. I'm a lifeguard on duty, and I have the duty to save you. Our two dogs, they are lifeguards too, they were trained in the famous Trinity School for dogs in Trieste, or was it on the Upper West Side? Here, Carol, here, we go. No, not yet. The fan. The fish. We must release the fish. Here, you do it, Carol, you're the youngest. You free the fish. Carol! Carol! Where are you? The fish, it has gone? Where? Where to? Alone? But it's impossible. We were to go together, all together. Carol. Carol. Wait. The room is so frail. It can no longer bear my weight.

C AN I SEE HIM?
        Yes, he's in his room. But you won't understand a word of what he's saying. Complete dyslexia. What a pity. He was one of our most talented young scholars.

He still is.

Hardly. The EM has destroyed his brain, and it's attacking his body. He doesn't retain anything. Within minutes he excretes everything we provide him with.

I beg your pardon, what does EM stand for?

The Earth Mania, a mental dissolution provoked by the Terra-retro-virus. It caused various fairly harmless illnesses on the Earth. Unfortunately, in our protected moon atmosphere the Ter-ret has mutated into a new form. It paralyzes all the mental control systems with the exception of the dream apparatus. A hyperreverie replaces reality with a flux of hallucinations affecting everything—the audiovisual as well as the tactile mechanisms. Because of the virus's origins, the mania is entirely focused on Earth, and as it progresses the sick subject begins to reject his moon identity and sees him- or herself metamorphosed into an Earthman or -woman.

That in itself doesn't seem so extraordinary.

You're wrong, it's extremely perilous and leads to disintegration.
Of what?

Of the subject's relationship with moon civilization. Furthermore, it incites the instinct of regression.

Regression to where?

To prehistoric terrestrial conditions. It kills all striving for progress —the ideal of our culture. We may excavate the Earth—we're by far too preoccupied with that—but no lunar person should forget that our main goal is conquering space, moving to other planets, tempering and architecturizing their celestial bodies, naked and either too hot or too cold.

I happen to disagree with your ambitious program. The idea of colonizing Venus and putting over her a disaster similar to what we have donned on the moon is simply ludicrous. And so is the concept of cooling Mars. The Earth, on the other hand, is recovering. Organic life, I'm told, is slowly returning to the water and soil, and so we may consider going back to our origins.

Never. No lunar government would ever approve of such a plan. As a matter of fact, what you say sounds like symptoms of the EM we combat. It's well known that mankind was always on the move. And certainly we, the modern lunaity, a superior stage, won't allow ourselves to be pushed backwards.

Had mankind been able to recoil, it might have survived. The same applies to us. But please show me the way to my sick friend.

I DREAM OF A SMALL SPACESHIP THAT IS BUILT TO RESEMBLE the interior of a boat. A steamer that can go full speed, or as slowly as a sailboat when there is no wind. Both are depicted in the *Moon Atlas of Earth Vehicles* they have removed from my room. The boat is taking me to Earth, back to Earth—the *Magna Mater,* as the Latin poet whose name I forgot called her. The drugs—they make me forget everything. I can hardly remember my name. What's the name of myself? Oh, I remember, the name of myself is Myloslav. It's easy, but I should repeat it: Myself—Myloslav, Myloslav—Myself. A pale moon-man and the *Magna Mater*—full of colors and smells.

My dear young friend, do you recall me?

My senior colleague? How kind of you to visit me here, in this strangely convoluted place, a labyrinth of white cubicles, neat and locked. A moon-maze for such maniacs as Myself and Myloslav.

Who's Myloslav?

Oh, I didn't tell you. I figured out that on Earth I was—and may still be—Myloslav, an unsuccessful architect with a gentle face. He built a church in the suburbs of this manmade island that was once so important in Earth history. A woman shot him, and so I know how he looks. His coat was blue, or rather gray-blue, and no, he didn't divide it. On a November day he measured the whole lot of century 21, and a woman helped him. He didn't care for her, but I have fallen in love with his female, and ever since I have been looking for her. Looking for a way of joining her on Earth—of escaping from here. To get outside. Into the open.

My sickness? Oh, it's nothing. I just suffer from the lunarphobia of our locked existence. No outside. Only inside. Haven't we talked about it a lot? Once, in another life, when I was still not counted among the maniacs, and the first letter of my name didn't yet stand for mortality. *Mors,* you know, is such an interesting word. In Latin it means death, but in another Earth dialect, a language I haven't been able to learn properly, it means a smooth sea animal. Or at least that's what I suspect it must mean, since in a half-burnt picture book there's a photo of such a lovely beast inscribed *Mors.*

So you continue your studies in Earth linguistics?

No, I don't. They have taken away all my Earth books. They inspire the mania, the doctor says. And you see, they force upon me so many drugs, give me injections and blood transfusions, replace my bone marrow, extract bits of my brain. By the time they cure me, I'll be another man, understand? No, I don't want to be cured. All I want is to escape. But how? Can you help me out of this rectangular white maze? The woman, she reciprocates my affection. She has sent a boat for me, or rather a small spaceship in the shape of an old-fashioned ocean liner. Or is it a sailboat? It's waiting for me. It's awaiting me on the shore of our Central Park lake, the one that imitates Japanese ponds and has in the middle an island. In its trees lunar pigeons, the descendants of the beautiful Earth doves, make their nests. It's there, her boat, but I cannot reach it. What a torture! Just one step down to enter it. Just one step. She has been waiting for me such a long time. But she can't wait any longer. No one can wait forever for anyone. No woman. No man. Here, look. See the soles of my shoes? They carry a picture of a bird and are inscribed with a word in an unknown Earth language. Part of the word has been rubbed out, but the first letter is an *H,* and the last letter is a *b.* I'm sure it means *dove,* and I know: it's a coded communication from her. That she waits, that she hasn't forgotten me.

How I got them? These are cheap standard shoes. The hospital furnished me with them. But only on the surface do the other patients' shoes look exactly like mine. In fact nobody else's soles are imprinted with the logo of a dove, and no other icon on the moon is inscribed with the eighth and the second letter of the Latin alphabet. So my theory is that the woman brought the shoes on the boat and gave them to the boat operator. And he smuggled them into the hospital. So that I might escape in them. Do you see what I'm driving at? She has organized it all—so well! But she hasn't foreseen that I'm not Myloslav—not myself anymore. The medication makes me forget who I am. Where I have come from. Where I'm to go. And the moon-maze—she hasn't foreseen that they'd imprison me here. Shoes with doves are fine. They're winged shoes, and I can fly in them straight into her arms. But first I must find a way out. You see, she has made a terrible mistake. Terrible! She sent me shoes, but first I need red thread, tons of it, and somebody to mark the way—the way out. You see what I'm driving at, my old friend?

My dear boy!

No, no. I am not asking you to lay down the thread. It has to be done by a stranger—a messenger from the Earth. You wouldn't succeed. They would arrest you, throw you too into this maze. In fact, I fear for your safety. You shouldn't stay here too long. No one visits me here, and for a good reason. The mania is contagious, I know, but that's not why. It's because they list the visitors who sympathize, who haven't abandoned us completely. They list all whom they suspect of carrying the potential illness within themselves. They list the future patients, understand? I'm moved by your courage, but I'm frightened too. Frightened for you. Look at the soundproof hiding place for the body-guard, inspect my cubicle. Its walls and screens are doubled, the floor is specially insulated. When I cry out, no one can hear me. Don't stay here. Don't!

I'll go now, but I promise that I'll do everything I can to get you out of here. To get you into the open. I'll phone the Lobby for Lunatics, I'll address the question in the media.

Don't. Nobody on the moon can save me. Only she can do it. She sent the boat for me. And the shoes. The shoes with the doves. But not the thread, the red thread she has forgotten. The thread of life. The red that would have embroidered my skin. She has forgotten it, and now it's too late. I'm not myself anymore, and I have forgotten my name. It's over. Before you go, ask them to bring me tea. Once a day I'm allowed a drink of my own choice.

I would enjoy having it with you.

Tea for two, as in the good old days. Yes, if you can spare the time. You're such an important visitor, so they may even grant us the favor of drinking terrestrial tea—not the lunatic piss, their speciality. I'm dying for Lapsung-si. Green and bitter and opaque. If you can convince them that you're really someone, they may give it to us.

Tea is served.

Oh, you did it! How wonderful. It's like on Earth! I close my eyes, forget where I am, and imagine that I have gone with my friend, a distinguished scholar, to a small teahouse overlooking a cherry orchard. We select a small marble table and two bamboo chairs at a fancy window. It has the shape of a tea leaf, light seeps through it like through a sieve, and we cannot take our eyes off the landscape in the frame—a pond which is being refreshed by a waterfall. Quick, shiny, luminous, the water flows, and time floats by. Sitting by the window, we're inside, but in touch with the outside—right at the borderline. It's enough to stretch out the left hand, and it's in the open, while the right balances the teacup. Made of the most delicate porcelain, it's round and hot, like the skin of a woman burning for a man. Flamboyant, she doesn't show any restraint. Why should she? A stranger in love with me, she ignores lunar frigidity. Soft but vigorous, she's a window, a boat, a dove, a cup of tea. She's here to escort me to Earth, to get into the open Myloslav-Myself.

M S. CHARLOTTE GOETHE
Globook, Semiotics and Semantics Section, Sydney University
2, Propertius Crescent
222 4694 Kangaroo Island, Australia

Dearest Lotte! June has arrived too soon in Kyoto, and its heat makes me tired. But I have inherited the habits of our late Myloslav and wake up before sunset. That grants me a few comfortably cool hours to wander around and water the moss on their grave. Did I ever describe it to you? After a life given to architecture, Myloslav designed Djuna's tomb as an homage to nature. A simple mound covers her remains, nothing manmade interferes with the soil and vegetation. The only reminder of his earlier career is a floral symbol. He selected two different sorts of moss, varying in shade and texture, gave the darker one the form of a cross and planted the lighter one around it. It's spectacular. The tomb rises on a slope that faces west and at sunset Kyoto's black contours are cut out against a flaming sky. Below a little pond is fed by a stream that passes just two steps away from the hillock. Everything is designed in such a way that there is enough moisture in the air, even in the hottest season, and the place doesn't really need watering. But the moss is like a baby, it sips and sips. As long as I'm around, I may as well take care of the green kid, especially when the weather conspires against it. Right now the source struggles for survival and the stream carries hardly anything. In panic, I water the grave daily.

What else shall I report? I lost the battle against the university and am teaching a class hatched in a French demi-mind. First I fought against it like a lion, but now I realize what life had taught me so many times before. That it's impossible to judge what's going to be good for us. Or, as Wolf used to say, *Ob der Vorteil nicht zum Nachteil, der Nachteil nicht zum Vorteil werden wird.* I have managed to modify the course. It no longer resembles an empty discourse, and I enjoy teaching young people. They tear me away from reminiscing about the death of our loved ones and my own end. Lotte, I really revel in my students, especially in the female ones. Young Japanese women are phenomenal! Creatures from another world. Emancipated and yet modest and full of warmth. Bright, eloquent. When we were in Rome I used to despair. I saw no future, just pollution and devastation, and our old Mediterranean world going down the drain. Well, it may disappear, but there are other cultures on the earth—ready to continue where we have stopped. The old Europe was obsessed with being flooded by the Asiatics—led by an Oriental Faust, a small yellow fist. But, perhaps, it's not a threat but a blessing.

Once I was the first to deplore the contemporary state of affairs. I ridiculed Wolf and his interest in the New World, a continent I considered then the embodiment of banality. When our Rome broke down and Kyoto invited me, I whispered to you: old-age beggary, final exile. But the exit has led me to a new start and today Moses, the stone I expected to go under, is a floating rock. Oh, Lotte, don't laugh at me! Of course, I'm an old fool changing his positions from one extreme to another—and always in accordance with my heart's beat. Yes, your guess is right, I have fallen in love with a female pupil of mine, a student of philosophy and a poet. To some extent that may explain my optimism. But it doesn't explain everything.

Remember Musil, Lotte? That summer—the first after Wolf's death —we visited him together in his tiny Swiss abode. Robert was sick, tortured by poverty and the inability to finish his *Man without Qualities.*

When you rang him in the morning, he refused to meet with us. But in the evening he called back. I picked up the phone and heard a hoarse voice: It's me again, Musil. Drop in tomorrow at five. The Chinese question, I wouldn't mind talking it over with you. So long. Next afternoon we bought a *Gugelhupf,* knocked on his door, and were treated to a monologue on the rising yellow tide, a more important topic than our European collapse.

Kant, Nietzsche, Schopenhauer, Robert roared, a rotten heap of thoughts running around in vicious circles. Let's have the guts to avert the glance from our Euro-souls and face the rest of the world. You, Frau Goethe, and you, Herr Professor, you of all people must grasp the enormous potential of the yellow avalanche, and the black avalanche too. The screaming about the *Untergang des Abendlandes* must end. Why shouldn't the West as we know it—with Christ in its mouth, Hitler in its bowels—be swept away? Why not? Empires rise and set. Today's Spartans overindulge in sweet Turkish coffee. The sons of the pharaohs are *Gastarbeiter* in Giessen. Why should you insist on holding on forever to your tetragrammaton, *mein Verehrter?* Why shouldn't you pursue Zen, *meine Gnädige?* Let's jump out of our skins, turn into clouds—it's a Chinese proverb—and support mountains.

I contradicted Robert and poured over him a whole tankful of polite contempt. I accused him of self-hatred, intellectual chameleonism, spiritual mystification. I insulted him, and a week later he died, and I couldn't take back my words. But you're my witness, Lotte. I'm taking them back now. Yes, Musil, it's excellent to study the plans of the Japanese gardens and the scope of Shinto. It's the best idea in the world to stand on an earthen bridge, overlook a lake, count the carp swimming in the water, delight in the cherry blossoms falling into it, follow a butterfly carried away by the wind, or a red maple leaf drifting away. Today I'm ready to admit, Lotte: I, the abstract rabbinic type, I have missed a lot of buses, and at last I look for guidance to Orientals. Isn't it funny, Lotte, the thing called life? It's setting traps for us, but in the end we fall into the traps we have set for ourselves.

I'm keeping in mind the invitation you and Florence extended to me. Certainly, I would like to browse with you through Globook. What an experience to see it all in one spot, in the soft stomach of a single machine, in one photo album. The dried magnolia petal Osia inscribed on one side with *Nadia,* on the reverse with *Ola.* The scrap of a letter Simone didn't send from Spain to Stalingrad. The broken shell, Carol's last work, with Myloslav's face. Chu's picture with a poem by Ezra and a comment by Karl. The palimpsest of a Lausanne aquarelle. Faust at the doorstep of your Weimar villa. The out-of-focus shadows of Ann and myself, stretched out on the Salamanca sand. The splinters of a glass Lowry broke in a Thai bar. He threw it at Conrad, but it hit the wall right behind Ernestine's head. Berenice's letter to Florence, asking her to adapt her Egyptian style to the taste of the American market. Assudin's sketch of Anna—executed a day before she threw herself under a train. Voronskoy's note to Goethe, describing his role in Afghanistan. The electronic simulation of Einstein, with *Anna Karenina* in his paws. The snap of our twins, in two identical white Sunday dresses, shot against a Warsaw ghetto wall.

Yes, I must visit this miracle, perhaps with a student of mine. I dread traveling alone. The airports, the passport controls, the immigration clerks—I cannot cope with them anymore. But won't you all burst out in laughter when I arrive with a grandchild of a girlfriend, her skin peachy as a baby's? Is there enough space to accommodate both of us? We need two rooms. I snore like an ancient sea lion, so loud that sometimes I wake myself up. Thus I insist on her leaving me after we have made love. Goodness! How indecent it sounds at my age! *Aber so ist das Leben,* Lotte: more fleeting than the glint of a withered windblown leaf—the thing called life.

D EAREST ITALO! The end is not the end is not the end. On Kangaroo Island dead souls buzz around me and Florence, but we still drink Earl Grey tea in the handpainted Meissen porcelain cups from Weimar, eat scones with orange marmalade or honey. The Muse, the Editor and you, the Eternal Student of Senility— we cannot die, Italo, so we guard the archives of a vanishing world. Sextus's cherry orchard yielded to electro-cutters, and when it was metamorphosed into a parking lot, I said to you: It's the end. Here we live in the neighborhood of a copter-port, its permanent noise torturing us day and night, but we have stopped complaining. We're afraid that if we say—that's the end, destiny will rush to unveil what's still in store for us.

Interestingly enough, I have completely reconciled myself to this relic of an existence. I find myself beyond resignation, accepting everything and cherishing small pleasures. A late breakfast with Florence— her fingertips blackened with ink, her gray cells bubbling with devilish editorial eagerness—on our luxurious terrace overlooking the Great Australian Bight. A letter from Kyoto describing Moses' patience in watering the grave of Djuna and Myloslav. A card from Joseph. He completes his last cruise around the world on board the *King Sobieski* in the company of Martin and Teresa Ingeneral, two former friends and saintly supporters of Carol and other unsuccessful artists. The trio enjoys pizza and disco in the Peppermint Saloon and participates in amateur talent nights in the Marco Polo lounge. Oh, I forgot, they are registered for two workshops: the Sea Saga Studio sabotaging Sunday sunsets, and the Maritime Modeling Manuf monotonizing Monday mornings.

Joseph's journey isn't without adventure. Today's *Kangaroo Times* reports that the *Sobieski* was trapped by a grounded Turkish tanker in Singapore. Isn't that the place where you were supposed to board? I hope the grounding won't prevent you from joining Joseph and arriving here with him. It's sad to have no men around. Even in old age, when everybody is *hors de combat,* the sexes need each other. Alone, men just stand and stare at the landscape that is themselves—the slopes of their noses, the defiles of their shoulders, the folds of their skin. If women don't tell them what is attractive in them, they forget it. If we don't remind them of the details that please us, they cannot put themselves together into a mosaic and remain a heap of fragments.

Two lonely females, we discuss men a lot. Which is more fitted for love, the handsome ones, or the ugly? Rose Selavy has always maintained that the male beauties aren't suited for sex because even at the last moment they'll wonder whether sex suits them. Those fitted for love are the great ugly things that carry their faces before them with pride, like masks. The great taciturns who behind their squareness and silence hide much or nothing at all. For they have bodies only at night and only in the arms of a woman. In daylight they are anonymous, but in the darkness they turn wild, their hearts tumbling in their chests, their cocks hardening to silver sables. A secret brotherhood of bears and bulls and bedriders who go berserk, they create in us the illusion of sex being the gravest dilemma. Do you remember Djuna's saying that the night does something to a guy's identity? But since they have no identity, the night does nothing to them. Where the handsome ones go impotent and blind, the ugly ones steel up. Giving off strong odors, they vacantly absorb us. All instinct, timid and aggressive at once, recoiling and advancing, they make the cookie crumble into panicky little bits. They brutalize our last ah-ah and turn it awful—a small death without consolation. They break the piece of art we hope to be, and abandon us—a readymade.

Oh, men! Their absence in Globook supplies our exclusively female discourse with a twist. Unfulfilled desire leads to elaborate denials, imagination blossoms. I dream of Wolf dressed in the most wolfish of all his outfits, and lick my lips. His presence is painful, an incurable malady—and yet a happiness. Italo, dearest, we await you with impatience.

By the way, Ann and Karl are still in Kyoto but plan to be here soon. It occurs to me that Eglizer contradicts the theory that male ugliness is endowed with the greatest sex appeal. A mix of Gérard Philipe and a decadent Renaissance sophist, he exudes irritating but immensely attractive fluids. His sex is grounded on impossibility, but women immediately recognize it as an act of passion in which agony and futility combine, but beauty is present. A figure of doom, with a pitiful smile on his lips, and stricken with the memory of what is no more, Karl incarnates that sublime seducer to whom we all want to succumb, although he confesses to nothing but melancholy doubt, promises nothing but the certainty of loss. Remote and noble, he has been navigating through the night sea with the precision of a blind seer, diving into the darkness and finding at the bottom shells filled with the music of the spheres.

No man has a better eye for female quality, for bringing to the surface an anima in distress and comforting her—without ever attempting to possess her. Disinterested, forgetful, Karl is after nothing but a woman's icon, to be acknowledged and deposited in the museum of his mind. A born aesthete, yet he's ready to infuse an essence into every female, cast her into significance. Adding to her a little extra of his own enlightened spirit, he receives back a little grace of his own making—as if it were all her own. So he unlocks doors, stirs in secret wells. Unobtrusive, he binds women to himself and lets time alter his affairs— from a passion to an elective affinity—all against Wolf's belief that great love is a mortal illness, since that which might heal it in fact makes it worse. Yes, affection can be retrieved from the ashes of sex, Karl proclaims or pretends.

Were you here, Svevo, you would laugh at me. I admit, the old romantic self of my youth is back. To continue here, in this paradise of pre-Edenic creatures and computers, every day I write about Weimar. But since my memory is gone, this recreation is a creation. Constructing a new German town out of particles popping up in my head, I realize the wisdom of Wolf who, still a young man, said to me: One cannot evade the world more effectively than by literature, nor link oneself to the world more effectively than by fiction. Indeed. The processing of words keeps me in touch with the world. Out of textiles a token of the past-present-future is born, tested, woven into a textile. Time changes before our eyes. Weaknesses become appealing, strengths turn ridiculous, familiarity replaces respect, and we begin esteeming what once irritated us, and grow fond even of perils.

No day passes without a discovery. Yesterday, in a bunch of letters Ann entrusted to me, I found an anonymous note in Karl's handwriting concerning her pregnancy—caused not by him. Under February 13th, I read: The child is to be called Otto. I'll adopt and raise him as my own son. What was kindred by spirit cannot be upset by physiology. I'll take him into my arms and look affectionately down at the infant, not a little surprised by the inappropriate color of his eyes and his striking resemblance to the other man. I'm sure Ann hasn't mentioned to him what condition she finds herself in. She isn't half as sure about him as she is about me. When equal affection there cannot be, let the more loving one be me. The too-much she gave to him, I'll return it to her. I'll ask Ann to keep from him the child's identity. That way I shall have my little triumph: I'll ask him to be our son's godfather. Oh, how I look forward to Otto's birth! Routine will be finally resolved, I'll retire from robotics. Riverside Park is around the corner. He'll crawl there, and run, and bike, and ski. Otto! In the imitation of his name's outer form outside he'll appear round and soft, but inside there will be a hard male core.

Today, Italo, Florence found a scrap of papyrus covered with writing, totally incomprehensible at first sight. Nevertheless I immediately identified it as Karl's handwriting on the stationery of a Cairo hotel. In the course of the morning I deciphered the short text. It's dated March 6th, and reads: Life has emptied Ann out and baptized Otto in blood. My son is no more. I say it, and still I don't believe it. In his strife for sterility, Saturnus has defeated us again. Smiling with satisfaction, he proclaims: That's what happens when some factors are not handled right. That's what happens when godfather assumes the role of dad. That's what happens when an elective affinity encounters blood and sperm. Ann has quickly rebuilt her old casual façade, but behind it I sense despair. She has become fully resigned and wishes to continue working, being agreeable to me and serviceable to her friends. Now that she has informed the man of what happened, her suffering was supplemented with an extra dose of pain. What she must have suspected became a fact: the man doesn't give a damn either about her or the child. She repeated to me her conversations with him, and I was shattered by his coldness. Upon hearing about Ann's miscarriage, he said: Perhaps it's better that way. I have always been just a fellow traveler in the car you were driving.

Had I not assisted Ann, not only the child but she too would have gone down the drain. When we love a woman, we dream of saving her from fire or flood. But Providence rarely provides us with such an opportunity. Therefore I'm grateful to fate. It obliterated Otto, but it saved her by putting me in her way. What more can there be in life? But how could someone specializing in house additions be so indifferent to what he had added to Ann? So it's *getan*. Death devoured my Otto. But the roundness of *o* and the straightness of *t*, bravely carrying his cross, promise endless couplings.

The screen flickers and the Lazer Whizzard prints my letter to you, Italo, in Gothic script. Kangaroo Island, the sea, and the salty wind contribute to the clarity of this instant. I'm not on board Globook anymore, I have been remitted home. A young woman, not yet thirty, who has become much thinner during your absence, I stand in my cherry orchard and on my face fatigue mingles with eagerness. Look at my smooth skin, Svevo. It won't last. Already I tumble back into my old, worn-out sack. On the edge of the horizon, where black waves leap up towards the glowing sun, the shadow of Singapore is outlined for an instant. Don't sink, my dear friend. Don't sink before you reach our shores. I chatter, nod my head, while the ocean begins to roll across the crimson disk. These aren't my words, Italo. Far from it. I speak with Joseph, the master of turbulent waters within, of the flood sweeping with a running darkness the faces of women and men. Now, a crested roller breaks with a loud hissing roar and the sun, as if put out, disappears. My voice falters and goes out with the light. In the sudden lull that follows the crash of the sea, Florence asks wearily: Tea for two? the cream-colored cups in her hands. In the gathering grayness of twilight a bulky form rises and begins marching on all fours with the movements of some big cautious beast. It's the invalid giant kangaroo whom we have engaged as our caretaker. Aye! aye! mesdames, he grunts encouragingly over us, benumbed and immobile, his eyes half open, his paws in his pouch.

In the sky the stars, coming out, gleam over an inky sea which, speckled with foam, flashes back at them the evanescent light of a dazzling whiteness born from the black turmoil of the waves. Distant in the calm that glitters hard and cold above the uproar of the earth, they gaze at the vanquished and tormented ships—sad and unapproachable as the hearts of humans. The hot south wind howls exultantly under the somber splendor of the sky, and as it dries our lips, I hear Florence mutter a quickly suppressed complaint. She never complains, so I'm alarmed, feel suddenly exhausted, yawn. Two elderly women, we sit side by side recalling the faces of our shipmates, catching the voices of the dead. The terrace is hot as an oven, and the immobility around us is animallike in its perfection. Kangaroo Island, this cute joke of a last haven, awaits the rest of you. Don't delay your arrival, Italo. Press Conrad.

Do I repeat myself? Perhaps. But I must tempt you, again and again. Join us here, in the maze of our mutual text, in the cage that imprisons the sweet birds of youth: Carol's out-of-focus snap Herr Géza shot before deflowering her. The Greek profile of Berenice's maid with the four-year-old Mezoros, a wooden crocodile in his hands. Karl in a *Matrosenanzug,* his hair neatly parted in the middle, a self-made steamer in his hands. A month-old Ann, naked, with a hint of a split between her legs. The future linguist picking red poppies for Florence on the meadows of Monte Casino, his hair flying in the wind and joining the curve of her cotton dress. Small Djuna, stuffing blackberries into her mouth, in an upstate wood. Osia—in *ushatka* and *walonki*—with a sled. Myloslav, age six, skiing with his mother in the Tatra. Ernestine, a smashing Redhood in a Trinity School production, her eyes fixed on the wolf. Moses holding his father's hand at the entrance to the Salamanca synagogue. And you, Italo, in short pants, tracing a girl's shadow with a pencil, your eyes dark and adult.

The end isn't the end isn't the end. The end is the beginning. We grow back into infants, and then, then we grow further back—into animals, plants, dust. Accomplishing the solidarity of *sein,* we come to rest side by side. Those of us who have persevered that long shall all have their graves on Kangaroo Island. May marsupial angels guard us until the end of time or, if they choose, reawaken and jump with us to another happier planet.

Before I leave you, Italo, a last postscript from Florence. She offers to edit your definitive version of *Senilità*—for free. To this I can only add: Accept her generosity, no text has ever been tormented by her in vain. Our love to both of you. Ch. & F., the future kangaroos.

I FIND IT DIFFICULT TO BRING IT TO AN END, KARL.
Your text, Ann?
No, ours. The fictional memoir of our time.

It's because we're still alive. It's not over yet, the thing called life, as Moses writes in his last letter to Lotte. Events and people still emerge from the past. The widow from Lausanne, for instance, such a minor figure in Wolf's life—here she's back. A distant relative of hers saved a shabby carton from the attic of her villa before it was auctioned. Inside— a homemade *Papiertheater,* a tabletop copy of the city theater in Weimar, painted in aquarelle and complete with a proscenium, a silk curtain, a set for *Faust* I and II, and Wolf's manuscript with the widow's notes. She cut his monumental drama down to the size of her paper stage and directed the actors, her own hands—the right performed Faust and Gretchen, the left Mephisto and Helen—in *Die Faust: A Duel.*

Miniatures are mirror images of suffocated souls—and a speciality of female amateurs. Yet once in a while they succeed in offering us something most professionals miss: a vista of the world threatened by mankind's arrogant fist. I wonder: did the widow teach Wolf more than the art of aquarelle?

Her sighs might have inspired the lines of his invisible female chorus. Remember how it cries out when Faust signs the pact with Mephisto?

Oh weh! Oh weh! Du hast sie zerstört, die schöne Welt, mit mächtiger Faust.

Perhaps it's in Lausanne, at the shore of Lake Leman, and in the widow's arms that Wolf wrote *Oh weh!* Perhaps she whispered it into his ear, when they first slept together, or when he parted from her. Perhaps it was her *oh weh!* he could never forget.

A million females, including our Lotte, repeated *oh weh!* a million times apropos our Wolf. First he caused them grief, then immortalized them in the *voce dietro la scena*—the female crowd eternally weeping in the backyard.

Or building mini-monuments to their broken hearts.

The widow's paper stage—the lightweight *Werk* of a born anti-archi-tect—made it to the shores of Australia, a tabletop bit of land, too large for an island, too small for a continent, together with us. Who would ever have thought that we'd end up on Kangaroo Island.

Which indeed has the shape of a kangaroo's snout and, in accordance with the rules of poetics, mediates between the sinister influence of Investigator Street, our sea to the left, and the more encouraging news from Encounter Bay, to the right. At sunrise Mount Kościuszko ap-pears at the horizon, like a patriotic reminder.

Absolutely. Once Conrad is here, you must both climb it and from its top swear that you'll abandon English—to rhyme *Pan Tadeusz* in Lithuanian.

The best occupation in a place like ours, no doubt. Sydney has graciously guaranteed our financial survival in the spacious and yet intimate pouch of Globook where amidst the dead souls we perform the living phantoms. To prevent the extinction of Old Europe's crème de la crème, it has been decreed that we should be left alone. No anthropologist is allowed to take our pictures, no Princeton postdoc can interview the survivors. Kangaroo Island is off-limits to mankind. How enjoyable!

It's a shame Goethe passed away without experiencing this ultimate simulation of the spirit.

Simulation?

Yes. They have us here to simulate the old good sense—that doesn't make sense anymore. And continuity—that has come to a stop. And the focus on the original image and text—in the Xerox age. We're like kids, Karl. We shout: Seek Truth, and hide in a zoo—south of the tropic of Capricorn where dwarf eucalyptuses fringe the tree-line and the soakages in the parched interior are indicated by a line of the same trees, stunted and struggling.

It's not a bad idea to rest amidst flying squirrels that make long, sailing jumps from branch to branch, the vagabond native bears—with long, soft fur, no tail, and no affinities to a bear—swans, black and thus belying the old Latin proverb Propertius liked to quote, and the graceful lyrebirds, their tail feathers spread in the shape of the Greek instrument. Kangaroo Island may be an ark older than Noah's boat, with species that have immigrated from other planets, more ancient than ours. No, I have nothing against settling down here.

You hope that the isle's fauna will keep alive your spirit of sarcasm, my dear Mr. Cogito.

And its flora soothe your soul, my dearest Ms. Anima. But right now I have to upset you, Ann. There is something you ought to add to Carol's archive: a letter I intercepted after her death. The envelope carried your address, but it contained a Kleenex and two dirty sheets of paper addressed to Myloslav. I recognized Carol's hand, opened the letter, read it—and decided to not hand it to you. Not straightaway. Ever since I have waited, but enough is enough.

Read it to me, Karl.

Then let's take out the deck chairs and sit on the veranda.

Dear M, the apple of my eye, the air of my lungs. The day of my death is so common. A commonplace, and yet a little event. A sign cut in your skin, an initial printed in red—it's ready to efface itself with a small gesture. Insignificant, and yet important. It's the egglaying season for moths and I wonder: shall I lay you an egg? An egg out of all proportion. A silk-moth egg whose odd color strikes me as the color of departure. My fore- and my after-wings overlap to make a deeper, creamier white. My wings flutter wildly in the wind. June too soon. But it's not too soon, dearest. The time is right and ripe with promise. The moth doesn't move. You strike her with your fist, and she falls like a leaf from a mulberry tree. In her life she fed on leaves. But in her death she can spin without having to eat. What an advantage!

Swarms of flies bob around the new decorative lanterns they have installed in Riverside Park. *The Snow Country,* a new Japanese movie, is being screened at the Metro Cinema, and you go to see it. Tell me, dearest, what is the film about? Is it about the egglaying season for moths and a man who visits a geisha? The range of mountains is already autumn red, she wears a pale pink kimono, her lips overlap to make a deeper green, and when he strikes her with his fist, she floats lightly up midway to the ground. But no, he doesn't strike her. He doesn't even touch her. Her skin comes off the screen because he refuses to put his fingers on her. Tell me, what glues together the man and the geisha? Maybe it's not too late, maybe I can learn something from their story.

No, I can learn nothing from it. No one has ever learned anything from someone else's story. The only story we can learn something from is our own story. The Hudson River flows from the tips of the trees, it's getting late, I must get ready. But, really, everything is ready already. The backpack, the text, the bricks. Finally my brain is ready too. It cannot wait until the beginning meets the end. Still, it awaits you still. Take your eyes off the screen, rush here! I am alive still. Still I can be saved. A kimono with a black and a white sleeve, I have no weight. Do you still wear the black shoes I gave you? Doves are hidden in their soles. White doves. Their wings touch the sky, and the sky touches the earth. It's night and they unite—the earth and the sky. It's night, let's unite, let me not go to the ground. Let me not, let me not!

Don't you know: I am sunlight and I pour over your face. Don't you know: I am a geisha and I celebrate the end of my term. Don't you know: a new teahouse opened in New Jersey, on our way to church. Don't you know: it's century 21, and you are only twenty-one blocks away from me. The number of your street is round, it imitates an eight, it mimics a nine. Yours is a female street, full of promise, but it's frozen and I'm afraid to walk on it. You, however, you skate to your house and inscribe the ice with 8s and 9s, while a horse looks out the window, an English smile on its face.

It's winter and a white foal resides in your bedroom. It climbed up the ladder, the dangerous metal ladder I used to fear, wrapped itself in a cream-colored silk sheet, and fell asleep on the first floor of your bed. The colt ascended to your bed, but I, I cannot ascend to it anymore. Were it just underwood and brush and moss, I could descend to it. But it's made from upperwood, hard and ready, and it's numbered: 41. A fatal number—it means: $4 + 1 = 5$. But did you ever see a bed with five legs? Yes, you reply, I saw such a thing, the fifth leg turned me off. But dearest, I cry out, don't you realize? I'm the fifth leg you cut off your table. No, you answer, I see nothing, I recognize nothing. I have a silk shirt and a sound sleep and an air conditioner and a part-time colt in my bed. I have what I need. A wooden leg? No one needs that. I have my own legs, I skate.

Stars skate down the river. No, June isn't too soon. To take one's life—the time is always right. Before we go down the drain—we prefer to speak in verse. *Man kann singen, man kann tanzen, aber nicht mit den zasranzen.* Faust, bite my belly! Good, good dog. Good, good blood. Let me sign the Kleenex for you, Mr. M. Drip, drip, drip. See the red sea of my mind sink? *Pani anima* leaves the vacuum cleaner clean. Wau, wau, Faust. I don't like your doggish dialect. Let us dialogue in *Deutsch*. No, don't speak! Lick my waterbed. Swim in my Persian Gulf. Here, Faust, I have a bone for you. Go, go after it. Jump! Jump into the waves! Ann, my brain! Karl, *mein Herz!* M, my moon! *C'est tout. Poisson sans boisson est poison.* Passion without drink is poison. Go, Carol, you're a coral fish. Drink! Water tastes sweet. There is a hell of a lot of it to quench your thirst.

Are you all right, Ann?
Yes, Karl.
Here, take it too. It's the Kleenex.
You want me to wipe my eyes with my sister's menstrual blood?
No. Here's a clean Kleenex. Soak it with your tears, and wash your face.

SOON CONRAD AND SVEVO WILL ARRIVE HERE ARM IN ARM. Their last cruise around the world ended yesterday. Any sec now they should be at our doorstep.

> Sundown, and a sound of cheering
> As the last ships make the port.

Quoting Wolf, Karl?
What else, Lotte? Since your performance of the *Papiertheater,* I'm immersed in *Faust.*
Me too. Last night I dreamt of our old dog. He licked my hand and spoke:

I see what is far,
I see what is near,
Moon, planet, and star,
The wood with its deer,
In all things perceiving
The charms that endure,
And, joy thus achieving,
My own joy is sure.
Dear eyes, you so happy,
Whatever you've seen,
No matter its nature,
So fair has it been.

Dr. Eglizer and Lady Lotte, I presume, reciting *Hofrat* Goethe?

Welcome, Italo. Let me kiss your senile cheeks. And where's Joseph?

On his way to or from the loo.

Here he comes, his arm around the secret of his success.

How do you do, my friends in intellect? I tear Florence away from the last bit of my *Narcissus* who, she claims, is as obscure as the *Nigger* and needs a lot of editing. So that's where the text has brought us? And it's vesper too, or am I the only Hemingway to hear the bells toll?

It's a recording, Conrad, a gift from Ernestine. She had taped the vesper chimes tolling at the chapel near their shack in Singapore, before she left it for a senior citizen home. Do you remember? You visited her there.

Of course, Lotte. Sundown, the last ships make port. In Singapore I looked for her, but found only a tin with her name—on the top shelf of a crematorium.

Would you like a glass of port, Joe? I saved the last bottle for your return. And there is a chilled bottle of Suave for Svevo.

A *Wyborowa* for Ann.

A *Gespritzter* for Karl.

A Mary bloodier than ever for the Editor.

And you, Lotte?

Ein Gläschen Schnaps.

I propose a toast to Malcolm's Edenic health!

To Moses' erotic tetragrammaton!

To Myloslav's moss-cross!

To Carol's *House of Time.*

To the moon scholar's escape from the moon!

To Faust's encounter with Einstein!

To Einsteins reading *Kareninas*!
To Vronsky in Anna's pouch!
To coincidence!
To Nadia's hope!
To Osia the woodchuck!
To Djuna's nightwood!
To Saint Simone!
To Sextus and sex!
To Eglizer's *Kirchenstaat* of robotics!
To the host of Hostia!
To the Hair of Berenice!
To Ann's apocalypse!
To Svevo's senility!
To Florence—the word processor of Petrarch and the other Poles!
To Wanda, the President of Vice!
To the semantics of semiotics!
To kangaroos and Kowalskis!
To *Century 21,* the text that never ends. For God's sake: end!
And begin: Sunset on Kangaroo Island. The red sea of my mind.

New York, May 5, 1988

From Globook Archive

ABC of International Vanity

BARNES, Djuna, b. 1892 in Cornwall-on-Hudson
BERENICE, Queen, b. 269 B.C. in Gaza
CONRAD, Joseph (Jósef Teodor Konrad Korzeniowski), b. 1857 in Berdyszów
EGLIZER, Karl, b. 1944 in Vienna Woods
FAUST (Poodle), b. 1769 in Weimar
GOETHE, Johann Wolfgang von, b. 1749 in Frankfurt am Main
GOETHE, Lotte (Charlotte Buff von Stein), b. 1742 in Eisenach
HOSTIA (Cynthia), b. 36 B.C. in Urbino
KAR, Ann, b. 1946 in Cracow
KAR, Carol, b. 1950 in Warsaw
KARENINA, Anna Lvovna, b. 1870 in Yasnaya Polyana
KOWALSKI, Henryk (Bel Bonafiducci), b. 1941 in Kielce
LOWRY, Malcolm, b. 1909 in Birkenhead, Cheshire
MAIMONIDES, Moses, b. 1135 in Cordova
MANDELSHTAM, Nadia (Nadezhda Yakovlevna Khazina), b. 1899 in Saratov
MANDELSHTAM, Osip Emilevich, b. 1891 in Warsaw
MOON SCHOLAR (Myself), b. 2988 in Morse, Moonomalaya
MYLOSLAV, M, b. 1938 in Frydek Místek
PROPERTIUS, Sextus, b. 44 B.C. in Assisi
SVEVO, Italo, b. 1861 in Trieste
WEIL, Simone, b. 1909 in Paris

Propertius in Peking (*Photo:* Es-ra Pon-du)

Professor M. Elephant & Carol Kar at Princeton University
(*Photo:* Bel Bonafiducci)

Moses Maimonides & Simone Weil at Universidad de Salamanca
(*Photo:* Anna Karenına)

Jean-Paul Sartre, Anna Karenina, and Simone de Beauvoir
(*Photo:* Count Vronsky)

Propertius & Queen Berenice in Gaza (*Photo:* Pharaoh Press)

Ann Kar & Karl Eglizer in Nanking (*Photo:* Chou En-lai)

The poster of *The Devil Incarnate* with Gérard Philipe at
The East Is Red cinema in Nanking (*Photo:* Karl Eglizer)

The corner of the Via dei Polacchi in Rome

In the *pizzicheria:* Olga Voronskaya, Osip Mandelshtam & wife, Anna Karenina, Sanzio Raphael (?) (*Photo:* Colonel Voronskoy, KBG. *Courtesy:* Paragon & Pentagon Polytechnic for Political Study, Stanford)

Ann Kar with mother (*Photo:* H. Kowalski)

Ann & Carol Kar with their dove Miła in Niebyłów

A Man Grows Old: Italo Svevo in Trieste
(*Photo:* Propertius)

Propertius in Venice (*Photo:* Italo Svevo)

Charlotte & Goethe in the Harz

Angelica, Faust, and Goethe on the Via Appia, Rome
(*Photo:* Ann Kar)

Myloslav in Frydek Místek (*Photo:* PTS)

Moses Maimonides in Kyoto (*Photo:* Djuna Barnes)

Djuna Barnes in Kyoto (*Photo:* Myloslav)

Carol Kar in Manhattan (*Photo:* M)

Charlotte & Johann Wolfgang von Goethe, silhouettes by
Louise from Lausanne

Otto Eglizer & Colonel Voronskoy in Kabul
(*Photo:* Nabullah Press Service)

Martin Ingeneral in the Peppermint Saloon of *King Sobieski*
(*Photo:* Joseph Conrad)

Teresa Polska-Ingeneral at the Sea Saga Studio
(*Photo:* Joseph Conrad)

Malcolm in Gabriola (*Photo:* Ernestine Lowry)

Conrad in Singapore (*Photo:* Teresa Ingeneral)

Moon Scholar, a cotton cloth by Carol Kar, installed by Moses Maimonides in the Two-in-One Pine Grove, Mishima Shrine, Kyoto

The black bikini, being shot by Ann Kar on the Salamanca beach

Myself in Moonomalaya (*Photo:* Mooma)